Pride Publishing books by KD Ellis

Out in Austin
Teddy's Truth
Shiloh's Secret

Out in Austin

SHILOH'S SECRET

KD ELLIS

Shiloh's Secret
ISBN # 978-1-83943-754-0

Interior text design by Claire Siemaszkiewicz
Pride Publishing

Published in 2021 by Pride Publishing, United Kingdom.

Pride Publishing is an imprint of Totally Entwined Group Limited.

SHILOH'S SECRET

Dedication

To Tiffanie, who was there for every word written,
And for Mart, who encouraged me to keep going.

Chapter One

Shiloh hiked the hem of his baby-doll dress higher as he leaned his knee against the back of the chaise. He knew the drape of silk pooling in the hollow of his thighs barely left more than a teasing shadow to keep him modest.

Not that anyone in the frat house cared. He'd seen each of the Sigma boys naked at one point or another, while either on his knees or his back. In fact, the only man here he *hadn't* seen naked yet was his bodyguard, a man who bought his muscles in a bottle of methyltestosterone.

Brad sat in the armchair across from him. He was scanning the crowd of drunk college students stumbling from room to room, supposedly keeping an eye out for cameras. In reality, though, Shiloh caught the subtle glances toward the chaise, the way his gaze lingered on Shiloh's exposed skin and the even-less-subtle looks into the corner, where a couple was doing lines on the glass side table.

Shiloh propped himself up on an elbow so he could see them. "Hey, Jorgie." Shiloh feigned a slur. He'd been nursing the same glass of cheap whiskey since he'd arrived over an hour ago, though he'd skipped to the kitchen for a half-dozen refills for the sake of appearance. "Kiss you for a line."

Jorgie, nearly as fabulous as Shiloh in a glittery pink tank and tight jeans, wiped his nose before grabbing the baggie. He stumbled over, his cheeks flushed, blue eyes nearly black as he leaned down. His lips were hot when they pressed against Shiloh's.

Jorgie lost interest quickly, dropping the baggie on Shiloh's lap as a girl Shiloh vaguely recognized stumbled past. Jorgie trailed after her, calling "Evie, those *shoes*!"

Shiloh popped the seal on the bag and turned it gently, letting the coke fall against the side. He shook out a crooked line on his thigh. By now, his bodyguard had given up all pretense of watching the room. Brad's gaze locked on the powder.

Slowly, Shiloh ran a teasing finger over his skin to straighten the line. He admired the way it looked, even paler than his sun-starved flesh.

"I don't mind sharing," Shiloh said suddenly into the silence between them, and Brad dragged his gaze up to Shiloh's. He wet his lips. He wanted it. That was obvious—wanted it even more than he wanted Shiloh. "I won't tell if you don't."

And that was all it took.

Shiloh was almost disappointed at how easy it was. Brad pushed his way to standing, stalking closer. Shiloh held himself still. Brad only loomed for a second before dropping heavily to his knees. There was the briefest hesitation then his bodyguard hunched over his thigh. He pressed one large finger against his left nostril, then the sound of sniffing made Shiloh wrinkle his nose in disgust.

He expected the man to sit back but Brad lingered, skimming his thumb over Shiloh's thigh. It would be sexual in another circumstance—foreplay, a tease—but Shiloh knew he was just grabbing the last of the powder. Brad lifted his thumb to his mouth, rubbing it over his gums.

Brad's brown eyes grew darker as the drug tightened its grip on him. Shiloh was on the clock now. He would be lucky if the drug stuck in the man's system for a half-hour, with everything else in his veins.

Shiloh pushed Brad back then slid off the chaise and into the larger man's lap in a single move. The thin lace of his panties was barely a barrier between them. He could feel the coarseness of his bodyguard's jeans and, beneath them, the rigid hardness of his cock. Shiloh felt nothing as he rutted against it.

"I see how you watch me," Shiloh mused, teasing one of the black buttons on the other man's shirt between his fingers. "Are you finally going to do something about it?"

Brad groaned, clamping his hands down on Shiloh's hips hard enough to bruise as he yanked Shiloh closer. He was grateful that years of ballet had left him with a flexibility most gymnasts would envy, because otherwise his hips would be screaming against the stretch.

Brad tangled his fingers painfully in Shiloh's pink hair and yanked his head back. Shiloh turned his wince to a grin, then had to struggle to hold back a laugh as

Brad growled—actually growled, like a wild animal instead of a man.

"C'mon, big guy," Shiloh teased, grabbing Brad's hand and yanking it free from his scalp, ignoring the painful way several strands of hair separated with it. "I'll go find us a room. You go clean up, yeah?"

Brad blinked then shoved Shiloh off his lap in his haste to find a bathroom.

Shiloh smirked at his back. He hadn't expected it to be difficult—seducing his bodyguards never was—but he'd thought it would be harder than that. Victor had lasted two months, and before him, Harry had made it almost four. Brad had only worked with him for one.

The cocaine helped, he supposed.

Shiloh slipped out of the party before Brad could come searching, not bothering to say his goodbyes to anyone else. Nobody there would notice he'd left until it was too late to stop him.

Shiloh dropped into the driver's seat of his Bugatti and double-checked the backseat for his bag. Then he pulled off the manicured lawn and onto the street, leaving the townhouse behind him. He'd lived in Austin his whole life, except for brief vacations with his father as a child, so it wasn't hard to find his way to one of the most exclusive clubs in the city.

He didn't bother finding a parking spot. He grabbed his handbag and left his car on the street, throwing his keys to a man in a red velvet jacket standing on the sidewalk who, he realized as he strolled up the carpet toward the bouncer, had better have been a valet and not a man with poor fashion sense. *At least Dad has good insurance.*

The bouncer was moving the velvet rope for him before he reached it. "Mr. Beckett," he rumbled, "always a pleasure."

Shiloh fluttered his fingers in acknowledgment, paused for a handful of photos for the paparazzi loitering nearby, then sauntered into the club.

He headed straight to the dance floor. There was a VIP lounge on the second floor, but he didn't come here to drink and schmooze. The strobing lights painted rainbows on his skin as he danced, his arms thrown carelessly into the air, rolling his hips, regardless of rhythm. He was a good dancer—more than good, *great* – but this wasn't ballet, and he wasn't performing. This was his attempt to briefly forget the real world and all the shit that came with it.

Three songs were all he allowed himself—three songs to be careless, three songs to lose himself in the bass and dance for nobody but him. Men groped his hips, ran teasing hands down his chest, even cupped his groin with grabby hands, but he didn't care. He danced with a single-minded lack of focus.

And when his three songs were up, he dropped back into his body like an automobile crash, peeled himself away from the grabby hands and crossed the dance floor with the ease of practice. He'd been coming here for years before he was legal, and he knew the tricks like the back of his hand—the dip and sway to avoid getting tangled with dancers.

He took the stairs down to the lower bathrooms. The hallway was dimly lit, bodies little more than silhouettes shifting from shadow to shadow. More than one couple was pressed against the wall, their pants lowered to their knees as they copulated.

In these halls, he could be anyone, just another faceless stranger in a crowd. He ducked into one of the bathrooms—no one here cared about gender—and closed himself in a stall.

He stripped out of his couture dress, swapping it for a pair of knock-off jeans so tight that he might as well have not been wearing them and a white lace camisole with a stain near the hem. He replaced his Miu booties with pink All-Stars. Finally, he pulled out a pink wig and held it between his knees to keep it off the floor while he filled the bag with his discarded clothes. He spent a few seconds pulling his real hair up under a skull cap before he tugged on the wig. He couldn't do much about his handbag. Hopefully people would assume it was a fake.

He stepped out of the stall and spent a few moments at the mirror readjusting the wig and touching up his makeup. He swapped his diamond eyebrow stud for sterling silver then stepped back, eyeing his reflection critically. He looked like himself, but…not. He looked like a knock-off of himself, which was exactly what he wanted.

He plastered on a grin and left the bathroom. The dance floor was even more crowded now. He merged into the sea of bodies, noticing several other wigs just like his. He grinned, enjoying the feel of anonymity as he started dancing again. Unlike earlier, though, this *was* a performance, every move just slightly *off* but geared to attract attention. He danced until sweat soaked his skin and thirst burned his throat.

He slid free of his current partner's grip, ignoring the man's groan as he headed for the bar. He pressed in tight between two men who were already waiting there, each brush of his body made to look accidental.

"Oops," he yelled over the music as he bumped the man to his left with his hand. With the gold watch on his wrist, he looked like he could easily afford to buy Shiloh a drink—then an hour of his time as well.

"I'm Shiloh," he introduced himself as the suited man looked down on him.

"Sure you are, and I'm Hugh Jackman." The man laughed. It wasn't cruel, but Shiloh feigned a pout. "What are you drinking, 'Shiloh'?"

"Do they got an appletini?" Shiloh asked, playing up the wide-eyed, innocent look and poor grammar that a man like this would go for.

"Sure, sweetheart." The man gestured to the bartender. Seconds later, a martini glass filled with the green cocktail appeared in front of Shiloh, complete with an umbrella.

"What's your name?" Shiloh asked, stepping closer to be heard over the music, using it as an excuse to brush his hand over the other man's hips. It was partly a tease, but also a subtle check. No gun or badge, at least not that he felt. He supposed a badge could be in the man's wallet, but, short of pocketing that, he had no way to check.

Even a whore had to draw the lines somewhere—and he wasn't a thief.

"Beckham." The man leaned against the bar but didn't try to escape Shiloh's fingers. Shiloh removed them long enough to take a sip of his appletini. It was an indulgence he couldn't allow himself often if he wanted to keep his figure. Then, he reached out and fiddled with a button on Beckham's jacket.

"Just get off work?" he asked, peering up through his lashes.

"What gave it away?" Beckham drained the last of what looked like Scotch before abandoning the empty glass on the bar to give Shiloh his full attention.

"The suit. Are you a lawyer? You are, aren't you?" Shiloh could tell a bespoke suit in one glance, and if Beckham's didn't cost at least a grand, he'd wear a pair of sweatpants out in public. Beckham lifted an eyebrow and Shiloh grinned. "I knew it. I knew you were a lawyer. Are you the kind that puts bad guys away? Or the kind that frees poor innocent people from behind bars?"

Beckham laughed. "Neither. I'm the kind who spends seventy hours a week cutting loopholes out of contracts—though I've been known to pick up a case or two to free up jail cells for the right price."

Shiloh scrunched up his nose. "Gross. Well, you must be stressed after spending that many hours *reading.*" Shiloh shuddered like the thought made him physically ill. "How about we go back to your place and do something more fun? Tell you what… For a sexy man like you, I won't even charge you full price."

If the lawyer was surprised Shiloh was a professional, he didn't show it. He just slid a handful of bills across to the bartender before putting his hand on Shiloh's lower back, guiding him out of the club. A few paparazzi lifted their cameras as he exited, likely spotting the pink hair, before lowering them with a frown and a shake of their heads. He smothered his smile with a duck of his head, adding an extra sway to his hips for the hell of it.

Chapter Two

Gage Tucker was a patient person.

He waited in line at airports without cursing too much, he could sit silently for hours in a swamp holding a rifle and not once in his twenty-eight years of life had he *ever* considered starting a fight at a Black Friday sale. But he swore to God, if he had to hear the lady next to him speak one more time, he'd lose his fucking mind.

He was going to be known forever as the angry American Airline's man. Some kid on his iPhone was going to post a video to TikTok or YouTube or something, and Gage would never hear the end of it. So instead of snapping, he crammed his cheap headphones farther into his ears and gritted his teeth.

It didn't help that he'd been in a foul mood already. Because, of course, besides being crammed into a sardine can of a plane—a fear not even two tours in Afghanistan had cured him of—he had to be stuck between the only couple on the plane going through a messy divorce.

Gage grunted as a sharp elbow careened into his ribs as the carrot-haired woman in the aisle seat leaned across him to snipe at her husband for the fiftieth time. Her speckled face was inches from his, which meant he couldn't avoid breathing in the stench of her heavy perfume. At least it drowned out her breath. Her voice was screechy as she said, "If you think I'm going to let you take Mr. Tibbles, you have another 'think' coming."

"I don't want your yappy little dog, Martha. Go ahead and take Oscar too, or I'm making bacon for breakfast." The man in the window seat beside Gage pounded his fist on the arm rest, narrowly missing Gage's wrist.

Gage took out his earbuds. "Are you *absolutely* positive you wouldn't prefer to—"

"I will *not* sit next to him!" Martha interrupted him.

"Then shut up and stay the hell out of my seat!" Maybe he said it louder than he'd intended, but seriously... He'd heard quieter grenades. He'd spent enough of his life in the middle of a war zone. He didn't need to be in one now.

The woman sat back in stunned silence. Just as he was about to congratulate himself on his success, she leaned forward again with a huff. The sweat-damp cotton of her blouse stuck to Gage's arm as she glared at her soon-to-be-ex-husband. "You're just going to let him speak to me that way? Say something, Earl."

Earl shoved his cowboy hat farther onto his head and grinned. "Honey, the only thing I want to say to this man is 'Thank you'."

"I hate you!" Midge's voice—or Martha's, whatever her name was—carried through the cabin, finally loud enough to attract the flight attendant. The attendant sighed and started down the aisle. She'd only made it three rows before Marge shoved to her feet and stormed toward the bathroom, her heels clicking loudly.

Gage hoped she got stuck on the toilet.

Earl bumped Gage's shoulder. "That woman, eh? Can you believe we were married for—"

Gage pinned him with a glare. "We are *not* friends, and I am *not* a couple's therapist." He was a patient person, normally. Any other day, any other situation and maybe he'd apologize, but being crammed into too-tiny seats for hours on end, unable to stretch his legs without indulging his desire to kick someone, didn't put him in a great mood—not to mention that the bickering brought up uncomfortable memories of his parents fighting when he was younger, before everything had gone to shit and he'd joined the Army to escape.

Gage was about to tuck his headphones in again when his phone rang, shocking him into dropping one of his earbuds. "For the love of *God*," Gage snapped as he yanked his phone up off his lap with one hand and dug for the earbud with the other. He groaned as he spotted the picture of who was calling. He just couldn't catch a break. Gage thumbed the green button as he replaced his earbud, which was already synced to his phone.

"Don't tell me the client died already," Gage said in lieu of greeting.

Mason Lockhart, Gage's boss and the head of Eagle Security, laughed. "No, not yet. How's the flight?"

"Flighty and dysfunctional." Gage shot a glare at his seat neighbor at the jab.

"Good thing I sent you with reading materials, right?"

"I haven't looked at them yet," Gage said. Mary, Mason's assistant and the woman in charge of handing out assignments, had only told him two things—that Gage would definitely recognize his new client and that she was sorry in advance. Opening the folder while stuck between fighting spouses who'd spent the majority of the flight half in his lap seemed like a shitty decision.

Mason was silent for a second. "Read it before you land."

Gage frowned but knew better than to argue. Mason rarely gave orders, so when he did, Gage knew to listen. He leaned down and pulled the manila envelope out of his carry-on. A quick glance at Earl, who was squinting curiously at the folder, validated his decision not to open it there.

"Hold on." Gage stood up and limped down the narrow aisle, picking his way around legs that spilled out like tripwires. Only one of the lavatories—he hesitated to call it a room—was unoccupied. He stepped in and locked the door behind him. The cramped space suffocated his tall frame, forcing him to hunch as he opened the folder. He arranged the contents on the small counter.

All it took was a glance at the photograph clipped to the front page to convince him that Mary had been right.

He *really* didn't want this assignment.

The kid—okay, so he *wasn't* a kid, was old enough to legally drink, but barely—had landed on more magazine covers than the Kardashians. Gage had purposefully avoided following any of the articles, and he still couldn't help but recognize him. With the pink just-fucked hair, the pierced eyebrow with silver snakebites and cerulean eyes that mocked Gage through the picture… He was *exactly* Gage's type—which was the last thing he needed when he was going to be stuck to the kid's side for the next eight to ten weeks, maybe longer.

"Seriously? You're putting me on *his* detail?" Gage picked up the photograph, hand clenching on the shiny paper until it wrinkled. He set it back down and tried to smooth it out.

"You *are* his detail," Mason corrected.

"I don't want it. Give it to someone else." Gage didn't get into personal security to keep spoiled little rich boys out of trouble. He'd much rather put them over his knee.

"You're the best I've got. And," Mason added, "you're already on the plane."

"What about Phoenix? He's used to paparazzi." Gage liked Phoenix. More importantly, Phoenix would like Shiloh. He was always bragging about this client or that one's exploits. He took pride in keeping them safe, especially when it was hard.

Gage had served with Phoenix. They had been riding in the same tank the day everything had gone up in flames. That was how the other man had gotten his nickname. His real name was Ashton, but after he'd walked from the still-smoking ashes without a scratch, Gage had jokingly gave him a new moniker. It was Phoenix who'd introduced him to Mason.

"He's already on a job in Los Angeles and I can't pull him for another month. Besides, I thought you'd be better for this one."

"Because I'm *gay*?" His voice was bitter. He wasn't ashamed of his sexuality. He was ashamed that even now, working for people he considered more family than friends, it mattered.

"Yes." There was no apology in Mason's voice.

And there didn't need to be, Gage reminded himself. Mason was gay too, so he hardly had the right to be angry. Mason continued to speak, yanking Gage from his thoughts. "I thought it would make the client more comfortable. His father said he doesn't like security."

Gage flipped the page to skim the bio. Shiloh's father was Anthony Beckett, the CEO of Beckett Industries, one of the leading tech firms in the country. It had started as nothing, just one more start-up among hundreds, until Beckett had developed a new gaming engine that had revolutionized the industry. The company had recently moved into designing training mods for the military, and ever since, its share value had skyrocketed. You couldn't pick up a smartphone without finding at least one piece of *BeckTech*.

"The kid doesn't like security, so you're punishing *me?* I didn't get into this field to be a media screen." There was nothing in the bio that Gage didn't already know—twenty-one as of January, no job, partied almost every night of the week and rarely attended his classes at the McCombs School of Business, where he was supposedly enrolled in the Science and Technology Management Program.

"It's not a punishment. The kid's in danger...real danger."

Gage turned the page to a small mountain of newspaper clippings. He started flipping past the headlines.

Son of Tech Tycoon Performs Striptease at Local Nightclub.

Shiloh Beckett Caught In Flagrante Delicto in Restaurant Bathroom.

Drunk and Disorderly Shiloh Beckett Causes Scene at Benefit Dinner.

The headlines continued. Most of them were familiar. Gage had been living in Seattle for the past three years and even there, the Beckett brat made headlines.

Gage kept flipping until he reached a sheet of paper with neat handwriting. It was a letter, nothing out of the ordinary. Addressed to 'Mr. Beckett', it was brief, just a 'Congratulations on your latest success', signed by someone who called themselves 'an admirer'. It was six months old. Gage flipped past it. The letters continued.

'Mr. Beckett' became 'Shiloh' in the second letter, making it clear they were meant for the kid, not his father, and '*an*' admirer became '*your*' admirer. Gage didn't miss the way it grew more possessive. Even the language changed. The longer the letters went unanswered, the more bitter they grew. It was textbook stalker behavior.

I liked you in that blue shirt. Wear it for me when we meet.

Or… *Who was that man you looked at in the bar? Do you know him? I don't want you to see him anymore.*

He flipped to the last one. Mason stayed silent on the line, letting him read.

Slut, you're not shy *at all. I saw what you did, and you won't get away with it. You are* mine. *If you like the taste of dick so much, I'll cut yours off and feed it to you.*

It was left unsigned, which wouldn't be odd since some of the early letters weren't signed either, except when the rest had 'Your Admirer', across the bottom. It was a drastic change.

"He's escalating. Has the family contacted the police?" Gage asked.

"Yes, but there's not much they can do besides keep an eye on the situation. They advised Mr. Beckett to increase his security. He has hired four bodyguards in the past twelve months and the kid keeps giving them the slip," Mason said, his voice leaking annoyance. Gage doubted that he would still have a job if he'd been the one to lose the kid.

"He's not taking the threat very seriously." Gage skimmed the folder a second time.

"Shiloh doesn't know about the letters, and his father wants to keep it that way. All the kid's mail goes through a personal assistant. They were able to remove the more threatening ones before Shiloh saw them. Mr. Beckett doesn't want his son worried about something he can't control. I informed him that we would not bring it up. However, he knows that it might have to come up in the course of you performing your duties, so don't let it hamstring you. Do what you need to do to get the job done."

"Yes, sir." Gage sighed. "I suppose it's an open-ended contract?"

"Yes. You'll be there either until they catch the stalker or until Mr. Beckett decides to no longer retain your services. I know I normally give you the evening, but considering the circumstances, I thought it best to have you get started immediately. Standard protocol applies."

Meaning Gage was on duty six days a week, every week, with an extended weekend off once every other month. Normally, that wouldn't bother him—while his clients were secured at home, he could take time for himself, so long as he stayed on the premises—but something told him that was going to change.

"I'm there to keep the kid safe, not to keep him out of the press and not to block him from the paparazzi," Gage clarified.

"No more than you would for any other client," Mason said. "Just do what you do best."

Gage flipped the folder closed. "Fine. I suppose it can't be as bad as the Deverill case."

"Nothing could be as bad as the Deverill case," Mason agreed.

"I want background checks on anyone who comes into regular contact with Shiloh—household staff, past bodyguards…the usual."

Mason agreed before Gage hung up, tucking his phone back into his pocket and stepping out of the bathroom. Ignoring the glare from the heavyset man waiting, he headed back to his seat.

Martha had returned, sporting a fresh coat of blood-red lipstick and a snarl.

"Ma'am, will you please move to the middle?" Gage asked, struggling to keep his voice calmer than he felt.

She crossed her legs, her small skirt riding up her pasty thighs, and shot him a smug smile. "No."

Gage rubbed the bridge of his nose and counted down from ten. "Fine." He dropped awkwardly back into the middle, his knees jammed uncomfortably against the seat in front of him. Cowboy Hat's wife twisted in her seat to face her husband.

Gage pulled out his phone and took a picture of her. He snapped one of Cowboy Hat next.

"What are you doing?" She blinked, stopping her rant only a few words in.

"Well, I figure one of you is going to end up murdering the other, and I might get called on as a witness."

The woman's face flushed scarlet, but she closed her mouth and turned away with a huff.

Chapter Three

Shiloh kept his eyes firmly latched on the roses dotting the nurse's scrubs as she withdrew the needle from the crook of his arm and started capping the blood-filled vials that lined the metal tray. It wasn't the blood that bothered him. It was the needles. He wasn't afraid of them—rather, years of using them for stress relief left his fingers itching to grab one to shove in deeper, until the pinch turned to burning.

The nurse gave him a bright smile. Her voice was high-pitched, too cheery for a woman currently unwrapping a pair of long cotton swabs. "Okay, just two left and you'll be all set to go." She held the first swab up. "Open up and say '*Ah*'."

Shiloh opened his mouth obediently and she quickly dragged the swab along his cheek. Then, Shiloh reluctantly bent over so she could slide the second swab between his *other* cheeks. He winced as it probed uncomfortably into his ass, which was still sore from last night's 'visitor'.

"All set. We'll text your initial results within the hour but do make sure to follow up with us again in three months. Have a great day!"

Shiloh doubted anyone that was showing up at the dingy clinic tucked between a UPS store and an out-of-business hair salon for an STI checkup after a broken condom mishap was having a 'great day', but he didn't bother arguing as he re-tucked his dick into his panties and tugged up his skinny jeans. At least he wasn't leaving empty-handed.

He shoved the scrip for a prophylactic antibiotic into his pocket, slid his designer sunglasses onto his face, then headed outside to his car. It was a short drive over to his favorite pharmacy where he left the scrip to get filled. Since he had time to kill, he decided to visit a few of his favorite shops in East Austin.

Not that he bought anything. He wasn't ready for his dad to track him down yet, and a purchase here would have a pair of goons on his tail before he could blink. He'd be lucky if his dad hadn't already put a hold on his credit card anyway, like he had after the *last* time he'd skipped out on dinner. For some odd reason, shit like that pissed the old man off. He wasn't sure *why*, since Dad never wanted to spend time with him anyway, unless there was a lecture involved.

Shiloh shoved down the frustration and started thumbing through the racks of clothing. He slung a few cute tops over his arms. He wouldn't buy them, but trying them on was nearly as exciting. It was fun at first, but after the third trip to the fitting room, it became just sad. Shiloh fingered a pretty pink chiffon scarf. He draped it over his shoulders, playing with the fringe where it fell over his chest.

"It suits you," a voice said from behind him.

Shiloh's mouth twitched into a smile as he slowly turned. The boutique attendant was older than him by a decade, his dark hair coiffed into a pompadour, and though his suit was clearly off the rack, it had been tailored to fit—not that Shiloh expected anything less from someone who worked at Vale. The boutique was known to cater to the rich and famous. Its employees had to look the part.

"It does, doesn't it?" Shiloh sighed and ran his fingers over the silk.

Ten minutes later, Shiloh was on his knees behind the cash register. Five minutes after that he was strolling from the shop, salt on his lips and with the pretty scarf draped around his neck.

Traffic snarled at the intersection and the sidewalk was cluttered with people. A man in a tie-dye 'Keep Austin Weird' shirt and cowboy boots ran into him at the crosswalk, hollering a pleasant apology over his shoulder. Shiloh blew him a kiss and kept strolling.

The glint of sunlight on a camera lens had him veering sharply to the right. It was probably a tourist, but it could be paparazzi. He didn't mind flirting with the cameras most days, since he knew each headline pissed his dad off a little bit more, but today his goal was to stay under the radar. As soon as his dad got wind of his location, he'd be back under lock and key again. It was early afternoon, and the goal was to make it home late enough that his father would be in bed and the guards too busy gambling in the guardhouse to pay him much mind.

He cut over a few streets, until he found one that looked paparazzi-free. It was the only benefit to living in Austin instead of LA. Too few celebrities meant fewer of the vultures—the downside, of course, being that there were too few celebrities to take the lenses off him. It didn't matter what he was doing, they found a way to twist it. Like last week, when he'd dropped his spoon under the table and they sold a pic claiming he was 'blowing' his date. Like Shiloh went on dates in the first place. It had been a boring dinner with his father's accountant at some restaurant he couldn't pronounce the name of.

It was ironic, really, how many times they'd twisted him doing perfectly normal things into a sex scandal, and yet, not once had they gotten a picture of him with a trick. He almost wished they would. Some days, he imagined himself tipping one off, getting caught with a fat, married man's dick lodged halfway down his throat. Maybe that would be the final straw.

He doubted it. He hadn't been disinherited yet, so the only thing it would get him was a tighter curfew and another guard who'd spend more time staring at his ass than guarding it. He had a plan to finally get out from under his father's controlling thumb, and it kind of hinged on him having a certain freedom of movement.

He stopped at an open-air stall along the sidewalk. An older Mexican woman named Rosa sat behind it, a bright red *rebozo* draped over her shoulders. "*Ola, Doña. Cuánto por esto?*"

She rubbed the scarf between her fingers, examining the weave with a critical eye. It wasn't the first time he'd sold to her, but she went through the same process each time. She harrumphed. "*Veinte dolares.*"

He switched to English. He'd taken the two credits of Spanish mandatory to graduate high school but remembered very little except for how to find the bathroom and how to count to twenty—which was the only reason he knew how much she was offering for the scarf.

"It's worth at least sixty," Shiloh bargained. Really, it retailed for over a hundred, but asking for that much would get him laughed away from the stall.

"Forty. No more." Rosa held up the bills. "Take it or go away."

He snatched the bills and regretfully passed over the pretty scarf. "*Gracias,* Rosa," Shiloh said before leaving the stall behind.

He really needed to come up with a better way to make money. He got tips for dancing at Envy, and that was nice, even if the tips didn't always amount to much. Lately, though, he'd found himself spending more time watching the johns in the audience than dancing, and that, more than anything, scared him.

If he couldn't dance anymore, where did that leave him?

Anger blossomed in his chest. Without thinking, he kicked the empty tin can that appeared on the sidewalk in front of his pink Chucks. Except…it wasn't empty, and when he kicked it, it went rolling out into the street, spreading nickels and dimes like a trail of breadcrumbs behind it.

"Come on, man. What the heck?" a young man whined as he scrambled after the coins, plucking them up and shoving them into his threadbare pockets.

"Shit, sorry. I wasn't paying attention." Shiloh crouched down beside the teenager and helped gather up what he could reach, but a good handful had already spilled down a sidewalk grate.

"Clearly." The kid glared at the grate like the force of his anger was going to make it cough the coins back up. He dropped back against the lamppost he'd been leaning on with a huff. "Whatever. Probably just pennies anyway,"

Shiloh shoved his hands into his pockets. Well, his fingers, anyway, since that's all that would fit in the tight pants he was wearing—and stared at the kid. The ragged hems of his jeans crept halfway up his shins, like he'd had a growth spurt since he'd first bought them, but the waistband gaped open over his skinny hips. And don't get him started on the sorry shape of his shoes. They were more air than cloth at this point. If he wasn't homeless, he was only one step up from it—and clearly starving.

"Can I buy you lunch?" Shiloh blurted. "Or, um...a coffee?"

The boy glanced up, trailing his gaze over Shiloh's outfit. Maybe he was embarrassed at the thought of being seen with a man fully decked out in pink or maybe he was looking for a weapon. In the end, he shrugged and stood up, hiking his jeans higher when they sagged. "Sure. I know a place."

Shiloh'd planned on an Italian restaurant a few streets over but didn't care enough to argue. He was likely going to charge the meal to his dad's card anyway. Instead of to a restaurant, though, the kid led him into an alley, stopping beside a dumpster.

"So how do you want to do this? You want a blow job, or...?" The kid hooked his thumbs in the waistband of his jeans and made to shove them down.

Shiloh immediately backed up, his hands lifted. "No, shit, sorry. I actually meant lunch, not..."

The boy eyed him warily. "People never mean lunch when they say 'lunch'."

"Look, kid—" Shiloh started.

"Not a kid," the kid growled. "I'm sixteen. I've been taking care of myself for years, so fuck off." He pushed past Shiloh, headed for the street.

Shiloh didn't think before he grabbed for the teenager's arm. He just knew if he let the boy out of his sight, he'd never see him again. The kid yanked his arm away, slamming into the alley wall in his haste to get free.

"Sorry, sorry." Shiloh lifted his hands again in apology. "Let me take you to lunch. Real lunch, with actual food."

"Why? If you don't want my ass, what's in it for you?"

"Well, kid—okay, sorry, not a kid—but it's not like I know your name, dude, so what else am I supposed to call you?" Shiloh rolled his eyes and planted his fist on a cocked hip, lifting a brow in question.

"Riley," the kid finally said. "You can call me Riley."

"Great. Well, *Riley,* I get to apologize for kicking over what was probably your lunch fund, and I get company for what would otherwise have been a boring meal at a taco stand or Tex-Mex or something. Nobody is sticking their dick in anyone, I promise."

After several moments of silence, Riley finally spoke, though his shoulders remained tense and his feet stayed pointing toward the alley, one step away from fleeing. "I guess you can buy me lunch. But I'm not fucking you. You promised."

* * * *

Shiloh bought Riley pizza. He only ate one piece, since even that would push him near to his carb limit, but the kid demolished the rest of it, as well as over half an order of breadsticks. Riley shoved his plate away and leaned back in the booth with a groan, his hands curled over his belly.

"That was good," Riley sighed, a belch punctuating his words.

"I was going to suggest dessert but I'm not sure where you'd put it." Shiloh drained half his Coke to smother a laugh.

"I could totally do ice cream." Riley sucked in his belly like that would prove he had more room left. But his face twisted immediately. "Maybe not."

"Next time," Shiloh promised.

Immediately, Riley's face shuttered, closing down at the words. "Yeah, I gotta go. Thanks for dinner but, yeah. See you never." He shoved up from the table like he thought if he didn't leave now, Shiloh wouldn't let him.

"Sit down, please." Shiloh wouldn't force the kid to stay if he really didn't want to. He'd spent too much of his own life being controlled by other people—but that didn't mean he couldn't ask.

Riley hesitated, clearly torn, but sank slowly back into the booth. "You promised no sex. You promised."

And damn if he didn't sound so fucking young when he said it that a little bit of Shiloh's heart broke for him. "I just want to talk."

"I'm not going back home," Riley immediately said, like he'd had this talk before and thought he knew where it was going.

"Sometimes home is the worst place you can go," Shiloh agreed. He didn't need to know the boy's life story to know that. Maybe home wasn't bad. Maybe the kid had parents that missed him and were worried about him. Honestly, Shiloh didn't give a fuck about the parents. If Riley thought he couldn't go home, then Riley couldn't go home. That didn't mean he had to be stuck on the streets selling his ass to whoever had a buck.

Riley looked surprised that Shiloh didn't press, because he opened his mouth but nothing came out.

Shiloh pulled the pen out of the black billfold the waiter had left on the table, then grabbed a napkin out of the holder. "I'm not saying you have to go home. You can walk out of these doors right now and go back to tricking, and I won't stop you. I won't even judge you, because I do it myself. But if you want to get out, there are other options." He scrawled an address on the napkin and pushed it across the table. Riley eyed it but didn't pick it up.

"That's to the Rainbow House. You can show up anytime, day or night, and they'll take you in, no questions asked. You can stay as long as you like. They'll never tell you you have to go home or send you back to your parents. They might ask you to help out with chores or something, but that's it."

Shiloh had stayed there himself for nearly a month, back when he'd been seventeen and had run away the first time. It had been one of the happiest months of his life. Of course, then his dad had tracked him down and dragged him back home, but that hadn't been their fault. It had been his own for being stupid enough to think he could sneak out of the dorms after curfew then getting spotted by the paparazzi, who'd tipped off the media, who'd tipped off his dad. Shiloh hadn't dared go back after that.

For Riley, though, it could turn out to be the perfect place.

"You don't have to go, just…think about it. They'll help you get your GED if you want—or find a job eventually, get you an ID and a social security number, if you need them." Shiloh forced himself to stop talking. The kid would go or he wouldn't. Instead, he cleared his throat and stood. He pulled out the pair of twenties he'd gotten for the scarf and dropped them in front of the kid. "So…stay out of trouble."

Shiloh left before he could talk himself into dragging the kid home with him. He was nearly out of the door when he saw Riley pick up the napkin and shove it in his pocket.

Chapter Four

Gage fought the urge to rub the skin below his left knee as he grabbed his luggage off the carousel. The old injury didn't bother him often, but four-and-a-half hours on a cramped plane had forced him to sit with his knees practically to his chest.

He managed not to limp as he started for the exit, even when someone dragged their suitcase over his leather boots. His client's first impression of him would not be that he was weak.

A wall of heat slammed into him as he stepped through the airport doors, the humidity nearly bowling him over. It was both too different from Seattle and too like his tours in Afghanistan. For just a flash of a moment, he was not in a bustling airport. He was choking on sand in the shadows of a forbidding mountain.

Then a horn beeped, and he was back outside the glass airport doors, staring at a sleek black sedan. An older gentleman in a suit stood beside it. He held a sign with *G. Tucker* written in a neat hand.

"Mr. Tucker?" the gentleman asked, scanning Gage's outfit.

Gage smiled politely. "Yes, sir." At least the black track pants and V-neck tee were clean and neat. He'd have worn something different if he'd realized he was being taken to meet his new employer immediately upon disembarking.

"I'm Henry. I was sent by Mr. Beckett. May I take your bag, sir?" Henry asked, holding out a hand.

"I'll keep it with me." Gage had his service weapon in the bag, as well as several expensive security devices. It wasn't that he didn't trust the driver, but—well, he didn't trust the driver.

"As you wish." Henry opened the back door instead, waiting for him to climb in before closing it and rounding the car.

As Henry left the airport lot and pulled onto the main stretch, Gage kept one eye on his surroundings. It was a holdover from his childhood, when he'd ridden with his father in his squad car, and one that had served him well as a Ranger. It was one of the few good things he'd learned from his dad. He didn't count the *other* things, like how the sound of a fist hitting flesh could be louder than gunfire, or how his own blood tasted.

It was a twenty-minute drive to Westfield. Henry turned into a subdivision, stopping at the gate to give his identification to a guard in a security booth. Gage wasn't surprised that the Becketts lived in a gated community. He was more surprised that the guard didn't bother to ask for Gage's ID. He would need to have a discussion with the security firm. He glanced at the logo. It was a chain company. He'd worked with subsidiaries across the country. They were decent at their jobs, but beyond the initial background checks, they had minimal contact with their employees.

The Beckett estate sprawled across two lots near the back of the subdivision. And estate, Gage decided, was the right word. It was an architectural marvel, all hard edges and glass, three stories of ultra-chic construction. A wrought-iron gate enclosed the house and gardens, more for style than security. Still, he spotted at least four cameras before Henry pressed a button on the dash and the gates parted, permitting them entry.

Henry pulled the car around the circle drive, leaving it to idle by the entrance while he exited. Gage didn't wait for him to round the car. He opened the door on his own and grabbed his suitcase and carry-on, stepping out onto the tumbled stone driveway. Henry looked disappointed as he reached his side and Gage *almost* felt guilty for depriving him of the opportunity to open the door. *Almost.*

"Would you like me to accompany you, sir?" Henry asked.

"I can find my own way." Gage grinned. His white-knuckled grip on the suitcase handle helped him ignore the pain in his knee as he carried it up the stairs to the wrought-iron-over-teak doors. He lifted his hand to knock but there was no need.

The door was already opening, revealing a gray-haired man in an expertly tailored suit. "Mr. Tucker?"

Gage held back his frown. Well-informed staff was a good thing, of course, since it meant unexpected company would be easy to recognize, but if he wasn't Mr. Tucker, he could now pretend he was.

"That's me," Gage said, after a long enough pause to be uncomfortable.

"I'm Thomas. Mr. Beckett isn't home, but he left instructions. If you'll follow me, I'll get you set up in your room then take you to the study to wait."

Gage followed Thomas into the house. The inside was even grander than the exterior, with large glass windows, stone staircases and marble flooring. Despite the extravagance, the foyer still managed to convey a sort of home that felt welcoming rather than intimidating. While it wasn't somewhere that Gage would ever willingly choose to live—he'd always felt most at home in the Army barracks—it still felt more like a home than he'd expected. Either the Becketts had a good interior decorator, or they had excellent taste.

He followed Thomas up the winding staircase to the second floor. "This is the East Wing, sir. The family has their residence here," Thomas explained, pointing out rooms as they went. He stopped outside a dark oak door. "Mr. Beckett set this room aside for you. I trust you'll let myself or Ms. Maria know if there is anything you require."

"It'll be fine," Gage said, opening the door and stepping into a room that belonged in a five-star hotel. The walls and carpet were taupe, accented with a blue comforter and curtains over the large windows. He bet he had a killer view. What did it say about him that he didn't bother to go look? Instead, he dropped his suitcase at the foot of the bed and returned to the hallway.

"Mr. Beckett thought it best if you were close to Shiloh," Thomas said, gesturing to the next door over. It explained the luxury. He had half expected to be relegated to a quaint room on the other side of the house, out of the household's hair.

Gage nodded. "I planned to have that very discussion with Mr. Beckett. This saves me the trouble."

Thomas hesitated, clearly debating with himself, before continuing. "Shiloh is a good kid. He doesn't deserve what those tabloids are saying about him."

"I'm sure he doesn't," Gage said, not sure he agreed. Shiloh was as bad as any other rich trust-fund brat with too much time on his hands and not enough discipline. The tabloids reporting his transgressions were exactly what he deserved, as far as Gage was concerned, even if he did think there were people more worthy of being reported on—like the Harvard doctor who'd developed a revolutionary new bionic prosthetic only to have his funding slashed or the students doing walkouts by the hundreds to protest the lack of stricter gun laws.

Gage followed Thomas to the study. "Mr. Beckett should arrive home any moment," the butler said as he held open the door.

Gage nodded and sank into the less-than-comfortable chair facing the wooden desk. "That's fine. I'm in no hurry." He pulled out his phone and opened the file he'd asked Mason to send him. It was a dossier on all the household staff, including short biographies, background checks and outstanding debts—anything their tech guy could get his hands on, which was pretty much everything.

The live-in staff was comprised of thirteen people. After Henry, Mr. Beckett's personal driver, there was Thomas the butler, and Maria the estate manager. Beyond that were the chief gardener, two chefs, three maids and four security officers.

Gage read through the entire dossier twice, flagging a few for further investigation, and still no Beckett. He glanced at his watch with a frown. It was nearing six in the evening, three hours after he'd settled into the study. Surely the family should be back from dinner by now. Thomas had insisted they'd arrive home at any moment. Gage wasn't technically on the clock yet, so there was little he could do but wait. He'd signed the non-disclosure agreement as required, but he couldn't sign the contract itself until Mr. Beckett was present.

Thomas stepped in twice to assure him that Mr. Beckett should be home at any moment. By the third time, Gage had moved to one of the more comfortable armchairs by the bookshelf.

The sky outside the window had long since darkened when the study door was finally flung open. A red-faced Anthony Beckett trudged into the room. He was tall and thinnish—not slender, but narrow in the way only a man who'd dropped a large amount of weight in too short a time could achieve—with a pair of wire spectacles perched on a regal nose. His tie hung crooked around his neck, his jacket unbuttoned. Just behind him was a man Gage recognized, but only from the dossier Mason had sent over. Sam Lawson was Mr. Beckett's personal lawyer. He'd been with the company since it had been founded. Whatever was bothering Mr. Beckett had not affected his lawyer—or his lawyer was better at hiding it. He was calm as he set down his briefcase.

"I'm very sorry, Mr. Tucker." Mr. Beckett sounded exhausted as he dropped down at his desk. Gage stood, his knees cracking, and moved to the chair opposite. "You arrived earlier than I anticipated."

"It's no problem," Gage lied. "I've just been reading over the background checks on your employees."

Mr. Beckett slumped back, swiping a hand through his thinning hair. "I had *hoped* to introduce you to Shiloh, but he skipped out on dinner last night and we haven't quite managed to track him down yet."

Gage stiffened in his seat. Was Shiloh missing like 'should have had a police report filed'? Or missing like 'ditched his guards to go get drunk'? Gage pulled out his phone and sent a quick message to his boss, alerting him to the potential disappearance of his client, then scrolled through recent news stories, relaxing slightly when he saw a tabloid post of the boy at a club late the past night. He hadn't been missing long, then.

"He'll turn up. He always does," Sam Lawson said from his spot near the edge of the desk. He wasn't sitting. He stood, his hip propped against the wood. His voice was bored. So probably, it was the second type. Gage wasn't surprised.

"It's different now and you know it," Mr. Beckett snapped, his eyes narrowing at his lawyer.

"Which is why you should tell Shiloh about the letters," Lawson said, exasperated in a way that made Gage suspect this conversation had happened before.

"I don't want him worried about something he can't control. There's nothing he can do about it," Beckett said.

"There *is* something he could do. He could stop slipping his security detail." Lawson pressed his lips together then turned to Gage, his eyes narrowing as they scanned his outfit. Gage had enough time that he could have changed, but he'd thought that as soon as he'd left to do so, Mr. Beckett would have shown up. And besides, they were paying him for his skill, not his suits. "Are you sure *this* one's going to be able to keep up with him?"

Gage smirked, answering before Beckett could. "Don't worry, Mr. Lawson. The United States military thought me more than capable to hunt down terrorists. I'm sure I can keep track of Shiloh." Something about Mr. Lawson put Gage on edge, and he liked to think he had good instincts. Maybe it was just that he was a lawyer. He'd never liked them.

"Lockhart assured me that Mr. Tucker was his best. I trust him to do his job, just as I trust you to do *yours,* Sam. Do you have the contract?" Beckett asked.

Lawson sighed and pulled a small stack of papers out of his briefcase, sliding it across the desk to Gage. Gage flipped through it. It was the standard contract, but he read it anyway before scrawling his signature across the bottom.

"Again, I'm very sorry for the inconvenience," Beckett said, standing. "I'm sure you're tired from your flight. Shiloh should be home in the morning." Beckett frowned like he wasn't certain. "We can discuss his schedule and our expectations then. If you need anything, the phone in your room connects to the kitchen. There's always someone there."

Gage decided that the first thing he would do was order something quick and easy, since airline peanuts were hardly filling, then he'd spend the rest of the evening doing as much research as he could. He had a feeling that this would be the last good night's sleep he'd get for some time.

Chapter Five

Gage jerked awake, his heart thudding in his chest—*whum-whumping* like the blades of the helicopter that had airlifted him from the bloodied sands of the desert—and for a moment he was still there. His throat closed on phantom smoke, cloying and black, before his mind oriented him. The loud *bang* was not a gunshot, not a roadside bomb, but a door slamming open.

He drew in a steadying breath and rolled to his feet. He heard the angry voice of Mr. Beckett next door, reassuring him that at least there was no intruder. It was just Shiloh, returning home in the early hours of pre-dawn. Gage eyed his watch. *Nearly three.*

"Where were you? Do you have *any* idea how immature that little stunt was?"

Gage left the guest room, peering into the hallway. Light spilled from the next room, painting the cream wall yellow.

"I just wanted to have a bit of fun. Jeez, Dad, lighten up a little." *That must be Shiloh.* His voice was softer than Gage had expected, less whiny.

"Fun? You were supposed to be at family dinner, not out having fun. What am I supposed to do with you, Shiloh?" Beckett's voice was as tight as a rubber band poised to snap. Gage wondered how much of the anger in his voice was really fear.

"It's not family dinner. *He's* not my family."

Gage imagined his client pouting. That full, pink lip, shiny with gloss, sticking out in a way that tempted him to bite it. Gage shook his head, struggling to clear the inappropriate image clear from his mind. That was exactly why he hadn't wanted this assignment. He hadn't even met the brat and he was already chasing away an erection.

"If you want to act like a child, I can treat you like one," Beckett threatened. "If you expect to keep your allowance, you'll watch your tone, and you will *not* talk about Sam that way. He's done a lot for this family."

Gage peered into the next room. Beckett was standing a few feet in, his back to the door. His fists were plastered to his hips as he loomed over the stubborn young man slouched on the edge of the bed. Shiloh was not pouting. Instead, his face was pale with anger, though he made no move toward his father, his hands clenched tight in the bedspread.

He looked younger than he did in the tabloids.

"If you say so, sir," Shiloh finally bit out.

"You will apologize to Sam in the morning for skipping dinner. Then you'll help Maria in the kitchen at breakfast," Beckett said.

Shiloh's head jerked up. "I'll help Maria, but I am *not* apologizing!"

Gage smirked. Now, with his eyes flashing, he was finally starting to look like Gage expected.

"You *will* apologize, and you *will* be polite, or I swear to God I will reconsider my decision to let you leave your room in the first place!" Beckett said.

Shiloh glanced away from his father, his gaze colliding with Gage's. Shiloh froze, his eyes widening before he jerked to his feet. "Who the fuck is *that*?"

Beckett glanced at Gage over his shoulder. "That's Mr. Tucker. He's your new bodyguard."

"Sorry to interrupt, sir," Gage said, He wasn't really sorry that he was caught eavesdropping, though he probably should have pulled on a shirt. "I heard the door slam and just wanted to make sure everything was okay."

"*He's* my new bodyguard? Where'd you find him, a Calvin Klein ad? I guess at least this one will be nice to look at." Shiloh leered at Gage's exposed chest. Gage refused to let the man fluster him. Rather than cross his arms, he straightened, allowing the muscles to flex. He knew he had a nice body. He worked hard to keep it that way.

"*Shiloh*!" Beckett sounded horrified. The glance he shot Gage was ripe with apology. "You will *not* speak to him that way—"

Gage interrupted. "Don't worry, Mr. Beckett. The kid didn't hurt my feelings."

"I'm not a kid," Shiloh said, crimson blossoming across his cheeks as he crossed his arms.

His chest wasn't as broad as Gage's. Instead, Shiloh was all lithe, lean muscle. He looked like a dancer. Gage wanted to let his gaze skim up and down the slender body but resisted. *One* of them had to remain professional.

"I'll stop treating you like a kid when you stop acting like one," Beckett inserted. "Get to bed. You have an early class."

"I'm not going." Shiloh flopped back on his bed, his arm flung over his eyes. "And you can't make me."

"Then you'll have plenty of time to help Mathew clean the pool," Beckett replied.

Gage backed out of the room and returned to his own as the pair continued arguing. He was more convinced than ever that Shiloh was nothing more than a spoiled, trust-fund brat.

Doubting he was going to be able to fall back asleep, Gage pulled out his tablet and powered it up. He'd spent two weeks in Austin a few years ago, right after he'd been released from the San Antonio Polytrauma Rehabilitation Center, and right before he'd taken the job working at Eagle Security. The brief visit had given him a vague knowledge of the city districts, which would be fine if he were here on vacation. He'd prefer a more well-rounded education on a job, though.

He pored over city maps until he was confident that he could navigate all but the most backroad of streets, then switched over to the University of Texas at Austin website. Shiloh was attending classes to get his business degree, so it wasn't hard to narrow down the professors he was most likely studying under and Gage start compiling a dossier. He'd send them off to Jason for background checks in the morning. Jason—or Sin, as everyone at the company called him—was their resident tech genius.

Gage supposed it was a good thing Shiloh's arrival had woken him so early. He had a lot to do to be ready for the morning and his first official day on the job.

Chapter Six

Threats from Mr. Beckett or not, Gage knew there was no way Shiloh was getting up earlier than noon, not with how late he'd straggled in the night before. He was fully prepared to wake up to another screaming match between the boy and his father. What he woke up to instead was the sound of the shower kicking on next door at a quarter to eight.

After pulling on his usual work uniform—a pair of black jeans, a black V-neck shirt and a pair of custom-made steel-toed boots—Gage stepped out into the hallway, just in time to meet his client.

Who apparently was already trying to sneak out. The shower was still running in his bathroom, and only sheer luck had made Gage step out when he did. Otherwise, the sleep-rumpled Shiloh might have slipped past him.

Gage's eyes traveled from his client's messy hair to the eyeliner still smudged around his blue eyes, then lower…past the sheer white blouse that barely hung on his shoulder to the threadbare jeans in a color he couldn't pronounce, somewhere between blue and red but not quite purple. "Cute," Gage said with a teasing grin.

"If you're done staring?" Shiloh said through gritted teeth, cocking out a slender hip so he could plant his fist on it.

"I don't know. An outfit like that is just begging to be stared at." Gage couldn't help it that Shiloh could have been pulled out of any one of his fantasies.

"Spoken like a man." Shiloh rolled his eyes, but Gage's were drawn down to the boy's finger, tapping impatiently on the thin strip of taut skin peeking out beneath the hem of his blouse. "Still staring," Shiloh snapped his fingers under Gage's nose.

"I'm memorizing your outfit. You know, in case you give me the slip and I have to make up a missing-child poster," Gage teased but finally lifted his eyes back to Shiloh's.

The answering growl was so cute that Gage couldn't help but laugh, which pissed off the kid even more. Shiloh's middle finger flashed between them. "Not a fucking child, asshole."

And thank God for that, Gage thought. Instead of voicing it, though, Gage shrugged. "Prove it."

"What do you want me to do, suck your dick? I have a better idea. Suck on this." Shiloh crassly grabbed his crotch, fabric stretching taut over what appeared to be a well-proportioned dick—not that Gage was looking.

"How about you do your chores like a good little boy. That'll show me how old you are," Gage suggested instead.

Shiloh gave a devilish grin as he backed down the hall. "I never claimed to be a good boy. You might have to spank me." Shiloh smirked and headed for the stairs, the heels of his strappy sandals clicking on the marble.

Gage adjusted the painful erection tenting his jeans. If he was forced to stare at the muscular globes of the brat's ass as it swayed down the stairs in front of him, he was going to go insane already. They were the perfect size for his palm, and he could just imagine how pretty the pale skin would look flushed with his handprints.

Which was a totally inappropriate thought that he needed to steer clear of, Gage reminded himself.

"You didn't shut the shower off," Gage called after the boy instead.

Shiloh froze at the top of the stairs. Gage was pretty sure he didn't imagine the curse the boy muttered under his breath before spinning on his heels and stomping back toward his bedroom. "You're my babysitter. Aren't *you* supposed to shut it off for me?" Shiloh asked.

"Next you'll ask me to give you a sponge bath, too. I hate to disappoint you, sweetheart, but that ain't in my job description." Gage snapped his fingers. "Pip pip… Better hurry if you don't want to disappoint Daddy."

Shiloh rolled his eyes but surprisingly went into the bedroom. A few seconds later, Gage heard the shower cut off.

"Happy?" Shiloh asked as headed back into the hallway.

"Ecstatic. All the grass in Austin thanks you profusely." Gage's voice was dry as he responded.

Shiloh just huffed and started down the hallway again. Gage followed him downstairs and along the corridors until they eventually found their way into a large kitchen. It could have been featured in any one of a dozen magazines, and quite possibly already had been. A young woman stood by the stove, whistling as she stirred what appeared to be oatmeal.

"*Buenos dias,* Maria," Shiloh said, snagging a piece of unbuttered toast off a plate before he hopped up on the counter on the other side.

"Your accent is terrible." Maria, without even looking, grabbed a spatula from beside her and swatted at Shiloh's hip. "Ass off my counters." Gage guessed she was second generation, like himself, because while she was clearly Latina, her accent was pure Texan.

Shiloh laughed but slid down. "Dad said to help you in the kitchen, so put me to work." He reached for another piece of toast, only to receive another swat on his hands.

"Eating is not working," Maria scolded.

Gage smiled as he watched the pair banter back and forth, sounding almost like siblings. They clearly had a good relationship, despite the fact that she was an employee. She teased him about his cooking abilities—or lack thereof—and he threatened to break the dishes instead of wash them, but all joking aside, they worked together well.

At least, until Mr. Beckett stepped into the kitchen. Shiloh's laughter withered, replaced by a set of crossed arms and narrowed eyes. "What? I'm helping Maria, like you said." Shiloh's voice dropped immediately into a snotty protest, a far cry from the friendly banter of a moment earlier.

Gage chalked the attitude change up to normal father-son tensions. After all, Shiloh was only barely not a teenager, and that was never an easy age. If Beckett had only recently started putting his foot down about his son's behavior, which seemed likely, given the tabloid exploits, there would of course be growing pains.

It wouldn't kill the kid to learn some responsibility. Someday, he might even thank his father for leading him off a dangerous path. Gage doubted it, but really, it wasn't his business. He was there to keep Shiloh safe, not teach him respect.

Though thinking of teaching Shiloh respect by putting him over his knee was not helping to curtail the situation growing in his jeans.

"Maria can finish up. It looks like you are making more of a mess than you're cleaning anyway." Beckett's gaze traveled from the soap suds on the counter to the water streaked along the tiles. "Come upstairs."

"Can't. Gotta go to class." Shiloh spun off the water and dried his arms on one of the linen towels that probably cost more than Gage had paid for his entire kitchen.

"I already spoke to the Dean. You can be late today." Beckett twisted his wrist to eye his watch, like this conversation with his son was pulling him away from something important. As the CEO of a company as big as Beckett Industries, maybe it was.

"Oh, I see. So when *you* don't want me to go to class, that's just fine, but when *I* don't want to go, I'm lazy and ungrateful," Shiloh muttered, looking one second away from stomping his foot.

"Kill the tantrum or I'm keeping your keys. Upstairs…now." Beckett didn't wait. Either he knew the threat would be enough of an incentive or he just didn't care if Shiloh followed, because he spun on his heel and stomped out of the kitchen. Gage heard his shoes on the stairs.

"Kill the tantrum or I'm keeping your keys," Shiloh mocked, his face twisting as he mimicked his dad's lower register voice. "Clearly, he's never heard of Uber."

Gage cleared his throat and Shiloh flinched like he'd forgotten Gage was there. He rolled his eyes. "I suppose you're going to drag me upstairs if I try climbing out of the window?"

"If you try climbing out the window, I'm going to laugh my ass off," Gage replied, glancing pointedly at the small square of glass he wasn't even sure opened. It definitely wasn't big enough for the younger man to crawl through, even as slender as he was.

Shiloh glared at him, but Gage didn't think he was imagining the small quirk of his lips at the corner. "Fine, whatever. I'll go upstairs. But not because he told me to."

"Of course not," Gage agreed, and followed his client.

* * * *

An hour later, Gage finally understood why Shiloh didn't want to go upstairs. His left knee was starting to ache from pretending to be a statue in the corner. He shifted his weight, trying to subtly ease the pain, then grimaced when it only worsened.

He'd stopped paying attention to Beckett's lecture after the first ten minutes. To be fair, he'd probably lasted about five minutes longer than Shiloh. The younger man was scraping his fingernail in circles around the arm of the wooden chair he was slouched in, not seeming to care that it was chipping his pink nail polish, sending minuscule flakes floating like dandruff to the carpet.

"Are you even listening to me?" Beckett snapped.

Gage watched the finger swirl around in circles again as an awkward silence filled the room. He glanced up to see three pairs of eyes on him. Beckett was frowning, Lawson had his arms crossed, wrinkling his suit jacket, and Shiloh was smirking.

"Who, me?" Gage clarified, grateful for his dark complexion. At least the flush that heated his cheeks wouldn't be visible. "Sorry… I thought we were still lecturing Shiloh about the importance of family bonding." He made air quotes around the last two words with his fingers.

Beckett glared, but it was worth it to hear Shiloh's giggle-snort, until he buried it into his palm. Beckett's face softened slightly at the sound.

"I was saying that Shiloh's going to be spending the evening with Sam as an apology for missing dinner the night before last, so you'll have the night free. Just make sure Shiloh's back here by six," Beckett repeated, then glanced at his watch again. "I have a meeting I have to get to, so you can go ahead and take him to school now."

The way the man spoke about Shiloh, it was like he was a possession or an employee—not a grown man with the power to make his own decisions. Although, given the decisions Shiloh had been making over the last few years, maybe that was why. If Gage had a son who was more likely to be caught at an orgy then at school, he might also not trust his decision-making.

Mr. Beckett held a set of keys out to Shiloh. Shiloh went to grab them, but Mr. Beckett held on for a second longer. "To school then straight back home or you'll get a driver again."

Shiloh rolled his eyes but snatched the keys. "Yeah, Dad. Whatever..."

Gage followed Shiloh out into a garage that held a dozen cars, each one worth more than most people's houses. When Shiloh went to open the door to a yellow Bugatti, Gage grabbed his arm to stop him.

Shiloh tried to yank his arm free, but Gage kept his grip. "Before we get in the car, we have to go over the rules."

"What are you, my dad?" Shiloh grumbled, giving up on pulling free but retaining his attitude.

"Think of me like a glorified babysitter," Gage replied, "here to stop you from doing anything stupid and stop anyone else from getting too stabby-stabby."

Shiloh looked pointedly around the empty garage. "So, was I about to do something stupid or is my car about to shiv me?"

Gage laughed. "The first one. You don't get into a vehicle that hasn't been checked. There could be a crazed fan in the backseat."

"There is no backseat," Shiloh pointed out dryly.

"Or," Gage continued like he hadn't been interrupted, "a bomb under the bumper."

"What is this, Baghdad?" Shiloh rolled his eyes. Gage's grip tightened on the boy's arm at the less-than-funny joke.

"I served two tours in Afghanistan. Never went to Baghdad, but I lost friends there," Gage replied, struggling to keep his voice calm at the casual mention of a place he'd seen soldiers cry from being stationed at.

Shiloh's skin flushed pink and he looked away, tucking his lip between his teeth before he muttered an apology. "Sorry. I just meant that I don't think anyone snuck in a bomb."

"And that's why it's my job to think that way for you," Gage pointed out. "But thank you for apologizing." For some reason, acknowledging his apology made Shiloh's cheeks flush even further.

Gage dropped down to his good knee, peeking under the frame of the car. Not that the kid was wrong... It *was* unlikely there was a bomb, but he wouldn't risk it. While he was down there, he slid his hand along the undercarriage, casually planting the small black device that would help him track the car if Shiloh pulled one of his famous stunts. Gage had only needed to use them a handful of times, but with each one, he'd been grateful for the foresight. A few minutes' difference in locating the GPS could be the difference in a client living...or not.

Chapter Seven

Shiloh cleared his throat and Gage glanced up at him. Shiloh's voice was husky when he spoke. "I can think of better things for you to do on your knees than eye fuck my car, Mr. Tucker."

"Not everyone wants to blow you, kid." Gage stood as soon as he felt his body reacting to the thought of following through, of leaning forward and tugging down the too-tight pants. He cleared his throat. "And call me Gage. Mr. Tucker was my father."

Shiloh gave a dry laugh and pushed by him to drop into the driver's seat. "Are you going to loom over me all day, Mr. Tucker, or are you coming?"

Gage was closer to coming then he'd like.

He cleared his throat before planting his hand on the doorframe. Before he could speak, Shiloh shook his head, already anticipating his next words. "We can stand here and argue for an hour, or you can get in the passenger seat. No one drives my Bugatti but me."

"You could get an Escalade," Gage mused. "It's safer. Lower profile. Then I could drive it."

"Why would I want that? Don't worry. My father forced me to take a class on defensive driving before he'd pay for my driver's license. You can just sit here and look pretty." Shiloh stroked the passenger seat in a way that had Gage burying a groan but rounding the car.

Gage needed to keep Shiloh safe and that meant building trust, not conflict. He slid into the passenger seat and buckled his seatbelt. Shiloh didn't bother, so while they waited for the garage door to creep its way up, Gage leaned over and tugged on the seatbelt, snapping it into place before Shiloh could protest.

Gage expected a certain level of indignant anger. What he did not expect was the immediate, primal reaction he got. Shiloh slammed his foot on the brake, hard enough the tires screamed in protest, despite them having barely been moving. His knuckles whitened on the gear-shaft as he threw it into park.

"Unclick it." Shiloh's voice was chilled steel, his words slipping out through clenched teeth.

"It's illegal to drive without a seatbelt." Gage frowned. This was not just Shiloh being a brat. His client's breath had sharpened into a ragged, broken pant, his eyes drowning in white. It was a panic Gage recognized, though he hadn't seen it in years. Then it had been from a fellow soldier. The man had been fresh from boot camp and facing down enemy bullets for the first time.

Shiloh unclenched a hand from the wheel and went to press the red button. Gage grabbed his wrist before he could. "You can't drive without a seatbelt, Shiloh. It's not safe."

"Let go." Shiloh yanked his wrist free, and Gage let him. Shiloh's skin was cold and clammy, and Gage feared he was pushing him toward the edge of something dangerous.

Shiloh opened the door, swiftly unlatching the belt and practically jumping free of the car. He'd rounded it and tugged open the passenger door before Gage could do anything but frown.

"Let's get some things straight," Shiloh growled. "You do *not* grab me unless you want a knee to the dick, and you are *not* my father. Do your job and keep the paparazzi off my ass or don't. I don't give a fuck, but *don't* tell me what I can or can't do. I don't wear seatbelts, and if you got a problem with that, you can fuck right off."

"I do have a problem with that," Gage said. "It's not safe."

Shiloh's laugh was pained. "Nothing's safe. That's life. I didn't ask you to tag along. I'll suck it up, but you need to *back* the fuck *off*."

Gage studied Shiloh. He wondered what had happened to make Shiloh so afraid of a seatbelt. He didn't remember reading anything in the file about a past car accident. Whatever it was, Gage knew pressing the issue would be a bad idea.

"Seatbelt or I'm driving," Gage compromised.

Shiloh huffed. "I don't speed, and I obey all traffic laws—even the stupid ones."

"This isn't a negotiation. Seatbelt or I drive."

Shiloh crossed his arms, mutiny in his eyes. But all he said was, "If you crash my car, you're paying my deductible."

Gage unbuckled and slid out, rounding the car and climbing into the driver's seat without comment. Shiloh collapsed into the passenger side. Gage ignored the pouting, the crossed arms, even the feet immediately propping on the pristine leather of the dash and started down the drive, unsurprised when a white van, probably filled with hopeful paparazzi, peeled out from the side of the road behind them as they left the property.

Gage kept an eye on the van just in case but didn't point it out. Instead, he brought up a topic he didn't want to leave for later. "I suppose now's as good a time as any to go over the rest of the rules."

Shiloh shrugged. "Whatever."

"The first thing we need to get straight is that I'm not here to keep you out of the tabloids." Gage knew Mason wouldn't like him blowing his cover in the first real conversation he had with the kid, but he couldn't keep Shiloh safe if he was more worried about ditching him then following basic precautions. He wouldn't tell him everything, obviously, just enough to get the point across.

"Yeah, right," Shiloh muttered.

"I'm a bodyguard. I—"

"If you say you guard my body, I'll kick you in the knee."

Gage ignored him. "I will do my best to keep the paparazzi from pestering you, but my primary job is getting you from place to place safely. I'm not your babysitter. I'm not here to tell you what you can or can't do, unless you're putting yourself at risk."

"That's what the other guy said. Then I blew someone in the bathroom, and he ran to my father," Shiloh said.

Gage forcibly restrained his lip from curling at the thought of Shiloh on his knees in a dirty bathroom. "I don't care what you do so long as you do it safely. I'm *your* bodyguard, not your father's. If you want to sneak out of the house, you take me with you. You have sex in a bathroom, you take me with you." Though God help him if that happened, because Gage wasn't sure he could handle standing back and watching that. "I'm not here to rat you out. I'm here to keep you safe—which leads me to my rules."

"Thought you weren't a babysitter," Shiloh mocked.

Gage ignored him. "I will enter all buildings and vehicles first so I can clear the area of threats." He paused, waiting for an objection that didn't come, then continued. "With a few exceptions, I will walk to your left, slightly behind you. There may be times this isn't practical, but we'll deal with that when it happens. If I ask you to do something, such as duck, freeze or run, I need you to immediately obey. I ask you these things because there's an immediate threat. If you want to know why, you may ask after."

"So if you say jump, *don't* ask how high?" Shiloh grinned.

Gage didn't.

"Exactly. If I say jump, you jump. I promise not to issue orders unless there's a direct threat, so long as you promise to obey them without question." Gage turned, watching the white van turn behind them.

Shiloh examined him in silence before giving a terse nod. "Fine."

"Sometimes, you might see something I don't. If you are uncomfortable but there is no immediate threat, you can say 'yellow' and I'll step in. If you can't speak or don't want to draw attention to it, tap your thumb to your middle finger twice, like this." He demonstrated the move to make sure Shiloh understood. "If you feel you are in immediate danger, say 'red' or bite your thumbnail. Understand?"

"Will that happen often? You missing a threat?" Shiloh asked. His voice was casual, but his eyes were sharp. He tapped a rapid beat on his thigh with his fingers.

"No. But you might perceive something or someone as a threat that I don't, because you have prior knowledge. It's better to prepare for it, just in case. And never, *ever,* leave for a secondary location without me, no matter how well you know someone."

"I guess that's smart," Shiloh grudgingly replied as Gage pulled the car into the university parking lot and circled for a spot.

"Do you have any questions before we leave the vehicle?" Gage asked as he parked.

"Can I nap in the car while you go to class for me?" Shiloh grinned.

"Only if you want to fail *Intro to Bio,*" Gage answered, stepping out. He held his hand out for Shiloh to wait, watching the white van slow. He was halfway to shoving Shiloh to the pavement at the sight of a scope emerging from the window before he realized it wasn't a gun but a large, expensive camera lens. Gage clenched his fist as he aborted the instinctive move, watching the camera flash like a strobe light as it took several pictures before the van sped away.

Shiloh followed his gaze, half leaning over the center console to watch the van curiously. "Nobody wants to see me being a good little boy and attending class. I'll be safe from them as long as I'm on campus." Shiloh paused before adding, "Unless I start taking my clothes off."

"Then I'd suggest keeping them on," Gage said dryly. He examined the surroundings—mostly students, a few teachers bustling about, all minding their own business, nobody that looked like a threat. Still, he was grateful that Shiloh seemed to be taking his warnings to heart and staying in the car. Just because it was clear now didn't mean there couldn't have been a danger.

He turned to tell Shiloh it was safe to exit the vehicle. Instead, he was forced to watch as Shiloh leaned over the seats to tug the driver's door shut and throw the locks. Shiloh gave a cocky grin as he settled into the driver's seat and threw the car in reverse.

Shocked, Gage watched the car narrowly avoid a collision with a silver Audi whose driver blared their horn in annoyance, then disappear into traffic.

He supposed he should have seen it coming.

Gage sighed and pulled out his phone, opening an app. Two minutes later, an Uber pulled up and he slid into the backseat, feeding the driver directions. He'd never been so grateful this quickly to have installed a GPS tracker on a client before.

Maybe he should invest in a tether. Either that or find a better way to convince Shiloh he wasn't there just for decoration.

Chapter Eight

Shiloh laughed at the surprised expression on his bodyguard's face.

Like he was really going to sit in the car and be a good little boy until he was given permission to climb out. *Fuck that.* He had better things to do with his time.

Shiloh angled the Bugatti into a narrow gap between a blue van and a silver Audi and peeled away from the university. As he drove, he thumbed through the contact list on his phone until he reached the one he wanted.

The stereo cut out as the Bluetooth connected to his radio. The line rang twice before a cheerful female voice came on the line. "This is Delia at Blood, Sweat and Shears. May I help you?"

"Delia, darling!" Shiloh angled his neck to glance both ways at the stoplight before he ran the yellow light. "It's Shiloh. I have a hair emergency."

"Oh no. Tell me you didn't…" Delia sounded too horrified to even finish her sentence. He'd joked with her after his last visit that he was going to try a new glow-in-the-dark hair dye that had been all the rage on Insta.

"I didn't, I swear. Cross my heart," Shiloh promised. "My hair just isn't pink enough. It doesn't match my new outfit."

"Oh, thank heavens. I can squeeze you in at four with Joel," Delia said.

"Perfect." Shiloh chatted for a bit longer before he heard bells through the phone. Rather than distract Delia from a customer, he said his goodbyes.

He had to kill time, but since it wasn't like he could go home anyway, so he might as well find something to do. He spent a few hours browsing boutiques, noting expensive things to charge to his credit card later. His dad had lowered the limit to a measly few hundred dollars. It was enough for him to grab lunch from a little diner tucked behind a laundromat and still afford the haircut later, but that was about it. The diner was his favorite place to eat—not because the food was good, because it wasn't, or because the staff was friendly, because they weren't, but because it was such a rundown little place that the paparazzi had yet to spot him.

Just in case, he wore his cap and sunglasses.

Finally, though, four o'clock rolled around. Shiloh strolled into the pink Victorian-turned-salon with a wide, only *somewhat* fake smile on his face. All but one of the stations was occupied by women of varying ages, though the stylists were a mixed bag. Shiloh waved to those he recognized—which was most, to be honest, since he came there regularly—as he headed toward the half-circle desk opposite the door.

Delia lounged behind it. Her half-laced Doc Martens were kicked up on the desk, and she had a book propped open on her knees. Shiloh leaned over and snatched for the paperback. Careful to keep his finger tucked between the pages to hold her spot, he flipped it over to see the cover. He scrunched his nose. "You should read the slash fic—more sex, less boobs."

Delia flipped him off with a grin. "You know I like boobs, Shy."

Shiloh pouted but couldn't hold the expression for long before he grinned. "Yeah, I know. How's Amy?"

"Still hot." Delia snagged the book back and propped it, spine up, out of his reach on the shelf behind her. "And unfortunately, still in Detroit with her mom."

"No fun." Shiloh straightened back up. "How's Maggie doing, anyway?"

"No change, still a bitch. Amy said she chucked a whiskey bottle at her yesterday. It upset her so much she left Maggie with the nurse. Then, of course, called me crying about how she was a horrible daughter." Anger flashed in Delia's eyes. "I told her that was a crock of horse shit. She doesn't owe that woman anything but a nice hard kick in the ass."

Shiloh was about to agree when a nondescript door behind the desk opened, distracting him.

Joel, Shiloh's usual stylist, stepped out from the hidden stairway. Shiloh still felt guilty for stereotyping the man before they'd met. He'd heard 'hair stylist' and had expected a slender, effeminate twink with a flair for flamboyant hand gestures. Basically, a carbon copy of himself.

Instead, Joel looked like he'd be more at home in a boxing ring. His blond hair was cropped close to his scalp and the wife beater he wore only made his muscles more prominent. For a whole two minutes,

Shiloh had nursed an unhealthy crush. Then he'd realized Joel wasn't an asshole, and now, they were almost friends.

"I hear you need a touch-up," Joel said as he moved out from behind the desk, leading Shiloh over to his station with a soft touch to his arm. His spot was tucked near the end, right beside the rinse area. Shiloh settled into the chair and allowed Joel to drape the cape around his shoulders.

"It's not pink enough." Shiloh pouted at his reflection in the mirror. "It doesn't match my new uniform."

Joel smirked back at him. He knew where Shiloh worked, though he'd not yet come out to watch him dance, so he knew that by uniform, Shiloh of course meant panties. "Are we adding highlights or doing an all-over?"

"All-over. I want it so pink I could be a flamingo."

"You *are* a flamingo." Joel ruffled Shiloh's hair affectionately.

"Thank you." Shiloh acknowledged the compliment and propped his feet up on the metal footrest.

"Are you coming upstairs after?" Joel asked, already mixing up the dye in a small plastic bowl.

"Only if you've prepped already," Shiloh said. "I'd hate to put you out."

"It'll be tight, but I have a bit of time before my next client." Joel started working the dye through the strands.

"Then that sounds great. I've been dying for a good workout." Shiloh relaxed against the back of the chair. There was nothing quite so soothing as getting his hair done. He loved the feel of fingers moving through his hair, even if it was only to make sure the dye was spread evenly, and the head massage that came with the shampoo was literally *to die for*. He couldn't wait.

* * * *

Gage tailed Shiloh in the Uber to a gay club. *No surprise there*. Envy was tucked in the middle of the Red River District. Relatively new, passing time hadn't yet faded the bright rainbow sign hanging above the door.

Of course, Envy wasn't the first place he'd tailed his client to. Shiloh spent an hour wandering through expensive boutiques, and by the time Shiloh had left the salon, hair still pink but brighter, Gage was wondering whether he would be coming out with any hair at all. Shiloh had eaten lunch at a small diner before the salon, large sunglasses glued to his face, and dinner had been from a drive-thru. Gage didn't bother making himself known. He could do his job whether Shiloh knew he was there or not. Actually, he could probably do it better in secret. At least Shiloh wasn't trying to ditch him now.

By the time Gage let the driver drop him off at Envy, he'd had more than enough reasons to cement his decision to rent a car for his stay in Austin and expense the cost. The Uber had cost a small fortune.

Gage followed the yellow sports car down an alley leading behind the bar. It was narrow, just wide enough for a single car to drive through, and dirty. It smelled faintly of beer and more so of urine. The single light mounted on the brick wall of the building flickered, ready to burn out. While Gage wasn't worried about getting mugged, this was certainly a prime place for it to happen. He didn't like the thought of his client wandering around here alone.

Thankfully, the alley was as short as it was narrow, and it was a quick jaunt to the lot behind the building. The yellow Bugatti was parked between a rusted red pickup and an old brown station wagon near a plain gray service door. He wondered why, of all the bars Shiloh could have picked, he'd chosen this one. It reminded Gage of the place he'd used to go to back when he had still been pretending to be straight, the one that had been just seedy enough that he didn't worry about running into anyone he knew.

Gage tugged on the gray door, disappointed when it opened easily. The hallway inside was plain. Two doors on the left were clearly marked as bathrooms, while one on the right was labeled *Employees Only.* Gage bypassed them, following the sound of music ahead.

The first sight of the interior of the club made Gage change his opinion. It wasn't seedy at all, regardless of the rundown exterior. The dance floor sprawled through the center of the floor, shadowed enclaves skirting the edges with little tables and booths peppered inside. Behind the bar, old murals on the walls glowed eerily under the black lights and strobes. It was hard to make out the original designs, especially with the shelves of bright liquors distorting them further.

A bartender in a bright, glitter-crusted top was wiping down the counter. Gage headed that way, dropping into one of the dozen empty barstools. Unlike most clubs, which smelled to him of vinegar and stale beer, this one smelled pleasantly of bitters and citrus. As he waited for the bartender to finish, he turned to eye the dance floor.

For as early in the evening as it was—barely seven—it was surprisingly full. The clientele was a motley group. As he searched for his client, he saw everything from young men in harnesses and spandex to men in suits, jackets unbuttoned and ties loosened, all the way to bears in their leather jacket, MC patches on their arms. There were even a few women in the far corner, away from the six platforms with barely dressed men dancing atop. It seemed Envy catered to everyone, yet no one in particular.

He absent-mindedly skimmed over the dancers atop each platform while he searched for his client. His gaze jerked back to the closest. That wasn't…

But it was.

The slender frame, the pink hair that matched the lacy boy-shorts that barely covered a straining erection, the piercings… The shiny silver mask did nothing to hide his identity. A fierce, clawing creature roared to life in Gage's chest, urging him to pull his client down and tuck him away somewhere safe, away from all the salivating men lurking too close. But this was just a job, he reminded himself, and he couldn't allow himself to be so easily distracted by a client.

So instead, he angled his body back to the bar, careful to keep his client in sight. The bartender came over, a bright smile on his lips. "What can I get you?"

"Just a Coke," Gage ordered.

"I'm Zach. I haven't seen you in here before." The bartender's eyes followed the line of Gage's tight black shirt and lower as he slid the glass over.

"Last time I was in Austin, this was a tattoo parlor, I think." Gage kept one eye on Shiloh as he chatted.

"Yeah, you can still see some of the murals when the lights are on." Zach followed his gaze out to the floor.

From the corner of his eye, Gage didn't think he imagined the disappointment on the bartender's face. "That's Shy. We're always busier on his shifts."

"I can see why." Gage watched as Shiloh dipped, spreading his knees obscenely. The pink lace stretched taut, leaving little to the imagination.

One of the watchers leaned forward, stretching out to grab Shiloh's ankle. Gage lurched forward, prepared to assist his client if he needed to, but Shiloh just frowned and tugged his ankle free. A moment later, the silver wrestling boots he was wearing slammed down on the grabby man's wrist. Gage heard the man yelp, even from the bar, then a bouncer escorted the guy out of the front.

"That happen often?" Gage asked. Shiloh's reaction had been quick, definite and surprisingly controlled, too much so for this to have been a one-time thing. He struggled with the urge rising inside his chest to turn caveman and drag Shiloh out of the club by his ear, to take him home and peel off those lace panties and turn the pale skin beneath just as pink. Gage cleared his throat, shaking free the unprofessional daydream.

"Once or twice a night. Shy's good at taking care of himself, though. And if things get too out of hand, the big guys step in." Zach nodded off to the side. Gage followed his gesture, easily spotting the three bouncers spread around the platforms. Two of the bouncers were watching the crowd. The third had just returned. He was the least burly of the three, with a dark patch on his neck that Gage thought was a tattoo. Rather than the crowd, this one watched Shiloh.

Gage leaned back against the bar again, taking a small drink of his Coke. Shiloh was a better dancer than the podium permitted. He was graceful in a way the other dancers lacked, even if his moves were overtly sexual. It didn't take a genius to realize that dancing was something the kid was passionate about. Gage just wished he wasn't doing it in a club. Surely there were other, safer outlets. It wasn't like the Beckett heir needed money.

Gage wasn't sure he could hide the reaction Shiloh's dancing caused in him if this became a daily thing.

"So…Zach, right? Shy dance here often?" Gage was curious both about whether the bartender would answer and what the answer would be.

"Oh, yeah, pretty often. Couple nights a week, usually. A bit less recently since Teddy's been off." Zach paused to top off Gage's drink. "Everyone likes it when Shy's here. I think Ian would let him work every night if he could."

"Why doesn't he?" Gage asked.

"I don't know. You'd have to ask Shy. But good luck with that. He's awful prickly…like a sexy cactus." Zach grinned. He dragged his eyes over Gage's body again. "But for you, he might make an exception, especially for the right price." Zach winked.

Gage didn't like the insinuation that Shiloh was fucking men for money but didn't press it. Maybe it made him feel safer, since a man who paid for sex was less likely to brag about it afterward. Instead, he rested his arms on the bar. "I'd be awfully prickly too if I had to fight off gropers every day. Anyone pay Shy *extra* attention? Buy him drinks, leave him presents… Stay near the back like he's afraid to draw attention to himself?"

Zach frowned, grabbing a glass and wiping it absently with a rag. "Who did you say you were again?"

Chapter Nine

The platform vibrated beneath his boots. Shiloh threw his head back, closing his eyes against the sight of the men watching. There was just him and the music. He was almost disappointed when Deak, the tattooed bouncer closest to his platform, reached out to tap his thigh, letting him know it was time for his break. If the heavier-set man's hand lingered too long, Shiloh ignored it like he always did and plastered on a smile.

The men grinding on each other by his platform groaned but made room for him to hop down. His skin was damp with sweat but that didn't stop them from reaching out to touch him, like they always did. He ignored all but the most intimate of gropes as he headed for the bar. He rounded it to grab a glass of water, planning to carry it back to the break room.

He hadn't seen his best friend Teddy in the club in weeks, and while he was still salty about their fight, if Teddy were loitering somewhere back there, he'd buckle down and apologize—or at least, break the ice. Sorry wasn't really his style, but if anyone deserved one, it was Teddy. He knew his friend had only been looking out for him, even if it felt a bit suffocating.

Before he could search out his friend, his gaze landed on the dark-haired man sitting at the bar, talking to a nervous-looking Zach—the very *familiar* man he'd sworn he left behind at the university this morning. Shiloh pushed all signs of his exhaustion clear from his face and cocked a hip instead, pasting on a grin.

"If it isn't my babysitter. Drinking on the job? Naughty boy." Shiloh stopped across from Gage, reaching out to snag his glass. Gage didn't stop him, just leaned back on the stool. And *damn* if he didn't look sexy with that mysterious, brooding way he had about him. Shiloh took a sip of what turned out to be Coke.

"You don't seem to be in any danger." Gage shrugged, stealing the glass back and downing it. "Are the masks just for your benefit?"

Shiloh grinned. "They were my idea. It was the only way I could convince the new boss to keep me on a podium."

"Pretty smart of you," Gage said. "I'm guessing your father doesn't know about this?"

Shiloh sobered quickly, his smile fleeing as he snapped, "No. And if he finds out, I'll know exactly how, won't I, Mr. *Not-a-Babysitter?*"

Gage just shrugged again. "He won't find out from me. I told you… I'm here to keep you safe, not stop you from making stupid choices."

"Dancing's not stupid," Shiloh argued, his anger swelling. *How dare this meat-headed, clumsy-footed—*

"No, but ditching your bodyguard to get a haircut is. And so is skipping class to dance on a podium in front of a bunch of drunks," Gage replied.

"It's barely seven. I doubt anyone is drunk yet." Shiloh flushed at the derision in the other man's voice. He didn't know why he cared what his new bodyguard thought. He never had before.

It had nothing—nothing at all—to do with the attraction Gage stirred up in him. He hadn't felt like this about a man in years—not since he was a teenager, just learning what that uncomfortable tightening below his waist meant. Apparently, it had just taken a tall, well-built guard to bring it back to life. He could almost picture Gage on his knees, giving him mouth-to…

No. He knew better than to go there. He needed to chase this one away like he had the others. Gage paid him too much attention. It had only been a day and already, Shiloh could tell Gage was going to make his plans harder. The others had only watched him if he was getting in trouble. And even then, it had only been to mitigate media exposure.

Shiloh didn't need his every move monitored. If his father found out what he was doing, a grounding would be the least of his worries.

Zach tapped his arm. "Everything okay, Shy? Your next set starts in a minute."

Shiloh blinked. How long had he been zoned out, staring at his bodyguard, for it to draw Zach's attention? He'd have to reach out to Teddy later.

His break was nearly over. "Yeah, it's fine. Can't wait to get back out there." He shot his bodyguard a sunny smile and hopped back over the bar, much to the delight of the waiting crowd. They cheered him as he strutted back to the platform.

And if they got a little too handsy as they helped him back up, it would put on a nice show for his babysitter. Because no matter what the man said, Shiloh knew better than to think that he wouldn't report back to his father. Shiloh knew better than to trust anyone for anything.

Shiloh couldn't feel the music anymore. He was too busy feeling Gage's eyes on his body. Gage, who wasn't a stranger. Gage, who wasn't fooled by the anonymity of the mask. Shiloh felt robotic, stiff and unwieldy. He wished it were a new feeling, but the only thing new about it was that it happened when he was dancing. This was his safe space and now, Gage had ruined it.

* * * *

Shiloh caught Deak's eyes, glancing pointedly toward the bathroom as he hopped off the podium nearly an hour later. He threw a finger—not the one he wanted to throw, but the one that meant hold on—toward Gage, then strutted down the hallway. The light above flickered, throwing him into a tenuous darkness.

The bathroom was grim and faintly malodorous. No amount of cleaning could strip away years of alcohol and vomit. Shiloh propped a hip on the faded blue counter and waited.

It didn't take long for Deak to join him. The squat, middle-aged bouncer glanced uncomfortably over his shoulder as he closed and locked the door behind him.

Immediately, an iron fist clenched beneath Shiloh's ribs. *Out,* the little warning voice in his mind urged. *Get out.* Shiloh gagged it.

"The letter will be in my locker." Shiloh was proud that his voice didn't stutter. He sounded confident, strong...not like the very thought of going through with his plan kept him twisted up each night with nightmares.

But he was in too far to back out now.

He didn't want to back out.

Deak fumbled with his belt, lifting his abdomen to slide it free and sag his pants enough that he could pull his dick out. Like Deak, it was short and squat, the head purple. "We gotta be quick," Deak grunted, leaning against the door for support.

Shiloh bit back his sarcastic comment that Deak was *always* quick and dropped to his knees instead. He held his breath as he swallowed Deak to the root. He worked the man's dick with his tongue, pulling out every trick he knew to make the man spill faster. Too soon, he was forced to breath in through his nose, cringing at the stench of old sweat.

Someone rattled on the doorknob.

"Yeah, hold your horses," Deak grunted. His breath came out in heavy pants, and he groaned as he got closer. He dropped a hand to Shiloh's head to yank him closer.

Shiloh jerked back, the dick slipping from his mouth as he glared up at the bouncer. "You better do a lot more than deliver some fucking letters if you want to touch me."

"Sorry, kid," Deak whined, lifting his hands off Shiloh and planting them on the door again. The doorknob rattled again.

"Occupied!" Shiloh snapped loud enough for whoever was there to hear him.

"You have fifteen seconds to open this door, Shiloh, or I'm breaking it down." The voice was too easy to recognize. His new babysitter didn't sound happy, either.

Shiloh swallowed Deak's dick again before the man had time to protest, reaching up to roll the wrinkled balls in his hand with a practiced twist of his wrist. It was enough to have the bouncer shooting bitter cum down Shiloh's throat just before his time was up. Shiloh spat it on the floor and stood, not bothering to clean it.

"Don't forget," Shiloh reminded the man as he shouldered him aside and pulled open the door, coming face to face with a livid Gage. Shiloh just patted the muscular chest as he slipped by.

"What were you doing in there?" Gage asked, following him across the hall to the *Employees Only* door.

Shiloh put his hand on the doorknob but didn't twist it. He spun to face Gage. "Taking a shit? Giving a blow job? Looking for the door to fairyland?" He shrugged, like each option was equally plausible. "I gotta change. You planning on watching?"

Shiloh turned his back to Gage, though it made spiders crawl down his spine, and headed into the staff locker room. Gage followed him in.

Shiloh sighed, spinning back around. "Look… I know a big dumb jock like you probably had a hard time reading in high school, so let me spell it out to you." Shiloh pointed at the words on the door. "*Em-ploy-ees On-ly.*"

Gage gripped him by the shoulders and forcibly lifted him out of the way. Shiloh squawked a protest, but before he could say anything else, Gage was already past him, examining the room. Shiloh tried to see it through Gage's eyes.

The locker room was small, but it was clean and brightly lit. There was even a painting on the wall between the two rows of lockers. It might have been of a naked man, but it was an *artistic* nude. Ian did a lot to make the bar a nice place for his employees. He even went so far as to not call them employees but *associates.* Each of the lockers had a name painted across it. Shiloh thought it looked nice. Much better than the old employee lounge with its mice and moldy carpet.

Gage pinned Shiloh with a disappointed look. "I'll be in the hall while you change. This will all go much easier for both of us when you realize I don't care what you do, as long as you follow the rules."

"I'm not good with rules." Shiloh couldn't stop his mind from skittering back to the *other* rules, the ones he could never break free of.

"We'll have to work on that," Gage said, then left him alone in the locker room.

Shiloh stripped out of his lacy pink boy-shorts. He went to put them in his locker when he paused, his focus catching on his name, scrawled across the small tag inside. You know, just in case one of the other dancers ever got it in their head to 'borrow' them.

He'd been trying to think of something to up the ante and these…these would be perfect.

Chapter Ten

All the lights at the estate were off. Shiloh slowly inched the Bugatti up the circle driveway. He'd go faster, but it was hard without headlights. The high walls that surrounded the lawn blocked out most of the jaundiced light from the streetlamps, and the nearest moonlight tower was too far away to be much help. He navigated from muscle memory and a small dose of hope.

He didn't bother opening the garage for fear that the noise would wake his father. Instead, he parked on the wilted grass beside it. He held his breath as he spun the key in the ignition, even though he knew he wouldn't hear stirring in the house from here anyway.

He jumped when Gage leaned over and whispered, "Are we having a sleepover in the car then?"

"No. Just...thinking. Sorry." Shiloh felt his cheeks heat and reached for the handle. *Why did I say sorry?* It had slipped out without any prompting from his brain. He didn't apologize. Ever. For anything.

"Can we think...inside?" Gage sounded far too amused.

Shiloh huffed, unbuckling the seatbelt he'd finally talked himself into wearing. "I guess. If you're tired of riding around in a Bugatti already."

"Don't listen to him, baby. He knows not of what he speaks," Gage said as if Shiloh had just insulted his mother.

Shiloh turned back in time to watch Gage lovingly stroke over the leather dash. "It's not a pussy. You can't turn it on by fingering it. You need the keys." Shiloh dangled them from his middle finger, wiggling them until they jangled.

The smirk that Gage shot him had Shiloh hardening in his jeans. He felt pre-cum dampen the lace of his panties.

"If I were trying to turn on your car, I wouldn't be fingering it. I have much more experience with shafts." Gage dropped his hand—with those thick, scarred fingers—down to the shifter. He rolled his palm over the bulbous silver head, then slowly curled his fingers around the shaft, stroking downward.

"Are you...?" Shiloh cleared his throat before continuing, "Are you saying you masturbate a lot?"

"No. I'm saying I'm gay." Gage climbed out of the car, leaving Shiloh to stare at the empty seat with his mouth gaping open like a fish drowning on oxygen. Gage, hand on the door frame, leaned down to stare at him, a shit-eating grin on his face. "You coming out or what?"

Shiloh snorted at the pun, then clapped his hand over his mouth at the embarrassing sound. "Been there, done that," he said when he finally managed to get himself under control, climbing out of the car as he spoke. "I'm still finding glitter in my ass."

"I see you chose the fancy package. Mine was far less exciting." Gage scanned the yard as he spoke, his focus lingering on the stretching shadows.

"Let me guess… You made a PowerPoint?" Shiloh teased, following Gage as he started around the garage for the back door.

"Nope. Got caught with Matt Romain in the backseat of my dad's patrol car. I couldn't sit down for a week."

"What'd he do? Take a belt to your ass?" Shiloh cringed at his own memory of his dad walking in on him as a teenager.

"I bet he wanted to, but no. Poor Matt got so scared when good old dad banged on the window that he fell off the seat, and trust me when I say you never want a dick to vacate your body like that."

Shiloh felt heat scorch his body at the thought of Gage bottoming. Gage was taller than him by over half a foot, his shoulders half again as wide and one of his thighs was bigger around than Shiloh's waist. Shiloh had no doubt that the larger man could crush him with ease. Shiloh couldn't help but wonder what it would feel like to be spread out beneath him, Gage's tight ass sliding down his cock like a vise…

He cleared his throat, shaking off the unlikely image as he reached around Gage for the door. "We should go inside."

Gage smirked and knocked Shiloh's hand off the knob. "Good idea." Then, he pushed it open and headed in. It opened into the laundry quarters. Shiloh knew what it looked like with the lights off because he snuck in this way at least once a week. There was a pair of fancy washers and dryers with lots of buttons and blinky lights, a half-full hamper of linens, since it was Wednesday, an ironing table still unfolded against the far wall. Shiloh stood on tiptoes to peer over Gage's shoulder and smirked when he saw he was right.

"Do you think you can make it upstairs without getting us caught," Shiloh whisper-yelled into Gage's ear, "or should I go first?"

"I've snuck into terrorist camps wearing upwards of fifty pounds of equipment in the dead of night. I think I can navigate the stairway." Gage shot him an amused look over his shoulder.

"Okay, but just be careful opening the door because there's—" Shiloh started to warn, but Gage was already moving, pushing the door open. It caught the leg of the end table beside it and Shiloh watched with horror as the cheap glass vase on top of it wobbled, then tumbled over the edge. He closed his eyes, waiting for a crash that never happened. After seconds of silence, he pried open one eye to see Gage bent over, the vase caught between two fingers inches from the marble floor. "An end table…" Shiloh finally finished.

"Dumb place to put an end table," Gage said as he returned the vase to its home and shoved the table over two inches to clear the doorway.

"Dad puts it there so I can't sneak back in," Shiloh explained. He closed the laundry room door, listening for the quiet *snick* of the latch engaging, then shifted the table back again.

"It really is like sneaking into a terrorist compound," Gage mused, curving up his lips. "I wasn't aware I had to watch for traps."

"There's a trip wire coming up." Shiloh pointed at the intersection of the next hallway. One direction led to the home gym, the other toward the library. Gage glanced down, and Shiloh laughed. "Made you look."

Shiloh continued to quietly tease his guard as they made their way through the lower floor, heading for the stairs on the other end of the house. His words died when he passed by the library and the light clicked on.

Shiloh froze, his heart thumping, as his dad's voice boomed. "Shiloh Anthony Marius Beckett, what in the Sam Hill do you think you are doing?"

Shiloh grimaced. "Going to my room?"

"I told you to be back by six." The sound of an armchair creaking warned him of his father's approach. "Sam waited around for over an hour."

"Poor Sam," Shiloh sneered, finally turning. He crossed his arms, refusing to back down. "Hope I didn't hurt his little *feelings.*"

"What has gotten into you?" Dad cursed, his face flushed red. "I don't know how you ended up this way, because it's certainly not how I raised you."

Sam, Shiloh wanted to scream. *Sam* was what had gotten into him, but nobody ever listened. Nobody ever cared.

"You didn't raise me. You raised your fucking tech empire." Shiloh clenched his teeth on the rest of the sentence, knowing it was too harsh, even if it was true. Nobody raised him. He was still a fucking child, and everyone treated him like it.

Dad's face got even redder, a feat Shiloh hadn't thought possible. "That tech empire is what pays for your designer shoes and the college classes you refuse to attend and— You know what, that's it. No more dance classes."

Shiloh's heart plummeted to his feet. "No, I didn't mean it. I'll...I'll go to breakfast with Sam tomorrow. I will."

"He has an early meeting tomorrow. You can go to dinner. *If* you behave and *if* Sam doesn't complain about your attitude, I'll consider reinstating your dance classes."

"I'll do it. I'll be good. Just...please don't cancel the lessons." Shiloh's skin itched at the thought of losing them. Some days, they were the only thing that kept him sane.

His dad didn't look convinced. He narrowed his eyes and stared at Shiloh for several long seconds. "I'll believe it when I see it. I'm tired of giving you chance after chance just to have you throw them back in my face."

"I won't. I promise."

"We'll see."

Chapter Eleven

Gage dropped Shiloh off at the door of a nice brownstone in Georgetown. Mr. Beckett assured him that Lawson had his own guards on premises. He would rather have met them, but officially, his shift ended at five and it was already half-past. Gage had no problem staying a bit extra, but both Lawson and Beckett had insisted it wouldn't be necessary. He'd stayed long enough to make sure Shiloh made it inside safely, then started the half-hour trip back into Austin proper.

Gage knew exactly what he was going to do on his first night off.

Nobody did guns like Texas.

Gage signed himself in and, after listening to a quick spiel on gun safety, he bought a box of ammo and headed into the range. It was nothing like the one he usually visited back in Seattle. It was larger and sleeker and clearly catered more to enthusiasts than professionals. The large sign advertising specials for bachelorette parties was his first clue.

But a target was a target, and he still put six paper silhouettes to death with his service weapon before he had to reload. The smell of gunpowder relaxed him like nothing else, bleeding away the tension from his muscles.

"You sure know how to handle your weapon," a flirty voice said as Gage was loading his gun for the third time.

Gage glanced at the booth beside him. The first thing he noticed was the man's gun. Not the one pressing into the crotch of his pants—*that* he noticed second—but the one held loosely in his left hand, resting on the table in front of him. It was pink and bedazzled with silver glitter.

"I've had some practice," Gage acknowledged.

"So have I, but I still can't hit the target," the young man pouted, fluorescent light highlighting the gloss on his lips. "I'm Will. Maybe you could show me what I'm doing wrong."

"Show me your stance." Gage holstered his weapon and stepped around the wall that divided their booths. A glance at the target down the range had him smirking. While Will's aim wasn't as good as Gage's, he'd hit the silhouette with a regularity that spoke of at least some skill.

Will obediently set his feet, but not without letting his gaze drift up and down Gage's body first. He cocked a hip. "Like that?"

Gage stepped closer, gripping the man's slender hips to align them properly. "Spread your legs."

He felt the man shudder as he shifted his feet farther apart. "Like that?" Will asked again, and Gage watched as the man slipped his tongue across his lower lip.

"Good boy." Gage moved even closer.

Will shifted backward, closing the distance between their hips. "You know, I don't think I have any bullets left. Maybe we could go back to my apartment and you could…teach me a lesson there?"

Gage hated himself as he agreed because, for just a moment, he imagined it was Shiloh.

* * * *

The door shut behind him with a quiet *click*. Shiloh wished it were louder. It should be louder. Nothing that quiet should scare him so much. The silence was heavy, settling on Shiloh's shoulders like a chain around his neck. He was drowning.

He took a deep breath, held it tight in his lungs for as long as he could, then dragged in another. He wiped his palms on his jeans, toed his shoes off on the welcome mat and hung his scarf on the coat rack.

He stalled as long as he could before wading into the depths of the house.

Later, when the only light in the bedroom was the sliver of starlight that slipped through the shrouded window, when his body was pinned to the mattress by the heavy weight of a naked arm, Shiloh didn't cry.

He'd run out of tears half a decade ago.

Chapter Twelve

Shiloh was sullen in the passenger seat. With his heel on the seat, a knee pulled to his chest and his face nearly resting on the window, he was a far cry from the spirited client Gage was used to. Not that he knew the boy well yet, a couple days was hardly enough time to have fleshed out all the personality quirks. Still... Something about the silence niggled at him, working its way under his skin like a tick.

"Was the dinner that bad?" Gage finally asked as he slowed to a stop at a busy crossroad, waiting for the light to turn.

Shiloh twitched at the sound of his voice, lifting his hand a fraction of an inch like he was startled. "Hmm? Oh. The caviar was old and stuck to my teeth. Absolutely terrible. Zero out of ten, would not recommend."

The boy's words were playful, but his voice lacked its usual animation. He was subdued. Gage felt guilty for the brief wish he'd had on the plane for a quiet client. He didn't want Shiloh quiet, not if it meant he was like this.

"To be fair, I wouldn't recommend caviar ever. Fish eggs..." Gage shuddered. "Gross." He pulled the flashy sports car into the university parking lot. This time, after he parked the car, he pulled the keys from the ignition and stuck them in his pocket. "Stay here," he told Shiloh as he opened the door.

Shiloh's hand snagged hold of his leather jacket, fear soaking his voice. "Where are you going?"

Gage hesitated, half out of the car. Immediately, he wanted to make a joke, to twist his words with sarcasm about running away, but there was a neediness to the younger man's words, hidden in the subtle shake at the end of the sentence. So instead, he offered a reassuring smile. "Just have to clear the lot. I won't be long."

Shiloh's hand lingered on his jacket a moment longer before he gave a jerky nod. "Okay."

Gage slid out of the car and closed the door. He didn't go far, just stepped a few feet closer to the sidewalk, scanning the students bustling back and forth. Behind him, the locks on the door engaged with an audible click. He wasn't worried, since he could unlock them anyway. If it made Shiloh feel more secure or like he was getting one over on Gage—with his client, it was hard to tell—then Gage would let him have it.

When he saw nothing suspicious except for a young professor—or he supposed an older student—clutching a backpack Gage suspected held some form of weed, Gage turned back to the car. He leaned down to peer at Shiloh through the window. His client had a smirk on his lips as he met Gage's eyes.

"Oh no. Whatever am I going to do?" Gage moaned dramatically and tugged at the locked door. "How am I ever getting back in the car?" He shoved his hand into the pocket of his jacket for the keys.

Shiloh grinned and held up his hand, the keys dangling from his forefinger. He jingled them just as Gage cursed, his own hand coming up empty. "Unlock the door, Shiloh."

"What's the problem? Lose something?" Gage watched Shiloh clamber over the gear-shaft and into the driver's seat. Now, they were only inches apart, separated only by a thin sheet of glass. Gage pressed his palms against the roof of the car and leaned closer.

"Unlock the door or—" Before Gage could come up with a good enough threat, Shiloh spun the ignition and revved the engine, drowning out his words. Shiloh waved, backing the car out of the spot before Gage could finish. "God damn it!"

The taillights flashed red in front of him as Shiloh turned the corner.

"Well, shit." Gage was never going to live this down.

* * * *

Shiloh was laughing his ass off in the passenger seat of the Bugatti, his feet kicked up on the dash, when Gage jumped out of his Uber ten minutes later. The brat had driven the car in circles around the university, from one lot to the next, before parking it beside the athletic center.

Gage stomped over, trying to keep his face impassive. Half of him was pissed. Shiloh had put himself in an unbelievable amount of danger for what amounted to a prank. The other half reminded himself that the boy didn't *know* he was in danger. If it weren't for the stalker, Gage might have found it funny.

He opened his mouth to yell or threaten, then closed it and dragged in a deep breath. It wouldn't work. It would just drive Shiloh further away. Likely literally, in this case.

"Please don't do this," Gage said instead, once again planting his hand on the roof. He wanted Shiloh to trust him—to be the one he turned to, not the one he ran from.

Shiloh was quiet for a long second, his eyes calculating, before he reached over and unlocked the doors.

"Thank you." Gage opened the door before Shiloh changed his mind and dropped into the driver's seat. He turned to face the younger man. "Can we talk?"

Shiloh slumped, shrugging a careless shoulder. "Yeah, whatever."

"No, not whatever. It's important. Do you not feel safe at school? Is that why you won't go?" Gage leaned in a bit closer, hoping Shiloh read his concern for what it was—honest. Mr. Beckett might claim Shiloh was unaware of his stalker, but it was obvious that the man had a strained relationship with his son. If Shiloh really did feel unsafe somewhere, Gage doubted he'd have told his dad.

Shiloh rolled his eyes. "No, I don't feel unsafe at *school.* I feel like a distraction to the other students and like I'm wasting my time relearning things I've already studied." Shiloh straightened slightly, eyes sobering. "My dad doesn't believe me, but I already made arrangements with all my teachers. I show up on test days and group assignments, but otherwise, if I have questions, I go to their office hours."

Gage didn't know his client that well yet, but something told him that Shiloh wasn't lying. "Okay," he said. "So what do you want to do today instead?"

Shiloh opened his mouth, looking like he was about to protest, then froze. "Wait. Really?"

"I'm not here to babysit you. I really am just here to keep you safe. So if you don't want to go to class, I'm not going to force you."

Shiloh's face broke into a wide grin. "I know exactly where I want to go."

* * * *

Gage didn't know where to look. There wasn't a whole lot creepier than a grown man lurking in the back of the room watching young, half-dressed women spin around in front of mirrors. Well, it wasn't all women…which made it worse for Gage in so many ways.

It was easy to ignore the women shooting him uncomfortable glances as they moved along the barre. He just shifted subtly to look as non-threatening as possible and made a point not to stare. They weren't his type anyway.

But Shiloh… Even when Gage tried not to let his gaze linger on the lines of Shiloh's body, on the swaths of peach-gold skin exposed by the nude leotard, he couldn't avoid the mirror.

He knew Shiloh caught him looking. Several times, their gazes locked in the mirror and the younger man's lips quirked up. He didn't think he was imagining the extra sway of Shiloh's hips or the fingers that seemed to graze accidentally over flesh.

He didn't know if he was grateful or sad when the music finally ended and the dancers straightened, their breathing labored, bodies glistening with sweat. He could watch Shiloh dance for days, but at the same time, another minute would have killed him.

Shiloh bounced over, his eyes bright, hair a pink halo around his head. He'd left the leotard on but was tugging a pair of tight black jeans up his legs. "Can we go get lunch? I'm sweaty and starving."

"I can only fix one of those things at a time," Gage pointed out. "So…food or shower?"

"Food. I don't have to smell me. So suck it up, buttercup, and take me to dinner." Shiloh grinned, tugging at the tight, low-cut collar of his leotard. Gage's eyes lingered on the way the damp fabric clung to Shiloh's chest.

"If I'm taking you out, then I pick the restaurant," Gage said, leading the way out of the dance studio and to the car. He waited for Shiloh to climb in before starting the car and pulling out into an intersection. *Bad idea,* his mind warned. *Client, remember? Not a date. Not a date.*

"No sushi," Shiloh immediately said, "and no curry. But other than that, I'm not really picky. Oh, and no pizza, I don't want to get sauce on my leo."

"Not picky, huh?" Gage teased, deciding on a diner nearby. He'd heard it had one of the best *pastelitos* he'd ever tasted. Almost as good as the ones his mother used to make, not that he would have dared say that to her before she passed. A native Cuban, she'd been religious in her adherence to traditional cooking.

A pang of melancholy struck him at the memory, and at the last moment, he changed his mind, heading instead for a random diner that advertised the World's Best Bacon Burger.

The only parking spot was on the street. He went to pass, but Shiloh pointed him toward it. Gage shook his head as they climbed out. "Aren't you worried someone will ding it?"

Shiloh laughed and ran a hand over the smooth paint. "Nah. My baby's stronger than she looks. Besides, that's what insurance is for, right?"

Immediately, Gage was reminded of the differences between the two of them. Only a rich kid would even think of saying something like that. Some of his thoughts must have shown on his face because Shiloh's shut down, dimming the humor that had lit his eyes most of the day. "I guess we're heading in then?"

Gage blinked and nodded. "Yeah." He held the door to the diner for Shiloh, examining the occupants through the glass and dismissing them as threats. There weren't many people anyway.

They sat at a booth near the back of the diner. The tablecloths were checkered and the laminated menus were peeling, but the server was friendly enough. Gage ordered a black coffee for himself.

Shiloh smiled a little too flirtatiously at the server and asked for a milkshake with extra cherries. "So I can pop them." Shiloh winked.

"You're going to get us kicked out before we even eat," Gage said as the red-faced server scurried to the back.

"Nah. No way he's not gay," Shiloh said.

"I bet he's dating the cook," Gage said, trying to peer—discreetly, of course—through the small window that separated the dining room from the kitchen. "And I bet the cook is a big, burly man with muscles the size of your face."

"Good thing I've got a bodyguard then, right?" Shiloh lounged back in his booth and looked *way* too pleased with himself.

"Good thing you didn't ditch me today."

"So… Tell me something nobody knows about you." Shiloh changed the subject abruptly, pulling the heel of his shoe up onto the bench.

Gage answered after a brief few seconds of thinking. "I hate scary movies. I jump every time I watch one."

Shiloh lifted his hand to cover the smile Gage clearly saw dancing on his lips. "Really? Weren't you a Seal?"

Gage glared. "I can't swim." Shiloh's mouth dropped open just as Gage grinned. "Just teasing. No, I was a Ranger. That's the Army," he added, like he thought Shiloh wouldn't know that.

"Ah." Shiloh nodded sagely. "Army. Right. That's the one with the planes?".

Gage laughed. "I feel like you're joking, but we were an airborne special operations force. So…yes. We had planes."

"Why'd you leave?" Shiloh asked.

Gage's laughter died. He lifted his fingers, rubbing unconsciously over the scar hidden in the shadow of his jaw. Phantom pains shot up his leg. "I wasn't ready, I'll admit. I thought I'd have two, three more tours in me. But life happens and I had to accept that, no matter how badly I wanted to stay. I was only going to slow my brothers down. They offered me a desk job, but I got a better offer from Mason—my boss," Gage clarified. "In the end, everything worked out. I might not be fit for Spec Ops, but doing this, protecting people? It's why I joined the service in the first place."

Shiloh picked at the peeling laminate on the menus. He peered up at Gage through the fan of his lashes. "I bet you never thought you'd be stuck with someone like me, right?"

Gage's face softened slightly. "I don't know. You're not so bad."

Chapter Thirteen

Mr. Beckett was waiting for them when they got back to the estate. The man paced the entry, the heels of his shiny black shoes clicking against the marble tiles. He spun to face them as the door opened, stalling Gage in his tracks. "Finally," Mr. Beckett said, adjusting his glasses on his nose. "Go to your room, Shiloh. I need to speak to Mr. Tucker."

"I'm not a kid. You can't send me to my room," Shiloh protested but Mr. Beckett's expression darkened like a thundercloud. Shiloh went silent, then rolled his eyes. "Whatever," he muttered, pushing his way past his dad to escape into the house.

"Let's go to my study," Mr. Beckett said, forestalling the questions he must have read easily on Gage's face. Gage followed him down the halls.

"Shut the door," Mr. Beckett said as he rounded the desk to sink into his chair.

Gage obeyed. "Yes, sir?"

"Have a seat." Mr. Beckett ordered.

Gage sat. "Is there a problem, sir?"

"The bastard left another little *gift* this morning." Mr. Beckett grabbed a small brown box from the floor and dropped it on the desk. "The police finally released it."

Gage reached for it. "May I?"

Mr. Beckett shoved it forward. Gage opened the flaps and peered inside.

Gage pulled out the plain white paper and set it aside, eyes already fixed on the rest of the box's contents. A small scrap of neon pink lace panties nestled atop a bed of white tissue paper.

"Those are Shiloh's," Mr. Beckett said. "His name's on the tag."

Gage didn't need to look to verify. He'd seen Shiloh in them, dancing at Envy. Gage wondered if the stalker was someone who had seen him there, his mind flitting back to the last letter.

You're not a shy boy at all…

You're not a *Shy* boy at all…

The more he thought, the more certain he became. He wondered if the police knew about the connection but doubted it, since Mr. Beckett refused to talk to his son and the man knew nothing about his son's side job.

Gage picked up the letter.

I'm sorry, my Shiloh. You just made a mistake. I've got our place all ready for you. We will be together soon.

Your Admirer

"The officer on the case…Officer Preston? Did he find anything useable?" Gage asked, tucking the letter back into the box.

"No fingerprints, no DNA. Nothing to bring us closer to the bastard," Mr. Beckett seethed, snatching the box back. "I'm going to burn the damn thing."

"Mr. Beckett, I know you don't want him to worry, but I really think—"

"No. Telling Shiloh will do nothing but scare him," Mr. Beckett said.

"If he knew about the stalker, your son might take better precautions." Gage thought that at this point keeping the boy uninformed was beyond stupid. It was blatantly reckless.

"Taking precautions is your job. That's why I hired you," Mr. Beckett said. "That's all for now."

"Yes, sir." Gage sighed and stood, heading for the door. He hesitated with his hand on the knob. If he spoke now, he would lose whatever shred of trust he'd built between him and Shiloh. If he didn't, though, and something happened because of his silence, he'd never live with himself.

"Look into a club called Envy, down in the Red River District." Immediately, Gage felt guilty for breaking his promise, but it was for the best. His shoulders slumped as he let the study door close behind him.

After checking on Shiloh—the boy was asleep on top of his covers, still fully dressed—Gage searched out the gym. It was better equipped than many he'd paid for in the past. He pushed himself farther than he'd intended, trying to work the guilt out of his system. When he finally switched the treadmill off, his legs were shaking and his tank stuck to his skin. He felt a bone-deep satisfaction that he only got after a hard workout. It made up for the limp he sported as he walked upstairs to his room.

He picked up the landline receiver on his nightstand and dialed, listening to the soft music play while he waited for it to connect him to the security office on the edge of the property. There was a *click* as it was answered.

"This is Henry," the aging Navy Seal in charge of security answered curtly. Gage had spoken with him before, knowing there'd be a few times when Shiloh was on the property that Gage would be unable to keep tabs on him.

"It's Gage. I'll be indisposed for the next hour or so. Could you keep an eye on the cameras?"

"Sure thing."

"I'll keep my cell phone nearby. Thank you." Gage returned the phone to the hook.

He grabbed his black silk pajama pants and a towel and carried them into the en suite. The bathroom was the only part of his rooms he'd bothered making changes to. Not out of any aesthetic desire, but out of necessity. He'd added a rubber anti-slip mat to the bottom of the oversized tub and a pair of suction-cup hand grips to the wall. A small stool waited to the side.

Gage hated all of it.

He hated the memories of how it used to be. Jump in, jump out. He hated the tacky bright-blue handles nearly as much as he hated the need for the grips themselves.

Therapy had helped.

Six years ago, when he'd woken in the hospital post-surgery, he'd been in denial. That couldn't be *his* leg. He had two feet, not one.

His leg didn't end below the knee.

His leg hadn't been left behind in some desert sands halfway across the world.

Denial had lasted until the pain medication wore off.

Now, he was stuck in some strange middle-ground. Still angry, always angry… He'd never gotten to the bargaining phase. How could he bargain with something like that? He felt guilty even thinking of it. He'd lost brothers that day, family bound together by bullets and fire and late-night promises.

If he could bargain for anything, it would be their lives, not his left leg.

Gage had learned to accept his new reality before they'd even fitted him for his first prosthetic. He was on his fifth one now. It was the newest model, still out of reach for most amputees. He didn't know what Mason had paid to get him on the list for the trial phase. He just knew he was grateful.

Gratitude only went so far. The best-fitting, most mobile prosthesis in the world was still just a prosthesis, though.

Gage perched on the edge of the tub and slipped his fingers beneath the silicone compression sleeve, breaking the vacuum seal to slide the artificial limb free from his stump. He set it carefully aside. Crafted from titanium, the prosthesis would hold up well in the water, but the compression sleeve less so.

He gripped the grab bars and swung his left leg, or what remained of it, over the edge. It was still awkward to kneel on the ceramic and swing his other leg over, then maneuver his way into a sitting position. Only when he was firmly seated did he turn on the water and lean back to enjoy the heat.

As he settled, he let his thoughts drift back to his client. There was something else going on there, something he couldn't quite put his finger on. He'd worked with some real knuckle-headed clients before, and he'd expected to be adding Shiloh to that list. He had all the warning signs—the alcohol, the parties, the sex. But now that he'd been working with Shiloh for over a week, he was being forced to reevaluate.

Shiloh drank, often to excess. That was the rumor, anyway, but so far, he'd seen the boy flirt with a single glass of whiskey, and that was it. He went to a different party every night—except he didn't, because except for dinner with the lawyer, he'd spent his nights at home. He blew strangers in the bathroom. Gage hadn't witnessed it, not yet anyway.

Shiloh was a mystery.

It was like putting a puzzle together upside down. And all the pieces fit, but when you flipped it over, the picture on the other side didn't match the one you expected.

Gage ducked his head under the water. His ears started ringing as the water flooded into them. When he sat up, the ringing continued. It was coming from the phone in his bedroom.

Chapter Fourteen

Shiloh darted down the hallway, his heart thumping in his chest, the words still echoing around his head. Gage had told on him, after he'd said he wouldn't—after he'd *promised.* Shiloh hadn't heard the whole conversation. It had taken him a few minutes to evade the servants bustling around the halls so he could press his ear against his dad's study door unnoticed, but he'd clearly arrived just in time.

Just in time to hear his bodyguard sell him out. A nasty grin cracked his face as he made a decision. If Gage was going to break his promises, then Shiloh would too—not that he'd promised Gage anything.

Shiloh was half out of the window before he realized there was no way his bodyguard wasn't going to check on him. He clambered back inside and closed the window, then flopped on top of his mattress just in time to hear his bedroom door crack open. He kept his breathing slow and steady and his eyes clamped shut, even though his face was turned away. It felt like an eternity before he heard the door click shut again.

Ten seconds later, Shiloh was down the lattice and halfway across the lawn. Once he got to the street, he flagged down a taxi.

"Where to?" the driver asked. He was a man of middling age and appearance, whose ID named him Jack

Shiloh glanced down at his outfit. "Walmart." His designer clothes needed to go. He didn't have his wig, but he'd figure something out.

The ride was short. Shiloh stared out of the window, watching the houses blur past. He wondered what it would have been like to grow up somewhere else—if his father had stayed middle income, if he'd settled down and remarried when Shiloh was younger, rather than been so wrapped up making sure his company was the top of his field. He wouldn't be the person he was now, that was for sure.

Maybe he would have been nicer. Maybe he would have been able to look at someone and not immediately wonder what they wanted him for or how they were going to use him. Was he going to be a steppingstone this time or a toy?

The taxi stopped outside the sprawling super-center, and he passed up a couple of bills to the bored driver. He opened the door to climb out before glancing back into the cab. "How much for the hat?"

"Hmm-m?" The man glanced back. He was wearing a dark blue baseball cap embroidered with a star for the Dallas Cowboys. Shiloh didn't care much for sports, but it would hide his pink hair.

"Your hat. I'll pay you for it," Shiloh said again.

"Not for sale, kid." The driver's annoyance leaked into his voice.

"I just *really* don't want anyone taking pictures. Please?" Shiloh said, hating having to beg. The last thing he needed was someone recognizing him.

"You some kind of celebrity or something?" the driver asked.

"Or something," Shiloh muttered. The driver tossed him the cap. "How much?" Shiloh asked, pulling a few more bills from his wallet.

"Just stay out of trouble, kid," the driver said, gesturing for him to shut the door.

"Where's the fun in that?" Shiloh grinned out of habit but obediently shut the door. He pulled the cap over his pink hair, stuffing as many strands below the band as he could. With the bill tugged low, he thought it might be okay. He didn't plan on being there long, just long enough to buy a quick change of clothes. The cab pulled away before he was finished. He waved at the taillights before heading inside.

Shiloh went straight to the skinny jeans. He flicked through the stack, pulling out a pink pair in his size. A teenage girl at a nearby rack watched him, giggling with her friend. Shiloh winked and grabbed a second pair in purple.

The girl giggled harder, waving as Shiloh walked away, jeans in hand. He grabbed a plain black T-shirt from the men's section and headed toward the checkout. Partway there, though, a shiver crawled down his spine and he stopped, glancing around.

A tall, spindly woman glared as she pushed her cart around him. He ignored her.

Someone was watching him. He felt the heavy weight of eyes. Paparazzi snapped pictures, fans giggled, homophobes glared... This felt darker. Dangerous. Had his bodyguard found him already?

An older woman browsed the greeting cards, a mother with a pair of young toddlers stood by the jewelry counter, a group of teen boys giggled by the lingerie. And… Shiloh's eyes sharpened.

A tall man was turning the corner of an aisle. He caught a glimpse of dark hair, and that was it. It could be nothing, but Shiloh had good instincts and they were screaming. It didn't look like Gage—the shoulders were too narrow—but before he could get a better look, the man was gone.

Uneasy, Shiloh hustled to the checkout, ordering an Uber while he waited. The danger was all in his head. It wasn't like he really had a stalker, but apparently his father's fear was rubbing off on him.

He carried his purchases into the restroom to change. The pink skinny jeans were looser around his thighs than he expected. He gripped the band, examining the thin gap between jeans and skin. He'd lost weight.

He stepped out of the bathroom and again, unease filled him. Glancing around as he thumbed open an app on his phone, he tried to spot anything unusual. Nothing stood out.

His phone *dinged* with an update, distracting him. He glanced down to see the message from his Uber app, sending him a picture of the driver and his name. Micah.

He was grateful to climb into the backseat of the silver sedan.

Micah was only a few years his senior, hair dyed a brilliant purple, eyes lined by a sparkly blue pencil. Shiloh thought about asking the twink for a ride on something besides his car.

Micah's eyes skimmed hot over his body, lingering on his pink jeans. "Where to?"

Shiloh told him.

Micah's leer widened. "Good choice."

Shiloh agreed and settled back against the seat. He stared out of the window. Nerves fluttered in his stomach like moths and he tapped his fingers against his thighs. He couldn't get the dark-haired man out of his mind. It was probably nothing to worry about. Probably, his bodyguard's worries had just infected him like a parasite.

Not a babysitter his *ass*.

"Everything okay?" Micah asked, putting an arm on the back of the passenger seat to turn around and look at him. His eyes were heavy with concern and Shiloh frowned, wondering why.

Then he glanced back out of the window and spotted the nightclub. No wonder Micah was concerned. He'd made the trip in total silence and hadn't even realized they'd arrived.

"Yeah. Sorry, long day. I must have drifted off." Shiloh plastered on a smile. "It was nice meeting you. It's not often I get a driver with fashion sense."

"Give me a call if you want to party sometime." Micah scrawled his number on the back of a receipt and held it back over his shoulder. Shiloh grinned and shoved it in his pocket before climbing out.

Micah waited until Shiloh was at the entrance to the club to pull away. Shiloh would have to leave him a great review later.

On the dance floor, Shiloh swayed to the music, the throbbing bass teaming up with the four shots of tequila he'd downed to urge him into motion. This was more than just a performance, more than just laying the groundwork. This was the part of himself he hated the most, the craving to touch and, more rarely, *be* touched. He would regret it later, when he was alone in his bedroom. But this parody of touch was all he allowed himself.

An unfamiliar pair of hands swallowed Shiloh's hips, urging him back against a familiar hardness. "Bathroom?" The stranger's gruff voice slithered into his ear, barely audible over the music.

Shiloh nodded. That was what he'd come here for, wasn't it? With a final sway of his hips, he peeled himself away, pushing through the sweaty bodies to the dark hall at the back of the club. He didn't need eyes in the back of his head to know his dance partner was following close behind. The crowd thinned and Shiloh glanced over his shoulder to get his first glimpse.

Tall and wide, not all his girth was muscle. Shiloh's gaze rose to the mess of curls on the man's head.

"Big Red," Shiloh murmured with a grin. The stranger shrugged, not offering a better name.

Shiloh joined the short line to the restroom, impatience making the wait seem longer. Soon enough he was falling to his knees on the dirty bathroom floor. None of the stalls had doors, as if the lack of privacy would prevent bathroom hookups. Maybe it did for some people but not Shiloh. The lack of privacy here was in itself a gift—*safety in numbers.*

Big Red fumbled with his zipper, freeing a short but stout erection, stroking it impatiently.

Shiloh pulled back. "Condom."

"It's just a blow job." Big Red gripped Shiloh's hair, trying to pull him closer. "Don't be a pussy."

"Condom or I'm out." Shiloh ignored the bristle of pain as strands parted from his scalp. He didn't go bare with paying customers, and he sure as *hell* wasn't doing it for free.

Big Red muttered a curse but allowed Shiloh to slide a condom over his shaft. Once covered, Shiloh let the man push into his mouth. Big red pounded his throat roughly. If Shiloh had a gag reflex, it surely would have been triggered by now.

Shiloh slid his hand into his waistband, stroking himself in time with each thrust. He was nearly there when Big Red's thrusts stuttered and he spilled into the latex. Rather than release him, the man's grip tightened in his hair, tugging until Shiloh's eyes watered and he was forced to look up, his mouth still stretched around the man's cock.

"Smile, slut." Big Red grinned, then Shiloh was blinded by the flash of a cell phone.

Shiloh strongly considered biting down around the delicate flesh still snug in his lips. Big Red must have seen the thought cross his mind because he was shoved free before he could act on it.

"Asshole," Shiloh seethed, pulling his hands from his softening dick to flip the man off.

Big Red just took another picture. "Think you'll make the cover this time?"

Of course he would make the cover. He *always* did. His father always said he should know better. Like he should *know* which of his hookups was going to fuck him and which was going to fuck him over. He resigned himself to another pointless lecture. Shiloh wasn't a monk, and he sure as fuck wasn't going to live like one.

I'm not a babysitter, Gage gritted his teeth. *It's not my job to keep him out of the papers.*

No, but the greasy tank of a man was certainly right in thinking that a picture of this—of Shiloh Beckett, heir to a Fortune 500 company, blowing a man in a bathroom—would make the cover of any tabloid he sold it to. And whether Gage was a babysitter or not, he could prevent that.

The question running over and over through his mind was, should he? The brat had snuck out of the house to go clubbing and hadn't thought twice at following a stranger into a club bathroom. At least the kid had used a condom. Seeing the proof of his stupidity in the papers would be a fitting punishment.

It would also, however, lead to Gage having to explain to his boss why he'd allowed it. And *"I'm not a babysitter"* wasn't a good enough answer. He was glad he'd thought to clone Shiloh's phone so he could track him without the car. He was even more grateful that the app had worked, since he'd never had to resort to using it before.

Gage cursed. No matter what he wanted to do, he knew he'd already made his decision. He stepped out of his stall, yanking the phone out of the large man's hand before they realized he was there. It took only a second to delete the pictures and toss the phone away. It skidded to a halt under one of the sinks, in the shadow of the rusted pipes.

The man swelled up like a pufferfish, his face red as his hair. "What the *fuck*!"

"I'm sure my client's lawyers would love to file a defamation suit if you make any allegations about his *alleged* behavior in this...rather shitty bathroom without proof. Shiloh, out. *Now.*" Gage growled and jerked his thumb toward the door.

He was shocked when Shiloh listened, scrambling out before the words had even fully left his mouth. Gage walked out with the stranger fuming, watching his back as he followed his client into the dimly lit hall. A security nightmare, even if it had allowed him to follow Shiloh unnoticed into the bathroom.

Gage grabbed Shiloh's arm and tugged him out of the back exit into an alley.

Shiloh stumbled over a loose flagstone. "Let…me…go!"

"No," Gage snapped, pulling him along until they reached the black sedan Gage had finally received from the rental company.

"I'm not going anywhere with you." Shiloh scratched at Gage's fingers.

Gage slammed Shiloh into the side of the car, fuming. "Do you even realize how much danger you could have been in? And not just from that idiot or the tabloids? You left the house *without* a bodyguard. You're drunk, and that idiot could have been anyone. You're damn lucky all he wanted was a picture."

"You're not my dad. You have no right to – "

"You are *lucky* I'm not your dad, I'd have you over my lap and your ass would be redder than a cherry. I've told you before and I will *not* tell you again. I am *not* a babysitter. Next time you pull a stunt like this, I'll let them keep the damn pictures." Even Gage was surprised at the vehemence in his voice at the threat.

Shiloh flinched before straightening, his eyes darkening with obvious anger. "They can have the damn pictures if they want them bad enough. It's not like anyone'll be surprised. Shiloh-the-Slut, right?" There was enough self-loathing underlying the words that Gage stepped back, dropping Shiloh's arm like it burned him. Shiloh didn't notice. "Maybe I should have invited you to the blow-job party. Then they'd *really* have a good picture."

"I don't give a rat's ass who you blow in the bathrooms," Gage said, forcing his voice to sound calmer than he felt. It was a lie. He *did* care, and he didn't know why. "Blow a whole goddamn football team if you want, just…don't be stupid about it. That man could have hurt you and no one in there would have lifted a finger to help."

"Nobody's ever lifted a finger to help me." Shiloh's face closed down as he spoke and he crossed his arms. "Can we go now?"

"Get in the damn car."

Shiloh got in the damn car. He slammed the door hard enough the windowpane rattled in the frame, but he was *in* the car. Gage took the driver's seat, grateful to be leaving the club behind.

He drew in several deep breaths then said, "I know you don't like me—"

Shiloh gave a harsh laugh. "*Like* you? What's that have to do with anything? Don't take it personally, but I don't even know you. I didn't *ask* to be famous. It's not my fault that my dad made that *stupid* gaming engine, but I'm the one who's being punished for it. I just wanted—" Shiloh broke off, halting himself from speaking further. Whatever he wanted remained a mystery. "I'm not stupid or careless. I never bring them home. I use protection. I just want to be able to do something…normal. And I can't. This is all I have."

Gage hadn't really considered it from Shiloh's point of view. He knew plenty of people who gave bathroom blow jobs… Hell, he'd done it himself a time or two when on shore leave. The only reason it was different for Shiloh was because of who his father was.

But he couldn't let his client keep putting himself at risk just because he understood the reasoning behind it, especially when Shiloh didn't understand the full extent of the risk he was taking.

Chapter Fifteen

Shiloh scrubbed at the bathroom grime that was still clinging to his skin, the water hot enough to burn. Music pumped through the in-shower speakers, joining with the running jets to drown out everything but the spiraling thoughts in his skull. He lingered until his skin was red and raw yet still didn't feel clean. But since he hadn't felt clean in years, he spun off the water.

He didn't bother drying off. He shook the water from his hair and collapsed atop his bed, pressing his face into the pillow. A silent, choking sob caught in his throat.

He had just wanted to blow off some steam—go out, dance, hook up, pretend for one night that he was normal. He knew better—*God,* did he know better—but he'd let himself get caught up in the fantasy.

As if he'd meet someone in a club who'd see him as more than just a bathroom blow job. He wasn't even good enough for *that*. He had to be their fifteen minutes of fame too. He hated this life.

He'd had a friend once, in middle school...Ryan Tremings. Like Shiloh, Ryan took dance at the local community center. Shiloh, because his dad refused to pay for better classes, and Ryan, because they were the only ones his parents could afford. They warmed the same bench while they waited for their rides.

Ryan's mom had always come in the same, rusted-out SUV packed with children—Ryan's seven little sisters, all being hustled from soccer practice and karate and ballet and tutoring—and she'd always had the same harried halo of carrot-red hair. But she'd always apologized for being late, and she'd *always* hugged Ryan when she'd finally picked him up.

Shiloh's dad sent their cook, Mrs. Tennison, except on the rare occasions she couldn't come, then he'd send his driver, a stern-faced man with little patience for a *"fruity little snot."*

Shiloh eventually started asking Mrs. Tennison to pack an extra sandwich for his friend, and in exchange, Ryan let him read his comic books.

The day everything had broken was carved into his brain. It had been right after his father's first heart attack, the *big* one, the one that had changed everything. It was just one more scar he'd never be able to get rid of.

Shiloh had been so angry, and Ryan had just kept pushing and pushing.

"Where have you been? You missed how to do a fouetté."

"My dad's in the hospital."

And Ryan had just kept going, telling him how *sorry* he was, and how glad he was that *"Mr. Lawson"* was able to take care of him, and wasn't it nice that *"Mr. Lawson"* had a pool and an Xbox, and could he come over and play with it?

Shiloh had snapped. He *wasn't* glad that Lawson had taken him in, and he didn't care about the pool or the Xbox anymore. He regretted ever telling Ryan about it.

And he *definitely* didn't want Ryan anywhere near that house.

So he'd told his friend that he wasn't allowed to come over, *ever*.

He may have said more. He remembered the seething anger, but he didn't remember the words, the insults he'd spewed about precious 'Mr. Lawson'.

He remembered the look on Ryan's face.

"God, you are such a baby. Why do you have to be so ungrateful? *I would do anything to have my own bedroom. I'm so sick of hearing you whine about all your spoiled, rich-boy problems!"* Then Ryan stomped off toward the rusted SUV and Shiloh, for just a moment, had actually felt *guilty*—guilty for not being grateful then angry, again, for that guilt.

He understood now. Ryan's jeans hadn't been artfully torn. They'd been frayed—because they'd been bought already worn through. The soles of his shoes hadn't been held together by duct tape because it was 'cool' or 'in fashion'. His mother simply hadn't been able to afford another pair.

Like a tidal wave, that same guilt swelled in his chest again. He had a multi-million-dollar trust fund—even if it was locked up tighter than a nun's pussy—a fleet of cars most men drooled over and a free ride to the best business school in the state. He had it so much better than any of his classmates.

Ryan had been right. Shiloh was a spoiled little rich-boy.

The tidal wave crashed, filling his limbs like saltwater and dragging him down. He was drowning, his lungs filling over and over with air he couldn't breathe. He found the dozens of small, pinprick scars lining the crease of his elbow and the fold of his knees, itching to add another. He didn't do drugs, had never needed to chase the highs and lows. They found him on his own. The only needles he stuck in his body had small, brightly colored heads and he used them to pin himself to the present. They would keep him from sinking.

Before he realized he had moved, the plastic box was open on the mattress. He grasped the blue pearl head and pressed. The shaft slid beneath his flesh, parallel to the crease of his arm. A burst of brilliant pain flared and he encouraged it, rubbing the skin over the small, raised line. Blood beaded near the blue head.

He added three pins before the numbness fled. He ran his fingertips over each ridge. The soothing gesture calmed the racing of his heart. He left them in until his muscles relented, then slid the bloodied metal slivers free. They dinged against the aluminum trashcan as he dropped them, one by one.

He was asleep before his head hit the pillow.

Shiloh is in the taxi again. The sky outside is a dark and foreboding gray, though Shiloh knows it should be blue. Shiloh blinks and he is on the sidewalk.

"Hey! Kid, you have to pay your fare!" the driver hollers after him. Shiloh remembers paying him in twenties, much more than the fare really cost. Now, he hands over brightly colored condoms. For a moment, the driver's hair is red.

Shiloh wishes he could stay in this moment, but he is shoved forward. The hospital doors yawn open like a mouth, swallowing him inside. He is running.

Past the desk where the woman gives him a toothy smile.

Past the flashing neon warning signs the real hospital never had.

Stop.

Go Back.

Danger Ahead.

He shoves open the swinging hospital doors. Just on the other side, a vise clamps down on his upper arm. It closes around a fading, finger-shaped bruise, and Shiloh flinches, tearing free. His back slams into the bile-green wall. Wanted Posters are plastered over the surface. The words are in his handwriting. The wall shoves him forward.

"Slow down, son. What's the matter?" the dark-haired man with the security badge asks. The guard's face twists, growing featureless and blank, a lump of flesh with a slit for a mouth.

"I want to see my father," Shiloh says through gasping breaths. He is falling apart...like every second he waits, pieces of him are dying. He needs his father. His father will fix it.

The faceless guard's slitted mouth opens. Shiloh knows what he's going to say. It's what he always says in these dreams. "He won't believe you, you know. Might as well just turn around and go home."

Shiloh turns away and goes farther up the hall. He urges himself to turn around, to wake up – to end this nightmare now.

The guard calls after him, "You're going to hurt someone."

Shiloh isn't running now. He shifts from foot to foot at the end of the hall, waiting for the elevator to descend. The neon red numbers crawl slowly downward.

"Come on. Come on..."

He stares at his reflection. He doesn't look any different. He doesn't move, but his reflection leans forward. Its voice is distorted, like white noise on a stereo. "Wake up, Shiloh. This never changes anything."

"Father will fix it." Shiloh is stubborn, even with himself.

"Father doesn't care. Wake up, Shiloh. Wake up." *The reflection lurches toward him. The mouth gapes open, the face cracking like bone China, dead and blackened fingers scrabbling at his breast.*

Shiloh slaps the skeletal fingers away.

A piercing bell dings. The elevator doors split open, screeching like nails on a chalkboard.

The phantom shatters like glass.

Shiloh doesn't wake up. He steps into the elevator. A pair of nurses in red scrubs are chatting in the corner. They stare at him.

The elevator moves. It climbs up and up and the walls close in. The nurses disappear. Shiloh is alone. The walls press into his shoulders.

The lights go out.

Shiloh is in a coffin.

The wood above him is rough. He can feel the slats where they join together. He pushes at the lid. It shifts. Grave dirt spills downward, pressing into his chest, his neck, coating his mouth until he can't breathe and he's swallowing it. It tastes like semen.

He claws his way upward. His arms breach the surface. He pushes clumps of earth free and pulls his way up. A blue sky hangs above him until it falls. It becomes a blue curtain, hanging in his face.

Shiloh knows what is behind the curtain, but he can't stop himself from shoving it aside.

His dad is child-sized in the hospital bed. Not even the wriggling, tentacle-like cords emanating from his body could distract Shiloh from the sight of the Monster's claws digging into the flesh of his father's shoulder.

Shiloh recoils, his breath forced from his lungs. He stumbles back but an invisible wall prevents him from fleeing.

"Sit down, Shiloh. We need to talk." Father is stern, unmoving as always. Above him, a bulb light sways back and forth on an iron chain.

"I... Dad, I need to talk to you." Shiloh's gaze skirts to the Monster. As always, it wears an Armani suit, well-pressed and well-tailored, but instead of a belt, a long strip of red jute rope encircles its narrow waist. Shiloh drops his eyes.

"Sam's already told me everything. Sit down," Father says.

A large, metal hook digs into Shiloh's navel and pulls him relentlessly forward. Pain blossoms in his abdomen, sharp and ugly, and he screams. The sound is bound in his throat, tied to his tongue. He is forced to perch on the edge of a blue-vinyl armchair.

"You haven't been following Mr. Lawson's rules." Dad sounds disappointed. "I've let you get away with a lot since your mother died, but you're not a child anymore."

Shiloh wants to tell his dad he is only fourteen. He is still too much of a child for that. *"You don't understand! His rules aren't – " Shiloh protests.*

"Fair? Life isn't fair, Shiloh. Sometimes you have to do things that aren't pleasant. All Sam is asking is that you don't just lie in bed and moan about. I really don't think it will kill you."

Shiloh tries one last time. "But, Dad – "

This time, he's going to say it. 'He raped *me.' The words laugh at him, crawling back down his throat like spiders.*

"Enough, Shiloh! Just do what he asks you until I'm home. If you insist on being a child, then Sam will put you over his knee." Father's cough bounces off the walls. It lands on the floor as a red ball gag and rolls under the hospital bed.

"I'm sure that won't be necessary, right, Shiloh?" The Monster's face twists in a leer. Shiloh's spine crumples into the chair as it approaches, looming over him. The words grow like mold in the air between them. "Do you think your daddy will look good in orange?" Nicotine-stained claws trail down his cheek.

Shiloh jerked up in his bed, his lungs heaving. His stomach joined them a second later as he rushed to the en suite to hurl his dinner into the toilet.

He rinsed his mouth in the sink and spat the foul-tasting water down the drain. There was no point returning to bed. He wouldn't be able to sleep now anyway. He grabbed a bottle of glass cleaner and a roll of paper towels, carrying them down the hall to his studio. He'd clean the floor-to-ceiling mirrors instead.

Chapter Sixteen

It had been three days.

Three days since Gage had ratted him out to his father, which was apparently how long it took his dad to decide to give a shit about what Shiloh was doing in his spare time. Shiloh supposed it was because his nights dancing at Envy hadn't hit the press yet, so his dad hadn't decided how big of a deal to make out of it. He must have made his decision, though, or Shiloh wouldn't be slouched in his study, waiting for his dad to make an appearance.

Rather than concentrate on the lecture that was surely coming, he watched his bodyguard. Gage was leaning against the bookshelf, skimming through the file Mason had forwarded for approval.

"What are you watching?" Shiloh finally asked, swinging his leg back and forth. "Is it porn? I bet it's porn."

"It's not," Gage replied absently, still fixated on the screen.

"Nobody stares that intently at something that isn't porn. Come on. You can tell me. I won't judge."

"It's the exit report from my last job. My boss sent it over for approval," Gage answered.

Shiloh tried to stay silent. He was still pissed that Gage had ratted on him, but...the quiet was uncomfortable, and he was genuinely curious. He blurted, "What's it like being a bodyguard? Does it get annoying having to follow someone around every day?"

"Are you asking if it gets annoying having to follow *you* around every day?" Gage finally tucked the phone away and eyed him with a smirk. Shiloh grimaced, trying not to let that hurt. He'd lined himself right up for that one, hadn't he? He shouldn't be surprised that yet another person was annoyed by him.

Gage's smirk softened to a smile. "I like my job, and when you're not trying to ditch me, you're a pretty good client."

"You must have some really fun stories." Shiloh started swinging his leg again, his pink converse striking the leg of the chair.

"A few," Gage finally said.

"You should tell me some. I'm bored." Shiloh shifted up in his chair, legs dropping to the ground.

"Sorry... I'd tell you, but you know—" Gage smirked.

"Then you'd have to kill me?" Shiloh finished, rolling his eyes. "So how would that work, actually? Would you have to try to protect me from yourself? You could be all like..." Shiloh sprang up from his chair, pretending to punch the air.

Halfway through the punch, though, Shiloh froze. He could never explain it to people, how it felt when inspiration struck. The closest he could come was that it was like a spool of thread in his brain that started to unravel. At first, it looked like a mess, just a jumble of knots and string, but the more he plucked at it, the more it started to stitch together an idea, a picture. He spun, scrambling for the doorknob.

"I'm not going to hurt you. What's—" Gage followed Shiloh into the hall.

"Just had an idea, I need to go to the studio, or I'll lose it," Shiloh called over his shoulder, pulling out his phone and scrolling through his music. It was the work of moments to connect it to his Bluetooth They weren't even in the studio yet when music, soft and haunting, filtered out into the hallway.

Gage leaned against the doorframe, unable to move further inside for fear of distracting Shiloh, not that Shiloh seemed to notice him. He was already dancing.

Shiloh moved like water—still at first, until the haunting music sped up. Then, Shiloh became a hurricane. He rose and fell like a wave, his muscles rippling. Sweat dripped between the sharply defined ridges of his abs. Like a parched man in the desert, Gage longed to drop to his knees and follow the drops with his tongue. The image filled his mind so clearly that his knees almost buckled.

Shiloh was a well with hidden depths. Behind the façade of party-boy, Gage had found something more, a vulnerability Shiloh kept carefully hidden. Dancing stripped away the mask, and with it, any illusions Gage held.

Shiloh was beautiful.

Gage's chest grew tight as Shiloh sank to the floor, crumpling as the music trickled off. In the silence, Gage was afraid to breathe. The moment stretched. Long before Gage was willing to break it, Shiloh stood, positioning himself again, and the music restarted.

Gage found himself sinking into the performance, hooked to Shiloh's body as it flowed across the wood. Each time the dance ended, Gage held his breath, certain that this time would be the last. Sweat made Shiloh's body gleam, plastered his pink hair to the back of his slender neck, and once, Shiloh fell hard enough that Gage knew the young man would wake up with bruises.

But Shiloh just stood and started again, more graceful each time.

It was a pity Shiloh only danced in clubs.

A low voice sounded behind him, and Gage flinched, cursing inwardly. He had allowed himself to get so pulled into the dance that he hadn't noticed Mr. Beckett approaching behind him.

"It's a pity he's so good." Mr. Beckett sighed, stopping beside Gage to watch his son dance. "I had hoped he'd outgrow it."

Gage frowned. "Why? He clearly loves it."

Mr. Beckett's eyes were fixated on his son, but it was like he didn't see him, like he was staring into the past instead. "My wife and I always wanted a whole house of kids, but Mariam had a lot of complications during the pregnancy, and we had to stop at one. I couldn't bear the thought of remarrying after she passed. Shiloh needs to concentrate on learning how to run the company. I want him to be ready, but the only thing he seems to put any effort into is dancing." Mr. Beckett sounded annoyed, but Gage saw the pained way his eyes followed the oblivious Shiloh around the small studio.

"If dancing is what he loves, have you considered letting someone else run BeckTech industries?" Gage asked.

"You know what I wanted to be when I was his age?" Mr. Beckett answered his own question without waiting for a reply. "A toy maker – to build little robots for kids to play with. Then I realized no one would pay for them. I enjoyed the work, but I was broke. Starving artist, you know? I don't want that for him."

"You'd rather he be unhappy?" Gage said without thinking.

Mr. Beckett stiffened, like Gage's pointed words dragged him forcefully out of the past. "I pay you to be his bodyguard, not to analyze my decisions."

"Yes, sir. Sorry, sir." Gage straightened, resisting the urge to throw off a salute. The soldier in him wanted to back down to his boss, but the man…? The man wanted to bundle Shiloh up and keep him safe from his father's disappointment.

"Tell him to see me when he's done." Mr. Beckett gave one last look to his son before he sighed, swiping his hand over his face.

"Yes, sir."

Chapter Seventeen

Shiloh felt the energy of the music ascending. His legs shook, but he knew this time he'd get it right. He planted his right foot, his toe pointing out, and extended his left leg forward, listening for the cue. He dipped into a *plie* before raising his right leg.

Then he leapt.

For a long, peaceful moment, he flew through the air, his legs stretching into a split. He knew as he landed that he'd pushed himself too far.

His right foot hit the ground and pain blistered up his calf.

"Shit!" he cursed, his knee buckling. He crashed into the wood. "God *damn* it!" It had almost been perfect.

He gripped his calf tight, working his fingers into the knotted muscles.

"Maybe it's time for a break." Gage moved into the studio, startling Shiloh. He'd forgotten Gage had been standing there—which, to be honest, was a first. Gage had stolen his attention since the first night they'd met.

"I can be better, though," Shiloh said, releasing his calf to stand. "One more run-through and it'll be perfect." Shiloh headed toward his cell phone to restart the song.

"You're limping and you skipped lunch." Gage grabbed the phone before Shiloh could reach it, tucking it in his back pocket. "Take a break. Grab a sandwich. Talk to your father. The studio will be here tomorrow."

Shiloh turned to Gage. A shiver spread down his spine as he realized, again, how much taller Gage was than him. He barely skimmed Gage's shoulders. Shiloh wondered what it would feel like to be tucked up against Gage's side, under his arm. To be pressed against that firmly muscled chest. Of course, he'd have to deal with the sternly disapproving look the man was shooting him.

"Yes, Daddy." Shiloh grinned.

Gage frowned. "I'm not that much older than you."

"How old are you? Surely not…thirty?" Shiloh doubted it, Gage didn't look a day over twenty-five.

"Twenty-eight." Gage held open the door to the studio to let Shiloh through. Shiloh paused in the doorway, only a breath of air separating the two of them.

"Really?" Shiloh reached out and ran his hand over Gage's hard, muscled chest. "Wouldn't have guessed."

"Yeah. So definitely not old enough to be a daddy." But the way Gage's throat moved as he swallowed, Shiloh wondered if maybe Gage wanted to be called Daddy more than he let on.

"I don't know. I think you'd look mighty fine as a silver fox." Shiloh regretfully removed his hand from Gage's muscles. He caught the red tint that spread across Gage's cheeks as he turned away. Maybe Gage wasn't as immune to him as he pretended.

Shiloh whistled happily and limped to the kitchen. It was a matter of moments to spread a thick coating of peanut butter on two slices of bread and slap them together. He took a bite before he realized that Gage hadn't eaten either.

"Want one?" Shiloh said around the mouthful of bread.

Gage eyed the sandwich, the corner of his lips curved up. "Are you offering to cook for me?"

"Nah, I can't cook. But I can make you a sandwich." Shiloh really couldn't cook, though he *had* tried. He'd given up after the Spaghetti Disaster of 2009.

"I wouldn't turn one down," Gage said. Shiloh sat his sandwich on the counter and went to work on Gage's. He spread the peanut butter carefully from edge to edge before pressing the pieces together. He went to pass it over but froze. What if Gage didn't like it? Which was stupid, because it was a *peanut-butter* sandwich.

Surely he couldn't fuck that up.

But, just in case, Shiloh put the sandwich back on the counter and grabbed the first thing he found in the fridge. He really wished it was something better than pickles, but now he was committed.

He slapped a handful of pickles in the middle of the peanut butter before handing it over. Gage stared at the sandwich in his hand, quirking his lips up at the corners, long enough that Shiloh second-guessed his decision to preemptively ruin it.

He reached for it, but Gage held it up out of his reach. "Hey now, if you want one, you have to get your own."

"But I made that one," Shiloh protested, really not wanting Gage to eat it. God, what was he thinking?

"For me. You made this one for me." Gage smirked as Shiloh lifted on his tiptoes but still couldn't reach it. "If I didn't know better, I'd think you didn't want me to eat this delicious sandwich you made for me."

"I…really don't. I regret everything." Shiloh grabbed the sandwich he'd made himself and waved it. "Trade you?"

"I don't know. You already bit off that one."

"I don't have cooties." Shiloh didn't mean for it to come out as a whine, but he couldn't take it back.

"But my sandwich has pickles on it." Gage waved it over Shiloh's head. "Does *yours* have pickles?"

"No, which is why you should eat mine and let me have that one."

Gage laughed before taking a giant bite of the peanut-butter pickle sandwich. His face twisted at the taste. "Yum," he said. His expression made it less convincing.

"I…didn't think you'd really eat it," Shiloh said as Gage finished the sandwich.

"Yeah, it was…delicious. Eat up, buttercup."

Shiloh grimaced but finished his sandwich. "I suppose I should head up to my lecture now." Shiloh sighed and started back upstairs.

"Are you sure it's going to be a lecture?" Gage asked.

"It's always a lecture. 'Do better in your studies, Shiloh. Shiloh, you've been skipping class again. Shiloh, I heard you sucked a nice big cock at the bar last night, naughty-naughty.'" Shiloh rolled his eyes.

"Have you thought about…*not* doing those things?" Gage opened the door to the study for him.

Shiloh dropped into the chair to wait. He rolled his head back, looking at Gage upside down. "Oh, I've *definitely* thought about not doing better in my studies. I think about it *every* day."

"That's not what I—"

Shiloh waved him off. "Yeah, yeah. Did you go to college?" Shiloh realized as he said it that possibly, it came off a tad offensive. "Sorry… I'm not being a dick. Just curious."

"No, I never went to college. Couldn't afford it. Figured Uncle Sam could, so I joined the Army. But college didn't seem as important by the time I got out," Gage said.

"I bet you looked good in camouflage." Shiloh let his gaze trail down his well-built body. He'd always loved a man in uniform. "Does it bother you if I thank you? My aunt was in the Navy, and she says it makes her uncomfortable."

"Personally? I don't need thanks. If you *really* want to thank me, you can stop trying to ditch me," Gage suggested.

Shiloh couldn't do that—not if he wanted his plan to work, and it *had* to. He couldn't keep living like this. He knew if he did, eventually he'd realize that he just…couldn't keep living.

He opened his mouth to crack a joke when the door opened, and his father headed in. He looked tired. Shiloh frowned and sat up a bit straighter in his chair. He recognized the dark shadows beneath his father's eyes. They were the same shadows that lurked before his last heart attack.

Guilt flashed in his chest. If—*when*—he followed through with his plan, it would hurt his father. Maybe it would hurt his father in a way he didn't want. There was a difference between a few days of anxious uncertainty and a literally broken heart. Maybe he should call it off or push it back, at least until his father's health cleared up.

No. He forced himself to remember the look on his father's face, and to remember every time his dad had sent him straight back to Lawson's dubious care. His plan wouldn't cause another heart attack because for that to happen, his father would have to care about his well-being—and he didn't.

He'd only care that the search would mean he'd have to take time away from the company. Maybe it'd be good for him. A mean thought crossed his mind. His dad would probably use the press to rack up the public pity points. He shoved the realization away before it could hurt him.

"You've been working too much, Dad." Shiloh scratched at the wooden arms of his chair.

"And you haven't been working hard enough," Dad said. If he sounded angry, Shiloh would make a joke, brush it off, but he just sounded so goddamn disappointed. "I don't know what to do with you, son. I've been patient, I've been lenient, I've been strict, but no matter which way I try to go, you don't learn. You don't listen."

I don't listen? Maybe if his dad had just listened to him *one* time in his life, just once, they wouldn't be here. Shiloh wouldn't be like *this,* wouldn't be so dammed broken all the time.

"And you." Dad turned on Gage while Shiloh was fuming. "I hired you to keep him out of trouble, and now a man by the name of…" He fiddled with a stack of papers on his desk until he found the one he was looking for. "Hank Prescott is threatening me with a lawsuit because, he claims, you 'assaulted him last night at a nightclub.' A nightclub, I'll remind you, that Shiloh never should have been allowed to step foot in. It leaves me to wonder, Mr. Tucker, just what in the hell you thought you were doing."

"It wasn't his fault," Shiloh started to protest, but Gage laid a hand on his wrist, silencing him.

"Mr. Beckett, if you'll look over my contract, it is clearly written that it is my job to protect my clients from physical threats. It is not my job to be a babysitter or a media shield. If you wanted a prison warden, you hired the wrong company. At no point last night was Shiloh in any danger. He just needed to blow off some steam." There was a joke there, but Shiloh resisted the urge to make it.

His dad opened his mouth but Gage continued before he could speak. Shiloh sat back and watched, impressed. Nobody interrupted his father, and nobody defended Shiloh, ever.

"This Hank character is lying. He was taking inappropriate pictures of Shiloh at the urinal, and when I demanded he delete the photographs, he threatened to sell them to a tabloid instead. I took the liberty of deleting them for him, but I never laid so much as a finger on that man."

His dad's lips thinned to a narrow line, but he didn't argue as Gage ended his only slightly fabricated speech, staring between the two of them. His eyes, blue like Shiloh's, were thoughtful behind his glasses. It was obvious he didn't believe them, but short of calling Gage a liar to his face, there was little he could do.

Shiloh must have looked too smug, lounging back in the chair, because his dad's gaze caught on his and held, narrowing his eyes farther. "I'm tired of cleaning up your messes. Whether or not this man is lying, keeping him from wasting my time on a lawsuit is going to be costly, especially to keep it out of the papers."

Shiloh shrugged. "So don't bother. He's lying. He won't win. And who cares what he tells the press? It's not true."

"My shareholders care."

"Once again, it all comes down to you and your precious bottom line, doesn't it?" Shiloh snapped, leaning forward in his chair, fisting his hands beside his thighs.

His dad's face grew redder as he replied, "Someday you will take over this company, if you ever figure out how to grow up, and when you do, it'll be *your* bottom line I'm worried about. Don't forget what keeps you off the streets."

Except it didn't, not really. Wasn't Shiloh still out there every week, cruising for tricks in seedy clubs? Wasn't he already taking it up the ass to make enough money to buy an apartment somewhere quiet, far away from his dad's reach?

"So yes," Dad continued, "I am worried about my bottom line. And because of that, until I've recouped the losses your latest stunt has cost me, I'm canceling your dance classes. You're dismissed."

Chapter Eighteen

Shiloh didn't go to class. He emailed his professor on his phone as he stomped downstairs, pleading illness, then shoved it into his pocket without waiting for a reply. Whether he could retake the exam or not, at this point he didn't care. It didn't matter anyway, whether he passed this class or the next one. He wouldn't be there to finish his business degree.

He'd already given Deak the down payment for a small apartment on the West coast. The man, for a fee, had put it in his name so Shiloh could disappear. As soon as he had enough money to pay for the rest, he'd be gone. His dad could stay here, chasing ghosts. In a few years Shiloh'd consider reaching out, maybe—just to let him know he was okay.

It wasn't a good plan, but it was the only one he had. He'd tried moving out once, just after he'd turned eighteen, but he'd only made it three weeks before his dad and his goons had shown up. The same thing had happened when he tried to get a job. Nothing was quite so embarrassing as teaching third position to a class of first graders and being literally dragged out. Dad seemed to think working was going to distract him from his lessons—or so he'd claimed. Shiloh thought really it was just that him having money would get him out from under his father's thumb.

"Shiloh, wait up." Gage didn't grab him but his voice halted Shiloh just the same.

Shiloh stopped halfway out of the front door, his hand still on the frame. "Why?"

"I'm sorry about your dance classes."

Shiloh drew in a deep breath, counting to ten in his head before he plastered on a smile. "It's fine. I don't really need them." It was only partly a lie. He didn't need them to perfect his technique, though he couldn't say he didn't learn things every now and then. He needed them for his mental health—needed the freedom to dance with the structure of the class to help settle his mind.

"Still… I thought getting rid of the pictures would make things better, and in the end, it made it worse. So, I'm sorry." Gage looked uncomfortable, like he didn't know what to say.

Shiloh shrugged, looking away. For just a moment, the soft expression on Gage's face, the genuine regret, had a decision solidifying in Shiloh's mind that he hadn't even realized he was considering.

He was going to trust his bodyguard.

"Will you go somewhere with me?"

****

Gage drove Shiloh to a blue house with white shutters. It had a quaint little wraparound porch that swallowed the small patch of land that called itself a yard. There was no sign above the door—or in the yard, or on the mailbox. There was nothing to set it apart from every other house in the suburb except for the small rainbow pride flag on a wooden stick stuck in the dirt of the little garden. In the driveway, a teenage girl was shooting hoops.

"Are we meeting a friend?" Gage asked.

"More like twelve friends." Shiloh didn't explain further. He just climbed out the passenger door and started up the sidewalk.

"Hold on a sec. We can't just waltz in there. It hasn't been cleared." Gage hurried to catch up.

Shiloh patted the bigger man's chest with a smirk. "Oh, honey, just wait. By the time we're done, they'll have had to clear *you*."

Shiloh wasn't lying.

They didn't let the two of them out of the entryway until the woman who introduced herself as Natalie, one of the House Mothers, had received an all-clear back from the company that ran their background checks and both of them were signed into the visitors' computer. Then Shiloh still had to promise to explain the rules before Natalie let them be.

Apparently, Shiloh volunteered at the Rainbow House, a home-between-homes for homeless LGBTQ+ youth.

Shiloh started rattling off the rules as he led the way to the rec room. "Okay, so the upstairs is where all the kids' bedrooms are, so it's off limits to visitors. Some of the kids stay here full time and some of them just visit for activities, but all of them have pretty rough home lives. Always ask before you join any activities, and don't get mad if they say no. A lot of them don't trust adults."

"How often do you volunteer here?" Gage asked as they passed a handful of boys who were sprawled over the couches, playing a racing game on the Xbox.

"When I have time." Shiloh shrugged and turned into the rec room, crossing over to the blue mats folded by the wall. "I don't do a lot, just run a couple of dance lessons every so often. No big deal."

"I don't know. I bet it's a big deal to the kids."

Shiloh paused partway through laying down the first mat. "Yeah, maybe." Gage grabbed another mat and lay it down beside the first. Between the two of them, they had them out quickly.

"So, how's this work? Do you have a schedule set up for volunteering?" Yet again, Gage was presented with another place that hadn't been vetted, a whole new slew of suspects who could be threatening Shiloh.

"No, just whenever I feel like it and have time. After I check in, the House Mother on duty lets the kids know I'm here for a session." Shiloh moved to the mat at the front of the room and dropped down onto it to start his stretches.

Shiloh's legs looked even longer as he pointed his toes toward the opposite wall, curling his fingers around the arches of his slender feet. The pink jeans clung to every well-defined muscle, and Gage couldn't help but stare at the strip of pale skin peeking from underneath his tank top.

Gage tore his gaze away and leaned back against the wall, shoving his hands in his pockets. Shiloh looked over but his eyes never got past Gage's hips. Feeling his face flush hot, he tugged his hands free, knowing he'd only drawn attention to the growing situation in his jeans.

Before he could make excuses, if he could even *think* of one, a girl in bright pink tights bounced into the room. "Shiloh, guess what? I got a scholarship to study dance at one of the studios downtown!" Her voice broke from excitement partway through, but she hardly noticed.

Shiloh grinned, looking even more excited than the girl. "That's awesome, Megan! I'm so proud of you."

Megan bounced up onto her toes before spinning to claim a mat. A few more kids slinked in behind her. Gage tried not to make it obvious he was staring while at the same time memorizing each of their faces. It was *extremely* unlikely any of them were Shiloh's stalker. They were too young, for one thing. Not that a teenager couldn't be a stalker, but the likelihood was low enough to be negligible.

Shiloh greeted each of them before he started walking them through their stretches. Some of the kids, like Megan, followed along easily, but a few were less confident, their darting eyes watching their neighbors like they thought they were going to be judged.

After almost ten minutes of stretches followed by Shiloh walking them through what he called 'positions', Shiloh finally turned on a radio in the corner of the room. A slow, classical piece started to play as he started taking the kids through a routine.

Gage heard Shiloh say they were going to do something 'simple' but it didn't look simple to him. After the third time the group watched him run it down from the top, he left his mat and started walking the room, making corrections as he went.

"And a one, two, three, four." Shiloh snapped his fingers to the beat of the music, counting them out as he moved. "Straighten that leg a bit, Jace. There you go. Can you point your toes a little? Good job, Stephanie."

Near one boy, Shiloh stopped, his smile gentling even more than it had with the others. The boy wore a baggy gray sweater that seemed to swallow him, his fingers tucked into the cuffs like he was hiding them. "You're doing well, Mason. Try a *bras-en courrone,"* Shiloh said in a voice Gage could barely hear.

Mason stiffly lifted his arms over his head, forming a circle. Gage stiffened when the boy's sleeves slouched down his forearms, dark bruises ringing his left wrist like a bracelet. And as Shiloh talked him from something called an *arabesque* to an *attitude,* Gage spotted the darker contusions on his lower back. He gritted his teeth and looked away, glaring at the wall instead.

He couldn't get involved. He didn't know the kid, and it wasn't his place. His place was to take care of Shiloh, and that was proving difficult enough as it was.

Maybe he would ask Shiloh about the kid later, see if there was anything he could do. If the police weren't involved—or social services—then they definitely should be.

"Relax your arms a bit, Mason. There you go." Shiloh finally moved on to the next kid, a girl with no bruises and a happy smile.

The lesson went by quickly, and soon, the kids were waving as they filed out. "You're really good with them," Gage said, moving up beside Shiloh and clapping him on the shoulder. Apparently, his hand had a mind of its own, his thumb stroking the Shiloh's nape before he caught himself and pulled away.

"No, I just understand what they're going through." Shiloh's skin went pink, and he bent quickly as if to hide it, folding up the nearest mat and dragging it over to lean it against the wall. "I mean, I guess it's not exactly the same. I've never been hungry like some of these kids, and my dad would never kick me out because I'm gay, but..." Shiloh trailed off, nervously running his finger over the rough stitching on the edge of the blue exercise mat.

"Pain isn't a competition. Just because you aren't hungry, doesn't mean you aren't hurting in other ways." Gage grabbed the next mat and helped lug it over with the others.

"Um..." Shiloh fiddled with the hem of his shirt. "Yeah, so... Okay, this is really awkward, and I'm not used to people being nice to me if they don't want something out of it, so will you be mad if we pretend this moment never happened while, inwardly, I cherish it forever?" Shiloh batted his eyes up at Gage and gave a bright smile, not waiting for an acknowledgment. "Okay, great. Now that we got that over with. I have one last thing to do here then we can skip out."

"I'm not in any rush."

"Great. Awesome. Okay, so... Yeah." Shiloh turned on his heel and headed out of the rec room. Gage followed him to the check-in desk, his curiosity growing. "Hey, Natalie?"

Natalie popped her gum and grinned. "Yeah?"

"Is there a kid named Riley here? 'Bout yay high, brown hair?" Shiloh's hand waved somewhere around his shoulder.

"You know I can't answer that, Shiloh." Natalie glanced down at her phone again, her thumbs continuing to tap a message.

"Oh, I know you can't. I was just hoping you'd nod or something on accident." Shiloh sighed and leaned against the desk. "Okay, so I guess I don't really *need* to know, but if he is here, can you tell him I stopped by?"

"Yeah, of course. *If* a kid named Riley is here, I'll let him know." Natalie smirked.

"Thanks, Nat." Shiloh started for the door. Gage was surprised when he stopped to let Gage exit first, for once following the rules he'd set up day one. Gage slipped by, stepping out onto the porch. It was dark out, the sidewalks lit by the amber streetlights. He started for the car.

Shiloh followed but stopped beside the passenger door, staring down the street with a frown on his face. Gage followed his gaze but there was nothing there, just normal Austin traffic, if a bit light for this time of evening.

Gage leaned on the roof of the car as the seconds dragged by. "Everything okay?"

"I'm not ready to go home."

"Okay. So we won't go home." Gage knew exactly where he wanted to take Shiloh, and while he knew it was a bad idea, he was going to do it anyway.

Chapter Nineteen

Lights flicked on along the darkened streets, leaving pools of light interspersed with shadow. Shiloh stayed silent, flickering his focus occasionally over to Gage, curiosity obviously alight in his eyes. Gage pulled into a small, pay-to-park lot and passed over a few bills to the attendant. He'd spent the entire drive trying to talk himself out of this stupid decision, but instead of driving them back to the estate, he'd ended up here. He told himself that it wasn't a big deal to go against Mr. Beckett's orders, that Shiloh likely would have snuck out again anyway, but sneaking around wasn't typically his style. At least he knew Shiloh would be safe with him.

"You wanted to show me a parking lot?" Shiloh asked as they climbed out of the car.

"Yes. It's the most marvelous parking lot in the land," Gage replied, shutting the door with a grin.

Shiloh laughed, the sound light and nearly carefree. Gage tried to think of a single time in the past week he'd heard it sound so real. "Where are we really going?" Shiloh asked.

"Dancing," Gage said, reflexively scanning the lot before he headed through the labyrinth of cars toward the sidewalk.

"Dancing? We're going dancing?" Shiloh hustled to catch up to him, excitement leaking into his voice. "*You're* going dancing?"

"Yes. You might not believe it, but I actually rather enjoy it. Think you can get us past the line?" Gage quirked up an eyebrow and gestured. The line wrapped around the building.

Shiloh glanced over at the glowing rainbow sign, his eyes brightening. "Fifth Storm? Not a problem." Shiloh didn't wait for him to follow. He bypassed the line and moved straight up to the bouncer. "Hey, Mike, room for two more?"

"Been a few weeks, Shy. Thought maybe you forgot about us." Mike was nearly as tall as Gage and half again as broad, tattoos decorating his bare arms and chest.

"I'd never forget about *you,* Mike." Shiloh grinned playfully up at the bouncer. Gage pushed down the instant flare of jealousy that he knew he had no right to have.

Mike unclipped the velvet rope and waved them in. "Don't get in too much trouble, boy." The bouncer swatted at Shiloh's ass as he walked past, and Gage buried a growl—or tried to, but he must not have done it as well as he thought. Mike lifted an eyebrow and winked.

Gage followed Shiloh into the club. Loud dance music pulsed through speakers and innumerable bodies gyrated under the strobing lights. Shiloh pushed right to the center of the dance floor, Gage at his back.

"Dance with me!" Shiloh hollered over the music, leaning back into Gage's chest. Gage acquiesced without protest, moving his hips in time with Shiloh's, though he was careful to keep his eyes on the bodies pressing close to them.

Shiloh didn't bother. He cast his head back, his eyes closed, swaying in time to the beat. For three songs, there was just them and the music. Then, the beat changed and Shiloh spun around, snapping his eyes open. They were bright and wild as he leaned up on tiptoes, his breath tickling the shell of Gage's ear. "I need a drink!"

"Come on then, *Shy.*" Gage tangled their fingers together, not willing to risk losing him in the press of the crowd. If it were just because Shiloh was his client, the lion in his chest wouldn't bother him, but his first thought was that someone else would snag Shiloh's attention if he were out of sight for longer than a moment. Only after that did he remember the real reason he should be worried.

Gage tugged Shiloh toward the curved bar at the back of the club. It took a few minutes for the overworked bartender to notice them, and when he did, his eyes slid right over Shiloh to Gage.

"Well, he-llo, *Daddy.*" The slim blond twink leaned across the bar, light glistening on his oil-slicked skin.

Shiloh burst out laughing. "Yeah, *Daddy.*"

Gage rolled his eyes. "I'll take a Coke. He wants a…" Gage eyed Shiloh for a moment, "a Manhattan."

Shiloh pouted, but there was enough of a twinkle in his blue-green eyes that Gage knew it was a farce. "What if I want a bourbon?"

"*Do* you want a bourbon?" Gage asked, lips twitching on a smile.

Shiloh made a face and shuddered. "No, it tastes like cough syrup."

"He'll take a Manhattan." Gage turned back to the still-waiting bartender.

"Coming right up." The man was quick to pour both. Gage paid, including a decent tip, and slid Shiloh his glass.

Shiloh drank without taking his eyes off Gage. "Not bad." Shiloh returned his empty glass to the bar. Gage placed his mostly finished one beside it.

They were turning to the dance floor again when the lights brightened and the music died. A voice came over the speakers. Gage glanced around, spotting the man in leather and little else on a stage across the room, microphone in hand. "I want to thank you all for joining me tonight, though I know it's not really me you're here to see, is it? Are you all ready for the fun to begin?"

The crowd called out its response, loud and exuberant. "Great! It's amateur night tonight, so any of you sexy men out there feeling confident enough to *bare* your talent for the crowd, the competition starts in ten minutes!"

"It's Thursday!" Shiloh spun to face him. "I totally forgot about this! We should go up."

"I'm not stripping," Gage answered immediately. He had no need to bare his anything for a crowd of people. No one would want to see that, anyway.

"Oh, come on. It'll be fun!" Shiloh was practically bouncing, gripping his hand and pulling him away from the bar, toward the stage.

"For you, maybe." Gage knew full well that Shiloh wouldn't have any problems *baring* it all for the crowd, and he wouldn't be in danger on the stage, not with Gage right there. "You go up. I'll happily stay down and watch."

Shiloh paused near the stairs, his eyes wide. "You...you'd let me go up there? You're not going to try to stop me?"

"Nope. I told you that I'm not here to babysit you. I'm just here to keep you safe," Gage said.

Shiloh's mouth opened but no sound came out. For the first time, what looked like genuine shock crossed his face. A second later, Shiloh let out a *whoop* of excitement and darted up the stairs and onto the stage. Several men were already waiting. Most were older than Shiloh, but not by much. Gage doubted any of them were older than him.

Shiloh joined the line. Over the next few minutes, three more men jumped to the stage, but then the lights over the crowd lowered again, leaving the stage illuminated. The leather-bound MC ascended. "It seems we have a lively bunch up here. Are you all excited to see them? I know I am!"

The crowd roared again. Several wolf whistles sounded. With each loud catcall, Shiloh preened onstage. Gage was torn. Part of him was proud of Shiloh, but part of him wanted nothing more than to drag Shiloh down and block him from the heated glances.

Following his instincts, though, would defeat the whole purpose of this experience. The leather man approached a well-built redhead with a cocky smile. The announcer muttered something, likely instructions, and the man grinned.

"Wanna tell the crowd your name?" the announcer asked.

"Dexter. But my friends call me Dex." Dex struck a pose, flexing well-toned muscles. Gage spared the man a few cursory glances as the music started and he began dancing, pulling clothes off and leaving them in a pile on the stage. There was no denying he was hot, but Gage found his eyes, more often than not, skirting over to Shiloh, even before it was Shiloh's turn.

Three people in, Shiloh stepped under the spotlight. Like the others, a cocky smile lit his face, though Gage knew him well enough by now to spot the nerves lurking beneath it. Shiloh's thumb ran circles over his forefinger when he was nervous.

Shiloh spoke into the mic. "Hey, guys, I'm Shy and—" Gage was glad that Shiloh was smart enough not to use his real name. Unfortunately, it didn't really make a difference.

Several voices in the crowd hollered, "Shiloh! Shiloh!" Gage heard at least one person whistle, and another yelled, "Take it off!"

Shiloh didn't seem surprised to be recognized. He did, however, look at Gage, and he seemed surprised that Gage made no move to pull him out.

"I guess I don't need an introduction." Shiloh passed the mic back and over the stereo, an overplayed pop song began. It was a struggle keeping his eyes off Shiloh's striptease and on the crowd.

After his next scan of the crowd, his eyes caught and locked on Shiloh. Shiloh was staring right at him, his face flushed, eyes heated. His black tank top was crumpled on the stage, right next to the skin-tight pink jeans that Gage longed to peel free from those lithe, toned legs. A pair of tight, pink panties clung to

Shiloh's hips, the large bulge in the front evidence of Shiloh's arousal.

Gage barely suppressed a moan as his jeans tightened painfully, his body reacting to the sight. He tore his eyes free, skimming back up Shiloh's body to his face again, uselessly hoping that Shiloh had missed him devouring him with his eyes. Shiloh wet his lips and he ran his hands over the panties, fondling himself before tugging at the waistband. He gracefully twisted, teasingly blocking his erection from sight while, at the same time, revealing the firm globes of his porcelain ass.

Gage bet it would fit perfectly in his hands. His palms itched with the desire to find out, heat coiling in his belly. He hadn't felt an attraction this strong in years, not since before he'd left the Army. Back then, it had been for one of his fellow Rangers, a man three years his senior and twice as high on the pay docket.

It seemed he had a thing for the forbidden. Shiloh looked coyly over his shoulder, his grin spreading when he locked eyes again with Gage. The brat shot him a wink and pulled his panties lower, hinting at the dark promise just below. Shiloh snapped the waistband back up on his hips and spun back around.

Gage wondered what material the thin scrap of pink lace was made out of to contain the straining erection Shiloh was sporting. Surely, the lace should have snapped by now. The spotlight highlighted every sculpted line of Shiloh's body, as well as the dark, promising wet spot dampening the material.

He was so engrossed in fantasies of what he *could* do to Shiloh's body, imagining the way he would writhe and moan beneath him, that he didn't realize the music had stopped until Shiloh bent down and scooped up his jeans, unashamedly putting his pants back on.

Gage cleared his throat, shaking himself free of the fantasy Shiloh was pulling him into, belatedly darting his gaze around the crowd again. Shiloh bounced off the stage, moving like a siren over to Gage.

"Dance with me." Shiloh grabbed Gage's hand again and pulled him back onto the dance floor. The amateur show continued but neither of them paid attention. Shiloh wrapped his fingers around Gage's hips and tugged him close, chest to chest.

"Dance with me," Shiloh said again, softer.

Gage's hands moved of their own volition, curling around Shiloh's hips as he moved with him. He felt the sweat on Shiloh's bare skin, the heat. He knew he should step back, put some distance between their bodies, but like magnets, they were drawn together.

Shiloh's eyes were mirrors, reflecting Gage's own desire. His focus dropped down to Shiloh's lips. They were full and soft, whispering his name. Gage longed to taste them…to see if they were as sweet as they looked.

Shiloh stretched up on his toes, stroking over Gage's chest to curl around his neck as their lips met. Then Gage had his answer. Shiloh *wasn't* as sweet as he looked, he was sweeter, like chocolate and wine. Gage could drown in the taste.

Shiloh tightened his fingers in his hair and the soft bite of pain cleared his head. *I can't do this.* Gage pulled away, taking a step back.

"Shiloh…" Gage started.

But Shiloh jerked away, his face stricken. "Sorry. I shouldn't have…" Shiloh spun and darted into the crowd, pushing his way through the dancing bodies.

Gage tried to follow but he was too big to be graceful. He shoved his way through, ignoring the curses that followed him, trying to keep his client in sight, but it was useless.

Shiloh was gone.

Chapter Twenty

Shiloh's eyes burned. He shoved his way through the sweaty bodies, tucking his head lower than the crowd to avoid being spotted. He was so stupid. Thinking a man like Gage could actually be interested in him was as bad as trusting a cocaine high. They'd both leave him broken like a china doll in an empty bathroom. At least the cocaine never promised him anything.

"Fuck!" Shiloh cursed as a laughing man in a bondage harness stumbled in front of him, spilling piss-colored whiskey over his bare chest.

"Sorry, mate." The laughing man swiped liquor-stiff fingers over Shiloh's skin, smearing the whiskey further over his flesh. Shiloh shoved him away and darted toward the neon-green exit sign. He spilled out into a dark, narrow alley, already fumbling with the ride-share app on his phone.

The door behind him had barely closed when it slammed open again, bouncing against the bricks. Shiloh's heart beat an allegro tempo in his chest as he spun around, coming face to face with a hooded figure whose face was hidden beneath a ski mask.

The man—it was definitely a man, despite the narrow shoulders—moved while Shiloh was frozen like an effigy in the dim, flickering light of the single streetlamp.

Shiloh's muscles were molasses, too slow and heavy to evade the grasping hands. One clamped around his arm while the other snaked around his throat, cutting off his airway. A hard shove sent him into the wall behind him then he was being lifted, the exposed bricks scratching his bare skin.

Shiloh scrabbled at the hand around his throat.

The masked man just laughed and released his arm, tobacco-stained finger lifting to molest Shiloh's cheek. "Pet, you've been naughty." Shiloh struggled harder at the sound of the mechanically altered voice. His feet barely skimmed the gravel, dangling like the broken limbs of a forgotten marionette.

A tongue, wet and slug-like, trailed over his face from chin to cheek, a trail of spit connecting him to the man's mouth. Shiloh cringed but only succeeded in slamming his head into the bricks.

The man breathed him in like an addict. "Careful, pet. I don't want you damaging your pretty face before I get to play with you."

Shiloh scratched his nails into the man's skin, leaving half-moon crescents behind. "Can't… breathe…" Shiloh gasped with his last breath of air, his head fuzzy. He was assaulted by the smell of menthol cigarettes and expensive cologne.

"It's time to sleep now."

Blackness crept along the edges of Shiloh's vision, blood pounding in his ears. This wasn't how it was supposed to happen. He didn't know who this man was. Had he followed Shiloh out because he had the opportunity? Would he have grabbed any random person who'd stumbled alone into the alley or had he picked Shiloh on purpose?

A loud crash sounded then Shiloh was flying, flung toward the gravel-crusted ground like trash. Stones dug into his knees and palms.

Two men towered over him. Shiloh cringed against the pavement, blinking his eyes clear of the haze. The figures resolved into recognizable silhouettes. Gage stood protectively over Shiloh, a gun clasped in his hand.

The man in the mask bared his teeth. "Get out of my way. This is between me and my boy."

Shiloh rolled, pushing his skinned hands to pavement. Dizzy and bleeding, he pushed himself up.

"I need you to back toward the street, okay? Stay behind me." Gage ignored the other man, speaking directly to Shiloh.

Shiloh stumbled away. He wanted to sprint…that, or fall to the ground and cover his head. It took everything in him to move back slowly. Gage stepped with him, staying between him and the man.

The masked man's eyes were ice. His mouth curved in a parody of a smile. "I know where you live, Shiloh. You might as well just come with me now."

Shiloh shuddered. It wasn't random, then, if the man knew his name. Of course, half the country knew where he lived, so it could be just…a crime of opportunity, but he doubted it. There was something dark in his assailant's eyes when they narrowed.

The man leaped forward, his shoulder colliding with Gage's stomach, just as Gage's finger squeezed the trigger. A piercing *crack* sounded, like thunder. Shiloh flinched as his ears popped painfully, deafening him to the sound of the bullet biting into the bricks. He watched Gage stumble backward, dropping the gun from his hand.

It slid across the pavement and both Gage and the stranger dove for the weapon.

Gage was a hairsbreadth too slow. The attacker's hand closed on the grip seconds before Gage landed, squeezing the trigger with little time to aim.

A second shot echoed through the alley, loud enough to pierce through the muffled white noise in Shiloh's ears, and Gage's leg jerked from the impact.

The attacker lifted the weapon again, preparing to fire, but Gage shoved himself up as if he hadn't just gotten shot.

Oh my God, he has been shot. Someone had shot Gage, trying to get to Shiloh.

Because of Shiloh. Because he hadn't done what he was supposed to do and stayed with Gage.

His breath came quick and heavy. There were weights on his chest, binding his lungs. Shiloh clawed at them, but his fingers met only flesh.

Gage grappled for the gun.

Sirens sounded from the street.

Shiloh watched the attacker give one last, futile attempt at snatching the gun from Gage's grasp before he turned to spring down the alley. Gage kept the gun pointed after him.

Shiloh gasped in a breath, loud and ragged, and the sound seemed to shock Gage into motion. Gage shoved the gun into its holster and spun, but Shiloh barely noticed.

He slammed his eyes closed as he struggled to draw in another breath. The broken silence weighed on his chest. Hands gently clasped the sides of Shiloh's face.

"I'm sorry. I'm *so* sorry," Shiloh burst out, his heart stuttering. He snapped his eyes open, scanning Gage for blood. But Gage was red—all red, red everywhere. "He shot you."

"Are you okay?" Gage tipped Shiloh's face to the side.

"He s-shot y-you." Shiloh couldn't stop the stutter. "I'm…I'm sorry, h-he shot you."

"You're going into shock." Gage urged him down to the pavement, maneuvering his head until it was cradled in Gage's lap. He stroked through Shiloh's hair and the feeling made him shiver. "Take a nice, deep breath."

Shiloh sucked in. It shuddered in his lungs. He shook as he exhaled. "I'm sorry. It's my fault. It's my fault he shot you. Oh God, this is my fault." Shiloh jerked, trying to push himself up to look at Gage. He must be hurt. "We need to stop the bleeding."

"It's okay. It's just a prosthesis. I'm fine. Let me take care of you for now, okay?" Gage urged him back down.

Shiloh sagged. "I'm sorry. I d-didn't mean to…"

"It's okay. Just breathe. The cops will be here any second."

"The cops! We need to call them…" Shiloh struggled to sit up again, patting at his pockets for his phone.

"I called them already, as soon as I stepped into the alley. They're on their way." Gage pulled out his own phone, showing him the screen, still connected to the emergency line.

Shiloh was going to be in so much trouble.

The sirens grew louder as a police cruiser pulled into the narrow mouth of the alley. There was barely enough room. The strobing red and blue lights were too bright.

Shiloh stared at the broken bricks over Gage's shoulder where the bullet had struck. *Am I going to have to pay for that?* Would his dad pay for it, once he knew what Shiloh had done?

Am I going to be arrested?

"Talk to me, Shiloh," Gage said, his voice distant, like it was coming from the other end of a long, dark tunnel.

Shiloh pressed his face to Gage's chest. His body shivered. It was summer. Summer shouldn't be this cold.

"What color's my shirt, Shiloh? Can you tell me that?" Gage asked.

"Red." Everything was red.

"Come on, Shiloh. Look at my shirt. What color is it?" Gage's hand ran through Shiloh's hair, brushing it off his face.

Shiloh blinked his eyes open. He tried to focus on Gage's shirt but the world was blurry, like looking through a kaleidoscope. He squeezed his eyes shut, nails scratching at the skin over his ribs.

Warm hands tightened around his wrists, tugging his hands away from his skin. "Stop. I can talk him through this." Gage's voice was muffled. All Shiloh's focus was on the restraining fingers. Like a scratched record, his mind skipped back and forth, past to present, *then* to *now*.

"We're going to have to sedate him."

A needle slid into the skin of his arm. Immediately, Shiloh relaxed, the pain centering him. He just needed another...but instead, a cold burning spread through his veins. His limbs grew heavy, invisible weights pinning him down—and he drifted.

Chapter Twenty-One

Red jute ropes tie his wrists to the wrought-iron headboard. It itches as he pulls, hoping to free himself before the door opens. His skin is chafed. The ropes tighten, twisting into snakes that hiss in his face, tightening around his wrists to keep him pinned. The door opens.

Mr. Lawson walks in. In one hand, he clasps a leather crop. In the other, a tube of super glue. "Time to learn your lesson, kid." Shiloh pulls at the snakes but they slither tighter, forked tongues flicking between venomous fangs.

The temperature drops. Shiloh swears he can see his breath as he pants from his mouth.

Mr. Lawson strips away his suit jacket and rolls up his sleeves. Latex gloves cover his hands. He straddles Shiloh's chest. It's hard to breathe.

"In the future, maybe you'll think before opening your mouth, hm?" He uncaps the superglue, smearing it over Shiloh's lips until it hardens.

Beep.

Shiloh strains against the red and yellow snakes. He tries to pry his lips apart, but the hand keeps them firmly closed, ensuring the glue holds.

Beep. Beep.

Mr. Lawson lifts his hand. Shiloh tries to force his lips open, pushing his tongue at the sealed skin, but he can't. Tears leak from his eyes, trailing down the sides of his face.

Beep. Beep. Beep.

"Shiloh?"

Shiloh flinched awake, tearing his arms free from the bindings. But there *were* no bindings. He was…in a hospital bed? Shiloh rubbed his eyes, opening them again to see if it had changed, but it hadn't. He was still in a hospital bed, an off-green curtain separating his bed from the rest of the room.

"Shiloh?" His father sat in a chair just beside the bed. Behind him, his face solemn, stood Gage.

"Dad?" Shiloh winced, dropping his hand to his raw throat. The skin was tender to the touch and memories flooded back. The man in the ski mask, the hands clasping around his throat. *It's time to go to sleep now…*

The gunshot echoing.

Shiloh jerked upright, scanning Gage. "He shot you."

"It's a prosthetic. Barely scuffed the titanium." Gage smiled but it was stiff. Shiloh vaguely remembered being told that already. His eyes dropped down to Gage's legs. It didn't *look* like a prosthetic. He supposed that was the point.

Shiloh's heart rate slowed to a reasonable level, a fact audible to everyone in the room, since the damn heart monitor insisted on sounding the chorus of beeps at full volume.

"Why am I in the hospital?" Shiloh asked, examining the few scrapes visible along the edge of the hospital gown. They didn't look deep enough for stitches.

"They gave you a mild sedative," his dad answered.

"Did…did they catch that man?" Shiloh looked past his father to Gage, who frowned but just shook his head.

"Don't worry about any of that, son. I'm sure it was just a…random mugging." His father shifted uncomfortably in his seat, looking, for a moment, almost *guilty*.

It *wasn't* a random mugging. "He knew my name, Dad."

"Probably recognized you from the papers, then. You were in them again last week." Dad smoothed out several wrinkles on his trousers. "We're going to have to talk about you sneaking out, as well."

"Dad," Shiloh spoke before his father could continue with a lecture, "he knew my name, and he called me 'pet'." Shiloh paused, taking in the strained look on his father's face.

Dad shifted uncomfortably in his chair. "Son, I don't think this is the best—"

"Place for this?" Shiloh interrupted. "Yeah, neither do I. Unfortunately, I wouldn't *be* here if you had just told me I had a goddamn *stalker* in the first place!" Shiloh was yelling by the end of the sentence, unable to stop himself.

He wasn't surprised his father hadn't thought it important enough to tell him. Shiloh had been dropping off creepy letters for half a year, and except for hiring a string of useless bodyguards, his dad hadn't said anything. A cold sweat broke out on his skin, and he shivered. How long had this man been following him? Had there been *other* letters? Real letters? Letters he hadn't written himself?

A young nurse popped her head into the doorway. "Sir, this is a hospital. I'm going to have to ask you to lower your voice."

"Don't worry. I'm leaving anyway." Shiloh grabbed the cords connecting him to the heart monitor and tugged, wincing slightly as they ripped free of his skin. The burst of pain helped clear the panic from his head.

"The doctor still has to—" his father started.

"The doctor can kiss my ass," Shiloh grumbled, scanning the room for his clothes. "Where are my pants?"

"The police took them," Gage answered.

"God *damn* it, I just bought those." Shiloh would just wear the stupid gown out. It wasn't like he hadn't been photographed in less.

His father stood abruptly, blocking his path to the door. "Wait, Shiloh. We need to talk."

"Too late, Dad. Probably should have talked to me, oh…when you *first* found out I had a fucking stalker." Or when he was fourteen. That would have been awesome.

"It's not safe to go yet. We're waiting for your new security officer. He should—" Father held up his hands to placate him. It didn't work.

"*New* security officer? I didn't want one bodyguard. What makes you think I'll let a second one hang about?" Shiloh stopped trying to get around his father, planting his hands firmly on his hips.

He removed them when he realized he probably looked like a pouting child.

"Mr. Tucker will be returning to Seattle."

Chapter Twenty-Two

Shiloh crossed his arms to hide the way his hands clenched into fists. "That's a shitty decision. Shouldn't you discuss this with me first?" Of course he would finally get a bodyguard he could even somewhat stand and his dad would try to get rid of him. Although he had to admit, if only to himself, that he could do more than *somewhat* stand Gage. Even if the rejection in the club still stung, he couldn't even pretend the man didn't have his best interests at heart.

"I thought it would be best." Dad trailed off when Shiloh glared at him harder.

"So you're firing him for doing his job." Shiloh narrowed his eyes as he pointed out the stupidity.

"If he'd been doing his job, we wouldn't be in a hospital right now!" Dad snapped, face flushing. Shiloh didn't care how angry his dad was right now. He didn't have any right to blame this on Gage.

"No, we're in the hospital right now because you couldn't trust me enough to tell me the truth!" Shiloh fired back at his father. "Maybe if you'd told me I was in danger, *real* danger, I wouldn't have tried giving him the slip in the club. You should be *thanking* him!"

"You shouldn't have been in the club in the first place! God, Shiloh, how many times have we gone over this? I shouldn't have needed to tell you that you were in danger. You should have just followed the goddamn rules! I don't ask that much from you. Don't skip class. Don't get mouthy. Don't make a fool of yourself in dance clubs." Dad was yelling now, his voice echoing off the paper-thin walls.

Gage moved to shut the door, but his dad didn't even notice. "What were you *thinking,* Shiloh? Dancing for tips in a gay bar? I'm not even surprised when I hear about these things anymore. You wonder why I didn't tell you? Because I thought if I told you someone was sending you letters, you'd go out of your way to get yourself in trouble, since that seems to be the only thing you're good at!"

His dad lurched forward and Shiloh flinched, unable to stop himself. His dad had never laid a finger on him, not once, no matter how much Shiloh had pushed him, but he couldn't help it.

"Son…" Mr. Beckett's voice softened but Shiloh was done listening.

"No. I want to go home." Shiloh pushed past his father and tugged open the door. He paused in the entryway only long enough to say, "And you're *not* firing Gage. He did his job the best he could. It was my fault—which you should know already, since all I'm good for is causing trouble."

He stormed toward the nurses' station. He heard Gage follow him but didn't look back. He slammed his hand down on the desk, feeling slightly guilty when the nurse jumped. "I want to go home."

"The doctor will need to clear you," the woman started to say, but her voice trailed off as she saw his expression.

"I'd rather not wait. Give me something to sign and I'll be on my way."

The nurse fumbled with some papers before silently handing him a liability waiver. He made quick work of filling it out, acknowledging that he was signing himself out against doctor's orders and wouldn't sue the hospital if he dropped dead on the drive home.

He thrust the paperwork back to the woman and turned toward the exit, but Gage caught his arm. "Officer Preston would like to speak with you. He's waiting in a conference room, if you feel up to it."

"I don't," Shiloh snapped, "but might as well get it over with."

Shiloh reluctantly followed Gage farther into the hospital. They stopped outside a small conference room. It appeared the officer had commandeered it while he waited.

Officer Preston was sitting at the round table, a folder open in front of him. He was older than Gage, though only by a few years. If he were more than halfway into his thirties, Shiloh would be shocked. His hair was dark but for the silver just starting to make an appearance by his temples.

Officer Preston looked up from the open file with a frown. "Mr. Beckett—"

"Shiloh," he corrected. "Mr. Beckett's my father,"

Officer Preston's frown deepened. "Shiloh. I'm glad you've decided to take time out of your *busy* schedule to finally sit down with me."

Shiloh allowed Gage to usher him farther into the room so he could close the door, confused at the anger in the man's voice. He'd only barely woken up, so it wasn't like he'd gone to a party and fucked around first. "Sorry that the sedative kind of knocked me out?"

Officer Preston flipped the file on the desk closed and stood. "If you refuse to take this case seriously, I have others I can spend my time on."

Shiloh flinched. It was exactly what Lawson had always said would happen. Why would the police bother listening to him about anything? "I'm sorry, Officer…" He glanced at Gage for a moment, struggling with the name.

"Preston," Gage reminded him gently.

"Officer Preston. I promise I am taking this *very* seriously." Shiloh might have pretended to have a stalker, but in no way, shape or form did he want to have a *real* one.

"This is the fifth meeting I've set up with you. Honestly, I'm surprised you decided to show." Officer Preston eyed his watch. "Sit down. I need to take your statement."

"Fifth?" Shiloh shouldn't be surprised. He felt a sharp stab of pain in his chest as he realized what had happened. "Let me guess… You were setting them up through my father."

"Is that a problem?" Officer Preston sat at one end of the table and reopened the folder. He shot Shiloh a pointed look, gesturing at the chair opposite.

Shiloh flopped onto it, wincing slightly as he landed on tender flesh. "Yeah, it is—since my father didn't bother telling me I had a stalker to begin with. I figured it out when some asshole in a ski mask manhandled me in an alley."

Officer Preston looked up from the file again, his gaze piercing. "You're saying that your father, knowing the danger you were in, intentionally kept you in the dark?"

Shiloh felt his skin warm. He didn't know what to say. He didn't want his dad to get in trouble. This was never about that. It was just about disappearing for a while. He shrugged. "I'm sure he had his *reasons.* He always does." Shiloh leaned forward, pointing at the folder. He tried to keep his voice innocent as he asked, "Did he send me letters or something?"

Officer Preston furrowed his forehead. He pulled out the small mountain of letters, each stored in its own evidence bag, and held them out. Shiloh read through them. The room was silent but for the sounds of crinkling plastic. He'd written these…every last one of them. Shiloh passed them back then curled his arms around his waist. If those were all *his* letters, then who was in the alley? Was it just…a coincidence? A crime of opportunity?

And would the police be able to find him if they were too busy investigating the fake crime? Should Shiloh tell the officer the letters were fake? If he did, would he get arrested?

Officer Preston seemed to stare closely at Shiloh. He tried to keep his expression open. "Why don't you take me through what happened today, starting from the time you left the house."

Shiloh obediently recounted everything, from his volunteering to their trip together to the club. Shiloh got to the end of the strip competition and hesitated. "So we danced a bit then…I left to go out to the alley and the—"

Officer Preston interrupted, scribbling on his notes, "Hang on. Why did you go out to the alley instead of leaving through the main doors?"

"It was...closer, and I didn't want..." Shiloh felt his cheeks flush, his focus darting to Gage. He didn't want to recount his stupidity, that he'd actually thought that Gage might like him. Might welcome a kiss, or more, from someone like *him.*

Gage finished for him. "There was a bit of a misunderstanding. I believe he thought he could lose me in the alley."

"Yeah." Shiloh bit his lip then continued.

"You said the man licked you?" Officer Preston looked up from his notes. "It's possible he left DNA behind that we could trace. May I take a swab?" He pulled out a small, orange-capped tube.

Shiloh swallowed at the memory before giving a brisk nod. "Yeah. Will it really help catch the guy?"

"If he's in the system. If he's not, we can still use it as evidence if we catch him."

"When," Gage corrected. "We'll get him."

Gage refused to consider the possibility that the man would get away or, worse, get to Shiloh. He was still fuming at the thought as they left Officer Preston and headed through the main doors. Everything went smoothly until they stepped onto the sidewalk. At least a dozen men and women with cameras and mics were waiting. Quickly, Gage stripped off his leather jacket and draped it over Shiloh's head and shoulders like a shield. He should have realized the attack would have hit the news by now.

It wasn't like Austin had a lot of celebrities, after all. He should have called for a car or asked about a back entrance. He was just grateful his jacket was so large. It fell nearly to Shiloh's thighs and, once Gage tucked the smaller man under his arm, would hopefully keep the paparazzi from getting any useable photographs.

He pushed his way through the reporters.

"Shiloh, is it true you were hospitalized for a drug overdose?"

"Shiloh, tell me about the man. Was it a boyfriend? Did you get in a lover's spat?"

"Shiloh, who's the new man in your life!"

"Shiloh!"

"Shiloh!"

They were relentless. Gage shoved away each mic forced into his face, pushing his way through the mass. He must have said "No comment" at least a dozen times before he finally reached the unassuming black sedan and hustled Shiloh inside.

Shiloh kept the jacket over his face, tucking his knees under it. Only his fingers, white, scuffed and clenched on the black leather, were visible for the photos. Gage climbed into the driver's seat as quickly as possible.

Unfortunately, the reporters had a death wish. They clustered around the car, camera lenses pressed right up against the glass, hoping for a picture they could sell to the highest bidder. Gage blared on the horn in warning but they didn't move. He considered just backing up anyway, but knowing the reporters, they'd let themselves get hit so they could get the settlement money.

"They're not going to move until they get what they came for," Shiloh said from beneath the jacket. Gage looked over in time to see his hands clench tighter.

"They'll move if the police escort them away," Gage said darkly.

"Cops have better things to do."

Gage heard him draw in a deep, shaky breath then he slid the jacket down. A forced smile spread across Shiloh's bruised face. The reporters were going to love the photos...the scrapes that spread across Shiloh's cheek, held together with butterfly bandages, made it look like Shiloh had gotten into a fistfight. Suddenly, Gage wondered how many of the newspaper headings he'd read before had told the real story.

Shiloh rolled down the window and Gage wanted to stop him. He wanted to tell Shiloh he didn't have to do this, but that wasn't his job. He wasn't, he reminded himself, a babysitter.

Shiloh smiled for the cameras as they flashed, nearly blinding, into the car. He answered a few questions flippantly, waved away the fake concern. Gage doubted the excuse Shiloh gave for the bruises—that he took a tumble down some stairs—would end up in any of the papers.

Shiloh just repeated himself until the reporters grew bored and left. Then, he rolled up the window and sank against the seat, the jacket pulled up to his chin. His face lost all glimmer of humor. "Can we go home now?"

"Yeah, Shiloh, we can go home."

Gage drove them back to the estate. He parked the sedan off to the side of the circle drive, behind a black car with a familiar dent on the rear bumper. He wondered why Lawson, Beckett's lawyer, was there when both the Beckett's were out, but didn't linger on the thought too long. Probably, he was just finishing up paperwork.

Gage waited for Shiloh to climb out but he didn't. He didn't reach for the handle. Instead, he locked his eyes on the sedan. Gage didn't think it was possible, but Shiloh grew even paler.

"I...uh...changed my mind? Can we go somewhere else?" Shiloh asked, his voice tinny.

Gage wasn't sure why Shiloh had changed his mind, and at the moment, he didn't care. He just nodded. "Yeah, we can go somewhere else."

Gage restarted the car and pulled out of the driveway. He didn't ask where they were going, just drove in silence for a while until Shiloh seemed to calm back down.

"Take the next left," Shiloh said as they approached an intersection. It was the first thing he'd said since they'd left the estate.

Gage obediently turned then followed Shiloh's muted instructions until they pulled into a lot outside a dingy, rundown apartment complex. A kid in a baggy sweatshirt and ratty tennis shoes sat on the steps. A cigarette dangled from his right hand and a bottle of liquor he didn't look old enough to buy was gripped in his left.

Shiloh climbed out before Gage could ask what they were doing here. Gage cursed under his breath and twisted the key, shoving it in his pocket. Shiloh was practically running inside, Gage on his heels.

"Shiloh," Gage called, "slow down. I haven't cleared—"

Shiloh stopped abruptly and spun around, his eyes wide. "Shit. Um, so this is my friend Teddy's place. He doesn't... I mean..." Shiloh swiped a hand through his hair. "Try not to scare him, please? I know you have to clear his apartment but can..."

"I'll be as polite as possible," Gage promised.

Shiloh's shoulders relaxed. "I know. I just feel guilty. I haven't talked to him in over a month because of a stupid fight. I hate bothering him at home. It just seems like an invasion of privacy."

"If you're really friends, he won't see it as bothering. I bet he'll be happy to see you."

Shiloh looked less certain. "I don't know. I've been too embarrassed to apologize. He's called a few times but..."

"Friends fight," Gage said. "That doesn't mean you aren't still friends."

Shiloh shrugged. "I guess. I've been a shitty friend lately."

Chapter Twenty-Three

The door looked the same as Shiloh remembered—the same rusted number right at eye level, the same ding by the broken deadbolt, the same scratches left by a neighbor's dog on the door frame. It had only been a couple of months since Shiloh had last visited.

The man who stood frowning in the doorway, however, was most definitely not Teddy. Shiloh stepped back as the door opened, right into Gage's chest. "Uh...is Teddy here?" Shiloh asked, trying to peer around the large man.

"Who the fuck is Teddy? You know it's like ten o'clock, right?"

"He...lives here? Or he used to." Shiloh frowned at the small fraction of the apartment he could see. That definitely wasn't Teddy's couch.

"Well, he doesn't anymore." The man slammed the door in Shiloh's face. He flinched at the sound.

Shiloh stared at the door in silence. "He moved."

Had Teddy told him? Shiloh was self-absorbed sometimes, but not *that* much. He wouldn't have forgotten that. He closed his eyes and thought back to the last conversation they'd had, but it was just Teddy telling him to be careful. But before that, Teddy had come to his house. Shiloh had been pretty fucked up, bruised up from a trick, but he'd swear Teddy hadn't said anything about being evicted.

He'd talked about the loan he'd taken from the cartel and the looming repayment, refused Shiloh's help a half-dozen times... Shiloh definitely would have remembered.

"Come on. Let's go back to the car. Maybe if you message him, we can figure out what's going on." Gage's hand was warm against his lower back. Shiloh followed him quietly. He couldn't believe that Teddy, his best friend in the whole world, would have moved without telling him.

Then again, Teddy *had* messaged him. Several times, in fact, and Shiloh had ignored him, at first too angry, then too embarrassed, to endure a conversation. It had been such a stupid fight, too, and he could hardly remember what they'd said. He knew Teddy had been worried about him staying with tricks, but Shiloh had never felt like he was in as much danger with a stranger as he felt in his own home. He remembered saying some things he wasn't proud of.

Shit, I'm such a terrible friend. Shiloh swiped his hand over his face as he dropped in the passenger seat, slouching against the backrest as Gage shut the door. He went to reach for his phone before he remembered he didn't have it.

No wonder the man in the apartment had looked at him like he was crazy. He was still in the hospital gown, Gage's jacket the only thing keeping him from flashing his ass at strangers. He flushed and turned to Gage as he climbed in. "I don't have my phone."

"Here." Gage reached into his pocket and passed it over. "Sorry. I forgot I had it."

Shiloh thumbed in his passcode and opened his contacts. Teddy was the top one—both the person he'd usually called last and definitely the person he'd called most often, before the fight. He hesitated over the call button until an accidental twitch of his thumb made the decision for him.

The phone started ringing. Shiloh jerked it to his ear and listened.

"Shiloh?" Teddy seemed worried as he answered before the second *ring* could even finish. "Is everything okay?"

"Yeah, yeah. Everything's fine," Shiloh answered, bending the truth only a little. "I just was in the area and wanted to say hi, but some asshole is living in your apartment."

The line went quiet for a long stretch of seconds. "I was evicted a couple of weeks ago. I've b—"

"Evicted?" Shiloh interrupted before Teddy could finish. "Where the hell are you right now? We'll come pick you up and you can stay in one of the guest rooms. You know Dad won't care." He might be a controlling bastard, but his father had always liked Teddy. Seemed to think he'd be a good influence on Shiloh, even though it never quite seemed to work out that way.

"It's fine, I've been staying with Ian." Part of Shiloh thought he should know this, since Ian's apartment was above the club, but the entrance to Ian's place was in the back, and it wasn't like Shiloh spent much time off the podiums. He still should have known, should have apologized to Teddy instead of hesitating.

Shiloh slouched back in the passenger seat as the tension leaked from his body. He smirked, even though he knew his friend couldn't see it. "With Ian?" He drew out the name like a song. "Well, well. No *wonder* you didn't call me."

Ian was their boss at Envy. He'd bought the place several months before and had remodeled the joint. More than that, though, he was Teddy's ex-boyfriend and the two had reconnected after he'd returned to Austin. It was nice to know they were still getting along.

"I know what you're going to say, and the answer is no, Shy. You can't watch, and you definitely can't be the meat in a Daddy-boy sandwich."

"Ew, you're like my brother," Shiloh shuddered. "I was going to see if you wanted to have a slumber party—do each other's nails, watch *Pretty Woman,* but I'm sure you've got more kinky things to do now."

"No, come over." Teddy rushed out the words like he thought Shiloh was going to hang up on him—which, to be fair, he probably would have.

"I don't want to interrupt. You and Ian have been circling each other for years." Shiloh remembered how upset his friend had been when the older man had left four years before for parts unknown, and how tied up he'd been since Ian had returned.

"Ian's out of town until tomorrow, anyway. Please come? I miss you," Teddy pleaded.

Shiloh glanced over at Gage. He was waiting patiently for Shiloh's decision. "Okay. I guess I can come over for a little bit."

Fifteen minutes later, Gage parked the car in the back lot of Envy and climbed out. For once, Shiloh actually listened, staying in the car while Gage scanned the alley for threats, only climbing out once Gage had given him the all-clear. He'd made enough mistakes.

Shiloh headed inside, going straight toward the only door he'd never walked through, the one that led to the upstairs apartment. Teddy was waiting for him on one of the bottom-most stairs.

Teddy's blue eyes narrowed as he spotted the hospital gown Shiloh still wore. He roughly brushed away a strand of his blond hair as he huffed, his face tight with concern. "What the hell, Shiloh?"

"It's no big deal." Shiloh waved him off. "I should be asking you that, though. I can't believe you got evicted and didn't tell me. You *know* I would have helped you."

"And *you* know that there's no way I'm taking your money. Besides, everything worked out in the end. My debts are all paid, I can start college classes next semester and I get to live with Ian." Teddy shrugged but his skin flushed pink. Shiloh knew how big of a deal all of that was.

Shiloh had only found out about it a few months ago, but Teddy had taken a loan from some dangerous people. The cartel had made him promises they had no intention of keeping, but Teddy had been eighteen and desperate. He'd used the loan to pay for his transition surgery, then the cartel raised his payments. And of course to make it all worse, the kid who'd introduced Teddy to the cartel had ended up eating a bullet. Shiloh didn't know the guy, just that he was about their age and Teddy's neighbor at the time, but he knew that Teddy used to have the biggest crush on the kid's older brother Ian.

The same Ian he was now living with… Shiloh didn't know if that was romantic or just awkward, but he was happy for Teddy.

"I'm really glad everything worked out," Shiloh said. He shifted, trailing the sole of his shoe back and forth over the linoleum. "I'm really sorry I haven't been around. I had no right to get pissed at you, and by the time I realized that, I was too embarrassed to apologize. I know you were just looking out for me."

Teddy feigned a punch to his shoulder. "So next time don't be an asshole about it, yeah?"

Shiloh slugged him back and laughed, hearing it for what it was, an acceptance of his apology. "I'm always an asshole. By the way, this is *my* asshole, Gage." Shiloh finally remembered to introduce his guard.

"Most people don't name their body parts, but I'm flattered," Gage said dryly.

Teddy laughed while Shiloh rolled his eyes.

"Come on up." Teddy stepped aside to let them pass. Shiloh started to go but Gage held him back, heading up first. Shiloh thought of protesting but decided to just enjoy the view instead. He headed up after.

Gage made them wait on the stairs while he cleared the apartment. Shiloh knew it was pointless. Teddy would never, no matter how pissed he was, invite Shiloh over if it were dangerous, but he didn't argue. It was his fault the man in the alley had almost shot Gage. The least he could do was tone down his theatrics for a bit until they figured out what was going on.

Gage returned a few minutes later. "You can go in. I have a few calls to make, so I'll be downstairs." He fixed Shiloh with a stern glare. Shiloh quailed beneath it. "Do *not,* under any circumstances, leave this apartment, and do not let anyone besides me inside. Do you understand?"

Shiloh nodded silently, something like shame welling in his chest. It was heavy and tight, tugging all the way up to his throat before dropping into his stomach like a stone. He didn't know why he cared that Gage didn't trust him. Shiloh had certainly not given him reason to.

Gage watched him for a long moment like he was looking for signs of dishonesty before he started back down the stairs. "Lock the door," he called back over his shoulder as Shiloh followed Teddy inside.

"Yes, sir," Shiloh answered on instinct, cringing even as the word left his mouth. He slammed the door before he could hear Gage laugh—or comment, or whatever he was going to do.

"Oh, does Shiloh have a crush?" Teddy teased him, a wicked grin on his face that faded when Shiloh didn't smile back. "Oh, shit. You really do, don't you?"

"It doesn't matter." Shiloh turned away from the door and eyed the apartment. "Nice place."

"Don't change the subject, babe. I haven't seen you genuinely interested in someone *ever*."

"That's because I haven't been." Shiloh moved into the living room and dropped onto the leather sofa. "And it fucking sucks. I don't know why anyone puts themselves through this. It's like… Gah. I don't even know what it's like." Shiloh went quiet for a moment. "Nobody's ever turned me down before."

"Of course not, you're freaking hot. But if he's your bodyguard, he probably was just trying to keep things professional. If he's a good guy, he wouldn't want to take advantage of you or anything." Teddy dropped down beside him, wrapping his arms around Shiloh's waist and squeezing.

Shiloh nearly sobbed. Teddy was the only one who touched him like this—the only one who hugged him, or held his hand, or just…didn't expect him to fuck him after. Shiloh gripped Teddy's forearms, where they clasped his stomach, holding on tight, irrationally afraid that if he didn't, Teddy would leave.

They sat like that for ages, until Shiloh's body was a melted puddle of goo on the couch, relaxed and boneless. Eventually, though, Teddy shifted, pinching a fold of fabric between his fingers. "Tell me about the hospital gown."

Shiloh sighed, knowing he was lucky Teddy let it go this long. Teddy was the only one he trusted with his secrets. It was Teddy who patched his cuts and bruises, who'd held him when he'd spilled his secrets in the middle of the night. He was the only one who knew Teddy's plan to leave.

"I'll tell you about the hospital gown if you tell me about this." Shiloh reached up to stroke the freshly healed cut at the corner of Teddy's mouth he'd only just noticed. It was small, maybe a centimeter long at the most, and still faintly pink.

"You first," Teddy retaliated, narrowing his eyes like he knew Shiloh would try to squeeze out of the deal if he was given half an inch.

"Some asshole grabbed me at a club, and I *maybe* had a panic attack," Shiloh finally said. So it was a bit of an under-exaggeration, but there was no point worrying Teddy about it, not when Shiloh didn't even know if there was anything to worry about.

"That doesn't explain this," Teddy replied, tapping his finger on the center of the gown, over Shiloh's heart.

"I might have swooned," Shiloh admitted.

"Aren't you a real southern belle," Teddy teased, his drawl thickening playfully. He slid his arm back around Shiloh's waist, urging him to relax again. "But you're okay?"

"Yeah, I'm okay." Shiloh pressed his face into the curve of Teddy's neck as the iron rod of tension still stuck in his spine finally dissolved. "Hospital was just a precaution. Tell me about yours now."

"My hospital gown? Sorry… I don't have one yet. Too fashion forward for me." Humor spilled from Teddy's voice like wine.

"Your *scar,* dick." Shiloh dug his elbow into Teddy's stomach, but Teddy just laughed.

"You want to see my scarred dick? We're friends, but I don't think we're *that* close," Teddy said, then laughed harder when Shiloh bit his shoulder.

"Come on. I told you mine," Shiloh whined.

"Fine," Teddy sighed. His body stiffened slightly with tension beneath Shiloh as he spoke, "So there might have been a little more to getting out of my debt to the cartel than I planned, but I'll take a little scar if it means they don't have a hold on my life anymore."

Shiloh leaned his head back until he could see Teddy's face. "You're okay, though? That's… They didn't hurt you anywhere else?" He'd heard stories about cartels and knew firsthand the horrible ways people could hurt other people without even leaving a mark. The thought of Teddy, his sweet, shy best friend, going through even a quarter of the things he'd been through made his heart break.

Even though he should have been the one comforting Teddy, it was Teddy who ran a reassuring hand through Shiloh's hair, soothing his worry with gentle fingers. "No, they didn't. Even this was an accident. Now come on, enough with the maudlin things. Wanna watch something?"

"*Glitter Nation*?" Shiloh suggested hopefully, immediately perking up at the thought of bingeing his favorite show. It didn't matter that he'd seen every episode at least twice and he could mouth along with all the lines of the pilot with the actors. The new season didn't start for another two months, and he felt like an addict in withdrawal.

Teddy smirked. "You and your silly crush."

"It's not silly," Shiloh protested.

"And yet you don't deny it's a crush. I guess I can handle watching it again."

"Like you don't love it." Shiloh shifted so Teddy could reach the remote, then slid down into the narrow space between Teddy and the back of the couch. It was a big couch, but was still a tight squeeze. Tonight, he didn't mind.

The opening theme started, and Shiloh was entranced. Todrick's voice was great, no matter what, but as the backing to the credits, it became magic in his ears.

It only took seconds for him to sink into the world of Adan, a self-professed Drag-Baby exploring his identity and sexuality in modern day Dallas after escaping from a tight-knit religious community. He wasn't sexually attracted to Adan, but there was something compelling about the young man's journey of self-discovery. He felt a kinship with the character he would never admit, not even to Teddy, though he suspected, by Teddy's oft-teasing comments, that he'd guessed.

It came in a tightness in his stomach and a stillness in his limbs, an almost-fear to move, like the smallest twitch would betray the feeling. It wasn't shame or embarrassment, but rather a feeling of exposure, as if the trials Adan trudged through on screen were a reflection of his own, each stumble a misstep by Shiloh's own feet.

Shiloh hadn't been raised religious, but his father was just as controlling as cult leader Abraham. He didn't live in a studio apartment with three other guys, but he knew what it was like to not feel safe in his home. And he might not do drag, but even his own community frowned at his feminine style of dress. Dressing in drag was the new fad, but only if you did it on the stage...only if you did it as an act. Heaven forbid he wear a skirt to class or heels to the club.

His father's wealth protected him from most physical violence, but it didn't stop the comments on the streets or the articles. He told himself he didn't care, told the *world* it couldn't hurt him, but he still remembered one article. One article out of thousands and it said nothing different, nothing new. It was just a picture of him standing at his father's side, in his shadow. Maybe it stuck with him because that day, he had toned it down. Except for a hint of eyeliner and the shiny pink belt, he could have been any guy off the street.

He couldn't tell you who wrote the article or what tabloid it had run it. He couldn't tell you the title or why he and his father had sat for the article, except that Beckett Industries had just released a new piece of BeckTech. But he could still remember what they'd written.

While BeckTech has quickly transformed itself into a household name since its break into the industry ten short years ago, it remains to be seen whether it can continue to hold its footing amid an ever-growing stream of competitors. CEO Anthony Beckett—shown above—must prove to shareholders and stockholders alike that he can maintain his control of the market, a daunting task for any businessman, but particularly for one whose lack of control over his own offspring begs the question of competency on a regular basis.

Maybe he remembered it so clearly because his dad hadn't even been angry. He'd just read the article and tossed it aside as if he weren't even surprised—as if he'd expected to be disappointed, as if Shiloh was such a constant source of criticism that one more hardly made a difference. At fifteen, though, Shiloh had yet to have started acting out. There'd been no semi-public blow jobs, no drunken frat parties or reckless driving charges—nothing but his love for pretty things.

So when the man in the hard hat onscreen jeered at Adan as he left a gig, Shiloh felt the fear in his own chest. When Adan locked himself in a small bathroom in his apartment and took a razor to his wrists, Shiloh's thighs tensed with the phantom prick of pins. And when, near the end of the fourth episode, Adan's future love interest scowled at him across the bar, Shiloh felt the hope crest in his heart.

Only to dash against his sternum a second later with the gentle knock at Teddy's front door. With it came the reminder that the only person Shiloh had dared to imagine might actually like him, might see him as more than just his wallet or his ass, didn't see him as anything at all.

Chapter Twenty-Four

Gage had left Shiloh safe with his friend, hoping that a familiar face would draw out the raw, jittery nerves he sensed brewing beneath the boy's surface. He'd rather make his phone call in the quiet of the alley, but even clearing the apartment above didn't settle his own nerves at the thought of being separated from his charge.

His *client,* he forced himself to acknowledge—if only for the next few hours, anyway. He'd had no right to lead Shiloh on, to dance with him as if he were the only man in the world, even if, to Gage, that was how it felt. He should never have let himself taste the sweetness that was Shiloh's mouth, to feel the sin that was his skin, soft under his fingers. Now, all he wanted was to go upstairs and take Shiloh back home—to press him to a mattress and claim him, to bathe in the whisper of each breath.

To reassure himself that Shiloh was safe and whole and, most of all, *his.*

But he had no right to even think it, so instead, he'd left Shiloh upstairs and retreated to the safety of the shadowed alley, pressing his tense back against the wall as he pulled out his cell phone.

He called his boss.

It was late, but Mason answered on the second ring, his voice as clear as ever. "I thought I'd be hearing from you."

"Did I wake you?" Gage asked, more to stall then out of genuine concern.

"It's barely midnight," Mason said, which Gage should have known. The stress of the evening made the two-hour time difference slip his mind, much like his sense of ethics had abandoned him earlier in the evening. "I can hear you kicking yourself from here. Knock it off."

"I crossed a line, and my client almost got hurt," Gage said bluntly. If he lost his job, he'd deserve it and more.

"You're human and your client ran. We knew he was a runner going in," Mason replied.

"He's a good man." Gage stiffened against the wall, immediately coming to Shiloh's defense.

"Never said he wasn't, but that doesn't change the fact that if he wants to give you the slip, he'll find a way. What matters is that you found him and kept him safe. We can only control so much in this job. You know that."

Gage dropped his head back to the distressed brick behind him and closed his eyes. "I know, but…he could have been hurt, Mace. I could have lost him."

"And that's never happened to you before. At least not on the job, so don't beat yourself up. You're a good agent, and you're good at what you do."

"Mr. Beckett wants me off the job," Gage admitted.

"I know. He has already called me. Do you want off the job? I already talked Mr. Beckett off the ledge. Do I need to talk you down too?"

Gage hesitated, closing his eyes and truly thinking about what he *wanted,* not what he thought he deserved. "I don't know. I don't want to leave him."

"But you want to be more than just a bodyguard," Mason observed astutely.

Gage nodded, then remembered to speak, "Exactly. I want to be the one to keep him safe, but…I want more than that. I want to hold his hand when he's scared and tease him when he's being a brat and…" Gage trailed off as he realized just how much he wanted to explore the burgeoning feelings he had for his client.

"Normally, I'd say TMI, but you're not Phoenix, so I know this is all new for you." Mason's voice held a gentle mocking, but it was more playful then mean. "While I would never encourage one of my employees to start a relationship with a client, I would also never force one of my employees to turn his back on his heart, either."

"You're such a sap," Gage replied around the lump in his throat.

"If you tell anyone, I'll kill you in your sleep." Mason's voice was dry, and though he was teasing, Gage was well aware he could do it. "If you want to pursue a relationship with Shiloh, just tell me and I'll send another agent down. Phoenix's contract is up at the end of the week, and he's already whining that he's bored."

"I can't ask you to do that."

"You're not asking. I'm telling you what I'm willing to do. Phoenix will take over as primary, and you can be secondary. There'd be no conflict of interest."

Gage struggled with the tug of war inside him, the feeling that stepping back would be failing when he knew it wouldn't.

Before he could answer, Mason continued, "I was thinking of sending someone down anyway, after hearing about the incident. If it was the stalker, he's accelerating. If it's not, then that's a new problem in itself."

"Okay. Send Phoenix. I'll talk to Shiloh tomorrow and explain what's going on. He might not even want to pursue anything with me anyway."

"You won't know until you ask," Mason said. "And, Gage? Good luck."

Mason hung up before Gage could acknowledge how much he needed it, so he shoved his phone in his pocket and started back upstairs. He knocked on the door before trying the knob. He cursed under his breath as the door opened. While neither of the boys in the apartment were ever in danger—nobody could get up the stairs without going past him—he wasn't happy Shiloh had disobeyed, even if it was by accident.

He walked into the apartment quietly. All the lights were off except for the lamp in the corner of the living room. At first, he thought the room was empty, despite the show playing on the TV, but as he stepped farther into the apartment, he spotted the young men cuddled up together on the couch. Teddy was on his back, Shiloh practically glued to his side, his face tucked up against his neck.

Jealousy flared hot in Gage's stomach, even as his mind rationalized that there was nothing sexual about the position. Shiloh had experienced a rough night. Of course he would seek comfort in his friend. Shiloh angled his head up a fraction to make eye contact, his cheeks flushing pink. Gage just tipped his head in acknowledgment and folded himself into the small armchair by the corner bookshelf, the only seat with a view of the door.

He watched as Shiloh dropped his head back down, locking his gaze on the TV. They were static, though, in a way that made Gage think he was no longer watching. A moment later, his mouth split in a yawn, and soon enough, his eyes drifted closed.

Gage watched the young man sleep. He looked calmer now, almost peaceful. A strand of pink hair fell over his forehead and into his eyes, and Gage struggled with himself not to go over and brush it away.

He didn't realize Teddy was watching him until the other boy spoke. "He likes you," Teddy said, his voice barely above a whisper. "So don't hurt him, okay?"

"I don't plan to," Gage replied, wishing he could say he wouldn't with certainty. He couldn't, unfortunately, because he didn't know how Shiloh would feel about him stepping back as security without talking to him. Would he even accept a new bodyguard?

"He needs someone to be patient—someone who cares about him, not his wallet." Teddy's eyes narrowed as he spoke, examining Gage with a critical eye, like he could see into his soul. Whatever he saw, whether it was longing on Gage's face or something else, made Teddy's eyes soften. They dropped back down to the boy in his lap. "He's more fragile than he lets on."

"I know." If it were anyone else, Gage would be angry at the assumption that he would intentionally hurt anyone, let alone someone who was starting to mean as much to him as Shiloh. Instead, he took a deep breath and found that instead of anger, something inside him was pleased that Shiloh had such a good friend.

Chapter Twenty-Five

"Baby, I'm home. I caught an early flight." A door slammed shut, jarring Shiloh from sleep. He flinched, jerking instinctively up, eyes wide and burning as his heart raced in his chest. Teddy grunted under him as Shiloh's elbow caught his ribs.

Shiloh was on his feet without registering the movement, blinking owlishly at the man in the doorway. It was Ian, of course. He was Shiloh's part-time boss at the club downstairs, so it wasn't like they were strangers, but he'd never seen the larger man like this. He was in a dark suit, a briefcase in his left hand, but his right was on his hip like he was reaching for a gun, though he dropped it as soon as he recognized Shiloh.

"Oh, did I wake you?" Ian looked between him and Teddy on the couch, before glancing over at Gage, who now stood in front of the armchair. The two men locked eyes in what felt like a challenge. Shiloh imagined this was what it looked like when a lion faced down a cheetah in the wild.

"Da— Ian!" Teddy corrected his initial slip as he scrambled off the couch. Probably because of Gage, since Shiloh had known since high school what kind of relationship his best friend wanted.

"Hey, baby." Ian dropped his briefcase to catch Teddy as he flung himself toward him. Shiloh, glad as he was that his friend was happy, couldn't help the flare of jealousy in his chest that grew stronger at the sweet kiss Ian dropped on Teddy's forehead.

"I should probably go anyway. I didn't mean to fall asleep," Shiloh said after several seconds.

Teddy broke away from his daddy with a flush. "You don't have to leave. They don't have to leave, right? They can stay the night?" Teddy looked up at Ian as he asked, his face hopeful, but Shiloh didn't plan to stay. His friend deserved to spend some time with the man he loved without Shiloh getting in the way.

A glance at the ornate clock on the wall showed that it was only just after three in the morning, so maybe he could go home now. He doubted Lawson was still there, and even if he was, he'd likely be sleeping.

"No, I can't stay anyway. You boys have fun." Shiloh plastered on a wide grin and started for the door. "Don't do anything I wouldn't do." He blew Teddy a kiss, then glanced to make sure Gage was behind him before he left the apartment, ignoring Teddy's protests.

They were quiet as they descended the stairs and went out into the alley. Gage cleared the car before they climbed in. Shiloh slumped into the passenger side, dropping his head back against the seat. "Can we go home now?"

"Sure." Gage started the car and stated driving. The city was quiet, only the earliest of commuters silently picking their way through the dark street. "Your friend seems nice," Gage said after several minutes of quiet.

"He's the best," Shiloh agreed. He leaned his head against the cool glass, streetlights blurring as they drove past. They didn't talk much after that, and too soon Gage was pulling through the gates and up to the estate. Shiloh obediently waited for Gage to clear the area before he followed him inside and up to their rooms.

When he hesitated outside his bedroom door, the quiet "Goodnight, Shiloh," from Gage spurred him into his room. He stood just inside his door and stared. It was familiar but not comforting.

He rubbed his hands over his chilly arms then glanced at his partially open window. He slammed it shut and shivered. It wasn't that cold. Austin rarely was. It was that he didn't remember opening the window recently, but he must have. He thumbed the locks closed, though it did little to cure his unease, then shoved the curtains closed as well.

It didn't ease the feeling of being watched. Shiloh closed his eyes and started counting, little good that it did him. Finally, he pinched the flesh of his thigh hard between his finger and thumb and squeezed. The pain shook him from his panic.

"Get a grip, Shiloh," he muttered to himself before stripping out of the hospital gown. He grabbed the first pair of underwear he found in his dresser and pulled them on before crawling into bed.

He closed his eyes, ignoring the prickling of his skin. Even tugging his comforter over his head didn't help. He squeezed his eyes shut, trying all his usual tricks—but nothing helped.

Finally, he shoved the comforter back and rolled onto his side, fumbling in his nightstand for his container of pins. He didn't need light to see. The cool metal was as familiar to his fingers as the barre. He slid the sharp pin into the skin of his inner thigh, the brilliant flash of pain like a drug—a ladder of ten on each thigh before the pinching pain fought off the fear and he finally fell into slumber.

The ghost of breath on the nape of his neck.

Phantom fingers on the hollow of his navel.

The press of a mouth on pin-struck thighs –

A stinging pain in his thigh tore him from sleep and he jerked up, heart thumping in his chest. A glance down made him curse. Carefully, he pulled the pins from his skin before dropping them in the trash beside his bed. He'd torn one free in his sleep, leaving a narrow, faintly oozing scratch near his groin. He pressed the sheets to it, soaking up the small drops of blood.

Vaguely, he was aware that his heart was still pattering in his chest, but he ignored it. A glance at his alarm clock made him groan. It was barely four-thirty. *Too early to be awake,* especially as tired as he still felt. He sighed and dropped back on his bed, rolling onto his side before freezing.

The curtain was pulled wide, moonlight casting stretching shadows like grasping hands across his floor and onto his mattress. Shiloh shuddered and rolled out of bed on the opposite side. He flinched at what sounded like a door shutting somewhere in the house.

"It's just Maria," Shiloh muttered but his heart rate didn't slow. He tiptoed over to the door and cracked it open, peering into the hallway.

It was empty. Shadows stretched from wall to wall, shifting as branches swayed in front of windows. It didn't help the nervous panic fluttering beneath his ribs. He remembered feeling like this when he was a small boy, before his mother died. She'd let him climb into bed between her and his father, like their presence could chase away the monsters in his closet.

He was old enough now to know there *were* no monsters in his closet. The real monsters were flesh and blood, and his father couldn't—*wouldn't*—save him from them. Shiloh's eyes slid to the next door over—but maybe someone else would.

Bad idea, a small voice in his head whispered. He tiptoed into the hallway. The wood floor was cold under his bare feet. He stopped outside Gage's door and lifted his hand to knock.

Then he lowered it. Gage had gotten up as early as he had and unlike Shiloh, he'd gotten *shot.* Even if it was just in a prosthesis, Gage probably wanted to sleep.

A shadow darted across the wall and Shiloh jumped. A small whimper escaped his mouth. Yeah...Gage probably wouldn't mind if he just...slept on the floor in his room, right?

But again, Shiloh lifted his fist to knock, casting a suspicious glance back down the hallway and froze. What if Gage was...*occupied?* That thought sent an image into Shiloh's head that didn't need to be there. Gage, lying on his mattress, his hand shoved under the waistband of a pair of tight briefs... Shiloh shook the image clear. Gage had made it clear exactly how he saw—or rather, *didn't* see—Shiloh back at the club.

Shiloh turned to walk away.

"For the love of— Just come in already." Gage's voice was exasperated as it sounded through the door.

"Sorry!" Shiloh winced. Even without trying to he'd managed to irritate Gage. "I was just—"

"Pacing anxiously outside my door." There was a thump then a few seconds later, the door opened. Gage was stormy eyed…and bare chested. Shiloh's attention fixated heavily on the latter.

"Um…" Shiloh forgot why he was standing there. Well, not *really,* but faced with Gage in all his muscled glory, his anxiety suddenly took a back seat, especially when he caught the flash of silver.

"Eyes are up here," Gage said. His voice, surprisingly, was more amused than angry.

"You have a nipple piercing," Shiloh dumbly stated, his eyes still fixated on the small silver barbell.

"Yeah. I remember getting it." Gage pushed Shiloh's chin up, dragging his eyes free. Shiloh felt his cheeks heat up. "Did you need something?"

"Um…it's stupid," Shiloh mumbled.

"I highly doubt that." Gage's expression softened. "What's up?"

"I… Okay, soIheardanoiseandIknowitwasMariabutnowIcan'tsleep." Shiloh sucked in a breath, knowing he was babbling too fast to be understood. "I heard a noise and now I can't sleep."

"Do you want me to tuck you in? I can check under your bed for monsters." Gage quirked his mouth up in a smile, but all it did was make Shiloh's mood sour. That was exactly what he wanted—or what he *used* to want, before he realized no Daddy would want a used-up boy like him.

"Never mind. I *knew* it was stupid." He spun on his heel and stomped back toward his bedroom.

"Shiloh, wait. I'm sorry. I shouldn't have said that." Gage followed him, reaching out to stop him. Shiloh flinched away. "I was just trying to make a joke. It's fine if you're scared. You've—"

"I'm *not* scared!" Shiloh lied. "I was just going to ask if..." He scrambled for a good excuse. "You wanted to go down and grab some coffee or something and...tell me what else you know about the bastard?"

"I can do that if it's what you really want." Gage looked knowingly at him. "Or you can come in and get some sleep and we can talk about it over breakfast."

"Besides, even if I *was* scared, it's not like I don't have reason to be. Someone just tried to kidnap me." *Stop while you're ahead, Shiloh,* he told himself, but his mouth didn't listen. "I think it's a perfectly normal and reasonable response to be scared after something like that. It doesn't mean I'm a...a kid."

"I know," Gage interrupted. "It's okay. I get it. I nearly pissed myself the first time someone shot at me. And I spent a good several months in therapy after I got out of the Army dealing with it all. You're allowed to be scared."

"I'm not." Shiloh shifted awkwardly. "But...can I sleep on the floor in your room?"

Gage held his door open. "Come on." Shiloh squeezed past. His embarrassment grew as Gage shut the door behind him. "No need to sleep on the floor. We're both adults." Gage passed him. Shiloh watched him straighten the covers on the bed. "I'm sure we can manage to share a bed."

A small part of Shiloh wanted to make a joke, but a much larger part knew it would get him kicked back out to his own room. "Are you sure?"

"Wouldn't have offered if I wasn't." Gage perched on the edge of the bed and bent, deftly cuffing up his pant leg. Shiloh's gaze dropped, snagging on the artificial limb. It was shining silver and, unlike what Shiloh expected, calf-shaped. He didn't have much experience with prosthetics, but the ones he'd seen on TV had looked like a metal rod connected to a plastic stump. This one looked more robotic. He bet it was expensive.

"Does it hurt?" Shiloh asked without thinking.

"Hmm-m?" Gage glanced up. "Oh, this?" He pressed a pin near the top and the prosthesis slid free. Gage propped it against the nightstand. "Not really. My old one used to chafe a bit. It aches a bit by the end of the day, but it's better than the alternative." Gage made quick work of tying the end of his pajama pantleg into a knot.

Shiloh's teeth worried at his lip. "Were you going to sleep in it?"

"Not tonight, but I have before. It takes too long to put on in an emergency." Gage didn't seem concerned about that now, which meant…

"Like if I sneak out." Shiloh frowned. He hadn't really thought about what his actions meant for Gage. He wasn't used to having to worry about anyone but himself.

"I wasn't going to say it." Gage's lips turned up at the corners.

"You should have. I'm not a *complete* asshole," Shiloh replied.

"Don't worry about it." Gage slid under the comforter, holding the other side up for Shiloh.

"Aren't…you going to put a shirt on?" Shiloh stuttered.

"You're lucky I put pants on," Gage said dryly, waving the comforter up and down a bit. "Come on. You're letting out all the heat."

Shiloh felt warm enough. "Is it hot in here?" He fanned the collar of his shirt.

"No. It's just you. Get in." Gage rolled his eyes but there was amusement in them too. Shiloh slid under the blanket, perching as close to the edge of the mattress as he could without falling off. While he would love to tangle himself up with Gage—because honestly, anyone who *wouldn't* must be insane—he didn't want to make Gage regret it.

Behind him, Gage chuckled. "I didn't realize you were religious."

"What? I'm not." Shiloh rolled onto his back to eye Gage.

"Well, you've left enough room for Jesus." Gage's eyes glinted with amusement. Shiloh rolled on his side toward Gage, closing the gap. Immediately, he was greeted with a subtle scent of leather and sandalwood. He drew in a deeper breath.

"Are you smelling me?" Gage asked, his brow lifting.

"Shut up." Shiloh swatted Gage's shoulder, failing to stop the flush that swelled across his cheeks.

"Aw, don't be embarrassed." Gage leaned forward. Shiloh's nose tickled the curve of his neck, then Gage drew in a deep breath. "There. Now we're even."

A laugh burst from Shiloh's throat as he shoved Gage back. "And you call *me* a kid." Gage laughed as well, and, just like that, whatever awkwardness had grown between them dissipated.

"Your briefs have Batman on them," Gage pointed out.

"It's laundry day!"

Gage laughed.

* * * *

Shiloh woke to the sound of glass breaking, his mind fuzzy. He was warm and comfortable. A heavy weight was slung over his waist like a blanket, and he snuggled into it…until the weight moved. Shiloh tensed, snapping his eyes open. They dropped to the arm wrapped around him, pinning him in place. The warmth at his back was a bare chest.

He sucked in a breath and shoved the arm off him. "No, no no *no no…*" He leaped from the bed like it was on fire, putting as much distance as he could between himself and…

Gage. Who was now sitting upright, blinking blearily at him, concern clearly written on his face. "Shiloh, what's wrong?"

Shiloh pressed the heels of his hands into his eyes and rubbed, drawing in a deep breath, then another, until his heart rate was fine.

"I…I thought I heard something," Shiloh muttered, dropping his hands and straightening from the crouch he'd unconsciously sank into.

Gage's face tightened and he slid to the edge of the bed, pushing what remained of his left leg into the prosthetic until Shiloh heard a loud *click.*

"What did you hear?" Gage asked, grabbing his gun off the nightstand.

"I thought it was glass breaking. I might have been dreaming," Shiloh answered, his eyes wide as he watched Gage prowl toward the door.

"Get in the closet. Don't come out until I tell you it's safe," Gage ordered.

Shiloh bit off the automatic joke—something about being shoved back in the closet—and obeyed in silence. The closet door clicking shut was as loud as a gunshot. Shiloh's breath came fast and loud.

If the glass breaking was real, then Gage could be walking right back into danger. Shiloh squeezed his eyes closed and pressed his forehead against the door. *It was just part of the dream.*

He was so tired of being scared. The whole reason he'd made this plan was so he could stop being scared. It wasn't fair. But, like father always said, *"Life isn't fair."*

Chapter Twenty-Six

Gage crouched outside the doorframe of Shiloh's room. He reached up to twist the knob. Pushing the door inward was awkward and undignified, but if it saved him from taking a bullet between the eyes, he didn't care.

He peered around the doorframe, then ducked back. It looked clear at first glance. A second look confirmed that it was safe to enter. Keeping his gun drawn, he stole inside. Across the room, the blue curtains billowed in the breeze from the broken window, the hem dragging itself through a small pile of shattered glass. Gage ignored it for the moment to peer under the bed and into the closet, then crept to the en suite. He nudged open the door. It was empty as well.

He returned to the broken window. Apart from a small white envelope planted on Shiloh's pillow and the scattered glass, nothing was out of place. Whoever had broken the window had done so by hand, not resorted to lobbing a brick.

Gage scrutinized the yard below. The ground was hard enough that he doubted the perp had left footprints behind, though maybe they could dust the trellis for fingerprints. He doubted they would find any. Likely, the perp had worn gloves. There was no sign that the man was still lurking about.

He picked up the landline on Shiloh's nightstand and rang the security office. Henry answered with a curt, "Make it quick, Shiloh, I've—"

Gage interrupted, not liking the chilly tone the former Seal spoke with, not knowing it wasn't Shiloh on the line. "Henry, it's Gage. Check the perimeter cameras ASAP. The stalker was just here."

The line went silent for a beat before Henry cursed loudly. "On it." A click sounded in his ear, followed by a dial tone. Gage returned the phone to the hook, then frowned at the letter. He needed gloves to open it, and the gloves were in his room. He should check on Shiloh anyway, to make sure he was fine.

He approached the closet carefully, not wanting to scare his client. "Shiloh, you can—" Before he could finish, the door burst open, and Shiloh crumpled into his arms. His hair was messy from sleep and, likely, unsteady fingers running repeatedly through it.

"Was he in there?" Shiloh patted down Gage's bare chest like he was searching for an injury. Not that Gage's body cared about the reason… All it noticed was that Shiloh's skin was on his.

Shiloh's hands were ice. Gage clasped them in his, rubbing them gently. "It's okay. You're safe. Listen to me." Gage could tell Shiloh was on the edge of a breakdown. "Everything's okay. I'm going to get a pair of gloves. You're going to sit in here and take some nice deep breaths."

"Gloves?" Shiloh's eyes widened and he pulled his hands free. They ran through his hair again. "I'm coming with you."

"You don't have to," Gage said.

"I don't *have* to do anything." Shiloh's lips thinned.

It wasn't the best idea, but he wasn't going to tell him no. He would just have to trust Shiloh to tell him if he needed to step out.

"Okay," Gage finally said. He slid on a pair of latex gloves. Shiloh practically walked on his heels into the hallway. "Wait here." Gage left Shiloh by the door to do another check of the room, just in case, then waved him in. Shiloh moved up to his side. They stared at the letter.

Gage picked it up and immediately he could tell this one was different. Not only was it on different paper—thicker, like parchment—but it was also handwritten. The lettering was sharp and heavy.

He read silently until Shiloh cleared his throat. "What…what does it say?"

Gage hesitated to read it aloud. *Will Shiloh panic again? Is it fair of me to think this is a decision I can make for Shiloh?*

He cleared his throat and started over.

"Pet, you looked so small tonight. Your bed almost swallowed you up. You were young again, innocent and untouched for just a moment. I could almost forget how much of a slut you've become. Don't worry. I won't hold it against you when you're mine for real."

Gage looked up from the letter just in time to see the stricken look on Shiloh's face. "I…" Shiloh's voice broke. Gage watched his throat move as he swallowed, then audibly cleared it. "God, the *curtains*."

Gage glanced at the blue swaths of fabric. "The curtains?"

"I shut them before I fell asleep and...and they were open when I woke up. I... God, he was in my room." Shiloh swiped his hands over his face hard enough to turn his cheeks red. "I didn't even realize..."

"Hey, it's not your fault. Why would you? You're supposed to be safe here." Anger surged in Gage at the realization that the bastard had been there, in this room, at the same time as Shiloh—that anything could have happened and he would have been right next door, not even knowing. *What kind of bodyguard am I?* "Don't worry, we'll find the bastard. This letter is handwritten, so maybe that will help the cops. They can look at the others and see—"

Shiloh jerkily moved forward, panic on his face. "It won't help. You don't understand. The other letters don't matter."

Gage thought about the look he hadn't been able to place the previous night at the hospital. He'd pinned it as unease, but could it have been something else? "I don't understand." Gage folded the letter and carefully tucked it back in the envelope. "You need to talk to me if you know something."

Shiloh turned his head away as he tried to avoid making eye contact. He tugged at the longish strands of hair. His cheeks grew so pink that they nearly matched it. Guilt rolled off him in waves.

"You can trust me." Gage stepped closer, reaching out to pluck Shiloh's lip from between his teeth, smoothing the soft surface with his thumb before he caught himself. Shiloh wasn't *his*. He was just his to protect. He needed to bury the warm feelings Shiloh stirred in him, and not just because they weren't appropriate for a working relationship. If he grew too attached, then Shiloh wouldn't be the only one getting hurt.

"I—I do trust you." Shiloh's eyes were wide, catching the light from overhead.

"Do you know who's leaving you the letters?" Gage asked gently.

Shiloh dropped his eyes again, teeth clamping on his lower lip again.

"Shiloh?" Gage prodded.

"I—" Shiloh took a large step back, bumping roughly into the side of the bed. His knees visibly buckled, and he sank onto the mattress. He buried his face in his hands. "It was a stupid idea."

Gage didn't comment, letting the silence stretch uncomfortably. Shiloh stayed quiet for a long span of moments, his shoulders shaking.

Finally, Shiloh continued. His voice was barely a whisper. "There's this guy named Deak. He's one of the bodyguards at Envy. I heard him talking a few months ago and... Well, he's involved in some...not exactly *legal* things sometimes?" Gage saw Shiloh peek through the spread of his fingers. "It seemed like a good idea at the time."

Gage held back the instinctive frown. "Did he do a job for you? Do you owe him money?"

"No, not... He said he knew a guy, who knew a guy who..." Shiloh sucked in a breath, then the rest of the sentence barreled out, words tripping over each other, "who makes paperwork for people who need to change their name or something—and he put a down payment on an apartment for me in Los Angeles and everything was supposed to be fine. There was just supposed to be a few letters so when I left, everyone would be so busy looking for a stalker that they wouldn't think to look for some kid named Simon in LA."

Gage stood in stunned silence for a moment. He hadn't seen *that* coming. He'd thought maybe the stalker was an old hookup of Shiloh's or someone he owed money to. Gage's spine stiffened, the full impact of the words striking him. He'd nearly shot that man back in the alley. Nearly *been* shot. Who was he? Some friend of Shiloh's who'd attacked to make it more believable? There was so much wrong with this whole situation that he barely knew where to start.

Gage's voice came out low and dangerous. "You're telling me that this whole entire thing was a *prank*? Fuck, Shiloh, someone could have gotten hurt! How could you be so selfish?" Gage turned toward the door. He needed to tell Mr. Beckett. Shiloh needed help, all right, just not the kind of help Gage could give him.

Shiloh clamped his hands around his arm, pulling him to a stop. Gage shook him off. If glares could injure, his would have been murderous.

"It wasn't a prank." Shiloh stumbled to get between him in the door, his face sickly and pale. "Dad won't listen to me. He *never* listens, and I was so tired of being scared and I just… I just wanted him to *listen."*

"And you thought faking a kidnapping was the best plan?" Gage crowded Shiloh against the door, bracketing the man's shoulders. "How was that going to help anything?"

Shiloh tried to push him back, but Gage didn't move. He wanted an answer. Shiloh eventually stopped trying, fisting his hands against Gage's chest instead.

"It was the only way to get out of here. I've tried everything I can think of. I've tried explaining, I…I ran away, and no matter what, he dragged me back, and…and—" Shiloh shuddered. "I c-can't keep doing this. I don't— It… God, it *hurts* too much." Shiloh's hand clutched at his chest. "My heart, it won't… Sh-shit, I feel like I'm dying."

Gage stepped back, not letting the panicked words break through his icy anger. "Did you think of what this is going to do to your father's heart? He's already had, what? Three heart attacks? Did you think about him at all, or were you too busy worrying about yourself?"

Shiloh looked stricken, like it would have hurt less if Gage had smacked him. Gage pushed down the desire to take it back, to soothe the wound his words had caused, and he stepped around Shiloh to open the door.

He walked away and didn't look back.

Chapter Twenty-Seven

"Did you think about him at all, or were you too busy worrying about yourself?"

The words cycled through Shiloh's head as Gage walked away. Shiloh clutched at his chest, where the hollow organ that claimed to be his heart stuttered away.

"Were you too busy worrying about yourself?"

I have to worry about myself...don't I? Nobody else was going to do it. Shame burgeoned in his chest, growing larger and larger, too big to be contained by the cage of his ribs, until there was no room left for anything else.

"Did you think of what this is going to do to your father's heart? He's already had what? Three heart attacks?"

Now it was Shiloh crumpling to the ground, his heart betraying him. He scrabbled at his skin. It wasn't fair. Why was it his responsibility to care about his father's health when his father certainly didn't care about his?

He'd thought—well, no, he hadn't, but he'd *hoped* that Gage would be different. That maybe, for once, someone would listen and actually be on his side. Was that so much to ask for?

Shiloh picked himself up from the floor and stumbled over to his nightstand. It took him two tries to tug open the drawer and his hands were shaking so bad that he dropped the plastic container of pins. It struck the floor with a clatter and opened. Pins scattered, brightly beaded heads cascading everywhere.

He'd pick them up later.

Shiloh winced as his scraped knees hit the wood. It was the *wrong* pain to clear his head, and he needed the right one. He picked up a pin. It was blue and silver, until he pushed it into his skin and blood stained it red. He added another. He built a ladder down the outside of each thigh this time but the pain in his chest was sharper than the small bites of the pins.

He needed something else, something stronger. He fumbled in the drawer of the nightstand, but apart from an old phone charger and a watch with a broken band, it was empty. Shiloh clenched his hands in his hair, tugging at the strands. His eyes caught on something glinting on the floor.

Broken glass from the shattered window.

He scrambled around the edge of the bed and picked up the largest shard that was two fingers thick and nearly as long. Maybe he should carve a smile on his face like a jack-o'-lantern.

His fingers spasmed at the thought and the keen edge sliced his palm. He barely felt it. Maybe instead of his face, he should take the glass to his wrists. It would be better than the alternative, he was sure. When his father found out what he'd done…

Shiloh shuddered, acid burning the back of his throat.

He'd rather die than spend another night at Lawson's.

Chapter Twenty-Eight

Why was he surprised that Shiloh had done this? Hadn't he cursed this assignment up and down before the plane had even landed? Shiloh was a spoiled, selfish party-boy. Pulling a stunt like this was very much in his wheelhouse.

That thought made Gage slow just outside Mr. Beckett's office. Before he'd met Shiloh, he wouldn't have given the situation a second thought. Now, he knew better—or he'd thought he did. He liked to think he was a good judge of character, and in the three weeks since he'd met Shiloh, he'd seen in him something else…something better.

The Shiloh he knew wouldn't do something like this without a good reason.

Gage hesitated, his hand on the doorknob. If he went into the study and told Mr. Beckett what Shiloh had been up to, he would lose any chance he had of figuring out the real reason…because his gut told him that there was more to it than just boredom with Austin.

If he opened the door, he would betray the little bit of trust that Shiloh had extended him, if walking away hadn't destroyed that trust already.

He cursed and paced back up the hallway, ending up outside Shiloh's door again. He had to know. Had his instincts finally failed him, or had he been too quick to jump to conclusions? Shiloh's face, lined with tear tracks, swam in his mind. Would Shiloh get so emotional over a prank? No. Something else was going on.

He opened the door and froze. Shiloh was crouched by the foot of the bed, rocking back and forth, a bloody piece of glass in his hand.

Gage moved without thought to drop in front of him. He gripped Shiloh's wrist tightly in his hand and pried the shard free. Except for a shallow slice on his palm, it didn't look like Shiloh had cut himself with it yet.

Shiloh whimpered, belatedly scrambling to grab the weapon back. "Please, I need it. I can't…" Shiloh's fear was so palpable that Gage could practically smell it on him.

"Hey, hey." Gage tossed the glass away. It only made Shiloh panic more. Gage relaxed his grip but didn't release him. "Calm down. Shit, what did you do to yourself?" He muttered the last to himself, taking in the neat rows of pins embedded up the length of Shiloh's thighs.

Trusting that Shiloh wouldn't lash out, Gage released his wrists and carefully scooped Shiloh up, carrying him into the en suite. He sat him down on the floor in front of the counter and fumbled through the cabinets behind the mirrors until he found a small box of Band-Aids and a partially full tube of antibacterial cream.

Shiloh had gone rigid and was still barely breathing. His eyes were focused off to the side, but when Gage tried to follow his gaze, he saw only the plain blue wall.

Shiloh didn't speak as Gage carefully examined the cut on his hand, applied the antibacterial medication, then wrapped it in gauze, nor did he speak as Gage plucked each pin from his skin. Gage washed the small specks of blood off the wounds, applied a small smear of ointment, then plastered a Band-Aid to each small puncture.

"Shiloh," Gage spoke softly as he smoothed on the last, "talk to me."

Shiloh blinked slowly, turning to face Gage, but his eyes were still distant. He looked like a doll, vacant and unseeing. Shiloh tipped his head forward, his hair cascading into his face like a curtain.

"He's going to be angry."

"Maybe." Gage brushed his fingers through Shiloh's hair, shifting the strands out of his face so he could see him. "But he loves you. That won't change."

Shiloh's hand clenched in his lap, then unfurled. "You were right. I'm being selfish."

"I shouldn't have said that," Gage admitted. "Just because I don't understand where you're coming from doesn't mean that the decision you made wasn't valid for you."

Shiloh blinked, his gaze sliding up to his. "I'm tired of being scared."

Gage knew he shouldn't do it, that it was crossing a line, that it would send Shiloh mixed messages, but he couldn't stop himself. He curled his fingers through Shiloh's, careful not to touch the gauze, and gently squeezed. "You don't have to be scared. I'm not going to let anything happen to you."

Shiloh gave a humorless laugh. It broke into a sob near the end, until he dropped his head and smothered it against his knees. "You can't stop this."

"I'm not going to let anyone hurt you—not your father, not even *you*," Gage promised.

Shiloh squeezed his hand. "I wasn't lying when I said I trusted you," Shiloh spoke into his knees, voice muffled. "But…I was lying when I said I didn't know who wrote the letters. I did."

"Okay. Tell me who wrote the letters, and we can tell Officer Preston. The sooner he finds him, the sooner we can get the whole situation cleared up."

"No, I mean, *I* did. I wrote the letters—not the last one, but the others. I typed them up and printed them at the library then dropped them off to Deak at the club. He said it needed to seem real or no one would buy it."

Gage ran his thumbs soothingly over Shiloh's knuckles, then up the backs of his hands. "You mentioned Deak before. He's the one who introduced you to the kidnapper?"

"You don't understand. There *wasn't* a hired kidnapper. I d-don't know who was in the alley. I didn't plan that." Shiloh didn't look up from his knees, though his hands tightened on Gage's. Shiloh started shaking. "It wasn't supposed to be this way."

"It's going to be okay. We'll talk to your father together, then I'll have my boss look into Deak." Gage didn't know if Deak would be much help, if he was just helping forge papers, but *someone* knew Shiloh was planning on leaving. How else would they know to try to kidnap Shiloh before he could? Otherwise, it was just a crazy, random coincidence. Gage didn't believe in coincidences.

Gage didn't understand what was so bad that Shiloh had resorted to faking a kidnapping, but at least they had a lead. He hesitated at the thought of passing anything he'd just learned over to the police. Filing a false police report was illegal. Not to mention, if they learned that the original letters were fraudulent, they'd take the situation less seriously now.

It may have started out as a complicated plot Gage still didn't quite understand, but it was now something much more dangerous.

Chapter Twenty-Nine

Fear was a familiar companion. They could go months without talking, but when it showed up, as it inevitably did, the threads of their last conversation weaved together into a bitter tapestry. Shiloh knew how fear tasted—of metallic copper and salt, of rusty nails and brine. He knew its scent—piss and sweat and cracked leather. Fear was an old friend.

It climbed into his shadow and clung to him as he followed Gage to his father's study. Like a thousand spiders, it crawled under the track pants he'd pulled on over the bandages. It swarmed over his hips and stomach, burrowed like termites into his chest. Shiloh embraced the fear, wrapping it around him and sinking into its familiar security.

Because his father didn't enter the study alone.

Shiloh's gaze immediately dropped to the gray carpet, then slid into his lap. His hands looked wrong, twisted. He picked at the gauze.

Gage, seemingly unconcerned, slid his hand into Shiloh's, stopping him from fidgeting. Shiloh clutched it like a lifeline. He didn't look up when his father sat down across the desk from him, and he didn't look up when Mr. Lawson moved to stand directly beside Shiloh's chair. His shadow fell over Shiloh. Shiloh fought to stay still and silent.

"I have a meeting in twenty minutes." Father sounded stressed. "I hope this is important."

Shiloh nodded mutely, throat closing on his words. He swallowed, but before he could find his voice, Mr. Lawson huffed. "Let me guess. You want to try to convince your father to release part of your trust early."

Shiloh jerked his head to the side. He knew better than to ask that again. He'd thought—*hoped*—that he could talk his father into letting him use the trust to pay his tuition at the California Institute of the Arts. Mr. Lawson had managed to twist Shiloh's words so badly that by the time the conversation was over, even Shiloh was almost convinced the money was going to be wasted.

"Shiloh has some information about the situation that could be helpful in catching the stalker," Gage answered when it was clear that Shiloh couldn't.

Across the desk, his father sighed and rubbed his eyes. "It has something to do with that club, doesn't it? The police are already looking into it."

This time Gage stayed silent, leaving it up to Shiloh to admit what he'd done. Shiloh squeezed Gage's hand tightly, wishing it could lend him strength. "I…" Shiloh gulped a breath of air. "I was the one writing the letters. I was going to leave and…I think that was why the man…"

He was such a fucking coward that he couldn't even say the words. *That's why he assaulted me in the alley.* Three words cycled through his head. *He assaulted me.*

His focus slid up to Mr. Lawson's and he froze in the cool blue gaze. *And* he *raped me.*

For the first time in years, the words filled his head unedited, not buried beneath his father's voice. Instead, he heard Gage's voice. Gage's promise. *"I'm not going to let anyone hurt you."*

Father's fist slammed into the desk and Shiloh flinched. "Are you even listening to me?" Father was saying, his face red. A vein throbbed in his temple. Shiloh cringed back. "I don't understand where I went wrong with you. I—"

Gage cleared his throat and disentangled his fingers from Shiloh's. He was angry, and this time, not at Shiloh. His narrowed eyes fixed on Father. "Mr. Beckett, you can be angry later. What's important now is that we try to identify the man. We—"

"What's the point?" Father jerked to his feet, his hands pressed firmly to the desk as he leaned forward. He was so angry that spittle escaped his lips with the words. Father's gaze shifted to Shiloh and hardened. "If you want my money so bad, then fine."

Father yanked open the desk drawer and pulled out his checkbook. He scrawled angrily across the paper then tore the top check off, throwing it onto the desk. "Take it and get out of my sight. No ransom needed."

Shiloh wished he could make himself smaller, invisible. His eyes took in the several zeroes on the check—an amount he guessed was roughly the same as what was in his trust fund—and flinched.

It was all the proof he needed that his father didn't know him at all.

"I don't want money," Shiloh said, his voice hoarse. It was hard to speak past the saltwater lump in his throat.

"Maybe Mr. Tucker should return to Seattle. If there's no stalker, then there's no reason to continue retaining his services," Mr. Lawson said, staring down at Shiloh. How could the man look so innocent, so *caring?* How come Shiloh was the only one who could see the devil beneath the smile?

"Shiloh should come to stay with me for a few days until this whole thing is sorted out." Mr. Lawson said it like it was the most obvious solution. He dropped a hand onto Shiloh's shoulder and squeezed, lingering his fingers on bare skin.

"Maybe that would be for the best," Father sighed.

Shiloh jerked out from under Mr. Lawson's hand, half falling out of the chair in his haste to get away. He stumbled to his feet, backing toward the door. "No. No, I'm not— I *won't* go back with him…not again."

He knew what was going to happen. If this were a movie, they'd be following the script perfectly. Mr. Lawson was going to shake his head, go on about how Shiloh needed to learn respect, and his father was going to tell him to grow up, and somehow, despite his protests, he was going to end up right back at Mr. Lawson's two-story hell factory, where he'd stay until he was broken. He didn't think he could keep putting himself back together afterward.

Mr. Lawson shook his head, his disapproval clear. "I'm really disappointed in you, Shiloh. I thought we really made a breakthrough last time you were over." He stepped toward Shiloh and Shiloh stumbled back another step.

Gage stood and stepped up beside him, uncertainty on his face. "I think it would be counterproductive to make any major changes. Shiloh's still in danger, maybe even more so than he was before. There's still a stalker out there."

"And I'm sure your desire to keep receiving a paycheck isn't in *any* way coloring your opinion on the matter." Mr. Lawson's voice was as dry as the Sahara. "As much as I appreciate your bringing this to our attention, I'm sure the police can handle it from here. This stalker is clearly part of Shiloh's latest prank."

Shiloh looked at his father, who was staring at Gage, deep in thought. "Dad," Shiloh said, "please don't make me go with him." Shiloh could leave, walk out now, but he had nowhere to go. He had a little money saved up, but it wouldn't last him long—and when it was gone, what then? Who would hire him with his reputation?

Father frowned and met his eyes. "I'm not sure you've left me much choice. He's the only one you listen to. You say you don't want money, but I'm at a loss as to what you do want." Father swiped a hand over his face. "Maybe staying with Sam will be good for you."

"No, no, no…" His knees buckled beneath him. He'd have hit the ground if not for Gage darting his arms out to catch him.

He wasn't going back there.

Chapter Thirty

Gage jerked forward to catch Shiloh's collapsing form. This wasn't a temper tantrum. This was panic—pure, undiluted panic. Lawson stepped forward as well and Gage couldn't stop the growl from spilling from his throat.

"Stay away from him." Gage didn't need to know anything else to realize that something was wrong. Maybe Shiloh was just overstimulated, still on edge from the attack. Maybe he just didn't like the lawyer very much. Whatever it was, Gage had made Shiloh a promise, and he was going to keep it.

"I've known the kid a lot longer, Mr. Tucker. If anyone should stay away, it's you," Lawson snapped, anger flashing across his face. It was gone a heartbeat later.

"Sam"—Mr. Beckett stood and rounded the desk—"maybe we should give him a second. He's had a rough night..."

"He's playing you," Lawson said, moving forward again. "I bet he thinks you'll feel sorry for him, and he'll get his way." Lawson grabbed Shiloh's arm, trying to pull him away from Gage. Shiloh trembled, pressing closer to Gage, like he could crawl beneath his skin and hide.

Gage knocked Lawson's hand free from Shiloh. "Touch him again without permission and I'll break your hand."

"Is that a threat?" Lawson's nostrils flared wide, breath hissing out.

"No. It's a goddamn promise. I think you should leave." Anger tumbled in Gage's stomach like a rockslide.

"I'm Anthony's lawyer and—"

"I'm not a cop, and Mr. Beckett's not under arrest." Gage pinned him with a glare.

"Then I'm his friend," Lawson said, moving closer again. Gage refused to step back, though he felt Shiloh cringe.

"Sam"—Mr. Beckett laid a hand on Lawson's shoulder, which the lawyer immediately shrugged off—"maybe you should go."

Lawson sneered at Gage before his focus dropped to Shiloh, his mouth twisting as he spat, "When you decide to do what's best for the brat, you know where to find me." Lawson spun on his heel, storming from the room.

Mr. Beckett stared after him with a puckered forehead. The door slammed, and both Shiloh and his father flinched. Gage stared at the closed door. He shifted through his memory of the lawyer's background check but nothing of note stood out—no history of violence or outbursts, no bad debts, no past or outstanding warrants. Nothing to imply that he was a danger to Shiloh, so why did Gage feel like the lawyer could be an even bigger threat than the stalker?

"Does he get like that often?" Gage finally asked.

"No," Mr. Beckett answered just as Shiloh nodded. Of the two, Gage knew who he believed. Shiloh was too scared, for one thing, and besides, when it came to lying, Shiloh wasn't good at it. He did this thing with his nose, like a twitchy rabbit.

"Son." Mr. Beckett hesitated. He awkwardly stepped forward, lifting his hand like he was going to pat Shiloh's shoulder, then dropped it. "Does Sam...talk to you like that when I'm not around?"

Shiloh flinched like his father had struck him. He pulled away from Gage and crossed his arms in front of his chest. "Like you care."

"Of course I care. If he's been making you uncomfortable—"

"*Uncomfortable?*" Shiloh interrupted with a humorless laugh. "I was *uncomfortable* when he called me squirt in second grade. I passed that when he stuck his dick in my ass. But you know, sometimes things in life just aren't pleasant, and all he asked was that I not... How did you phrase it? '*Lie in bed and moan about?*'"

A stunned silence descended on the room. Fury flashed in Shiloh's eyes, until they widened, the spark swallowed by fear.

Gage felt a roaring anger surge through his veins, the words repeating over in his head. He didn't know—and didn't *need* to know—the context of what Shiloh was saying to know that it was messed up. Mr. Lawson was twenty years older than Shiloh. Whatever had happened between them was dubious, at best. At worst...

Gage didn't want to think of it, but he couldn't stop the images from playing, over and over, in his mind. Shiloh on his knees, on his stomach, on his back beneath Lawson. Shiloh, gasping and moaning or, worse, bruised and bleeding.

Gage fought the urge that overcame him to track the bastard down and introduce Lawson to the barrel of his gun, to shove it down the man's throat like a cock and squeeze the trigger.

Mr. Beckett lifted his hand to his chest, his mouth opening and closing like a fist. His skin turned gray, sweat beading above his lips. "*Shiloh,*" Mr. Beckett gasped, then stumbled back a step. His knees bowed and he collapsed, clutching the fabric of his shirt. Gage and Shiloh both leaped forward, but Shiloh was faster.

"Dad!" Shiloh clutched at his father's arms, keeping him upright. "I think he's having a heart attack."

Gage pulled out his phone and called for an ambulance, then phoned security to make sure someone would immediately escort the paramedics to Mr. Beckett's study. Then, he knelt beside the fallen pair to grip Mr. Beckett's wrist. His pulse was there, but fast and erratic.

"Does he have medication?" Gage asked.

"Yeah. It's— It's in the top drawer of his desk—aspirin...and his angina medication. It's called—fuck, um—nitroglycerin." Shiloh helped Mr. Beckett lean against the desk. "Come on, Dad. I didn't mean it. I won't talk about it anymore, I'm sorry."

"No, Shiloh, that's..." Mr. Beckett gasped in a breath.

Gage tugged open the desk drawer and fumbled through a half-dozen orange pill bottles, looking for the right medication. His hands were steady as he sorted them, pushing aside a cigar case and several takeout menus in the process. The calm that descended over him was bred out of years of practice in emergencies, though he knew fear hovered just beneath it—not just fear that Mr. Beckett would die before an ambulance could arrive, but fear for Shiloh, that losing his father would push him over the cliff he was already poised at the edge of.

"I didn't know. He..." Mr. Beckett's words trailed off into a wheeze, his face growing blotchy. His eyes fluttered shut.

Gage grabbed the right bottles and rounded the desk.

"I'm sorry, Dad. Please don't leave me." Tears spilled over Shiloh's cheeks. "I'm sorry."

"Stop, Shiloh." Gage dropped to his knees beside the pair. "You haven't done anything to apologize for." He twisted off the childproof caps and poured a little pill into his palm from each bottle.

"This is my fault. I gave him a heart attack." Shiloh reached out and shook his father's shoulders. Mr. Beckett moaned, his eyes slitting open.

"Stop, Shiloh, it's not your fault. Twenty-five years of red meat and cigars gave him a heart attack." Gage pressed the first pill into Shiloh's palm. "This is aspirin. He needs to swallow it." Shiloh fumbled the small pill, coaxing it into his father's mouth until the man swallowed it. "This is the nitro. It's sublingual, so just put it under his tongue."

"Okay..." Shiloh's fingers shook but he carefully slipped the tiny pill beneath Mr. Beckett's tongue.

"Here... Help him lean forward." Gage carefully guided Shiloh's hands into position on Mr. Beckett's back, helping him arrange his father correctly, then moved across the room to grab a pillow from the small armchair in the corner. He propped it behind Mr. Beckett, then helped Shiloh convince the gray-skinned man to lean back against it.

By the time the paramedics rushed into the room and loaded Mr. Beckett onto a stretcher, the older man was unconscious.

The paramedics offered to let Shiloh ride with them. Gage felt guilty declining, but he couldn't risk it. The attacker was still out there, and he didn't trust the paramedics to be enough to keep Shiloh safe. Instead, he bundled his client into his black sedan and followed the flashing lights to the hospital.

Chapter Thirty-One

Shiloh hated hospitals like some people hated the dentist or the dark. He couldn't think of a single good reason to ever be in one. At least at the dentist he walked away with clean teeth and a new toothbrush. The hospital was just filled with the sick and dying—and people like Shiloh. The weren't sick or dying, but wishing they were.

He was a horrible son. He'd watched in a state of shock as the paramedics wheeled his father in then immediately back through the swinging double doors. Definitely a heart attack. The paramedics hadn't said much else. A young doctor—too young, surely, to be a doctor?—had come out once already, just to tell him that his father was going into surgery.

Shiloh buried his face in his hands.

Then Gage knelt in front of him, gently tugging his arms down and away until their eyes met. "Let's go down to the cafeteria. You need to get something to eat, and it'll be a few hours until he's out of surgery anyway."

"I'm not hungry." Shiloh couldn't bear the thought of eating, of being down in the cafeteria doing something so…so *normal* when—*if* his father didn't make it.

"Then come to the cafeteria and watch me eat."

Shiloh felt Gage's fingers slide through his hair, and he struggled against the urge to lean into the touch. He didn't deserve the comfort.

When he didn't answer, Gage tugged lightly on the strand and said, "I don't like hospitals anymore. They have this…smell that sticks in my throat. Reminds me of the weeks after my injury. The cafeteria smells like coffee…"

Shiloh suspected that only some of that was true, and that mostly, Gage just wanted to get Shiloh out of the grim waiting room. But it was enough to make Shiloh hesitate to decline again. "Okay."

Gage ran his hand through Shiloh's hair one last time before standing. Shiloh swayed as he pushed himself to his feet, struck by a sudden wave of lightheadedness. Gage caught his arm and steadied him.

The cafeteria was nothing special, but Gage was right. It smelled like coffee and faintly, beneath that, of antiseptic. Gage loaded a pair of plates with a small selection of everything, then guided Shiloh to a small round table near the door.

Gage picked at the stack of fries on his plate. "I used to like hospitals."

"Nobody likes hospitals," Shiloh said.

"I did. My mom was a nurse. Sometimes, she'd take me to work with her, when she couldn't find a sitter. They'd let me sit in the gift shop. I got to help deliver flowers. I thought hospitals were these magical places where people went to get better, and doctors were wizards. I was certain that when I grew up, I was going to go to college and learn magic, just like they did."

A few weeks ago—before he knew Gage, before all of this—he would have laughed and certainly would have ribbed him outwardly, even if secretly, he thought it was sweet. "I've never thought of them like that before. What made you change your mind?"

Gage's smile dimmed. "My mother died. They rushed her to the emergency room but couldn't save her. She died before anyone even told me she was there. It made me realize that doctors weren't magic after all."

"How—? I mean wh-what—?" Shiloh stuttered, choking off his words as he realized how inappropriate that question would be.

"It was a car accident. My father drank himself under the table at the bar. Ma went to go pick him up. Some asshole ran a stop sign and hit her head on." Gage shrugged like it was old news, but his face said otherwise.

"I'm sorry."

Gage smiled. "It was a long time ago."

Shiloh shrugged. "Doesn't really go away though, does it."

"No. Not really."

They stayed in the cafeteria for nearly an hour. By the time Gage sighed and pushed his plate away, Shiloh had helped pick the second plate clean. He didn't remember tasting it, only vaguely noticed he'd eaten it in the first place. But it helped. He hadn't eaten since yesterday morning, between one thing and another.

Shiloh spent the next two-and-a-half hours pacing the surgical waiting room before the door opened and the young doctor from earlier entered. He looked tired but pleased.

"Good news," Dr. Holden said as he approached. "The surgery was successful. You're father's sleeping. We're going to keep him in the ICU overnight and probably for the next few days for observation, but I think we caught it in time to curtail any long-term effects. He was very lucky that you were there and recognized what happened so early. We'll be meeting with his cardiologist in the morning to discuss changing up his medication, but once he's home, things should return to normal."

Shiloh doubted that.

"You can go see him if you'd like. He can have one visitor at a time. Just try not to wake him."

Shiloh immediately shook his head and stepped back. Now that he knew his father was going to make it, the thought of seeing him… Of having to face his father after what he'd admitted… He didn't think he could handle it.

"I'll— Maybe tomorrow. He's sleeping."

"We can come back tomorrow," Gage agreed.

Dr. Holden frowned, looking between the pair of them for a moment. Shiloh supposed it wasn't often the family declined to enter the ICU after surgery.

A few minutes later, in the car, Gage spun the heat to high. Shiloh still shivered and hunkered into his seat. Gage turned to face him, but Shiloh avoided eye contact. After a few seconds, Gage said, "I think it would be best if we went to a hotel for a few nights—somewhere under the radar, until we can find your assailant."

"Okay. If you think that's best." Relief struck him. He hadn't realized how much he dreaded going back to the manor until Gage said they didn't have to.

When Gage said 'under the radar', Shiloh expected him to drive them to some seedy motel where the cockroaches were as big as rats and you paid by the hour. Instead, after they'd grabbed a few necessary belongings, Gage drove them to a run-of-the-mill hotel Shiloh drove past daily but had never been inside.

There were no cockroaches, and Gage paid the room up for a week.

Chapter Thirty-Two

Gage watched Shiloh sleep. He could try to convince himself that it was just part of the job, watching over his client, but what was the point? Shiloh was so much more to him than just a paycheck and that, more than anything, scared him. He didn't let people get close to him…not anymore.

The last person he'd let get close was Ashton, his former Army buddy and current coworker. After their tank had rolled over the IED, Gage had shoved him away with both hands and not just because he was afraid of losing him, though that had been part of it. He'd been overwhelmed by a sense of inadequacy. He couldn't help feeling like he was missing more than just his leg. Therapy had helped, but his relationship with Ashton had missed its chance. They were still friends—good friends—but nothing more.

Already he felt an attachment to Shiloh that was too strong to deny. He wanted to protect him, not just from the mystery assailant, but from the world. But he couldn't wrap him up in bubble wrap and tuck him away like a doll.

Shiloh rolled onto his back, scrunching his eyes shut as he yawned. "What time is it?"

"A bit after nine in the morning." Gage turned and dug through one of the shopping bags he'd picked up the previous night before they'd checked in. He wasn't looking for anything, except to look like he *wasn't* staring at Shiloh creepily.

Shiloh sat up, his feet dangling over the edge of the bed. "What are you looking for?"

Gage pulled out a toothbrush and waved it. "We should talk about the plan for today."

Shiloh's gaze dropped into his lap, where his fingers were busy plucking at the fabric of his pajamas, then lifted again. A fire blazed behind his eyes and he stubbornly set his jaw. "I want to go to Blood, Sweat and Shears."

Gage didn't think going to a hair salon, especially one Shiloh frequented often, was a good idea, but if all Shiloh needed was to feel normal, who was he to stop him? Maybe it would do the boy some good.

"Okay."

Shiloh looked shocked at the acquiescence before bounding out of bed and into the bathroom.

Gage watched Shiloh carefully paint on his mask of a shallow socialite. He lined his eyes with a glittery pen, dabbed his lips with an insane amount of lip gloss and threw on an exceedingly skimpy pair of shorts and a pair of blue Chucks. A pink, off-the-shoulders blouse completed the look. Shiloh blew himself a kiss in the mirror, then spun on his heel.

He shot a wide, careless grin at Gage that fit him like a mask, then they left, riding the elevator down into the parking garage.

Shiloh directed him to the same salon Gage had tailed him to his first day on the job. Gage kept a careful eye on the car mirrors, searching for anyone acting suspicious and made sure to give the small parking lot beside the salon a similar treatment. He spotted nothing unusual and waved Shiloh out of the car.

Despite that, Shiloh still darted his eyes nervously around until they'd safely entered through the salon's front door.

Gage had never seen a salon like this before. Built out of what had once been a house—a fancy one, definitely, but still a house—most of the interior walls had been stripped out to leave an open floor salon. Each of the three walls were different and yet somehow, still managed to provide a unique backsplash to the otherwise-modern salon.

Shiloh's tense expression smoothed out as soon as the door closed behind them.

The salon wasn't busy. A single stylist worked with a client at a station nearby while another touched up her makeup in a large mirror. Behind the desk, a young woman with magenta hair and rainbow-painted nails was reading. A small silver name tag identified her as Delia.

She looked up as the bell over the door dinged.

"Shiloh!" Delia bounced up with a bright smile. "It's been a few weeks. I wasn't sure you were coming."

"Yeah. It hasn't started yet, right?" Shiloh picked up the paperback book from where the girl had flung it. "Oh, I *like* this one," he said, then returned the book to the desk. Gage couldn't read the title, but he could clearly make out the two male chests on the cover.

"I do too, so far. But no, you've still got time." Delia eyed Gage for a moment. "Is your friend joining you?"

"Yeah," Shiloh answered before Gage could say no. He was perfectly fine with his hair the way it was.

"There's plenty of room." Delia looked Gage up and down with appreciation. "Certainly looks like he could handle himself."

Delia waved a hand at a nondescript door behind the desk. "You know where to go."

Shiloh went to go through the door, but Gage gripped his arm, tugging him to a stop to enter first. He saw Shiloh roll his eyes before Gage started up the narrow flight of stairs. Shiloh didn't argue. He just followed him with a small huff. At the top, Gage pushed through a second door, expecting to find another salon—maybe a better station, or just one more private. Instead, he walked into an open-plan room with a cement floor and gray walls. Large, foldable blue mats were spaced across it, most already occupied with women of varying ages. There were a few men, but not many.

Shiloh brushed past him, walking with purpose to an empty mat near the wall. Several women called greetings that Shiloh returned as they passed.

"Grab a mat. I think you'll like this." Shiloh dropped down and started stretching. Gage mimicked him.

"This doesn't look like a root touch-up," Gage commented partway through the stretch.

"Nope. This is a *self-defense* touch-up." Shiloh's small smile dimmed. "I froze in the alley."

"Knowing self-defense is different from using it. There's nothing to be ashamed of."

Shiloh just pressed his lips together and looked away, clearly not convinced. Before Gage could say anything else, a man near the front stood. His arms were bared by the tank he wore, showcasing his rippling muscles. Combined with the toned thighs peeking out from the black basketball shorts, he was one hell of an attractive man. Strangely enough, Gage's attention instead found its way back to Shiloh.

Shiloh, who was currently twisted into what would have been a painful position for Gage, was staring back at him with a thoughtful expression on his face. Gage cleared his throat and looked away.

"I see a couple of new faces out there, so for all my returning friends, bear with me. My name is Joel and I'll be your instructor." Joel went on to list his qualifications as a teacher.

"He was intimidating when I first started coming," Shiloh murmured beside him. "But he's a giant teddy bear."

Gage examined the instructor again. "I wouldn't call him a *bear.* Maybe a bull."

"Is that your type?" Shiloh's lips curved upward.

Gage lifted his brows in amusement and gave Shiloh a very thorough once-over. "I'm surprised you haven't guessed my type." It was Shiloh exactly…twinks with an attitude problem.

Shiloh looked flustered. Crimson burned across his cheeks. "Oh. Well…back at the club, when I tried to… I mean, you wouldn't… Then you didn't try anything last night when we…"

"Not wanting to take advantage of you doesn't mean I'm not into you." Gage's stomach twisted at the thought that Shiloh was so used to it that he expected it. "It just means that I'm not an asshole."

"Taking advantage... Jeez, is it the 1940s?" Shiloh laughed. "It's not taking advantage of me when I wanted you to."

"It is when you're trusting me to keep you safe." There was nothing *illegal* about starting up a relationship with a client, but it was certainly unethical. He could reevaluate when Phoenix arrived.

"Everyone grab a partner. Spread out, and leave yourselves some room," Joel said. There was an uneven number of members. A young man, barely in his twenties, if that, was left standing alone. His hands picked at the edge of an oversized sweater that hung off one shoulder. Joel waved the kid forward. They spoke too quietly for the class to hear.

After several moments, Joel raised his voice to a normal volume again. "Chase is going to help me demonstrate the right and wrong way to stand when you are first confronted by an attacker."

Chase hesitated, his cheeks pink, then dropped into an aggressive-looking stance, his knees bent, fists clenched in front of him. Nervousness took much of the threat from it, but it was a good attempt.

"Some teachers will tell you that this is the stance you should start with. Prove you're a threat, that you're willing to defend yourself if necessary. That's not *wrong*, but it can escalate a situation faster. Instead, try to find a more passive stance."

Joel walked around Chase, nudging his legs into a more stable position, tucking his elbows in closer to his sides. He gently encouraged Chase to unclench his fists so his palms were open and facing outward, one closer to his face, one outstretched. "From this position, you can still protect yourself, still block any punches, but you look more open. Try to calm your attacker down.

Say things like 'Stop' and 'Wait'—or 'I don't want any trouble'."

Joel moved back around in front of Chase and dropped into a similar stance. "It might be less aggressive, but it's also more secure for you. If I take *this* position"—Joel clenched his fists and adopted the original stance—"see how far my fist has to travel to get to Chase?" He, very slowly, demonstrated the difference.

Chase flinched, then froze.

"But look at Chase," Joel continued as if he didn't notice. "His hand is right here. He could slap me, strike my ear, dig into my eye… A lot of defensive moves involve simple moves to the face. Chase has the advantage, and his attacker doesn't even know it. So while it *looks* passive, it's actually not."

Joel demonstrated a few more beginner techniques, then broke the class up to practice.

Shiloh faced Gage. "Go ahead and show me what you got." Shiloh dropped into the passive stance.

"Do your worst." Gage moved calmly and slowly, telegraphing his moves before he made them. This was *practice* for Shiloh, not real life, and Gage had enough experience to hurt him if he wasn't careful.

Shiloh put full effort into practicing each move, trying it over and over until it was perfect. Gage wasn't surprised. Shiloh was a harder worker than he'd ever given him credit for. His gaze trailed over Shiloh's body, taking in more than just his form.

Shiloh noticed his distraction and whipped out his leg, catching it between Gage's just as he sifted. Gage tumbled backward onto the mat. He managed to snag Shiloh's wrist on the way and pull him down with him.

Shiloh landed with a soft *oomph* on his chest, winded. Gage quickly rolled over, pinning Shiloh below him.

"Almost." Gage's voice was a purr in his throat. For the first time, Gage noticed the gold halo hiding in the dancing, steel-blue eyes. They pulled him in, like they were a pair of magnets, irrevocably drawn to each other.

Gage's lips met Shiloh's and he didn't know who kissed whom, and now he was drowning—drowning on the taste of mint toothpaste and strawberry lip gloss and, underneath both, a sweetness that was distinctly Shiloh. Gage's hands were no longer pinning, but caressing—cradling the slender line of Shiloh's neck, tracing their way across muscular shoulders and down his toned chest. Gage wanted to breathe Shiloh in, like the most pristine fragrance, like oxygen. He wanted to devour him, to exist only in this moment, until just the two of them remained.

Gage wanted everything, then a disapproving throat cleared above them. He broke away.

What on earth am I doing?

Chapter Thirty-Three

Shiloh stared up at Gage, warmth burning in his chest. It tangled with the feeling of Gage's lips on his. That warmth curdled into ash as Gage wrenched away, the heat in his eyes turning to horror. Gage leaped off him like he'd been burned. The expression on his face seared itself onto Shiloh's retinas. Gage turned his face away, incapable of even looking at him.

"I'm…sorry. That was beyond inappropriate. I'm just going to…" Gage sucked in a breath. "I'll wait downstairs."

And he left. Gage *left* him, alone in the converted studio, with Joel looming over him.

Shiloh abruptly sat up, darting his arm out to stop Gage from leaving before he froze. He let it drop. Gage, like so many others, had *left* him.

Pain, sharp and biting, flared in his chest and he gasped, curling into it, clutching at the fabric of his shirt. He wanted to tear it, to ruin something in the same way that he was ruined. Instead, he sucked in a breath, then another. With each one he forced down the hurt and confusion, burying it beneath the knowledge that this was always how it was going to end.

It just hurt so much more because, for the first time in ages, he'd let himself think that *maybe* this would be different. Maybe *Gage* would be different.

"Shiloh." Joel's gentle voice was a balm to the pain in the same way aloe vera soothed a knife wound.

Shiloh looked up from the floor. He hadn't noticed the studio emptying until only he and Joel remained. Joel crouched beside him, uncertainty on his face. Shiloh plastered on a cocky smile. "Sorry, man. Guess I couldn't keep it in my pants, huh?"

"Cut the shit, Shiloh. I've known you long enough to know better. Who was he?"

"My bodyguard." Shiloh allowed the smile to fall from his face. Joel was one of—scratch that, pretty much the *only*—man Shiloh felt comfortable letting his guard down around besides Teddy and the other dancers at Envy. And that was because he knew that Joel had been harboring a flame for someone else for months.

"Looked like more than that," Joel said.

"Yeah, right." Shiloh grimaced and looked away. His hair tumbled into his eyes. He didn't bother brushing it away. "I gotta go."

"If you ever need to talk..." Joel offered.

"I know where you work. I know." Shiloh waved in acknowledgment and headed back downstairs.

Gage stood stiffly by the entrance. Shiloh wanted to push past him but hesitated at his side instead. No use tempting fate—or in this case, a potentially homicidal and definitely crazed mafia-adjacent psycho. "Ready?"

Gage nodded curtly. "It's all clear."

Shiloh brushed past him and headed out to his car, collapsing into the passenger seat. Gage dropped into the seat beside him. "Shiloh—"

"I don't want to talk about it," Shiloh snapped.

"I think we—"

"I already know what you're going to say. Let me guess... "That was a mistake. It shouldn't have happened, totally unethical, blah blah blah. But we can still be friends, right?'" Shiloh mocked, unable to hide his anger. It wasn't like this was his fault. Gage had kissed *him,* not the other way around.

"No. I was going to tell you that I already spoke to my boss. I put in my notice as your guard." Gage's voice was annoyingly gentle.

And still, it cut deeply. "Fine." His voice came out strangled and he cleared his throat, trying again. "That's just fine. Great even. I was getting b-bored with you anyway." Shiloh ignored the stutter that betrayed him.

"Shiloh—"

Why did Gage have to sound so *nice* even in the process of breaking Shiloh into a million pieces? "I said I don't want to talk about it!" Shiloh snapped and folded his arms across his chest. "Can we go already?"

"I'm not—"

"If you say another fucking word, I'll run." Shiloh thumbed the lock and gripped the door handle to prove he's serious. "You can try and catch me on your busted-up leg."

Gage pressed his lips together. He didn't look happy—in fact, looked decidedly *unhappy*—but he nodded and started the car. Shiloh turned away and glared out of the window.

Gage didn't drive them back to the hotel. Shiloh didn't notice where they were going until Gage had pulled the car into the underground parking lot below the hospital and by then, it was too late to do anything but protest.

"I said I didn't want to come here," Shiloh hissed, crossing his arms and glaring at Gage, who just tucked the keys away and rounded the car to tug open his door. "I'm not going in there."

"Yes, you are. If something happens and your father passes away before you can talk to him, you're going to kick yourself for it forever. Trust me." Gage held the door open wider, a dark, guilt-ridden expression flashing over his face. "I know how that feels."

Shiloh glared down at the pavement to avoid reaching out to comfort Gage. It didn't stop the words from escaping his mouth. "Your mother?"

"The last thing we did was fight. She'd asked me to leave the movies early to go pick up my dad. She had a migraine. I threw a fit, told her she should make him walk and hung up on her. Every day I wish I could take that back and tell her that I loved her instead, that I'd gone and picked up my dad so she'd stay home. I know how painful regret can be. I don't want you to regret not talking to your father." Gage's hand twitched toward him and for a moment, Shiloh deluded himself into thinking that Gage was going to touch him.

But he didn't. He just dropped his hand back down to his side and waited patiently.

"Fine. But not because you told me to." Shiloh crossed his arms.

"Not because I told you to," Gage agreed. "Stay here." Gage stepped away, starting his check of the parking lot. Shiloh leaned against the car door and debated pulling out his phone.

Before he could decide, a shadow separated from the corner of the parking garage. Shiloh opened his mouth to call out a warning, but he was too slow. The sound of the gunshot pierced through the quiet air.

Gage crumbled in a spray of red.

Shiloh's breath came out in a horrified scream. His bare knees scraped along the sidewalk as he scrambled to Gage's side, his palms stained red where they clutched at the holes in Gage's body. "No, no no…"

Chapter Thirty-Four

"It's just a scratch," Gage told Shiloh for the millionth time in the last hour as the boy fussed at the side of his hospital bed, offering him water, or the remote, or threatening to call the nurse for pain meds. The bullet had barely hit his shoulder, a 'through-and-through' that left a lot of pain but no long-term damage. Gage was more worried about how close the stalker had gotten to grabbing Shiloh than the wound itself. If it hadn't been for a pair of hospital visitors hearing the shot and coming running, scaring the man off, he didn't know what would have happened. He'd blacked out for a moment, coming to on the pavement.

Shiloh's eyes were red-rimmed. "It's not *'just a scratch'*. There is a *hole* in your arm." He crossed his arms stubbornly, his jaw set.

"Barely. I've nicked myself worse shaving," Gage lied, just as a doctor walked in with his chart and a wide smile on his young face.

"Good news, Mr. Tucker. You won't need surgery. We just got your X-rays back and there were no bullet fragments left behind. You got really lucky. I'd still take it easy for the next few weeks, but we should be ready to release you as soon as the police get your statement."

Thankfully, it only took the detectives a few minutes to wrap everything up, since as a Personal Protective Officer, getting shot was part of the job. He promised to come speak with them again later in the week at the precinct to finish his statement, and the officers left.

Of course, Shiloh still fussed at him as he helped him put his shirt back on without jarring the injury. Gage finally couldn't resist pulling the boy in and enclosing him in his arms until he stopped shaking. "Everything's okay. I'm fine."

"He... You could have *died.*" Shiloh spoke into Gage's chest, the words a barely understandable mumble.

"But I didn't. We're okay. But I was thinking"—Gage spoke the idea that had just come to him—"rather than going back to the hotel, we could go somewhere else. Get out of town for the weekend."

"I...I don't know." Shiloh tensed in his arms. "I... What if something happens to my dad?"

"Then we'll come right back," Gage promised. "But I'd feel more comfortable if we could go off grid for a bit, until my arm isn't so sore and backup can get here from Seattle."

He didn't think it was possible, but Shiloh tensed even more, trying to disentangle himself from Gage's arms. "I forgot," the boy said, his voice cracking like his heart was breaking, which made Gage's shatter in his own chest. "You're not my bodyguard anymore, are you?"

"Hey, no. That's not what's happening." Gage sank back onto the hospital bed and tugged Shiloh into his lap, ignoring the pain it caused. "I'm still going to be here, okay? I told my boss to send another guard because it's not safe for you if I'm distracted by my feelings for you. I can't engage in a relationship with you the way I want and keep you safe the way you need. Mason is sending Phoenix down to take over as your primary. I served with him in the Army and he's a good man. He'll be your primary guard, and I'll drop back to secondary. I'll still be here, but…it means I can take you on dates and just be here with you—if that's something you want."

Shiloh went still and quiet for so long that Gage got worried, then flung his arms around Gage's neck with a broken sob. "You mean that?"

"Yeah, honey." Gage draped his good arm around Shiloh's waist, rubbing his back.

"Shit, your arm." Shiloh jerked back, nearly toppling off Gage's lap as he eyed him with concern.

"It's fine and worth it to get to hold you." Gage smirked at the blush on Shiloh's face. "So, will you go somewhere with me? Just until Phoenix can get here?"

"Yeah. Yeah, I'll go somewhere with you."

Chapter Thirty-Five

Shiloh clenched his teeth hard enough to hurt his jaw, his fingertips leaving dents in the leather armrests as the plane lowered itself to the tarmac. He hated flying, hated the loss of control that went with it even more.

"Relax, Shiloh. We've landed."

"Still moving…" Shiloh grunted, his eyes closed. He felt the spinning, jerking motion of the plane as it shuttled down the landing strip.

"Oh, sweetie, we've been stopped for a while now. We're the last ones on the plane."

Shiloh pried his eyes open and saw that Gage was right. His heart slowed as he took in the empty seats. "Oh, thank God."

"I didn't realize you hated flying," Gage apologized, "or I wouldn't have suggested Seattle."

"Humans were never meant to fly," Shiloh grumbled as he stood on shaky knees to grab his carry-on, following Gage down the aisle and off the plane. "If we were, we'd have wings."

"Well, I already knew you were no angel," Gage teased, grabbing Shiloh's hand in his free one. Shiloh was grateful they had no luggage, even though everything in him had protested about leaving with so little clothing. Gage had promised to let Shiloh shop all day the next day in exchange for leaving with just the change of clothes he already had at the hotel and nothing else.

If he thought Shiloh wasn't going to hold him to that, he was insane.

An older man was waiting for them at the departure doors—older than Shiloh, at least. He was in his young forties, maybe, his hair still black with only the smallest streaks of gray. He held a small sign that said only *G. Tucker*.

"You have a driver?" Shiloh asked in shock.

Gage laughed, the sound more boisterous and carefree than Shiloh had ever heard. "Hell no, that's my boss. Shiloh, this is Mason Lockhart. Mason, this is Shiloh," Gage introduced, a grin still on his face. "He thought you were my driver."

A twinkle glinted in the older man's eyes as he laughed. "Well then, should I open the door for you, sirs?"

Shiloh flushed and glared at the pavement at the good-natured teasing. "You didn't have to tell him," he muttered, elbowing Gage in the ribs.

"Ow, I'm injured, you fiend." Gage chuckled and ruffled Shiloh's hair. "Come on… Perk up. I had to tell him. We all make fun of him for the suits."

Shiloh swatted Gage's hand away. "You'll mess it up." Shiloh brushed the strands back in order but stopped pouting. "So, uh…this is your boss?" He straightened up and smoothed out a wrinkle in his shirt, wanting to make a good impression.

It was useless anyway, he knew, since the man had probably read the papers, and even if he hadn't, he would have gotten a file with all his indiscretions from his father—if he hadn't heard about them from Gage directly. He felt his cheeks warm at the thought. He'd never cared what people thought of his antics before, at least not in years, so the feeling was brand new.

Mason held out his hand to shake. He had a firm grip but didn't try to break his fingers with it. "Nice to meet you. I've been wanting to see my man here settle down for years, so I feel like I owe you a cake or something."

Shiloh's flush deepened but he finally found his confidence, even if most of it was a farce. "I like chocolate, but I'd settle for red velvet."

Mason laughed. "Chocolate it is. Hope you can eat a bunch, because my husband will go crazy with it. Speaking of… Gage, Ryder insists that you bring your boy to dinner tonight."

"Is he cooking…or are you?" Gage asked, humor evident in his voice.

"You know he is," Mason said, rolling his eyes.

"Then of course we'll come to dinner, as long as Shiloh's up for it?" Gage looked down at him in question. "If you'd rather go straight to my apartment, we can. I know flying can knock me on my ass sometimes."

Shiloh didn't want to disappoint Gage by admitting that he was, in fact, tired. More than that, though, he wanted to see Gage around his friends, wanted Gage to get to spend an evening where he could just relax and not worry so much about him. So, rather than say he wanted to go to the apartment, he smiled. "I want to meet your friends."

"Okay, but if it gets to be too much, you tell me and we'll go, okay?" Gage squeezed his hand and Shiloh nodded his agreement.

* * * *

Shiloh yawned, drifting in and out of the conversation. He wasn't paying enough attention to the discussion to say what it was about, but it was soothing to just sit in the armchair and listen to Gage speak and laugh with his friends and not be expected to participate—to not have to reach for a bottle of Jack or a line of cocaine just to fit in. He'd thought it would just be Mason and his husband at dinner, but there were several others there as well, all people Gage greeted with a hug or a slap on the back.

They were all nice to Shiloh, but not *too* nice—not the kind of fawning, obsequious nice that was never real, just an attempt to pry open his wallet or his jeans. They were nice like you were to that friend of a friend you didn't know but had heard of a few times.

They'd eaten burgers grilled on a barbecue on the small back patio and drank beer from a can while the Seahawks played on TV. The room was warm and filled with laughter, and Shiloh didn't mind being forgotten in his armchair in the corner. Especially because he knew he wasn't *really* forgotten, since Gage wandered over at one point to drape a throw around his curled-up body, asking if he wanted to leave.

Shiloh had just shaken his head and pried his eyes back open until Gage, hesitantly, returned to his friends. But Gage's eyes drifted to him more often than not, always with a smile on his lips and affection in his gaze.

"Come on, sweetheart. Time to go home." Gage nudged him awake, and Shiloh saw him crouched in front of him. The room was dark, empty except for Mason and his husband, the much younger Ryder, cuddling on the other couch. It was late—or it felt like it—and Shiloh yawned, stretching up.

"Time to go?" he mumbled, his mouth filled with cotton.

"Yep. Time to go." Gage barely waited for Shiloh to stand before he pulled him to his side, under his arm where it was safe and warm.

"M'kay. Was nice to meet you," Shiloh said through another yawn to the couple on the couch as he trailed along beside Gage, stumbling over his suddenly heavy feet. Gage bundled him into the car and the next thing he knew, Gage was shaking him awake again. They were parked in a large garage, a lawnmower right outside his door.

Shiloh's whole jaw cracked with his yawn. "Come on, sleepy boy. Let's go upstairs," Gage prodded him along. Shiloh wanted to look around, to take in the house that Gage lived in, to see how what secrets it revealed about its owner, but he could hardly keep his eyes open.

He barely registered Gage helping him into bed before he passed out on the pillow.

He'd snoop through the house in the morning.

Chapter Thirty-Six

Gage draped the blanket over Shiloh's body, careful not to wake the younger man. Shiloh huddled farther beneath it with a sigh. Gage was only just beginning to realize how many masks Shiloh wore throughout the day. Only in sleep did they seem to drop fully. Shiloh looked softer in repose, bringing all Gage's protective instincts to the fore.

A strand of pink hair fell over Shiloh's face and the boy scrunched his nose where it landed like it tickled. Gage brushed it back, tucking it behind his ear, then forced himself to leave the room. He could stare at Shiloh for hours, memorizing each swath of smooth skin, each curl of hair, but he had work to do.

Work he'd rather do while Shiloh was sleeping, for now. Shiloh had made some serious accusations. It wasn't that Gage didn't believe him, because he did, wholeheartedly. There was too much fear in Shiloh's eyes around Lawson, too much panic. Now, looking back, so much made sense—why he skipped the so-called family dinners, why he didn't want to go home when he saw Lawson's car in the driveway.

Gage cursed and slammed his office door. It also explained why Shiloh had been so fucking quiet after he'd spent the night with Lawson. While Gage had been having fun, getting off with a stranger, Shiloh had…had been… Gage grabbed an empty glass off his desk and chucked it, darkly satisfied at the sound of it shattering.

He picked up his phone and dialed as he dropped into his chair. He'd clean the glass up later, when he was less likely to cut himself from carelessness. After a handful of rings, Mason answered.

"Gage? Everything okay?"

"Not really. Shiloh's sleeping, though, so I figured it was a good time to update you."

"Are you finally going to explain the last-minute trip to Seattle?"

Gage hadn't told his boss anything except that they needed to get out of Austin as quickly as possible and informed him of his injury so that he wouldn't be surprised by the hospital bill. They had insurance, but it would still show up as an invoice.

"Yeah." Gage swiped his hand over his face. "The situation's changed." Mason didn't fill the long silence that followed, letting Gage get his thoughts together. "It's a bit of a story, so bear with me."

Gage spun in his chair to stare blankly out of his window. "There was no stalker to start out with. Shiloh admitted that he's been writing and dropping off the letters himself, which explains how they were able to bypass security."

"Shit, you mean—"

"There's more," Gage interrupted, knowing Mason would likely have the same initial reaction he did without the context. He didn't want to hear him disparage Shiloh. He was still cringing over his own insensitive words. "Apparently, Beckett's best friend... You know the lawyer? Lawson? He's been assaulting Shiloh."

"Hitting him," Mason asked, "or is it more than that?"

"Sexually," Gage grimly clarified. "I don't know very many of the details yet. I don't think Shiloh meant to even admit it. His dad and Lawson were coming at him from both sides about the letters, and he let it slip. I haven't pressed yet, because Beckett went into cardiac arrest right after, and I don't want to push. I need to sit him down and get more details. Whoever attacked him in the alley wasn't the stalker, and the latest letter is real, so I'm at a loss."

"Well, the first thing we need is more information. If you don't feel comfortable asking him, you can bring him out here in the morning and see if he'll talk to me. The real attacker might have been random, if not for the newest note, so he's still in danger, but if we throw out all the other letters, we have to start creating a profile from scratch. I'm assuming you haven't spoken to the police yet?"

"No. I don't want them to take the case less seriously. And until I got more information, I didn't see the point. If...I don't know... If the situation with Lawson is as bad as I fear, the police will need to be involved there as well." Gage ran a hand over his scalp. His hair, usually buzzed, was longer under his palm than he was used to.

"He didn't say much. Just"—he closed his eyes to remember the exact wording—"that *'he was uncomfortable when Lawson called him squirt in second grade, but he passed that when he put his dick in his ass.'* It could have meant they had a drunk hookup he regrets, but…he said something about telling his dad, and his dad telling him to deal with it and not just lay there. It sounded a lot more ominous than that. I think maybe Lawson was molesting him. If that's the case, he should be prosecuted." *Or castrated,* Gage thought, but didn't say it out loud.

"Which could be difficult," Mason said, his sigh audible through the phone. "Even if the police are willing to believe Shiloh, which will be difficult with his history—"

Gage's growl interrupted his boss as anger flared at the insinuation, "Shiloh wouldn't lie, not about something like this."

"I'm not saying he would, but the prosecutor will have to convince a jury that the playboy troublemaker they've seen in the tabloids isn't the real Shiloh, and you know how hard that will be. Hell, remember how you felt about him before you took the job?"

Shame welled inside him at the memory. "Sorry, boss."

"So even if the police are willing to open an investigation, Lawson is a well-respected member of the community. He has ties to dozens of charitable organizations, donated thousands to the mayor's reelection campaign and has a history of being a shark in the courtroom. We'll need more than Shiloh's word to get the police on board. I'd say talk to your boy and get as much information as you can. I know a few private investigators we can bring on if we need to.

There's a good possibility that if Lawson isn't behind the new kidnapping plot, he knows who is."

"Shit," Gage cursed. "I hadn't even thought of that."

"If you're right, and Lawson's been molesting him for years, not just a one-time thing, then he could be angry. Maybe he thought the stalker was going to grab him out from under his nose or maybe he just got tired of limited access. Maybe your boy threatened to come clean. He might not be involved, but I don't want to leave an obvious stone unturned."

"I'll talk to him in the morning…if he'll talk to me." Gage frowned, knowing Shiloh well enough to realize he might not. Shiloh wasn't great at communication on the best of days.

"Impress upon him the importance."

"Will do, boss. Can you look into a bouncer at the club Envy? All I know is his name is Deak. I believe it's short for Deacon? Shiloh was using him to get paperwork together, so he might be involved as well." Gage wanted as much information as possible to get this all sorted without further injury.

"I'll get Sin on it in the morning. Oh, Ryder says to give him a hug and see if he wants to go shopping later." Mason's voice lightened with the last sentence, and even Gage smiled. Ryder was twenty years younger than his husband and the definition of a hipster, from his nerdy chic glasses to his man bun, to his custom suspenders. All he needed was a flannel shirt and beard to complete the look. He was not what Gage had expected his boss's husband to look like, but somehow, they made it work.

"I think he might be Shiloh's new best friend." Gage smiled, though it brought up memories of his *real* best friend, the young man who'd lectured him about not hurting Shiloh. Now, knowing what he knew, it made more sense than ever.

Gage frowned and spun back around in his chair, opening his laptop. He'd scanned in all the files already, so it only took a few moments to find the file for Teddy de Luca, formerly known as Theodora. He skimmed the bio until he found a phone number. "Hey, Mason, I gotta let you go. Tell Ryder I'll give Shiloh his number, okay?"

"Keep me updated." Mason hung up without saying goodbye.

Gage thumbed in the numbers and lifted the phone back to his ear, listening to it ring. It almost went to voicemail before a confused voice answered, "Hello? Who is this?"

"Hey, Teddy, this is Gage. Shiloh's bodyguard?"

Immediately, the other man's voice grew thin with tension. "Is everything okay? Is he hurt?"

"Nothing like that," Gage hurried to reassure. "I just had a few questions I was hoping you could answer."

"Oh, okay. Um, sure. Go ahead?"

"Have you ever noticed unexplained bruises on Shiloh? Or has he ever talked to you about being hurt by someone?" It was a long shot, but if he could get his friend to testify on Shiloh's behalf that Lawson was abusing him, the police would have to listen.

The long silence that followed made Gage certain that Teddy knew something. Finally, Teddy replied, "Is this about Lawson?"

Gage didn't know whether to be pissed or pleased that Teddy knew immediately what he was asking about. It meant Shiloh had confided in someone, but it also meant that his dad had to have known…or suspected. That, or he was absolutely oblivious when it came to his son, which might be worse. "Yes, it's about Lawson."

"I never saw Lawson hurt him, but…I have pictures of the aftermath. Would those help? I've been trying to get him to go to the police, but he says they won't believe him. I started a file back in high school."

Gage closed his eyes and dropped his head back to the chair. *High school?* How long had this been going on, if he'd been taking pictures since high school? And as much as he needed that file, he didn't want to see the photographs, not if the bruises were obvious enough that Teddy knew to take pictures.

"Can you mail the file to me?"

"I um… I scanned most of the photos ages ago. I can email them to you? Would that be okay? Or I can send you the originals if that's better…" Teddy sounded hesitant.

"Email would be perfect. Do you have a pen?"

"Yeah, one sec." There were a few moments of rustling. "Okay."

Gage relayed his email address, then wrapped up the call. It didn't take long for his computer to *ding* with an incoming email.

He opened the files and immediately felt like vomiting. He'd seen worse, both in the deserts of Afghanistan and at home—but this was Shiloh, someone he cared about. Someone he might, someday, love. And beyond that—beyond the black eyes and split lips, beyond the bruises wringing a very young Shiloh's wrists and neck—they stirred up memories from his own childhood. Memories of his mother covering the marks his father had made with makeup, memories of himself wearing long sleeves and sunglasses.

He closed the file only halfway through, unable to stomach looking at the images. In some, Shiloh couldn't be more than fifteen. He'd go through them later, he had to, but for now, he just sent the file to Mason and shut his computer. It was late, and he didn't want Shiloh waking up alone.

Chapter Thirty-Seven

Shiloh woke knowing exactly where he was—which was strange, because he was in a new place, and in all the books he's read, that meant he should be wondering. He had before, when he'd stayed over at a trick's. Admittedly, that was rare, but something about Gage's apartment just felt like home. He hadn't even seen Gage's bedroom with the lights on. He couldn't tell what color walls it had, or carpet, but he could tell that the bed was big and soft, the blankets were warm and, best of all, Gage was in it.

Very much in it, if the erection jutting against his ass was any indication. He shouldn't—he knew he shouldn't—but he rubbed against it, enjoying the way Gage's arms tightened around his waist, enjoying even more the soft groan against his ear.

"What are you doing, brat?" Gage murmured, though he didn't let him go, so he couldn't mind. *Right?* In fact, Gage just slid his hands lower, gripping his hips and pulling him back hard, stilling his own movements so Gage could take over. "Tell me to stop," Gage ordered.

"I don't want you to stop," Shiloh groaned when Gage thrust harder, his voice breathy.

Suddenly, Shiloh was on his back, blinking up at the naughty grin on Gage's face. "What do you want, Shiloh baby?" Gage teased. Shiloh wanted Gage over him, rather than just pressed against his side. He wanted…

"I want your dick in my ass," Shiloh answered crudely, reaching down in an attempt to squeeze the dick in question, but Gage just grinned, grabbing Shiloh's hand and gently restraining it. Shiloh could pull away, but he didn't want to. He trusted Gage, knew that if he struggled, Gage would let him go—knew in a way he'd never felt before that Gage would never hurt him.

"You have such a dirty mouth, baby." Gage didn't sound like he minded.

"Then maybe you should find a way to shut it," Shiloh suggested. "Let me suck you?"

"Not today. This morning, I want to take care of you." Gage shifted until he was lying between Shiloh's thighs. "I want you to grab the headboard. Don't move your hands. Can you do that for me?"

"Yes," Shiloh breathed, his heart thumping at the subtle display of dominance. It was what he'd always imagined sex would be, before he'd grown too afraid to let his guard down. He reached up and curled his fingers around the wooden rods of the fancy headboard. "I won't let go."

"If you do, I'll stop. Okay?" Gage said, and Shiloh didn't know if it was a threat or a promise.

Shiloh nodded frantically, tightening his fingers on the wood. "Okay. Don't stop."

Gage gave him a devilish grin, then worked the jeans Shiloh had fallen asleep in down his legs, throwing them off the bed to land on the floor. He didn't lower Shiloh's panties, just pulled the blue lace taut over his straining erection. A swipe of his tongue over them made Shiloh buck his hips with a gasp.

Gage worked over the lace until it was damp with pre-cum and spit before he finally peeled them off, sliding them far too slowly down Shiloh's thighs. They joined Shiloh's jeans on the floor, and for a horrible second, Shiloh felt exposed. Bare, in a way that nudity had never made him feel before. But then Gage licked up his length and the moment passed.

"More," Shiloh demanded, thrusting his hips, seeking a friction Gage denied him.

"You'll get what I give you," Gage said, shifting back until only his breath teased along Shiloh's hot, throbbing shaft.

Shiloh keened at the loss of touch.

"You know what to do if it's too much. Let go of the headboard and I'll let you finish yourself," Gage said and again—was it a threat or a promise?

"No, not too much," Shiloh breathed, heat burning in his chest like an open flame as his heart pounded.

Gage grinned and went back to teasing him. He swiped his tongue over Shiloh's crown, gathering up the pre-cum before releasing him, letting Shiloh's cock slap back onto his stomach. Then, he slowly licked him from head to hilt, swirling his tongue over Shiloh's balls, sucking one then the other into his mouth, but never doing enough to let Shiloh come, just building the pleasure higher, and higher, edging him until he was sobbing.

"Please," Shiloh whimpered. "Please, please…" He repeated it over and over, spewing nonsense until finally, *finally,* Gage sucked him in to the root. The warmth of Gage's mouth followed by the sweet suction tipped Shiloh over the edge immediately and he was coming, his body twitching like a marionette on strings.

Gage swallowed everything Shiloh gave him, then pressed a kiss to Shiloh's hipbone. As Shiloh came down from his high, the aftershocks fading from his twitching muscles, he apologized, "I should have warned you."

"You were perfect," Gage promised, dropping a kiss onto Shiloh's stomach, tongue dipping into his navel in a ticklish swirl. Shiloh cursed, his hips spasming as it sent a last, coursing pleasure to his dick. "No warning necessary for a treat that tasty." Gage winked up at him.

Shiloh unclenched his hands from the headboard and covered his face as he laughed, embarrassment heating his skin. "That's so cheesy."

"No, that will be the omelets I make when we get our lazy asses out of bed. Shower first or food?"

"I'd say both, but soggy eggs aren't my jam." Shiloh felt high, like he'd taken the best drugs, but he was completely sober. "Shower, then food. Then shopping."

"Speaking of, Ryder's been dying for a shopping buddy. Think we can let him tag along?"

"You just want someone else there so I don't try to dress you up, don't you?" Shiloh accused but couldn't help his grin. He didn't have a lot of friends, not real ones. Teddy was basically it. Ryder, from the little he'd seen of him at the party last night, seemed like maybe he could be another.

"Well, I know I'm a doll," Gage teased, then lightly swatted the curve of Shiloh's hip. "Out of bed, lazy bones."

"You just want to see me naked." Shiloh sat up and dragged his blouse off, letting it join the rest of his clothes on the floor. "There. No shower needed."

A high-pitched shriek fled his mouth as Gage shoved him back, forcing his arm up to bury his face in Shiloh's pit. "No, shower *definitely* needed," Gage joked, digging his fingers into Shiloh's sides until Shiloh cried for mercy from the assault.

"Stop! Stop! I'll shower!" Shiloh cried.

Gage relented immediately and allowed Shiloh to roll off the bed. Shiloh turned to examine the room. It wasn't flashy, but it was nice. Kind of plain, but the walls were a pretty blue and the furniture complemented it well.

"I'm not here enough to decorate," Gage explained without being asked, watching Shiloh with a satisfied smile. His erection still tented his pants, but he didn't seem to notice.

"Shower with me and I'll take care of that for you," Shiloh offered, gesturing to the impressive bulge.

"Maybe if you're good today, I'll let you take care of it tonight." Gage winked as he climbed off the bed, graceful as a panther. He shoved his pants down his thick thighs, carefully disentangling them from his prosthetic. Shiloh tried not to stare, not wanting to make Gage self-conscious, but the way he averted his eyes must have been too obvious.

"Come here and you can look at it," Gage said, not sounding angry or ashamed—not that he should be. There was nothing to be ashamed of.

Shiloh moved closer, small steps taking him back across the room. "Kneel for me," Gage murmured, his voice quiet. It was a demand hidden in a question, a test with no wrong answer. Shiloh knew if he refused or hesitated, Gage wouldn't be mad, which was the only thing that let him sink to his knees, his ass on his heels.

Immediately, calmness radiated through him, starting in his chest before flooding his muscles as he relaxed into position. He'd knelt for others, for tricks who paid double to get the experience, to the bastard whose name he refused to think of while in this room that promised safety…but he'd never knelt for himself, knelt because he wanted to, knelt to please a person he cared about.

"Good boy."

Gage might look down *at* the kneeling man but would never look down *on* him. Heat coursed through his veins at Shiloh's unexpected obedience. It was quiet and unassuming, not the joke Gage had expected. Shiloh looked up at him with wide, youthful eyes. He suspected this was the first time Shiloh had knelt for a lover—or at least, the first time he'd *meant* it.

"Good boy," he praised, his voice a pleased murmur. He lowered his hand to Shiloh's head, running his fingers through the tousled pink hair. "All you have to do is tell me to stop, and I will." He tipped Shiloh's head up with a finger to the chin. "All you *ever* have to do is tell me to stop. Do you understand?"

"Yes, I understand," Shiloh promised.

Gage dragged his thumb over Shiloh's plump lower lip, a gentle pressure all it took to tell Shiloh to open his mouth, then the younger man was sucking on it like a lollipop, his eyes blissed out. "Good boy," Gage praised again as he removed it. "Look at my prosthesis."

Shiloh's skin turned a lovely pink, like a cherry blossom freshly bloomed, but his gaze moved down, lingering on Gage's erection where it jutted near his face, before lowering with what seemed an obscene amount an effort to Gage's lower leg.

He was quiet, but his flush deepened, wetting his lower lip with his tongue. Gage smirked, a fantasy growing in his mind that no longer seemed quite as out of reach. "If you're a good boy for me, maybe I'll let you worship it with your mouth."

Shiloh's breathing sped up at the words, darting his eyes up to meet his and back down. He didn't seem disgusted. If anything, his dick plumped back to life.

"Would you like that, baby?" Gage prodded, reaching down to take his erection in hand. Not stroking, just squeezing the base. "Would you like to taste the metal under your tongue?"

Shiloh whimpered. "Can I?"

"Go take a shower, baby." Gage grinned at the crestfallen look on Shiloh's face. Not because he liked disappointing the younger man but because of the way Shiloh's cock got even harder at the denial. "I'll be in the kitchen making omelets. Clothing is optional," he added, and that seemed to spur Shiloh into motion.

Gage couldn't hold back his laugh, however, when the first door Shiloh opened wasn't the en suite bathroom but his closet, and the second led out into the hall. Shiloh huffed and tried the last, glaring death daggers at him over his shoulder as he shut the door firmly between them. It opened a second later and Shiloh peered around it with a sultry grin. "Just in case you decide to join me," Shiloh said before disappearing.

Gage wished he could, but shared showers were a thing of his past. He'd soak in the bath later, if he had time. He pulled his pants back up and headed for his kitchen. It was a nice kitchen—not chef quality, but he wasn't a great cook. There was a fridge, a stove and a toaster oven. *What more does a person need?*

It was easy enough to whip up a pair of omelets and set the table. He was pouring black coffees into mugs when Shiloh strutted into the dining room, naked as the day he was born. Gage's cock, which had partially deflated while cooking, stiffened to a steel rod beneath his pants.

He'd seen Shiloh in varying stages of undress, of course—in just his panties at Envy, in his tights in the studio, in just his shirt this morning—but never fully nude. Gage wanted to pin him to the table and ravish him, taste every inch of smooth skin exposed to his eyes, but he wouldn't—not until they'd had a conversation.

"Like what you see?" Shiloh asked, his voice teasing, though there was insecurity in his eyes.

"I could eat you right up," Gage replied, holding out one of the mugs, "but I'll settle for the omelet."

Shiloh's pale skin flushed pink as he took the coffee. He took a sip without looking away from Gage, his face twisting a moment later at the bitterness. "Bleh, is this black?" Shiloh didn't wait for an answer. He just moved toward the coffee pot, opening doors until he found the sugar. He doused his coffee liberally with it before moving to the fridge, his hips swaying enticingly. And when he bent over to grab the creamer, Gage couldn't stop the groan from spilling out of his mouth. He took a sip of his own coffee to cover it, but Shiloh's smirk said he'd heard it anyway.

Gage's table was small, one of those breakfast nook things that sat in the corner. He didn't entertain guests, and to be honest, he was rarely home. Even when he was, he was more likely to be eating takeout than anything that required a plate. Compared to the fancy table that sat twelve with ease back at the Beckett estate, it was practically quaint. Part of him expected Shiloh to laugh at some point or realize how much better he could do than Gage, but he knew he should give the younger man more credit. Not once had he seen Shiloh act like a snob.

Shiloh sat down beside him, his skin pinking further. Gage grinned. "Problem, sweetheart?"

"The chair is cold," Shiloh whined.

"Would you rather sit on my lap?" Gage asked, pushing back slightly from the table. He didn't know who he was teasing now, him or Shiloh. The curve of Shiloh's ass pressing down on his dick as he draped himself over Gage's lap pushed him nearly to the edge.

Shiloh knew it, too. He smirked over his shoulder and wiggled. Gage gripped his hip to still him and Shiloh literally giggled. "Sorry. Something is poking me," he taunted.

Gage swatted his hip. "Eat your omelet, brat."

"Ooh, pet names already." Shiloh shoved a bite of omelet in his mouth. "It's good," he mumbled through the food.

"Don't talk with your mouth full," Gage scolded, though the grin tugging on his mouth gave away his lack of concern.

"Yes, *Daddy,*" Shiloh replied, taking a smaller bite.

"Is that what you're looking for?" Gage asked more seriously. "A Daddy?"

Shiloh turned to stare at his plate, like hiding his face would make the question go away. Gage didn't press, even when Shiloh stayed silent for several minutes, picking at his food. Finally, he shrugged. "I don't know? I used to think… But then…" Shiloh sighed. "What Daddy would want a boy like me anyway?"

"Any Daddy would be lucky to have you," Gage said firmly, reaching up to tip Shiloh's face back toward him. "You're kind, talented and so fucking smart."

He felt the warmth flooding to the boy's skin at the compliments. "I'm a brat. That's what I am. Besides, Daddies want their boys to be untouched little virgins." Shiloh rolled his eyes at that, though the way his shoulders hunched made it clear he wasn't taking it so lightly.

"I like that you keep me on my toes. I'd be bored if you were a perfect little angel all the time," Gage said, then reached up to curl his fingers in Shiloh's hair, tugging lightly on the pink strands. "And besides, I like your dirty mouth. Why would I want a virgin when I can have someone who can keep up with me?"

"You're going to be the one keeping up with me, old man." Shiloh brightened considerably at the reassurance. He went back to wiggling, and Gage didn't have the heart to chastise him, even if it made his cock throb painfully.

After a particularly dedicated shift of Shiloh's hips, Gage gave up on his omelet and curled his hands around Shiloh's waist, holding him steady while he thrust against his ass, only the thin fabric of his sleep pants keeping him from penetrating.

Shiloh moaned, his fork clattering to his almost-empty plate. "Please," Shiloh moaned, dropping his hands to Gage's knees for support.

"Tell me what you want, baby, because I'm not going to last long," Gage said, his voice taut. He'd planned on making both of them wait until after they'd talked, but clearly, that plan had failed miserably.

"I just... Can I touch myself? Please, I'm so close already..." Shiloh's voice broke on a whimper.

"Yeah, baby. Get yourself off," Gage groaned, the thought that he was giving Shiloh permission...that Shiloh had *asked* for permission in the first place, had him wound even tighter.

He heard Shiloh spit into his palm, then the sound of his hand slipping back and forth over his dick, but it was the small gasp as Shiloh came, shaking in his arms, that pushed him over the edge.

He thrust once, twice, against Shiloh's ass as he shuddered, spilling into his briefs. It was warm and sticky and vaguely uncomfortable but worth it for the way Shiloh slumped against his chest. Gage let go of his hips to grab Shiloh's wrist, bringing the limp hand up to his mouth to lick it clean of the salty cum.

"Such a good boy, coming for me like that," he praised, then dipped his tongue between Shiloh's fingers, gathering the last few drops. "Open your mouth, baby."

Shiloh obeyed, his eyes glazed. Gage pressed his lips to Shiloh's, slipping his tongue into the younger man's mouth, exploring, teasing. Shiloh moaned, tangling his fingers into Gage's chest hair.

Gage pulled back slightly. "Can you taste yourself, sweetheart?"

Shiloh nodded. "Yes..."

"See how good you taste?" Gage dropped his hand down into Shiloh's lap, giving his cock a last few strokes, milking out every last bit of cum before Shiloh whined in protest. Gage licked his fingers clean.

"Let me clean up breakfast then we need to have a talk," Gage said. Shiloh immediately tensed until Gage dropped a kiss to his shoulder. "Not a bad talk," he promised.

"Is this where we talk safewords?" Shiloh laughed uncomfortably.

"Yes, and a few other things." Gage patted Shiloh's hip. "Meet me in the living room. Grab a throw so you don't get cold."

Chapter Thirty-Eight

Shiloh grabbed a blanket like Gage had suggested but he couldn't sit down. His body itched to pace from wall to wall, but he refused to give in to his insecurities. He knew what Gage wanted to talk about. He wasn't stupid. He was going to ask Shiloh about Lawson, about the accusation he'd made in his dad's study. He should be grateful Gage had let them wait this long, that he hadn't pressed at the hospital, or at the hotel, or even on the plane.

He heard Gage's soft footsteps on the carpet behind him, but he didn't turn away from the window. He didn't need to look at the man as he told his story. If he saw disgust or, worse, *pity,* it would break him.

"I was fourteen," Shiloh said unprompted, answering the unasked question. "My dad had just had his first heart attack and I went to stay with Lawson. I thought it was going to be so cool." He swiped a hand over his face, like he could wipe away the memory of his naivety. "He used to bring me fun things—video games, new toys, something different each time. I thought… I thought going to his house for a week or so was going to make everything better." Shiloh laughed at his stupidity. "I was so stupid."

"You were a kid. You had no reason to think anything different," Gage murmured behind him, closer than Shiloh expected.

"But I should have. He was always touching me—my hair or my shoulder. I should have realized there was something wrong." That was what had made Shiloh hate himself the most, how he'd fallen right into Lawson's trap. He hadn't asked a single question when Lawson had told him he had something for him. He'd just followed him stupidly up to his bedroom.

"You were a child." Gage gripped Shiloh's arm. Shiloh didn't fight to free himself, allowing the larger man to guide him over to the couch. He sat at Gage's urging, though he kept his eyes averted. "You couldn't have known. He was a predator, and I doubt anyone would have guessed what he was up to."

Shiloh tugged a throw pillow into his lap. "Logically, I know that."

"But it doesn't help in here?" Gage reached out and touched the center of Shiloh's chest, over his heart. Mutely, Shiloh shook his head. A moment later, Gage scooted closer on the couch and pulled Shiloh into his lap until he was tucked under his chin. Shiloh tensed but when Gage made no move to do anything but comfort him, he slowly relaxed.

"It wasn't your fault," Gage said. "I'll say it as many times as I need to for you to believe that."

"Okay," Shiloh agreed, his voice sounding small in the silence. He dug his teeth into his lip before gathering his frayed nerves again. He needed to finish his story or he never would. "Lawson took me upstairs.

He said he had a new game to play. I thought he meant on the PlayStation, so I followed him. But…it wasn't a video game. He… I told him no. I told him that I didn't want to do it, but he just laughed, like he thought it was funny that I tried to fight back. Like he *enjoyed* it."

Shiloh shuddered at the memory, bile rising bitter in his throat. It was like he was back in that room, Lawson laughing, pinning him down, telling him to scream, licking the tear tracks on his cheeks.

"Hey, stay with me." Gage tightened his grip on Shiloh, not hard enough to hurt, just enough to ground him in the present. "I'm right here."

"He told me that he knew my dad was in trouble for insider trading and that if I told anyone about what he was doing to me, he'd make sure Dad went to prison," Shiloh admitted. "He was lying. I knew he was lying. My dad wouldn't do that." He spun to look at Gage for the first time, knowing it was important that Gage believe him. "He wouldn't do that," Shiloh repeated.

Gage nodded his understanding. "I know, baby."

"So when Lawson finally left the room, I managed to squeeze out of the bathroom window. I stole some money from his nightstand to pay a cab to take me to the hospital and went to see my dad, but Lawson was already there. When I tried to tell my dad, he said Lawson had already told him. That it wouldn't kill me to have to follow some rules, and that I needed to grow up." Shiloh stopped talking as the pain at those words flared up again. "I…I don't think Lawson really told him what happened," Shiloh admitted for the first time, both out loud and to himself. "I think he told him I was being a brat or not listening. But it sounded like he knew at the time."

Gage didn't say anything. He just ran his fingers soothingly through Shiloh's hair, letting him gather his thoughts. Shiloh tugged the throw blanket tighter over his lap, nervously running it through his fingers.

"Lawson superglued my lips together after that. Said if I couldn't keep them shut, he'd shut them for me. He was really good about finding punishments that wouldn't leave a mark or only leaving bruises when my dad was away. I tried running away but the cops found me pretty quick. Guess it was pretty suspicious for a teenage boy to try buying a one-way train ticket. When I was eighteen, I thought it would get better, because I could move out, but Lawson talked my dad out of it. Said I wasn't mature enough, that if I lived on my own I'd become a drug addict. I tried getting a job so I could pay for a place, but my dad just sent his security to come drag me home. He said I should be concentrating on school instead."

"Oh, sweetheart." Gage held him tighter. Shiloh felt his lips brush his forehead and even though he liked it, he had to force himself not to pull away from the touch. "I'm so sorry."

"I didn't want anyone to get hurt. I just didn't..." Shiloh trailed off.

"You didn't think you had another choice," Gage finished for him.

"Exactly. It wasn't going to be forever. I thought if they were looking for a stalker, they wouldn't be looking for me, then I could get an apartment and a job all set up and everything would be fine." Saying it out loud made him feel even more foolish.

"You don't have to worry anymore. I'll keep you safe, from Lawson and whoever is actually after you," Gage promised.

"What if my dad dies?" Shiloh blurted out. "What if this time he doesn't pull through, and I'm not there because of my stupid idea?"

"Dr. Holden said he expected a full recovery. He's stable and awake—won't stop asking for you," Gage reminded Shiloh of the phone call they'd had the day before. Shiloh hadn't spoken to his dad, but he'd listened quietly while Gage had it on speaker.

"I'm not ready to see him," Shiloh admitted.

"Whenever you're ready." Gage didn't press, didn't ask why. Either the answer was obvious, or he knew Shiloh wouldn't want to explain.

"Can we go to bed?" Shiloh blurted, plaintively changing the subject, then clarified, "Just to sleep?"

Gage held his hand the whole way back to the bedroom and the simple act made Shiloh feel younger, more innocent, like the past seven years had just been a bad dream. Then he let Shiloh fall asleep curled up at his side.

* * * *

Ryder Lockhart was the devil—an actual demon, sent to sway Shiloh into bad decisions. At least Shiloh was going to be the best-dressed sinner strutting into Hell.

"You have to try this one. With your complexion—which I am *so* jelly of, by the way—the color will really pop." Ryder shoved another shirt, this one a cerulean, off-the-shoulder silk blouse, onto the growing pile already dangling off Shiloh's arm.

Shiloh flipped the tag over, his mouth dropping over at the price. Was *reverse* sticker shock a thing?

"Come on. Let's go try these on." Ryder grabbed Shiloh's arm and practically dragged him to the changing rooms.

Shiloh couldn't help glancing over his shoulder, looking for Gage, not that he thought he was in danger. Even if he didn't trust Ryder, the man only came up to his shoulder and weighed half as much, which was saying something as thin as Shiloh was. He couldn't help the instinctive need to know where Gage was. He felt safe with him.

Gage was sitting in the same bench by the door he'd dropped into when they'd started shopping over an hour ago, reading something on his phone. As if Shiloh's gaze was a physical weight, Gage looked up, lifting his brow in question.

Shiloh felt his cheeks flush and he turned away quickly, embarrassed to be caught staring, *again.* He allowed Ryder to tug him to the changing rooms, watching the other man make quick work of procuring a key.

"Just one? Feeling voyeuristic?" Shiloh asked with a grin.

Ryder rolled his eyes. "You'll show me an outfit, then I'll show you one. Otherwise, how will I know if it looks okay? Normally I make Mason come with me, but he just sits and grunts like a caveman for every outfit then tries to talk me into a quickie. One time I picked out the most hideous lime green bellbottoms and he told me they looked great. Can you believe that? I definitely need someone with fashion sense."

"If anyone could pull off lime-green bellbottoms, though..." Shiloh let his comment trail off as he gave the other man a critical once-over. "I can see it."

"Oh God…" Ryder looked devastated. "I thought… I thought I finally had *someone* who knew fashion."

"No, seriously. Wait… I'll prove it." Shiloh spun on his heel, refusing to let Ryder believe he was in any way fashion challenged. It only took him a second to find the pants Ryder was talking about—unless there were two pairs of neon bellbottoms in the store. It was, admittedly, a challenge to find the right pairing, but finally, he carried his choices back to the fitting room.

"Here," he said, passing them over. Ryder looked skeptical but retreated into the changing room.

A few minutes later, Ryder strutted out. The hot pink crop top left a few inches of bare skin visible over the high waisted pants, a tease more than anything, while the white over shirt, unbuttoned, toned down the colors.

"See?" Shiloh smirked, the look even better than he'd anticipated. "I couldn't pull it off, not with this hair, but you make it work."

Ryder beamed. "Your turn now."

They each paraded out several of their outfits. In the end, Shiloh's armload of 'maybe's' had turned into a slightly smaller armload of 'definitely buying'. And, to make everything even better, the total cost of what he could mix and match into fifteen or so outfits, was less than he normally spent on a single pair of shoes.

Ryder walked out of the store with less, but only because he claimed he was running out of closet space and Mason would *"Literally murder me with a clothes hanger"* if he brought any more home.

Shiloh followed Ryder out to his car, a pink Jeep with a ton of bumper stickers. They chatted while Ryder stuffed the trunk with his purchases, his bags stacked only slightly precariously to fit.

"You have to come over to dinner again before you go back to Austin," Ryder insisted as he shut the trunk. "Tomorrow night, maybe? We can make the guys cook while we do each other's makeup."

Gage laughed, "Oh, I see how it is. You guys get to pamper yourselves while we slave away in the kitchen."

Shiloh batted his eyes. "How else do you think we stay this pretty?"

"I assumed we were in a Disney fairytale, so you woke up like this. Don't the birds help do your hair?" Gage answered dryly.

Shiloh blinked at him. "What about my life leads you to think Disney fairytale?"

"The pink hair?" Gage asked.

Ryder laughed. "That's anime, dude."

"Isn't that the thing with the tentacles?"

"Are you talking about porn?" Shiloh wondered, choking on a laugh. What on earth did Gage watch when he jacked off? Shiloh had assumed he watched twinks getting railed by bears with tattoos…

Gage's cheeks turned red. "I didn't say I watched it."

"You didn't say you didn't," Ryder crowed.

"It's not fair if you two gang up on me." Gage crossed his arms and frowned, and damn if it didn't look like he was pouting.

"Aw, now he's talking about a gangbang," Shiloh teased. "Jeez, who knew you were so kinky."

"I didn't say—" Gage started to defend himself, but Ryder didn't let him.

"I'll have to ask Mason. He gets jealous easy." Ryder tugged out his phone like he was going to text his husband.

An expression of pure horror spread over Gage's face, and he jerked forward, arm reaching like he meant to snatch Ryder's phone.

Ryder pulled away too quickly, his eyes gleaming. "Uh-uh, I already asked him." As he spoke, his phone *dinged,* then *dinged* again. "Mason says that... Oh. Hmm-m... Well, he says he wants to see you and to ignore the giant bazooka. It'll only hurt a little."

"I'm going to die," Gage said. Shiloh laughed at the still slightly horrified but mostly resigned look on his face. "I never should have introduced you two. Mason's going to kill me."

"Oh, don't worry," Shiloh purred, shifting all his bags to one arm so he could pat Gage comfortingly on the shoulder. "I'm sure Mason will only kill you a little bit."

For some reason, Gage didn't look like that made him feel better.

Chapter Thirty-Nine

Gage listened to the laughter spilling out from the open bathroom window above him, unable to hold back his smile. It was nice to hear and to know that, despite everything he had gone through, Shiloh could still laugh. Ryder, too, since Gage knew just enough about his boss's husband to know he hadn't had an easy life either.

"It's nice, isn't it?" Mason said from his place near the grill.

"I'm just glad they get along. He needs a friend," Gage admitted, taking a sip of his beer. He didn't drink often—couldn't when he was on the job—but even off the clock, he never drank anything harder.

"So does Ryder. He spends more time on his computer than with real people," Mason said as he flipped the burgers. Ryder was a Penetration Tester for the NSA—which, from what little Gage understood, was basically a hacker, but legal. When he wasn't off working for the government, though, Gage knew he spent his time searching the dark web for his older brother, who'd gone missing when Ryder had been in middle school.

"While the boys are occupied, though," Mason started, clearing his throat as he put the spatula down and turned to face Gage full-on, "What are your plans after the weekend? Phoenix is available to fly down to Austin any time after Monday. Will you be heading back then or staying longer? We love to have you around, but I need to get flights arranged and such."

"I'm not sure yet," Gage admitted. "Shiloh seems to be enjoying himself, and it's nice to see him relax, but I know we can't stay forever. Even if his dad wasn't in the hospital, the paparazzi will catch up to him eventually, and he'll be in danger from the stalker again."

"Did you talk to him yet?" Mason asked.

Gage nodded, jaw clenching painfully until he forced himself to answer. "Yes." As much as he wanted to, he couldn't keep what Shiloh told him a secret, not if he wanted his boss's help. He relayed what he'd learned, ending with, "Shiloh's friend Teddy sent me the copies of the pictures I sent you. While there's no proof the injuries were caused by Lawson, they'll at least prove that *someone* was hurting him."

"It's better than nothing," Mason agreed. "If it were me, I'd convince him to head back on Monday and go to the police. They'll need more evidence, but at least he can start a report. I'll also work on some short-term housing. Until we figure things out, I'd rather Shiloh not stay at his dad's or anywhere someone might think to look."

"I don't see a problem with that. Especially—" Gage cut himself off as the thundering sound of feet on the stairs inside signaled Ryder and Shiloh's descent from upstairs. And he hadn't stopped a minute too soon, because the door opened and the two laughing men spilled out onto the back patio. Shiloh was in front, racing to the yard. Gage caught only a glimpse of what looked like vivid blue eye shadow on one eye then he was past him.

He got a better look at Ryder, who looked like a poorly done up drag queen, if their makeup had been done by a toddler. Bright red lipstick spilled over his lips onto his chin and his eyeliner stretched nearly to the hair line.

"You didn't let me finish!" Ryder hollered after Shiloh.

"You'll have to catch me first," Shiloh called back, glancing over his shoulder with a manic grin.

Gage laughed out loud. He didn't know what Ryder meant to do, but Shiloh looked like a circus clown, blue eyeshadow all the way up to his eyebrows, red circles in the center of each cheek and one on his nose.

"Be careful, boys or you'll—" Mason started to chastise the pair as they chased each other, but before he could finish, Ryder's foot caught on a clump of grass and he tripped forward, tackling Shiloh to the grass.

Gage jerked forward, about to go check on him, when Shiloh started laughing. "I thought you said you couldn't play football? That was a hell of a tackle."

Ryder rolled off Shiloh and stood up like he was on fire. "Oh, gross," he whined, glaring at his grass-stained knees in disgust.

Gage watched Shiloh glance down at his hands and chuckled at the face he made. "Oh, gross," Shiloh repeated his friend's words.

Mason shook his head and started into the lawn, Gage on his heels. Mason took Ryder's hand and started leading him back inside. "Come on, baby. Let me take care of those before they stain and you become my little green-kneed monster."

Shiloh watched his friend walk off, his eyes widening when, before they were properly inside, Ryder said, "But, Daddy, I'd make a great monster."

Gage crouched down in front of Shiloh. "Will you let me clean you up, baby?"

"Like..." Shiloh glanced up at him, then back toward the door. "Are they...?"

"Normally, I'd say it's not my business, but I don't think Ryder would mind me saying that yes, Mason is his Daddy." Gage wouldn't usually out anyone, but Ryder never made it a secret. He called Mason 'Daddy' whenever he was feeling little, no matter who was around.

"And...you'll help me clean up like...like Mason is going to help Ryder?" Shiloh asked, and his voice was filled with longing but also fear.

"If you'll let me."

Shiloh didn't answer for so long that Gage thought he wasn't going to before he finally gave a small nod. "Okay."

Gage couldn't restrain his smile as he stood and helped Shiloh up, leading him inside and upstairs to the bathroom. "Here... Sit down, baby." He helped Shiloh sit on the closed toilet seat, even though he didn't really need the assistance. But something inside him crowed when Shiloh allowed it.

Gage wet a washcloth with soap and water then started slowly cleaning the dirt off Shiloh's palms, making sure to get in between his fingers and over his knuckles, even though they didn't need it. As he slowly washed away the dirt, he crooned, "You looked like you were having so much fun playing with your new friend."

"I was," Shiloh admitted, watching Gage's hands.

"I'm glad. You should be more careful, though. I don't like it when you get hurt." Gage lifted Shiloh's hands, kissing the palm of one, then the other. "There…all better."

"Thank you, D—" Shiloh froze before the word could slip free, twisting his face in panic, but Gage kissed his forehead and it seemed to calm Shiloh down.

"Come on. Let's go downstairs. The burgers should be nearly done by now."

Shiloh followed Gage downstairs, but he wasn't paying much attention. All he could think of was the feel of Gage's fingers on his. Nobody had helped him wash his hands in…God, he couldn't even remember. Maybe his dad had, when he had been really little, but he didn't remember. His dad had always too busy with work.

He was still reliving the moment in the bathroom when he sat down at the patio table beside Ryder. "It's weird at first," Ryder said quietly without prompting, "letting someone take care of you."

"Is it that obvious?" Shiloh asked, feeling warmth spread through his face. He could dance nearly naked in clubs, blow men in bathrooms, see his face on cover after magazine cover, but something about this made him feel exposed.

"Not really," Ryder admitted. "Maybe a little, but only because I've been in that seat before. When I first ran into Mason, I was adamant that I was going to do everything on my own. I didn't need anyone to take care of me. Now, coming home and letting Mason be Daddy is the best part of my day."

"It doesn't make you feel weak?" Shiloh asked, then kicked himself as the words came out, hearing how they sounded. "Not that I think you're weak... I just mean..."

"That you feel weak letting Gage take over sometimes." Ryder's smile was gentle, not teasing at all.

"Yeah...like I'm failing somehow if I give in. Or..." Shiloh hesitated as the thought finished in his mind. He took a steadying breath. "I feel like by letting Gage take control now, I'm saying that I wanted what happened when I was younger."

Ryder looked sympathetic. "I don't know what happened before, but I promise it doesn't mean that. It's okay to want to let someone you care about care for you. I like being spanked, but that doesn't mean it was okay for my dad to hit me when he got drunk, right?"

Shiloh, halfway through lifting his glass of wine to his mouth, slammed it back to the table at the thought. "No! He sounds like an asshole."

"Exactly." Ryder gave a bright grin. "You're allowed to want what you want with someone you trust."

It was like a weight was lifted off his chest. He was sure he'd heard it before, but it had never clicked for him, never made sense the way it did now with Ryder saying it. Maybe it was because he didn't know Ryder well, or maybe it was because he trusted Ryder more than he did his old friends, except for Teddy. But he rarely spoke to Teddy about things like this—probably because he knew what Teddy would say, but he hadn't been ready to hear it. Not then.

He glanced at Gage. Maybe he was now.

Chapter Forty

Something had changed over the course of the evening. Gage noticed it immediately. Shiloh was... calmer. And on the ride home, he seemed distracted, staring out of the window the entire drive but stuck in his own head. Or so Gage assumed, based on how he opened the passenger door for Shiloh and still had to tell him that they were home three times before Shiloh blinked and came back to himself.

"Sorry," Shiloh mumbled.

"No need to be." Gage held out his hand. "Come on. Let's go inside."

Shiloh took it without protest and allowed Gage to lead him in, following him mutely into the living room. "Are you thirsty? I can get you something..." Gage trailed off as Shiloh spilled like water off the couch onto his knees and blinked up at him through shuttered eyes.

"I don't need anything to drink. I just need you." There was a brief hesitation before Shiloh drew in a breath and added, "Daddy."

It was like the world froze for just a second, then everything inside Gage heightened. Shiloh had called him that before in jest and he'd protested, but this felt different. He'd been in power exchange relationships before, but not like this—not one that felt this real.

He groaned, threading his fingers through Shiloh's hair, using it to tip his face back so he could see it better. "You mean that, baby?"

"Every word," Shiloh promised. "I trust you to take care of me."

And that was exactly what Gage wanted, more than fucking, more than breathing. "I will, baby. I promise."

"I trust you," Shiloh said again, but this time, like he was speaking to himself, and he sounded surprised—like it was something he never expected to say out loud, let alone mean. It both broke Gage's heart and at the same time, filled him with a need to take Shiloh, claim him and never let him go.

"If you tell me to stop, I will," Gage promised, tightening his fingers in Shiloh's hair as he spoke, tugging until Shiloh leaned closer.

"My safeword is red," Shiloh blurted, his skin turning pink at the admission.

"Such a good boy for telling me that," Gage praised. He let go of Shiloh's hair to run his fingers across Shiloh's cheek and down his neck instead. "Now tell me your limits, baby."

Shiloh's skin warmed even further under his hands, but he didn't take long to answer, rattling it off in a rehearsed spiel. "No bathroom play, no permanent damage and I don't do bareba—" Shiloh broke off, teeth digging into his lip. "Sorry," he finally whispered.

"You don't have anything to apologize for," Gage assured him, prying the soft lip free from Shiloh's teeth.

"I'm used to answering tricks and hookups, not..." Shiloh trailed off again, looking embarrassed.

"Not your Daddy?" Gage finished for him.

"Not someone who matters," Shiloh agreed. "It makes everything seem...bigger. I trust you not to hurt me, so I think my limits will be different, but... everything seems so much more real now. I know I'm good at sex, but I suck at *feelings.* I don't want to disappoint you."

"You could never disappoint me." Gage smiled confidently down at Shiloh. "I want everything to seem more real now, because it is. *This* is real. *We* are real. So I don't want you to worry about anything. I'll take care of you."

Gage straightened back up, letting his smile hint at the wicked turn his thoughts were taking. "Now, you were such a good boy at dinner tonight, and I believe I made you a promise." He dropped his hands to his belt and unbuckled it, slowly unthreading it from his belt hooks and letting it drop with a *thud* to the floor behind him.

Shiloh's focus locked on his fingers as he popped the button on his jeans and lowered his zipper one microscopic centimeter at a time. His grin widened when Shiloh whimpered. Gage hooked his thumbs into his pockets, feeling his jeans sag lower on his hips, his fly gaping open only inches from Shiloh's face.

Shiloh swayed forward but Gage stepped back, out of reach, and *tsk*ed. "Naughty boy, I didn't tell you that you could touch me yet."

Shiloh's whole body shuddered at the mock disappointment in Gage's voice, but his eyes stayed locked on the triangle of skin revealed by Gage's jeans. He wasn't wearing briefs and he knew it would take only the smallest tug on his pants for his throbbing erection to pop free. He was dressed to the left today, and he knew Shiloh could tell from the prominent bulge.

"Please?" Shiloh begged, only barely seeming to restrain his hands from reaching out to touch. He fisted them on his thighs instead.

"Please what?" Gage pressed.

"Please let me touch you, Daddy." Shiloh's voice was needy.

"You want to worship me?" Gage asked, reaching inside his jeans and fishing himself out. His cock was thick and throbbing, flushed red at the tip.

Shiloh nodded, slipping his tongue free to wet his lips. "Please, Daddy, can I?"

Gage shucked his jeans, kicking them somewhere behind him. There was something powerful about standing nude in his living room while Shiloh knelt, fully clothed, in front of him. Gage took himself in hand and stroked, enjoying the way Shiloh's eyes followed the movement and the soft, needy whine that spilled from the boy's mouth.

"I'll give you a choice," Gage decided. "You can worship my cock and let me come down your pretty throat, or"—he grinned—"you can worship my prosthesis, and I'll come in your tight little ass."

Shiloh groaned and practically collapsed onto his stomach in his haste, no hesitation before his mouth was on the sleek titanium that made up Gage's lower left leg. Gage couldn't feel it, but the sight sent electric shocks straight to his dick. There was no disgust on Shiloh's face, no revulsion, just a determination to do a good job. And any questions of whether the boy was enjoying it were immediately quashed at the sight of Shiloh humping his hips against the carpet.

Gage shifted his leg forward, out from under Shiloh's mouth, sliding it lower instead, until he could prod Shiloh's stomach gently. "None of that, baby. Good boys don't hump the floor."

Shiloh whined, "But, Daddy…" He blinked up at Gage, his eyes wide and face flushed with arousal.

"Aw, does my baby need something?" Gage shifted his leg forward a bit more, until the cool titanium butted right up against the crotch of Shiloh's jeans. "Go ahead, baby. Use Daddy's leg to get yourself off."

Gage watched closely, wondering if he'd pushed too far, too fast, but Shiloh just shuddered and obediently humped his hips against Gage's leg, the sounds spilling from his lips not even words, just needy whimpers. Shiloh's face was pink, and even though his embarrassment was obvious, the arousal was even easier to read.

Shiloh gasped, his eyes glazed. "Daddy, I…I'm so close. I need…"

"Aw, baby, tell me what you need." Gage loved how simple it was to send Shiloh tumbling into submission. He looked so needy, flushed red like this as he humped Gage's leg, his hips moving jerkily. The only thing better would be if Gage could feel his heat against his skin, but this was a close second. It had taken him years to accept his prosthesis, to learn to trust it as a part of himself—to be thankful for the ways it improved his life instead of regretful.

"I don't know," Shiloh whined, gripping Gage's thighs, his fingers curling and uncurling against his skin.

"Take yourself out. I want you to rub your hot, needy cock against me. Think about how nice the cool metal will feel against your soft skin." Gage practically purred at the frantic way Shiloh hurried to obey, tearing open his jeans to release his smaller cock. It was nearly purple, and pearly fluid beaded at the tip. When he obediently began to rub it over Gage's prosthesis, it left a glistening trail behind that made Gage moan aloud. "Such a good boy, tell Daddy how that feels."

"It's so hot, Daddy," Shiloh panted, his hips jerking erratically.

"Go on, baby. Come on Daddy's leg," Gage coaxed.

Shiloh came with a keening shudder, his eyes fluttering closed as his cock pumped shot after shot of cum onto Gage's leg. Gage stroked Shiloh's hair through the aftershocks, humming with approval. After a long stretch of seconds, Shiloh opened his eyes and stared at the proof of his orgasm on the silver metal.

"I…I made a mess, Daddy," Shiloh finally said, eyes skirting up to his and back down.

"Maybe you should clean it up," Gage suggested.

"Yes, Daddy," was Shiloh's answer, and he leaned forward again, licking his seed off the metal until it shone.

"Such a good boy," Gage continued stroking Shiloh's hair, enjoying the way Shiloh leaned into his palm.

When Shiloh deemed the prosthesis clean, he blinked upward, his eyes stalling on Gage's cock, hard and throbbing. "Are you going to fuck me with that?" he asked in a breathy voice.

Gage gripped the base and rubbed the tip over Shiloh's pretty mouth. "Are you going to let Daddy put it in your tight little ass?"

"Yes, Daddy, I want it." Shiloh was still soft, still sated from his orgasm, but Gage wouldn't have been able to tell from the needy look on the boy's face. His breath against Gage's slit made him grit his teeth.

"Then go into the bedroom and lay in the middle of Daddy's bed. I want you hard and waiting for me by the time I get in there," Gage ordered.

Shiloh pushed himself to his feet and scampered down the hall, the firm globes of his ass wiggling in his hurry.

Gage took his time following, pausing to fold his pants and put them in the laundry room and to fish a bottle of lube out of the hallway bathroom. He doubted it would take Shiloh long to get hard again, but half the thrill came from making him wait. He wanted Shiloh aching before he finally claimed him.

Shiloh was sure aching. He was already half hard when he threw himself onto the mattress in Gage's bedroom and it only took a handful of strokes to get all the way there. He'd never felt like this, like he was just going to die if someone didn't fuck him immediately. Sex had been good, before. It wasn't like he'd been a martyr. He didn't fuck a trick if he didn't think he'd get *some* pleasure for it, but it had always felt like a means to an end. Have an orgasm, make some money, go home.

The orgasm had never been the be-all and end-all part of sex. It had been nice, something to hope for, but not necessary. Not something that felt like he'd die without…and it wasn't even *his* orgasm he was craving right now, not after the way he'd exploded in the living room.

He wanted to feel Gage lose control…to *make* Gage lose control because of *him.* Humping Gage's leg like a dog in heat should have been embarrassing. More than embarrassing, it should have been humiliating. Instead, it had been the hottest moment of his life.

Shiloh let go of his dick to trail his fingers lower, circling his rim. Hadn't Gage said he'd wanted Shiloh hard and waiting for him? That meant he was allowed to touch himself *there,* right? Would Daddy be mad if he put his fingers in his tight little hole?

Just the thought made him moan. Needing permission to prep himself was nothing he'd ever considered erotic before, not even in his fantasies. He wanted Gage to walk in and punish him for playing with himself without permission.

He'd barely slid the tip of his forefinger inside his hole when Gage stopped in the doorway. It made Shiloh feel even smaller on the bed and he moaned, slipping his finger deeper.

"Getting started without me, are you?" Gage grinned, not sounding angry at all. "Maybe I should just sit here and watch."

"No, Daddy, I want you to fuck me," Shiloh protested, immediately pulling his finger out of his hole and spreading his thighs. He knew how he looked like this, wanton and slutty, and a part of him wanted to feel shamed by that. A larger part of him didn't care. Gage knew what he was…*who* he was…before this whole thing had started. If he wanted Shiloh to change, he'd tell him. Until then, he was going to be a slutty little brat if he wanted to be.

Chapter Forty-One

Gage stalked into the room like a a large cat, and Shiloh felt like his prey. The thought sent a shiver down Shiloh's spine, and he fisted his fingers in the comforter beneath him to keep from touching himself. Gage crawled up onto the bed and between Shiloh's thighs, hovering over him with a wicked smirk.

Shiloh tilted his hips, the tip of his erection dragging along Gage's abs. It sent a double shock of electricity straight to his balls—one from the feeling, and a second following closely behind when Gage *tsk*ed, pressing Shiloh's hips back to the mattress with a firm hand.

"You'll get what I give you," Gage said, his voice far too calm. Shiloh wanted him panting, desperate—like Shiloh was.

"Then give me your cock," Shiloh demanded. Tried to demand, anyway, because it came out like a plea.

"Oh, don't worry, you'll get it." Gage did something with his hips, a slow, rolling thrust that slid his cock just right against Shiloh's.

"Fuck," Shiloh gasped at the feeling.

Gage landed a sharp slap on Shiloh's hip and the pain made everything sharper. "Language, baby."

"F…fudge?" Shiloh tried to correct but it felt like his brain was offline. All he could think was *more, more, more…*

"Such a good boy," Gage practically cooed down at him. It was…not *quite* condescending, not in a way that made him feel less. Just in a way that made him feel small and that feeling slid under his skin like needles. It should have been painful but instead, it was as calming as it ever was.

Gage laid his hand on the center of Shiloh's chest and for a long stretch of moments, it rested there, like he was feeling the patter of Shiloh's heartbeat. Heat flooded Shiloh's body, warming his cheeks and neck as the flush spread, but Gage finally started to move. He flicked Shiloh's right nipple. Shiloh sucked in a sharp breath at the feeling, his nipple beading. When Gage flicked his left, Shiloh couldn't help but arch up into it.

"Nuh-uh, baby, stay still. Take what Daddy gives you." Gage grinned and Shiloh knew he was enjoying himself.

"Is Daddy going to give me his cock soon?" Shiloh wondered aloud. "Because otherwise I'm going to explode."

"I'll teach you patience eventually." Gage slid his hand lower, trailing down each already-taut muscle of Shiloh's abs.

"Does it have to be today?" Shiloh whined as goosebumps spread over his skin wherever Gage touched.

"No, baby, it doesn't." With that, Gage took a firm grip on Shiloh's cock and pumped it until Shiloh was leaking. He shifted back on his knees so he could slip his other hand between Shiloh's thighs, taking the opportunity to roll Shiloh's balls in his palm.

Shiloh keened, his body quaking at the dual sensation. "Daddy, I can't… I'm going to come. I'm so close, Gage, please, *please.*"

Immediately, Gage released him, and the loss made Shiloh cry out, while pumping his hips into air. Gage gave him several moments to calm down before he took him in hand again. This time, one hand closed around his dick and the other dipped lower. Shiloh felt Gage's finger circle his rim, pressing gently but not entering. He shifted his hips, trying to fuck himself back on it but Gage didn't allow it. He just made gentle, teasing circles until Shiloh was a desperate, writhing mess, then he pulled away.

Shiloh whined at the loss then Gage was back, and this time, there was no hesitation. Gage slid a lubed finger into Shiloh's waiting ass. Shiloh clenched around the probing digit, heightening the sensation even further. "More, Daddy," he gasped, thrusting his hips as much as he could.

"You ready for another, baby?" Gage pulled out but slid in a second finger before Shiloh could miss him. The stretch was doubly intense but still, not enough.

"More," Shiloh demanded.

"Greedy boy." Gage didn't look angry, though. If anything, he looked hungry, a wicked glint in his brown eyes. Gage gave him three fingers and Shiloh rode the burn, the feeling in that halfway place between pleasure and pain.

After several long seconds, Shiloh let out a breath. "I'm ready—Oh, God." Shiloh broke off with a moan as

Gage crooked his fingers, stroking Shiloh's prostate in a way that made him see stars.

"I'm not a God, but I might let you worship me," Gage mused, his eyes glinting, but he slowly removed his fingers. Shiloh watched with hooded eyes as Gage sheathed himself with a condom and leisurely coated it with lube, as if he weren't just as desperate as Shiloh, but the flush of his skin and the steely hardness of his cock betrayed him. He was just as needy as Shiloh. He was just better at hiding it. It made Shiloh feel better about his own panted breaths.

The blunt head of Gage's cock pressing up against his hole felt like a baseball bat. Shiloh could take it—knew he could—but for just a second, it felt too big, too *real.* Before he could tense, though, Gage was sliding inside him. There was no stopping him, but Shiloh didn't want him to stop, not until he'd taken every last inch. And take it he did.

Soon, Gage's balls were pressed against Shiloh's skin, their hips nestled together. Gage was big. Not the biggest Shiloh had ever taken, but he was no size queen. It was almost too much, his whole body strung tight as a drum.

"God, baby, you're so fucking tight," Gage breathed, clamping his hands on Shiloh's hips to still the instinctive rocking of his pelvis. He couldn't help it. He needed Gage to move. "Wait, baby," Gage murmured.

"I can't. You feel so good." Shiloh reached between them to take his cock in hand. He didn't stroke, just gripped tight at the base, the only thing that kept him from coming. Maybe Gage could tell and that was why he didn't protest.

"I'm not going to last." Gage might sound like he was disappointed by that, but Shiloh wasn't, because he wasn't going to last long either.

"Just give it to me, Daddy, I want it. We can have a marathon later, but I'm ready now..." Shiloh was so ready. He could feel the way his balls had drawn up tight to his body, the only thing keeping him from shooting the hand he had gripped on his cock like a vise.

"Go ahead, baby. Come for me. Show me how good you feel," Gage said before lowering his face to the crook of Shiloh's neck, mouthing his skin.

"So good, Daddy," Shiloh bit out, but that was all he could say before he was spilling onto his chest. Lightning shot through his body from his cock to the soles of his feet and all the way back up to his clenched jaw.

Before he'd come down from his own orgasm, Gage's hips stuttered as he joined him, digging his fingers painfully into Shiloh's skin, the bite of pain dragging the pleasure out even further.

Gage slumped across him, draping over Shiloh like a warm blanket, and Shiloh wished they could stay like that forever. Unfortunately, he knew from experience that there was nothing sexy about being cum-stuck together.

Gage must have thought the same, because he allowed them to stay pressed together for only a few minutes more, languidly stroking along Shiloh's skin, before he pulled away with a sigh. "Time to go clean up, baby."

"Do we have to?" Shiloh asked, wishing they could stay together for just five more minutes.

"Yes, baby. Move your butt." Gage rolled off him and stood, holding out his hand. Shiloh groaned but took it, allowing Gage to lever him off the bed and lead him into the bathroom. It was smaller than the one Shiloh grew up with, but the bath was larger, taking up almost a full half of the room. The shower that Shiloh had used the day before looked small in comparison, tucked into the corner.

Shiloh glanced between the two, then back at Gage. "You can't take a shower with me, but…we could take a bath, right?"

Gage hesitated, the expression on his face the closest thing to fear Shiloh had ever seen. A soft, warm feeling spread through his chest, and he stepped closer, wrapping his arms around Gage's waist. It felt odd, but not bad. It had been so long since he'd touched someone without it leading to sex.

There was several seconds of silence before Gage cupped a hand on the back of Shiloh's neck, the other stroking gently down his spine. "If that's what you want."

"Is…it what *you* want?" Shiloh asked. He didn't want to make Gage uncomfortable.

"Yeah. Yeah, I think I do." Gage gave one last stroke down Shiloh's spine.

Gage hadn't taken his prosthesis off in full view of another person since he'd gotten out of rehab. If he had to, like back at the estate with Shiloh, he tried to keep his stump under the hem of his pants. He wasn't embarrassed, but he just knew some people were uncomfortable by it, and he never wanted to see that look on someone's face, especially not someone who was important to him. But, if he wanted this to work, he had to trust Shiloh.

He sat on the closed toilet lid before depressing the button on the side of his prosthesis and working it off, leaning it against the wall between the tub and the toilet where he could reach it easily, then peeled off the liner. As much as he wanted to immediately climb into the tub, he didn't.

Instead, he glanced over at Shiloh, nerves sparking in his belly, but the boy didn't look disgusted or pitying. Instead, Shiloh had a hand curled around his steadily growing cock. "God, you're like sex on a fucking stick," the boy moaned, wetting his lip with his tongue. "Are you sure we have to get cleaned up?"

Any lingering fear Gage had dried up and he laughed. "Yes, baby. You've got cum stuck to your skin."

"We could add some more," Shiloh said, but it came out like a question…or a plea.

"Come here," Gage ordered, and Shiloh did, and the thrill of that, more than anything, brought Gage's cock back from the dead. "On your knees."

Shiloh dropped, locking his eyes on the growing shaft. Gage gripped it, angling the head of his cock down. "Is this what you want, baby?"

"Yes…" Shiloh moaned, swaying closer.

Gage dropped a hand to Shiloh's throat. He didn't squeeze, simply halted the forward motion, keeping Shiloh's mouth only just close enough to feel the breath on his dick. "Here's what's going to happen. You're going to help me into the tub, and we're going to get you all clean. Then, if you're good, we'll get you dirty again."

Shiloh moaned, but the sound was all agreement.

Chapter Forty-Two

It could have been nerve-racking, helping Gage into the tub, but instead, it was erotic. Gage spent the entire time in between issuing gentle instructions, running his hands over Shiloh's body, teasing him until he could hardly think. But they both ended up safely in the tub, Shiloh nestled between Gage's thighs with his back against the hard chest. The head of Shiloh's cock was red and flushed where it peeked out of the water.

Of course, Gage ignored it. He ran a washcloth down one of Shiloh's arms, then the other, over his chest. Everywhere but where Shiloh wanted his hands. And, when he finally did wrap his cock in the washcloth, it was only for a quick stroke, cleaning off the old cum but leaving him wanting.

"Your turn, baby. Wash Daddy." Gage pressed the washcloth into Shiloh's hand and leaned back.

Shiloh twisted around, excited to get his chance to tease Gage now. He ignored the small splash of water that overflowed onto the floor as he reached for the body wash, adding it to the cloth and working up a lather. He ran it over Gage's flesh, careful around the still-bandaged arm, regretting that the fabric separated their skin. He wanted Gage panting, moaning under his—

"That's enough," Gage ordered.

Shiloh whimpered as he dropped the washcloth. "Seriously?"

Gage landed a swat on Shiloh's bottom. "Don't sass."

"You like my *sass,*" Shiloh teased, rocking his hips against Gage's.

"Yeah, I really do," Gage agreed, then he was cupping Shiloh's ass, kneading the flesh and that was really all Shiloh could concentrate on. Just the feeling of his fingers digging in, then pulling apart his cheeks until water rushed in against his sore pucker, then massaging again… It was driving him crazy.

From the smirk on Gage's face, he knew it.

"Don't tease me," Shiloh groaned, pushing his ass back into Gage's hands. "I need…"

"I know what you need," Gage agreed, and he did. He slid a finger into Shiloh's crack, circling around his hole before sliding into the still-loose rim. Shiloh hissed at the sting but then Gage's other hand was gripping both of their dicks together in a loose fist and it was exactly what he wanted.

"Take what you need, baby." Gage finally give him permission to move, so he did, rocking into the steady grip, then back onto the probing finger, until each movement had him either fucking or being fucked.

But it was the expression on Gage's face that finally tipped him over, the intensity mixed with the desire. When he spilled, it was everything he never knew he needed, then Gage followed him, his cum mixing with Shiloh's into the water.

Quivering with aftershocks, Shiloh folded over onto Gage's chest, breathing hard. He could stay like this forever.

Or at least until the water went cold, which it inevitably did. It led to another quick wash up before they drained the tub and Gage allowed Shiloh to help him out. Allowed, Shiloh realized, because Gage was fully capable of taking care of himself. If a gunman had burst in halfway through, Shiloh was fully confident that Gage would have been able to defend them both, leg or no leg. That Gage would allow Shiloh to help made him feel warm inside, like he mattered.

He dried Gage off, and Gage even let him help reattach his prosthesis. It was intimate, more intimate than sex. On instinct, Shiloh dropped a kiss to Gage's kneecap. Gage ran his fingers through Shiloh's hair in return.

"Ready for bed, baby?" Gage asked. Shiloh's answer was a yawn.

He slept a rejuvenating, deep sleep then woke in the dark, before dawn had even crested on the horizon. He was not a morning person by any means. He'd sleep until noon if his lifestyle allowed it. This morning was different, though. Maybe it was that, for the first time in years, he woke with no secrets and no threatening shadows in his mind. Maybe it was that Gage's arms were still around him like a suit of armor.

Either way, he felt like he was finally ready to face his dad—and his past with it.

"Thinking deep thoughts?" Gage asked, breaking the comfortable silence that settled between them.

"I think I need to go home," Shiloh said. "I'm ready to see my dad."

* * * *

The flight home was just as terrifying as the flight out, and this time he didn't even have the destination to look forward to. It wasn't that Shiloh didn't want to see his dad, because he did. He loved him. But he didn't want to see pity in his father's eyes or, worse, any disbelief. Maybe it was the fear of flying, but it was like every ounce of bravery he'd summoned fled before they landed.

His hands were shaking as he pulled his luggage off the carousel. Even Gage looked tense, though probably for different reasons. It was like he'd been able to relax in Seattle, away from the threat of a stalker, but now that threat was back threefold.

He scanned the airport like at any second, a dozen men were going to burst out with guns and nets to snag him. Shiloh almost made a joke, but he refrained, knowing Gage was under a lot of stress trying to keep him safe. For once, he didn't feel like making that job harder. Gage had agreed to coming back early, but Shiloh knew he wasn't happy. He'd heard the muted conversations Gage'd had with his boss, arranging flights and hotel rooms and making plans to keep them safe until Shiloh's new guard could fly down.

So he let Gage lead the way, doing everything Gage asked without question, even if it didn't make any sense to him. He trusted Gage. By the time they were in a rented sedan pulling away from the airport, even he was nervous, scanning every person. Did that man look suspicious with his briefcase and tennis shoes? Was that woman's baby just a little too still? If this was what Gage went through every day, if this was what *each* of his guards had felt like, he was almost ashamed for the hell he'd put them through.

Almost.

Some of them had deserved it.

Gage's voice pulled him from his thoughts. "Mason's laying some rumors in Seattle that you're going to be attending a ballet tonight, so I'm hoping no one will realize you're back in town. But, just in case, we're not going in through the parking garage this time. I'm going to park on the street and we're going to get inside as quickly as possible. When we leave, I'm going to call us an Uber and we'll arrange to have the car picked up later. If anyone *is* looking for the car, maybe they won't notice we've left."

"Sir, yes, sir." Shiloh snapped off a salute. He flashed a cocky grin to make sure Gage knew that while he might be joking, he was definitely listening.

"Brat," Gage teased as he parked the car against the curb. Shiloh resisted the urge to jump out and waited—impatiently, but waited—for Gage to round to the sidewalk and open his door for him. Gage hustled him inside to the front desk.

For a second, everything slowed. Shiloh was fourteen again, coming to see his dad, fear like acid in his throat, but then the receptionist lifted her hands from the keyboard with an overworked sigh and he was back in the present. "Can I help you?"

"Can you tell me what room Anthony Beckett is in?" Shiloh asked. Gage shifted so his back was to the desk, eyes scanning the lobby.

The receptionist's fingers clattered on the keys, then she frowned. "I'm sorry. I'm not at liberty to release that information."

"Please, I'm...I'm his son." Shiloh fumbled around his pockets for his wallet to free his ID and held it out.

The lady sighed again but took it, comparing it to something on her screen before she finally gave it back. "He's on the third floor. Room 396."

Shiloh started for the elevators. Vaguely, he heard Gage mutter a 'thank you' to the woman. He felt guilty for forgetting but not enough to turn around. It was bad enough having to stop at the doors to let Gage clear the elevator first. He held back the snarky remark about a murderer hiding in the ceiling tiles. The joke would have come out flat, since it wasn't funny, and Shiloh was legitimately afraid.

Not of stalkers hiding in ceiling tiles, but of facing his father—though there was a small part of him worried that the bastard from the parking garage would be back. He shoved that fear aside, because otherwise, he knew he'd be rocking in the corner until they locked him up in a crazy ward.

It was easy to find Room 396—not just because the signs were large and complete with arrows, but because his dad's head of security was sitting in a folding chair outside the door, playing with his phone.

It was significantly harder to convince himself to enter. Gage finally laid a comforting hand on Shiloh's shoulder, which spurred him to move. He stepped through the doorway.

It was a private room. Dad's hospital bed was to his left, midway down the wall. It was tucked between a small wooden nightstand and a steadily beeping heart monitor. The door to the attached bathroom was ajar.

Dad had the head of the bed inclined, the covers slouched over his lap. His hospital gown was baggy, sensor cords exposed at the neck and creeping out the arms. One tangled around his elbow as he shifted and Shiloh watched as his dad absently shrugged it away, too wrapped up in his phone call to pay it any attention.

"The Core Prototype was supposed to be rolled out six weeks ago, so not only is your team late, but you've also gone nearly twenty grand over budget. I've tried to give you leeway, but our investors are starting to get concerned." Dad's voice was calm and professional, but his fist was clenched in the sheets.

Shiloh stepped farther into the room and the movement must have caught his dad's eyes, because he said abruptly, "I'll give you a one-week extension." Then, he hung up and tossed his phone to the side, not seeming to care where it landed. "Hello, son. I wasn't sure if you'd come. Not that you had to… I understand if…if you need time."

Shiloh wasn't ready to talk. They needed to—God, did they need to—but not today. Instead, he moved to sit in the armchair by the window. "I'm here, aren't I?" he said, regretting it immediately as Dad's face fell. "I mean, I *want* to be here." Shiloh corrected, picking at his jeans. "I heard you on the phone," he said, changing the subject. "Is everything okay?"

It hadn't sounded okay. The last thing his dad needed while recovering from heart surgery was stress. Shiloh had enough stress for both of them.

Dad waved him off. "Just a delay with the newest line of gaming software we're hoping to drop. Nothing to worry about."

"*You* sounded worried. You're on a leave of absence, remember?" Shiloh hated how accusatory it came out, but he couldn't take it back. He hadn't had a pleasant conversation with his dad in years. He didn't even know how to start one.

Dad looked away. "I know you don't want to work at the company. I shouldn't have tried to push it on you. I shouldn't..." Dad shuddered in a breath. "I should have known what was going on."

Immediately, Shiloh knew they weren't speaking about the company anymore. His muscles tensed and he clenched the armrests. He couldn't talk about this. He didn't want his dad to know at all, and he definitely couldn't talk about it.

"The *company,*" Shiloh stressed, "can live without you for a few weeks. *You* need to concentrate on getting better."

Dad looked constipated. "Do you know how many dumpster fires I'll have to put out? I can't afford to be hands-off right now, not with Sam—" Dad's jaw clamped shut so hard on the words that Shiloh could hear his teeth click together. He turned his head away from Shiloh.

"You can't afford *not* to be," Shiloh corrected, resolutely ignoring the second, unfinished part of the sentence. "I'll set up a meeting with the board myself and make sure everything is on track. I'll even get with Tommy first." Tommy was his dad's personal assistant. Shiloh disliked him intensely, because it always seemed like Tommy was judging him. Still, he'd suck it up if it meant his dad stopped stressing.

Dad didn't look comforted, so Shiloh added, "Dad, I know the company's portfolio. Don't worry. I also know that quarterly earnings are down by half a percent from projected because of project delays, but we're slated to acquire a new app development company next month that should bump them back up. I can keep going."

Dad looked shocked. "I didn't realize you read them."

Shiloh shrugged, aiming for a nonchalance he couldn't quite feign. "I'm not as dumb as I look."

"You're not dumb at all," Dad immediately protested, his expression pained. "I know I haven't been that good of a dad, but I'll try to be better. You shouldn't... You shouldn't feel like you're not good enough just because you want different things than I want for you." Dad closed his eyes and took a deep breath, wincing. "I know I criticize your dancing, but I see how much you love it, and...and you're good. More than good."

Shiloh dropped his eyes to his lap and glared at his jeans. It was exactly what he'd always wanted to hear his dad say, but now that he had, he realized how little it changed. It had taken his dad another heart attack to get to this point—and if he were honest with himself, he knew that wasn't even the real reason. It was learning about Sam, and that cast a pall on the moment.

He didn't want his dad to let him pursue dancing because he felt guilty or, worse, because he *pitied* him. It felt almost like...like a bribe. Or a payout. *Oh, my best friend raped you for years and I didn't listen? Here's a few extra dance lessons, I guess you can finally make a few decisions about your own life. #Oops?*

Shiloh clenched his fingers on the armrests. It wasn't rational. He knew his dad loved him, that he never would have wanted anything bad to happen to him, but that didn't change how it *felt.*

Rather than make any of the snotty comments tickling his throat, he cleared it and said, "I'll call

Tommy. I'll rein in the board. I'll also see if I can set up a few meetings with some new law firms for once you're back in the office. Until then, I'll set up a temporary contract with Kabbot & Michaels. I know you'd prefer an exclusive contract, but you can negotiate that yourself when you're back in the office."

Dad grimaced. "He always calls me Tony."

Shiloh rolled his eyes at his dad. "It won't kill you. Just start calling him 'Dick' and I bet he'll stop real quick." Richard Kabbot was the type of man to spend his weekends golfing and drinking Scotch with the 'good old boys'.

Dad chuckled. "I might have to do that."

A nurse in floral scrubs peeked into the room. His already-smiling face brightened further when he spotted Shiloh and Gage. "Mr. Beckett, you have visitors! I'll just take your vitals *super* quick then get out of your hair!" He bounded into the room and over to the side of Dad's bed and...

Shiloh's eyebrows shot up at the way his dad smiled. "No need to rush, Jamie. You know you're my favorite visitor." His dad's voice was practically dripping with charm. *Oh God, is my dad flirting? With his nurse? Who's a* guy?

A young guy, who, Shiloh had to admit, was actually kind of cute, in that nerd-chic way that was more and more popular lately. If it were anyone but his dad lying in that hospital bed, he'd be shipping it so fast.

Instead, he stood abruptly. "Well, we have to go anyway, so *we'll* be getting out of your hair. Right, Gage?" Shiloh looked to his—*boyfriend? Are we dating?*—for help. Gage smirked but opened the door and checked the hallway.

Shiloh wanted to be insulted that his dad just waved him off with a simple goodbye, but the pheromones building in the room were, quite frankly, grossing him out, so he just darted into the hallway.

"Oh my God," Shiloh said to Gage as they headed to the elevators. "My dad has a *boyfriend.* Or…he wants one at least. That's so weird."

Gage laughed. "That he's flirting with the twink?"

"No, that he's flirting at all." Shiloh shuddered. "He's a parent. He's supposed to be boring." And besides, his dad wasn't gay, not that there would be a problem if he were. Shiloh would be nothing but supportive, but he *wasn't.* Dad was the one who'd kept trying to talk him into settling down with a 'nice girl'. And dad was the one who'd told him that it didn't matter what he felt, only how he looked. He'd always said that people would never look deeper than the easiest answer, so he needed to be careful.

Maybe he was speaking from experience. Shiloh had never met his grandparents. They'd died before he was born, but he knew his dad's father had been a minister. He wondered how much of his dad's concerns about his sexuality stemmed from insecurities of his own.

The look Gage gave him was amused, pulling him from his thoughts. "Poor, naïve Shiloh. If parents were *boring,* everyone would be an only child."

"No. I'm not thinking of my dad having sex." Shiloh followed Gage through the elevator doors, letting Gage press the button to send them down to the lobby. "Instead, let's talk about the logistics of how to get me back to my dad's house so I can fetch my suit."

"Shouldn't be too hard. We'll just get in the Uber and go." Gage smirked. "Security has been there twenty-four seven. We won't stay long, but it should be fine."

The Uber was already waiting outside the hospital. Gage checked the ID, even texting a picture of it to someone on his phone before he let Shiloh clamber into the backseat, following him in. Gage relayed the address to the driver, then sat back.

Shiloh slid a bit closer on the seat, suddenly feeling shy. He knew Gage wouldn't care, but for a second, he expected him to ask what he was doing. Instead, Gage just took Shiloh's hand. "That went well," Gage commented—not pressing, just opening the door to a conversation if he wanted.

"I think so. Dad's stubborn, though. I'll probably have to tell Tommy to stop answering his calls if I want him to *really* not work." Shiloh frowned. "And I don't know. That might stress him out more."

They spent the rest of the ride in a companionable silence. Shiloh wished the drive could go on forever, just him and Gage—and the Uber driver, who was kind of cute but mercifully silent—and the open road. All too soon, however, they were pulling up to the ornate gate. Gage rolled down his window and spoke to the guard house. The gates opened to allow them up the driveway.

Since Shiloh was on his own property, he didn't wait for Gage to round the car and open the door for him. He wanted to get in and out as quick as possible. He started for the door while Gage was still arranging for the driver to wait.

"Ten minutes and I'll double your tip," he heard Gage promise.

Shiloh pushed open the door and moved quickly through the atrium. He could hear whistling from the direction of the kitchen, probably Marie preparing lunch for the groundskeepers, house security and the other live-in staff. Other than that, the house was eerily quiet. Without his dad working in his office and staff bustling around preparing for his dad's meetings and business dinners, Shiloh's footsteps seemed to echo louder. Faintly, he heard the front door close downstairs, probably Gage following him in.

Shiloh turned down the hall toward his bedroom. He slowed when he saw his door was cracked open but couldn't be positive he'd shut it when he was in there last. After all, he'd been a bit preoccupied.

He pushed the door open further, then froze. In the shadow of the closet, someone was moving.

Chapter Forty-Three

It was Lawson.

Shiloh didn't need to see more than the cut of the suit and sliver of jawline to recognize him. Shiloh sucked in a breath, fear mingling with anger in the pit of his stomach. "What are you…?" Shiloh clenched his fists, realizing immediately that he didn't really give a shit *what* Lawson was doing. "Get the hell out."

Lawson turned toward him, shoving something in his pocket, a scrap of blue lace—one of his favorite pairs of panties. Shiloh couldn't bring himself to care. He just wanted the fucker gone. Lawson moved toward him, a sneer on his face. His shoulders were narrow, and he was only centimeters taller than Shiloh, but he seemed to suck all the air out of the room with his presence.

Shiloh stumbled backward into the hall, bumping into a wall when he expected to meet air, but then the wall moved, grabbing Shiloh's shoulders to steady him, and he flinched away. A darted glance over his shoulder had him relaxing when he realized it was Gage. Gage wasn't watching him, though. Instead, his eyes were narrowed on Lawson, who loomed in the doorway.

Lawson just smirked, tugging a pack of Dunhill Blacks out of his jacket pocket. Slowly, as if he didn't have a care in the world, Lawson flipped the carton open and slid out a cigarette, placing the filter between his lips as he lit the end. The ember burned red.

Shiloh flinched, the sweet smell sticking in his nostrils. He'd always hated the smell of tobacco, but something about *this* smell was worse. And worse, it was…familiar.

"It was you in the alley," Shiloh said suddenly as the scent clicked.

Lawson just flicked ashes onto the carpet and smirked. "What alley?"

Shiloh snapped. He shoved the bastard back with two hands. Lawson stumbled, surprise flickering over his face before it mutated to anger. "You best watch it, pet. The police don't look too friendly on assault."

"Assault? Assault!" Shiloh's voice raised to a near shriek. "You… You fucking raped me, you asshole, and you want to talk about *assault*?" He stepped forward to shove Lawson again, but Lawson grabbed his wrist in a bruising grip, using it to propel Shiloh backward.

A second later, Shiloh was free, Lawson's hand knocked off his wrist with a quick, barely seen motion of Gage's. "Keep your hands off him," Gage snarled.

"Tell your client to do the same." Lawson's face was a mask again.

"Touch him again and you'll have more than the police to worry about," Gage replied, his voice as serious as Shiloh had ever heard it.

"The police?" Lawson laughed. "I'm not worried about them. There isn't a cop in this town who would write me so much as a speeding ticket." He brushed past Shiloh and Gage. He was halfway down the hallway when he stopped, shooting a mean grin over his shoulder at them. "Oh, and Shiloh. Someone left a mess in your studio. You might want to go clean it up."

Shiloh took off at a run.

His studio was more than just a mess. It was trashed. The mirrors were shattered, cracks spiderwebbed across the glass, distortion his reflection, and paint, like blood, had been spilled over nearly every surface. Every surface, except for a circle in the center of the floor.

Shattered glass had been piled inside in a jagged heap, and on top was a small tube of super glue.

Shiloh went cold, then hot.

The message was crystal clear… *Keep your mouth shut.* He couldn't keep his breath from escaping his lungs faster than they could fill, his vision bleeding black at the edges.

He felt Gage backing him out of the room, heard his voice though he couldn't understand the words, but then they were outside and the fresh air hit him like a semi. He sucked in a breath, reaching up to wipe dampness from his cheeks from tears he hadn't realized were falling.

Gage was still speaking. Shiloh tuned in partway through a sentence, blinking up at him. "For me, okay? Take a breath. You can do it."

Shiloh concentrated on his breathing, nodding his head in a jerk to show he was listening. "I'm…I'm sorry. That was… I don't know what came over me."

"You have every right to be upset right now," Gage assured him.

"I know," Shiloh agreed. "It's just… That was my safe place and…"

"I get it." Gage gathered him close to his chest, stroking his fingers through Shiloh's hair. "How about this. I'm going to text Thomas and have him grab your suit and bring it down, and I'll let him know about the studio. They can get it cleaned up and arrange for the mirrors to be replaced, whatever they need to do."

"I…" Shiloh hesitated. He didn't know if he'd ever be able to use it again, after this. "Yeah, okay," he agreed, even though he wasn't sure. It would need to get cleaned up regardless. "Actually," Shiloh said abruptly, "don't bother having him bring down the suit, I'm pretty sure I spilled tequila on it. Can we just… Can I just get a new one?" he finally asked, plaintively.

"Yeah, baby. We can get you a new one." Gage grabbed his hand and squeezed it. "Let's get out of here."

They got out of there.

* * * *

Gage watched Shiloh adjust his tie for the sixth time since they'd entered the large conference room on the top floor of Beckett Industries. After tightening it further, Shiloh started fidgeting with the portfolio that was open on the table in front of him.

Gage walked over, laying a hand on Shiloh's, stilling his fingers. "You've going to do great. You've gone over the numbers how many times now?"

"Seven," Shiloh answered quietly, eyes still scanning the papers. "But I could have missed something."

"You didn't." Gage pushed a lock of Shiloh's hair behind his ear. Shiloh sighed. Before Gage could say anything else, there was a knock on the conference room door. Gage stepped back, a mask of professional sliding over his face. Right now, he had to be Shiloh's bodyguard, not his boyfriend.

A young woman with wire-frame glasses and a shock of curly red hair stepped into the room. She had a travel cup in one hand and a pad of paper in the other. "Good afternoon, Mr. Beckett," she said, placing the cup in front of Shiloh, who looked nonplussed. "Rumor has it you like hot chocolate, so I brought you a peppermint one. I hope that's okay."

She kept going before Shiloh could speak, and Gage almost smiled at her tenacity. "I also took the liberty of ordering you a feta and walnut salad with cranberry vinaigrette dressing for after your first meeting. Speaking of… You have a meeting with Mr. Yax from marketing to approve the final ad layout, but don't worry, he's made minimal changes from the original design approved by Mr. Beckett."

She leaned in like she was telling him a secret. "He changed the font from a fifteen point to a seventeen." She rolled her eyes. "Honestly, I doubt Mr. Beckett would have noticed. I'm sorry, Mr. Beckett, but that is going to get confusing. Should I call you Mr. Beckett?" Her face dropped with the question, like she was worried she would offend Shiloh.

Shiloh, however, looked like someone had just hit him over the head with a plank. "Um. I'm sorry. Who are you?"

The girl widened her eyes, and Gage had to fight back his snicker. "Oh shoot, I'm Madeline. I'm your personal assistant."

"What happened to Tommy?" Shiloh asked.

"Oh…Um…" Madeline looked flustered, glancing down at the pad of paper in her arms, visibly uncomfortable. She gathered herself. "Tommy felt it would be a conflict of interest for him to work with you instead of your father. If… If you'd rather, I can have HR send up someone else?" It was clear even to Gage that she didn't want to.

"No, it's fine. I just didn't realize that I had a personal assistant?" Shiloh said it like a question, voice lifting at the end.

"Oh, of course! I mean, I haven't had much to do yet. I've mostly been sorting your mail for you and handling PR, what I can anyway." She hesitated. "This is my first job since college, and I was lucky enough to get pulled from the intern pool. I'd understand if you'd rather have someone more experienced."

Shiloh waved her off, finally relaxing. "Not at all… We can learn together, right? And please, call me Shiloh."

She cheered back up at finally getting an answer to her question. "Great! Then if everything's all set, I'll gather the board and tell them you're ready for them."

The board, it turned out, was predominantly male, predominantly old and predominantly white. There was only one woman, a dark-haired female who sat near the door and rarely spoke. And when she did, the men beside her tended to turn away, muttering to each other rather than listening. The youngest man in the room was forty if he was a day and seemed to be a junior member.

In other words, it was exactly what he'd expected.

What he didn't expect, considering Shiloh's nerves prior to the meeting, was how well Shiloh handled their disdain. Shiloh took firm control, laying facts and figures out clearly and refusing to let the board railroad him. While Gage didn't understand half of what Shiloh was saying—he'd never been much into tech—it was obvious that Shiloh knew what he was talking about, and by the end of the meeting, at least half of the board walked out with sour faces.

It was clear they'd expected to be meeting with an incompetent boy they could walk over. Instead, they'd found a poised, knowledgeable man who hadn't hesitated to light a fire under their asses.

As soon as the door shut behind them, Shiloh sagged back into his chair. "I think that went well," he said, but Gage thought it sounded like he was reassuring himself.

"I think it did," Gage agreed. "You made them take you seriously. I'm proud of you."

Shiloh flushed, peering at him through his lashes. "Yeah?"

"Of course." Gage finally broke his stance by the wall to crouch beside Shiloh's chair. "Baby, you are so smart. You could do anything you put your mind to, so I'm not surprised you handed them their asses."

Shiloh finally grinned. "I kinda did, didn't I. God, I hate the board. They're so stuffy and old-school. There are so many things we could be doing if they'd just let us."

"I noticed they were a bit…" Gage hesitated.

"Old? Rich? White?" Shiloh snorted. "Yeah. I mean, I get it, because as much as I hate to say it, Dad is conservative when it comes to his business. These are the people who had his back, as it were, when he was just starting out, but I think they're starting to hold us back now."

"Have you spoken to your dad about it?"

Shiloh shrugged. "Not yet. I didn't think he would listen. I…might have misjudged him."

"Maybe, but you still have time. Your dad will be out of the hospital soon and you'll be able to be as involved, or not, as you wish." Gage reached out to squeeze Shiloh's hand.

Shiloh frowned, uncertainty clear on his face. "I…I don't know. I think that there are a lot of changes that could be made to make BeckTech stronger, like diversifying the board and broadening our reach into more spaces, but"—Shiloh rubbed the center of his chest—"I don't have the passion for it that Dad does. Not right now. I…want to be a dancer. Maybe I'll be more active in the company eventually. I know ballet is a short-lived career, but…I just don't know."

"And you don't have to know." Gage dropped his hand to Shiloh's knee. "We'll figure it out together. I'll be here, no matter what decision you make."

Chapter Forty-Four

The interrogation room was cold.

Shiloh slumped farther down in the uncomfortable metal chair, making the back of his suit jacket bunch up near the middle of his back. He wiggled in an attempt to straighten it out. "Shouldn't there be a *better* place to do this?" He plaintively whined to Gage, who was seated beside him. Unlike Shiloh, Gage looked right at home.

"Like what?" Gage asked, the corner of his lips quirking up.

"I don't know, somewhere with more comfortable chairs?" Shiloh shrugged, glaring at the mirrored walls. "I feel like I'm two seconds away from being put in cuffs. I'm the *victim*" – God how he hated that word – "but this room makes me think I need to call a lawyer."

"The atmosphere helps make people reconsider lying to us," a voice said from the doorway behind them. Shiloh spun around in his chair with a start. Officer Preston stood with a dossier in one hand and a coffee in the other. Once he had Shiloh's attention, he moved into the room, dropping down into the chair across from them.

A portly man Shiloh didn't know trailed along behind him. The other officer had carrot-red hair and a pudgy face, with a sour expression twisting his thin lips. He looked like he'd rather be anywhere but there.

"So, Shiloh, Mr. Tucker set up this meeting because he said you had some new information for us regarding your case. Care to share?"

Shiloh slouched even farther in his chair, his heart thumping. He didn't want to admit that he'd written some of the letters, that the whole thing had started out as a...not a scam, exactly. He hadn't ever expected to get a ransom or anything like that. A way out... That was all he'd wanted. He'd never intended on lying to the cops, though maybe he should have realized it might come to that.

Maybe they wouldn't ask about the letters, and he wouldn't have to admit anything. It wasn't lying if he just...didn't bring it up.

"I know who tried to grab me in the alley," Shiloh blurted.

Officer Preston's gaze pinned him in place, something calculating behind his blue eyes. "You said he was wearing a mask."

"I did. I mean, he *was*. But I've been thinking about it"—more like reliving it, over and over, like a movie playing on repeat—"and there are other things. Like, he smelled like cigarettes. Fancy cigarettes."

"Lots of people smoke," the other officer grunted, tapping his pen on the desk. "This is a waste of time."

Officer Preston frowned at the man. "We don't know that yet, Andy." Andy just rolled his eyes and went back to tapping his pen. Officer Preston looked back at Shiloh. "Go on. He smelled like cigarettes…"

"Dunhills," Shiloh specified. "And I *knew* his voice sounded familiar but…there was so much going on that it didn't click at the time."

Officer Preston leaned forward. "Okay. So you recognized it? Can you tell me who it was? Someone you know from school, or—"

"It was Sam Lawson."

For a second, the room froze. Nobody moved. Nobody breathed. Joy like a phoenix rose in Shiloh's chest at finally, *finally,* saying the words. It was like a weight lifting off his shoulders, but then it crashed back down when Officer Preston's face dropped and Andy made a scoffing noise in his throat.

"Pull the other one, why don't ya, kid?" Andy slouched back. "You expect us to believe that Mr. Lawson, of all people, dressed up in a mask and waited in back of a fag bar to try to grab you?"

"Andy!" Officer Preston snapped. "Watch it."

Andy rolled his eyes again. "Sorry. A *homosexual* bar."

Officer Preston sighed. "While I *don't* approve of the language my partner chooses to use, I do have to agree with the sentiment." He turned to Shiloh, a frown on his mouth. "I do find it hard to swallow that a well-renowned figure such as Sam Lawson would be involved in such a scheme. Do you have *any* proof? Or any reason *why* you think Lawson would attempt to kidnap you?"

Shiloh felt like he was walking a high wire. He could fall to one side and lie, say he made a mistake, let Lawson get away with it and not deal with the shame of having to talk about *it* and see their faces as he called him a liar. Or he could fall to the other side and tell the truth, admit what Lawson had done to him. No matter which way he fell, he knew he would crash at the bottom.

He gripped the arms of the chair and straightened his spine. If he was going down, he was taking Lawson with him—one way or another.

"Sam Lawson has been raping me for the past seven years." Shiloh stuttered as *that* word left his lips, the word that sent spiders down his spine and rocks into his stomach. It hit the air like a gunshot.

For a moment, the room was silent, then Andy huffed, his face twisted in disgust. "You expect us to believe that Samuel Lawson, an upstanding member of the community, who has donated thousands of dollars to the city and is close, *personal* friends with not only the police commissioner but the mayor, forced a"—he looked down at his notes, probably doing the math—"fourteen-year-old boy to engage in sexual relations." It wasn't a question. Officer Patches had already made up his mind.

"You don't believe me." Shiloh's voice was blank, emotionless. It wasn't like he was surprised.

"Officer Thomas just means that you're making a very serious accusation. Without evidence, it comes down to your word against Mr. Lawson's, and with your reputation..." Officer Preston winced. "Well, you'll need to be prepared that it will be an uphill battle convincing anyone to give us a warrant."

"They won't believe you, brat. Nobody will." Mr. Lawson had told him that, over and over. For a moment, Shiloh was on his stomach, Lawson's breath moist on the back of his neck as he grunted into his ear,

the words repeating in time to each harsh thrust of his hips.

"I'm not saying I don't—" Officer Preston started to answer.

Officer Andrews interrupted, his voice angry. "No, I don't. We have *real* crimes to investigate. You were probably drunk. Maybe you regretted it the next day, but that doesn't mean anything except you're a slut—"

Officer Preston hissed, "Andy!"

"You've seen the photos the same as I have," Officer Thomas snapped back, his arms crossed.

Gage slammed his hand down on the table and stood, looming over the table. "You think you know him, but you don't." His face was angry and despite that, a thrill surged through Shiloh. Gage was defending him. *Gage* was defending *him.*

"I've spent every day for the past few months with Shiloh, and he's more than just a...just a party-boy. If he says that's what happened, then that's what happened. Maybe you should spend more time trying to figure out how to investigate this and less time calling him a liar."

"I didn't—" Officer Thomas went red with anger.

"You didn't treat my client with even a shred of the respect or dignity that he deserves, and if you think that I won't be lodging an official complaint with both your boss and the Office of the Police Monitor, then you are as delusional as you are stupid."

Officer Preston laid a hand on his partner's arm, stopping whatever argument he was clearly about to spout, and said instead, "I don't think he's lying. But without evidence—"

Shiloh drew in a breath. It rattled in his lungs like broken glass as he said, "He made videos."

* * * *

Shiloh kicked the brick wall outside the police station, concentrating on the pain that spread through his foot rather than the scream building in his lungs. "I *knew* they wouldn't listen." He went to kick the wall again but Gage wrapped strong arms around his middle as he pulled him away.

"They promised they'd look into it," Gage pointed out, though even he didn't sound certain.

"Oh sure," Shiloh scoffed. "They'll *look into it* in between going for donuts and reading about me in the tabloids."

"I swear, between me and Mason, we'll be on their ass about it until they do," Gage said, spinning him around until his back was to the wall. "I promise, okay?"

Shiloh nodded. He knew Gage would do it if he said he would. Gage wouldn't lie, not to him. It was the cops he didn't have faith in. They clearly thought he was lying, or at least exaggerating. There was no way they were doing anything more than what they absolutely had to.

He knew what he had to do.

* * * *

Gage woke to the sound of groaning bed springs as Shiloh slowly rolled off the bed. He kept his eyes closed, curious what the boy was up to. He heard the sound of drawers sliding open, so slowly he could tell Shiloh was attempting to be stealthy, which immediately made him suspicious.

Shiloh had a habit of running, and he wasn't going to let him—not this time. Gage had…not suspected, exactly, but he had thought that this was a possibility. It was why he'd gone to bed with his prosthesis still attached and his shoes by the bed. It was also why he'd arranged for a simple black sedan to be left in the parking garage in case he needed it.

It seemed he would.

As soon as the room door clicked closed, Gage rolled off the bed and slipped into his shoes. Getting kitted out and ready to go in less than two minutes was almost easy after being in a combat theater for four years. Slip on boots, and grab his gun off the nightstand. There were no helmet or heavy pack to don, no binoculars or compass to keep track of.

By the time he stepped into the hallway, the elevator doors were only just closing. Gage bypassed them, taking the stairs instead. They jarred his stump, but he couldn't afford to wait. As it was, Shiloh would likely end up in his Uber before Gage could get out of the parking garage. Gage thumbed open the tracking app on his phone as he reached the lower levels, relieved when he saw the red dot was active.

The black sedan was exactly where he'd been told it would be, keys in the console. He spun them in the ignition. As soon as his phone connected to the cars Bluetooth, he hooked the navigation up to the screen before quickly making his way out to the road.

He supposed he shouldn't be surprised that the street they ended up on was familiar. The rows of brown houses were dark. The streets were quiet in the way they only were in that hazy period after the bars closed but dawn had yet to crest.

A blue Ford lingered outside a house near the end of the lane, its headlights on. Gage cursed, hoping Shiloh was still in the car and that he hadn't made a bad decision not stopping him at the hotel. He'd wanted to see where Shiloh was going but now that he knew—straight to Lawson—he wished it had remained a mystery.

Gage angled his car in front of the Uber, leaving it running as he popped out of the car and moved straight to the other. He yanked open the back door as soon as he spotted Shiloh still in the back seat. The boy was staring into his lap, an expression on his face Gage couldn't quite pinpoint. It was like a cross between fear and anger with a dash of devastation hidden beneath both.

The Uber driver threw open his door, yelling something at him that Gage didn't care to pay attention to, just as Gage tugged open the back door. Shiloh looked up with a start, fear more pronounced until his eyes landed on Gage.

He looked resigned for a moment before relief took over. "Gage," he breathed, "you followed me."

"Of course I followed you, stupid," Gage said, tugging on Shiloh's hair. "You think I was just going to let you sneak out alone?"

"Hey, I don't know what's going on here." The Uber driver climbed out of the car, his fists planted on his hips. "But you need to leave, buddy."

Shiloh was just as content to ignore the driver as Gage was. "I thought I could do this but then I got here, and I can't."

Gage half-pulled, half-guided Shiloh out of the car so he could smother him in a hug.

"I got other rides, man." The Uber driver shoved the back door shut, nearly clipping Gage as he did, then dropped back into the driver's seat. Gage pulled Shiloh back onto the sidewalk as the Uber driver threw it into reverse before peeling away.

"Shit, baby," Gage breathed, burying his face in Shiloh's hair. "You scare the living shit out of me sometimes."

"Sorry," Shiloh mumbled into Gage's shoulder. "I thought I could get the evidence and get out."

"You can do anything you set your mind to," Gage said dryly. "I just wish you wouldn't put your mind to some things."

Shiloh's laugh was quiet and pained. "You might be right."

"Let's go back to the hotel." Gage walked Shiloh over to the rental car and helped him into the passenger seat. They didn't talk until Lawson's house was out of sight behind them.

Suddenly, Shiloh hit the dashboard. "God, why am I so fucking stupid?"

Gage hit the brakes, angling the car over to the side of the road with little care to the surroundings, then throwing it in park. "You are *not* stupid. You are so fucking smart, Shiloh, it blows my mind. I didn't understand half of what you told the board yesterday, and I could never even *dream* of getting an SAT score like yours. And you're so goddamn talented. It wasn't stupid to think you could get the evidence from Lawson. If he still has the videos, they probably *are* somewhere in his house."

"Oh, I know they are," Shiloh said, a dark expression crossing his face. "He makes me watch them sometimes. Keeps them in a floor safe in his office. I *hate* it! I hate that he has them."

Gage frowned, the spark of an idea growing in his mind. "So he definitely still has them and watches them?"

"He likes to rub it in that he watches them every night before bed. He knows I hate it."

If Lawson watched them every night, then Gage wouldn't have to worry about how to get in the safe. He'd just have to make sure he was in the house when *Lawson* was in the safe. He could grab the videos and get out.

The only question was what to do with Shiloh while he was preoccupied.

He waited until Shiloh was asleep before going into the hotel bathroom and hitting his speed dial.

"Phoenix? How soon can you get to Austin?"

Chapter Forty-Five

Gage felt a deadly calm settle over him. It was as familiar to him as breathing, and it had been missing for the past few years. It was nearing dusk, the perfect time for infiltrating an enemy base. Night raids had become increasingly more common prior to his discharge. Gage knew this wasn't the same… He wasn't capturing insurrectionists and bringing down terrorist operations. What he was doing was so much more critical. He was bringing to justice the bastard who raped the man Gage loved.

Gage's heart thumped louder. The man he loved… Because, suddenly, he realized he did. It made this moment so much more critical. He wasn't fighting for some ambiguous concept of justice, but one he could hold in the palm of his hand.

All he had to do was get inside, grab the evidence and get out.

Simple.

Gage was dressed in the closest thing to tactical gear it was legal for a civilian to have and practical for him to have carried with him. He had it on good authority—Shiloh's—that the black cargo pants cupped his ass like a second skin, and Shiloh had literally moaned when Gage tugged on the leather gloves. He didn't want to leave behind any fingerprints.

The gear had a purpose beyond turning Shiloh on, of course, but he couldn't deny it was a happy side effect. He'd promised Shiloh the boy could strip him out of it when he got home safely.

Gage had researched the security company that monitored Lawson's house. It was an expensive one, and while it would have been nearly impossible to sneak in with the system activated, he had no problems sliding open a ground-floor window and dropping through it into a laundry room. It was one of the main flaws the company had, and the reason he never encouraged his clients to buy it.

Once he was inside, he had free rein. Gage knew Lawson had no visible security cameras, but just in case, Gage had a black tactical hat on his head and a dark neck gator pulled up over his face. He could be anyone on camera. He pictured what they'd see.

Male, average height, average weight. Indeterminate age, indeterminate race. No logos on his clothing, no fingerprints to leave. He'd specifically worn boots a half size too large with thick socks in a brand sold at every department store in the country. There was nothing traceable, even if he left a footprint.

His plan was to grab the evidence and get out—no violence, nothing broken. Mitigate the charges he'd risk facing if he couldn't talk the cops into immunity in exchange for the evidence. He knew it was a possibility, but it would be worth it.

Gage cracked the laundry room door and listened. Faintly, he heard muffled noises from the left, in the direction he knew Lawson's office was located. Gage had spent the last week doing recon. With Phoenix in from LA and officially set up as Shiloh's primary—and after having extracted a solemn promise from the boy not to ditch him—Gage had spent every waking minute trailing the lawyer. Except, of course, for the day he left the man in court to sneak in and plant a camera in Lawson's office.

It was trained at the floor and now, thanks to the camera, Gage was in possession of the safe's six-digit security code. Gage would have rather done this while Lawson was out, or at least later at night while the lawyer was asleep, but there was only a limited window when the security alarm was deactivated. His hope was that he could get the evidence to the police and get a warrant issued before Lawson even knew it was missing.

The lawyer, he knew, would be smart enough not to stick around otherwise, and he wanted to see the bastard in cuffs. Or, he admitted to himself, in the ground, not off on some beach in Maui sipping Mai Tais.

It meant doing this in the early evening when the bastard was both home and awake, but Gage refused to allow himself to worry. If he couldn't handle sneaking into a civilian's barely defended house, he didn't deserve the tan beret he still kept in a place of honor back home.

Gage slid into the hallway and carefully shut the door behind him. If Lawson stuck to his usual schedule, he should be finishing up in his office within the next ten minutes. Just to be safe, Gage ducked into the hallway closet. It was directly to the left of Lawson's office. From there, he'd be able to hear when Lawson left, and stay out of sight until then.

Unfortunately, it also meant he could hear every sound that came through the computer speakers, each accompanied by the disgustingly familiar sound of a man jacking off. If Gage hadn't hated Lawson before, hearing him pleasure himself to Shiloh's cries and pleading made murder seem an even more viable option.

He clenched his fists to stop himself from punching the wall or, worse, storming into the next room and throttling Lawson as the crying got louder.

"Please, it hurts. Please take it out, please…" Shiloh's voice sounded younger but it was definitely Shiloh, and Gage thought he was going to vomit at the sound.

"I'm going to tear this little ass up. You're not going to be able to let anyone else in by the time I'm done." Lawson grunted over his own words.

Gage tried not to listen, but the video kept going and every sound hit him like a bullet. Shiloh should never have had to go through that. *No one* should have to go through that.

Finally, the only sound from the office next door was faint crying that clicked off to silence. It didn't take long after that for footsteps to head from the door and out into the hallway. It sounded like Lawson was heading toward the living room.

Gage waited a second before he twisted the knob and cracked open the door. The hallway was clear, so he moved into the next room. The computer was off, the safe covered by a plain blue rug. Gage swiped it away, entering the code he'd made sure to memorize, relieved when the little green light flashed and the lock disengaged.

Gage yanked open the safe, cringing at the loud creak that sounded. Rationally, he knew it wasn't loud enough to be heard outside the room—he hadn't heard it from next door—but it still made him work faster. He didn't bother finding out what in the safe was evidence and what wasn't. He could sort it out later. Or, rather, let the police figure it out. Instead, he just shoved every flash drive, DVD and what looked like scrapbook into his backpack and closed the safe. He replaced the rug, climbed back through the laundry room window and left without getting caught or, regretfully, putting a bullet in Lawson's spine.

Chapter Forty-Six

As much as Gage wanted to, he couldn't take the pilfered evidence back to the hotel to comb through. Not only would he rather not get caught with it, just in case Lawson had better security than he'd anticipated or decided to check his safe a second time, but he also wasn't sure he could stomach watching it twice.

He called Phoenix, double checking that Shiloh was still fine, then drove straight to the precinct. He parked in the visitor lot, dumping his hat, mask and gloves into the center console. Then, he picked up his phone and dialed.

"Is your guy there?" Gage asked immediately, in place of greeting.

"Almost. Don't go inside without him. He should be there in less than five," Mason answered.

Gage tapped his fingers on the steering wheel. "Got it."

"I know you're not going to listen, but I'm going to suggest one last time that you drop the evidence on the stairs and drive away."

"And hope they find it, hope they watch it, hope they don't then throw it in the trash to protect the reputation of a substantial donor…" Gage listed all the flaws to the plan.

Mason sighed. "Do what you think is best. My guy will keep you out of hot water, as much as he can anyway."

"I appreciate it," Gage said. A black SUV pulled into the lot and parked near the door. "Your guy look like he should be off playing soccer somewhere?" he asked abruptly as a man in a finely tailored suit climbed out of the vehicle and glanced around.

Mason let out a bark of laughter. "You'll never guess what his name is."

"Mm?" Gage reached into the passenger seat and grabbed the backpack. "What's that?" He slid out of the car and through the sack over his shoulder.

"Beckham!" Mason's laughter blended with Gage's.

Gage's laugh died quickly in face of the seriousness of the situation. "I gotta go, Mase."

"Good luck."

Gage hung up and shoved his phone in his pocket. "Beckham?"

"You must be Gage. Mason explained the situation on the phone. Is that the evidence?" Beckham glanced down at his watch.

"Yes."

"You've watched it?" Beckham finally looked up.

"No. I *may* have heard Lawson listening to one, though, and…there'll be enough to get a warrant and then some." A new wave of anger swelled in Gage's chest. He clenched his jaw to hold back a curse.

Beckham glanced at his watch again. "Let me do the talking." He didn't wait for a response. He spun on his heel and started to the door, opening it in a flourish. Gage followed in his shadow.

"Excuse me," Beckham said as he marched up to the front desk, where an officer was doing a crossword. "I need to speak with the officers in charge of Shiloh Beckett's case. I believe their names are Officer Preston and Officer Thomas."

"I'm sorry, but those officers aren't currently available. I can arrange a meeting tomorrow for you," the desk officer said after checking something on his computer.

"That won't work for me. I'm willing to wait"—Beckham looked at his watch—"exactly thirty minutes. Tell them that new information has surfaced that is extremely time sensitive. If they don't show, I'll be forced to take it to the police commissioner and the press instead." Beckham didn't wait for an answer. He headed to the lobby instead, gesturing for Gage to follow with a tip of his head.

"You think they'll show?" Gage asked quietly as he sat down beside him.

"They will. Trust me. They know better than to let evidence end up in the press instead of their case files." Beckham didn't sound worried.

And, in the end, he was right. Barely twenty minutes had passed before a disheveled Officer Preston burst through the front doors. It looked like he'd come straight from the gym. He bypassed the desk, heading straight for Gage and Beckham.

"You'd better hope this evidence is good," Preston snapped as he approached. "This was my first evening off in over seventy-two hours."

"It is," Gage snapped back. He didn't particularly care if the officer was upset about working on his day off. Maybe if they had been doing their jobs while they were *on* the clock, he wouldn't have had to do it for them.

Beckham cleared his throat and shot Gage a pointed glance. "Maybe we should go somewhere private. My client would like to turn over some evidence that he believes will be of help to an ongoing investigation."

"And how was this evidence obtained?" Preston immediately questioned, clearly suspicious.

"Irrelevant," Beckham countered. "My client will agree to hand over this evidence only under the provision that he suffer no consequences relating to how it may or may not have been obtained, and he will be answering no questions about its source. He believes the contents will be enough to assist your case on their own."

Preston frowned, clearly hesitant. "Surely you must know that without a clear chain of custody, most evidence would be inadmissible."

Beckham shrugged. "As I stated, the content of the evidence itself, pending proof of authenticity, will be all you need."

"Let me arrange a conference room." Preston finally stomped away. Gage didn't get the impression that he was unhappy they'd brought evidence. It seemed more like he was worried it wouldn't stand up in court. Gage wasn't concerned. He hadn't even *watched* the videos and he'd been able to tell that what was happening was clearly rape. They'd have no trouble getting a computer forensics analyst, or whoever ended up with it, to authenticate the tape. If Gage believed Shiloh, which he did, then he knew there was no question.

Eventually, Preston returned to lead them to a small conference room. Gage was grateful it held a television already, though Preston could only have assumed that what he brought would need one. But the officer seemed like the kind of person to be prepared for any instance.

"Okay, show me what you have," Preston said, sitting down across from Gage.

Gage carefully tipped the bag, letting the contents spill out onto the table. "I haven't watched them yet," Gage admitted.

"My client," Beckham said before Gage could say anything else, "brought it straight here after its discovery."

A calculating glint lit Preston's eyes. "And how was that again?"

"Irrelevant," Beckham immediately replied. "And I would like it noted that my client has been nothing but cooperative in bringing forward this evidence."

"Noted," Preston smirked, but it died quickly when the door behind him burst open. Preston's partner, Officer Thomas, strolled inside, a coffee in one hand and a bag of donuts in the other, a walking stereotype.

Gage could hear the audible sigh Preston let out as Thomas dropped into the chair beside him. "What we got here?"

"Possible evidence in the Beckett case," Preston said quietly, bringing his partner up to speed.

"Hmm." Thomas sat back, looking bored as he scanned the pile of DVDs and photo albums. He reached for one, but Preston gripped his wrist.

"Gloves, Andy."

Thomas huffed but pulled on a pair of black nitrile gloves. He grabbed one of the albums and slid it over, flipping open to a random page halfway through. The man's formerly ruddy complexion paled to a sickly gray. Even with the photographs upside down, Gage could see what was so disturbing.

It looked like a still captured from a video, the way Lawson's left hand, holding a belt, was slightly blurred. The boy tied to the bed with red ropes wasn't Shiloh, but he was clearly underage. From the way his skin stretched taut over bony ribs, he was likely either homeless or impoverished. His skin was mottled with lash marks and reddish-purple bruises. His face was toward the camera, tears shiny on pale cheeks.

Thomas flipped the page, growing even more pale, if that were possible. It was another still from a video. Lawson loomed over a bound teenager even younger than the first, pulling the kid's hair as he forced him toward his crotch.

Each page Thomas flipped was similar. Sometimes, it was the same boy for a stretch, sometimes there was only one picture. Eventually, Thomas shoved the book away. "Clearly these are fake." His voice was adamant, but the paleness of his skin made it obvious he didn't believe it.

"I'd strongly suggest you allow a certified analyst to make that call. I'd hate to think the police department would disregard evidenced of child pornography and assault to protect an influential donor. I'm sure the press would be interested to—" Beckham didn't need to say more to get his point across.

Preston interrupted, "That won't be necessary. I assure you the *entire* police department"—he shot his partner a glare—"will be taking this seriously."

"I certainly hope so. I'd hate to see another Devon Butcher incident..." Beckham's threat was clear. Even Gage winced.

The Butcher had made it to national news after a young man had been brutally murdered then cannibalized in the basement of Devon Butcher's house. If that were *all* that happened, it would have been a tragedy, but not national news. Except then it was discovered by a journalist covering the horrific murder that three other men had gone to the police in the months prior to report a hookup gone wrong. One said he'd gone back to the man's house and had sex, but then the man tried to lead him to his basement, and he'd escaped. Another escaped after the man tried to chew into his shoulder mid-sex and was spotted by a neighbor, naked and bloody, running away.

Each time, the police either discredited the victim, saying that it was either consensual and therefore not worth investigating, or derided the man for choosing to go to a strange man's home for sex. After the Butcher was finally arrested, they found the bodies—what was left, anyway—of at least four other men on the property.

The police were still being dragged in the press over a year later for failing to take the initial reports seriously, and even more so for the blatant homophobia obvious in their actions.

Neither cop wanted their department to be the next Clanton County, Michigan.

"I promise you that we will be taking this case *exceptionally* seriously," Preston promised. "Won't *we,* Officer Thomas?"

Thomas grimaced but nodded. "Of course." He pushed away from the table. "I gotta take a piss." He left the room, but Gage swore that before the door was fully closed, he saw the officer tug his cell phone out of his pocket.

"How long will it take you to get a warrant with these?" Gage asked abruptly.

"By the morning, I'd imagine. Earlier if I can get a judge to sign one after hours." Preston frowned at the stack of DVDs. "Of course, going through the evidence could take all night."

Gage shifted uncomfortably. "Yeah, you might want to speed that up. I might be wrong, but I'm pretty sure your partner just tipped off Lawson."

Preston went blank for a second before a violent curse slipped from his mouth. "That *motherfucker.*" He grabbed his cell phone and checked the screen, then stared at the DVDs. "As long as I assume this evidence will be authenticated, I can make the arrest without a warrant." Saying it out loud seemed to validate whatever thought he was having, because he stood up. "Thank you for bringing this in. I'm going to need you to vacate the room so I can have the evidence processed and logged, but I promise we will be taking this *very* seriously."

Preston hesitated, staring at Gage critically. "I shouldn't tell you this, but something tells me if I don't, you'll take things into your own hands…" The *again* at the end of the sentence was left unsaid but obvious in Preston's glance at the evidence. "As long as I can get the Chief to sign off, I can make an arrest without a warrant."

Gage appreciated the information because Preston was right to worry. If he thought there was a chance the police wouldn't get involved, he would, legal or not.

Chapter Forty-Seven

Shiloh paced back to the window, yanking the curtain aside to stare down at the sidewalk. Like the last twelve times, there was no sign of Gage.

"Dude, if that carpet had vocal cords, it would be screaming about wear patterns right about now..." Phoenix broke the silence they'd fallen into an hour ago, after he'd tried to convince Shiloh to order dinner and Shiloh had told him to *"mind his own fucking business."*

Of course, then he'd immediately felt guilty, but he'd never been good at apologizing, hence the awkward, stilted silence.

"Shouldn't he have been back by now?" Shiloh said, ignoring the comment about the carpeting. As much as he was paying to rent this room on a nightly basis, the hotel could damn well replace it when he left.

"Not necessarily. Real life ain't like TV. Cops move slow." Phoenix didn't *sound* concerned. He was sitting—if lying upside down on an armchair with his legs flung over the back could really be considered *sitting* – with his head dangling over the seat, his scarlet Mohawk nearly touching the floor.

Shiloh huffed and dropped the curtain, moving back to collapse on the mattress. His leg angled up, automatically presenting his body at an agreeable angle, one he knew left his v-cut prominent. Immediately, guilt set in and he folded in on himself. He would never cheat, but it was just habit by now to seduce his bodyguards. After all, they couldn't forcefully take something he freely gave.

If Phoenix noticed, he was considerate enough not to comment. Shiloh rolled onto his stomach and yelled into the pillow, then crawled off the bed to pace back to the window. He yanked aside the curtain.

Still nothing.

He was halfway back to the bed when his phone started ringing. Hoping it was Gage with an update, Shiloh snagged it up. The caller ID said it was the hospital and his heart dropped.

"Am I speaking with Shiloh?" a male voice said as soon as he answered.

"Yeah. I mean, yes, this is Shiloh. Is this about my dad? Is he okay?" Shiloh grabbed his shoes and started tugging them on, not even worrying about socks, then scrambled to put his jacket on one-handed without letting go of the phone.

"It appears he's had a bit of a setback. We've had to move him to a new room for monitoring. We just wanted to keep you—" the man said. His voice was familiar, making Shiloh wonder if it was one of the same nurses he'd spoken to earlier in the week, because it wasn't Dr. Holden. The voice was too mature.

"I'll be right there. Thanks," Shiloh interrupted.

"He'll be in room 218."

Shiloh thanked the doctor again before hanging up. "We gotta go," he said to Phoenix, who had started pulling on his shoes and jacket when Shiloh had. "My dad's being moved rooms. The doctor said he had a relapse."

Phoenix didn't waste any time arguing. He just led Shiloh down into the parking garage, doing a quick sweep before they climbed into a plain sedan and left for the hospital. Waiting for Phoenix to clear the hospital lot made his leg bounce with impatience, but he knew, objectively, that it didn't take that long before they were riding the elevator up to the second floor.

The hallway was quiet. He heard the faint *beeping* of heart monitors and the low voices of nurses chatting at the nurse station, but that was it. He had a moment of concern stepping into his dad's room about the lack of guard, but by the time he'd processed it, it was too late. There was a painful prick in his neck, a flash of movement then his vision went blurry.

He felt himself falling.

* * * *

Gage was halfway back to the hotel when his phone dinged. A quick glance at the screen had him turning away toward the hospital. Phoenix's message was terse.

At hospital, S dad had setback. Bng mvd to Rm 218.

Gage didn't like it. He knew a lot of the worry that swelled in his chest was irrational. He didn't like the idea of Shiloh leaving the hotel without him, even if Phoenix was perfectly capable, but it was more than that. What were the odds that Shiloh's dad would have 'a setback' the same day that everything with Lawson had come to a head?

He wished Phoenix would have waited, but he understood how hard it would be to convince Shiloh to hold off if his dad were doing worse. Still, something wasn't setting right. He thumbed the green button on the steering wheel to dial the hospital, listening to the receptionist rattle off her greeting.

"Hello, my name is Gage Tucker. I'm a personal security officer hired by Anthony Beckett, one of your patients? I would just like to verify the security protocols in place on his new room."

"One moment, please," the bubbly receptionist said. Several seconds later, she came back on the line, clearly confused. "I'm really sorry, Mr. Tucker, but I'm not sure who told you Mr. Beckett was being moved. He's still in room 396."

"Shit," Gage cursed and hung up the phone, immediately calling Phoenix. Or, rather, trying to. It rang straight to voicemail. "Fuck," he cursed again and sped up. He knew there was a risk of getting pulled over, but he was worried the risk of delaying was worse.

He left the car on the sidewalk and raced into the hospital. He bypassed the receptionist, ignoring the shout she sent after him to stop running. He took the elevator, knowing with his leg it would probably still be faster than the stairs. On the ride up, he double-checked the room number.

It took him less than a minute to make it to room 218, and less than a second after entering to know immediately that something was *very* wrong.

Chapter Forty-Eight

The curtain was mostly pulled, but through the gap, Gage spotted a pair of worn combat boots. He yanked it aside to see Phoenix sprawled over the hospital bed, blood oozing from a lump on his forehead, unconscious.

For what felt like the thousandth time that day, Gage loosed a curse and ran back to the hall. "I need a doctor!" he called. Immediately, a handful of nurses and orderlies ran by him, into the room.

"What happened?" one asked, a man in dark blue scrubs, a stethoscope hanging around his neck.

"I'm not sure. He's my partner. We're both Protection Officers with Eagle Security. He came with our client to visit his dad." Gage lifted both hands to his head, locking his fingers behind his skull as he gritted his teeth. "I need to speak to security." He spun on his heel, leaving Phoenix with the medical staff.

"Sir, you can't leave. The police will—" a nurse called after him.

"I have to find my client," Gage snapped. He dragged his phone out of his pocket and called Mason. He kept it terse, just giving him an update on Phoenix and that Shiloh was missing.

His voice broke as he said the words. He was struggling to maintain the distance he needed to the situation to think rationally. He couldn't afford to get emotional, but he didn't know how to treat this like a job.

Shiloh was so much more than a job. He was… He was everything—everything Gage had never known he wanted, never known he *needed.* He couldn't lose him.

It didn't take much more than showing his PPO license to the head of security to get them to show him the security tapes.

"Fast forward a bit," Gage said, watching the time stamp. "There. Slow it now."

The man obediently slowed it down and Gage watched as a man in a white jacket and blue surgical mask entered the empty room. Several minutes later, he watched, heart thudding in his chest, as Shiloh and Phoenix exited the elevator.

His breath was shaky as he drew it in. Poor Shiloh was clearly anxious as they moved down the hallway and into the room. "Are there any camera shots into the room?" Gage asked.

"No, we try to protect patient privacy as much as possible," the Head of Security replied.

Gage kept watching. It took about three minutes to see anything else. The same man came out pushing a gurney, a white sheet pulled up over… Gage drew in a shaky breath. He couldn't fall apart, not if he wanted to help Shiloh. "Follow that gurney."

They tracked it down the elevator and into the parking garage, where Gage forced himself to watch the man in the white jacket load the gurney into the back of a nondescript silver van. With the way it was angled, he could only see the first three letters of the license plate.

He borrowed a sticky note from the security guard and scribbled down the make and model, along with the partial plate number, then pinned his eyes to the screen, hoping he'd get the rest of the letters. Maybe off a reflection, or if it would turn just right, but no luck.

He slammed his hand on the desk and stormed out of the room, already calling Officer Preston.

The man answered after a half-dozen rings. "I can't give you any information about an active investigation—"

"Shiloh's missing," Gage interrupted. "He got a call from the hospital saying his dad was being moved. I found his other bodyguard knocked unconscious in the hospital bed and security footage shows an occupied gurney being removed from the room by a man in a surgical mask and white coat. I have a partial plate—"

"Give it to me." Preston sounded completely serious. Gage passed along the little bit of information he had as he moved into the stairway to start down to the ground floor. He passed on the landing when Preston added, "I shouldn't tell you this, but Lawson wasn't at the scene. There's been a BOLO issued, but with the evidence we have and what we were able to recover from the scene, I believe Lawson had been planning his getaway for a while."

Gage cursed, striking the cinder block wall with his fist hard enough to split the skin on his knuckles. "I'm going to check the tracking app. One sec." He pulled his phone down and pulled up the app. The slim hope he'd held died a quick death when the map was blank. Clearly the battery had been pulled from Shiloh's phone.

"No luck," Gage said into the phone, moving down the stairs again. "I'm coming to the precinct. If Lawson was prepared to run, then he had to have prepared somewhere to run *to.* He's not just driving aimlessly."

Preston was silent for long enough Gage was nearly to the car when he finally spoke. "I'll get permission from the captain to bring you into the investigation. I'm *assuming* you have a PI license?"

"Of course." Gage started the car and peeled into the street.

"That'll make it easier. I'll meet you there in twenty."

The call disconnected.

* * * *

"It's been twelve hours." Gage rubbed his eyes, dropping the latest stack of obscene photographs on the desk between him and the cop.

"I know." Preston sounded exasperated—whether at him or the situation, Gage didn't know.

"I feel like I should be out doing something." Gage grabbed the next scrapbook of horrors with fingers like ice.

Preston frowned. "Like what? Drive around the city and cross your fingers for luck?"

"I don't know," Gage snapped, flipping the page harshly. He skimmed the photographs, pain tearing through him with each one.

He didn't want to look. He saw Shiloh's face on every broken boy, Shiloh's tears on every red cheek, Shiloh's cries spilling from each cut and bleeding lip. Each picture detailed a horror he didn't want to imagine Shiloh going through but couldn't stop. And the worst part was that imagining Shiloh's face imposed over each boy's was almost better than seeing their real faces, each one so young. They should have been at home, riding bikes down suburban sidewalks or fighting about doing their homework, not *this.* He didn't want to know what happened to them.

Were their bodies buried somewhere in the woods so often pictured in the photographs, left to rot where no one could mourn them? So many boys, he knew they must be runaways—street kids with no one to keep them safe, no one to report them missing. There was no way this many boys—fifteen, at least—could be unaccounted for.

Or were they dumped somewhere afterward with words of warning to keep their mouths shut, some unimaginable threat enough to keep them quiet? Were they now back home with their parents, going to Boy Scouts and school as if everything were normal, hiding this…this *nightmare,* from everyone? Did their parents attribute their children's sudden fear of the dark to the horror movie they *knew* he was too old to watch last week but had caved anyway? Did they think this new world-weariness was a sign of maturity?

Did they even notice?

Gage gritted his teeth and went to flip the page but froze after a glance back at the top photo. It was taken outdoors, which wasn't unique. Several other photographs were similar. The picture was of a young teen. His hair was a dark blond, a shade or two darker than Gage guessed Shiloh's would have been at that age, his face dotted with freckles where it wasn't red from crying.

He didn't want to look at the poor boy, tied naked to a tree while Lawson tortured him, but… "Look at this." Gage shoved the book toward Preston. "Do you see what that says?" He stabbed his finger at the corner of the photo, where a blurry wooden sign was peeking through the foliage. "Can you read that?"

Preston grabbed a magnifying glass and held it over the photo. A second later, he broke into a dark grin. "We got the fucker."

Chapter Forty-Nine

Shiloh woke to acid burning his throat as he hurled over the edge of a bare mattress. He curled around his stomach, tears spilling from his eyes at the bitter taste. He was still dry heaving, his throat convulsing, when his head was yanked up by a hand gripping his hair. He blinked at the brightness of the lights, a blurry silhouette slowly coming into focus.

Lawson sneered down at him. "Aw, don't cry, baby. We've barely started."

Shiloh flinched hard, strands of hair parting from his scalp, at the sound of Gage's pet name for him on the bastard's lips. He tried to pull away, jerking his hands up to grab Lawson's arm but was stopped halfway. Cuffs he didn't realize he was wearing tightened around his wrists, the chains pulled taut.

"Now what was that for, hmm?" Lawson *tsked,* patting Shiloh's hair like a misbehaving pet. "Was it something I said?"

"You damn well know it was, you mother*fucking*–" Shiloh's angry words were cut off by a violent slap. He cried out, more from the shock than the pain.

"Watch your mouth, pet," Lawson scolded. He gripped Shiloh's hair again, yanking his head closer. "Unless you want me to gag you again." Shiloh gagged as Lawson dragged his fingers down the side of his face, digging into his cheeks until he was forced to open his mouth and allow them to slip inside.

Lawson roughly explored his mouth with his fingers, scraping over his gums and along his teeth, forcing his tongue down flat. "God, I've missed your mouth." He removed his fingers, dropping them to Shiloh's neck and squeezing instead. "If you bite me, I'll remove your teeth with a pair of pliers. You're mine now. I don't need to keep you pretty for your 'daddy'."

Shiloh paled. Lawson had never exactly taken it easy on him before, but now... He shuddered to think what his life was going to turn into. He darted his gaze around the room, looking for anything that could help him escape. They were in what looked like a cabin, with rustic wooden walls and hardwood floors, but nothing that could help him.

Pain burst through his jaw as Lawson gripped it tight enough to bruise, forcing his face back to him. "Look at me when I'm speaking, pet." Reluctantly, Shiloh obeyed. "Here's what's going to happen. You're going to show me how much you missed me and how happy you are to be here. Then, if you do a good job, I'll give these some slack"—he rattled the chains that kept Shiloh bound to the bare mattress in the corner of the room—"and let you clean up the mess you made." Lawson sneered. "If you're not, I'll take the mattress away and make you sleep in it."

* * * *

Shiloh swallowed the bile that rose in his face at the smell of his own vomit as he struggled to scrub it out of the cracks in the hardwood. The bucket Lawson had brought him was only half full of cold, soapy water. By now, it was cloudy and chunky, and just the thought of sticking the sponge back into it again disgusted him.

Then Lawson dropped a dry towel in front of him and gratitude filled him, immediately followed by anger that he would in any way feel grateful to the bastard, particularly for something as small as a towel to dry up his vomit.

He refused to feel anything positive for the fucker, especially now, when he still had the taste of Lawson's cum staining his tongue.

Lawson crouched in front of him. "I've got to get my pet cleaned up now, don't I? We can do this one of two ways... You can be a good boy and let me give you a bath, or I can bring in the garden hose and spray you down right here."

"Bath," Shiloh bit out.

"Say please." Lawson reached out to tweak Shiloh's nose, laughing when he flinched back.

"Bath, please," Shiloh corrected snappily, glaring. He should know better than to goad the man, but he couldn't stop himself. He wasn't going to just roll over and take it. One way or another, he was getting out of there.

"*Tsk, tsk.* You don't sound very happy about that. Say, 'I'll be a good boy and take a bath, please.'" Lawson interlaced his fingers and waited.

Shiloh struggled. He couldn't say it, *wouldn't* say it...but if he didn't, he knew Lawson would make good on his threat. And while it wouldn't kill him to be sprayed down with a hose, he just *knew* Lawson would make him stay on the soaked mattress until Shiloh *did* say it.

He clenched his jaw hard before finally biting out, "I'll be a good boy and take a bath, please." Consoling himself with the idea that pretending to cooperate would maybe have Lawson lowering his guard was the only way he could get the words out of his throat.

He should have known better.

It shouldn't have surprised him when Lawson let out a mean laugh and stood. "I just don't believe you," he said, turning on his heel and strolling out of the cabin door just ten feet in front Shiloh but so far out of reach.

Shiloh *shouldn't* have been surprised, but he was, and it *hurt.* It snapped something inside him, some little thread of steel he didn't realize he was still carrying around in his chest, and its loss had him sagging forward, dropping his face to the mattress as small, silent sobs shook his shoulders.

After all these years, he finally let go.

Some minuscule part of him had still held on to memories of *before* like a shield. He hadn't even realized it until now, when it shattered. Every time Lawson hurt him, he'd convinced himself that at least it meant the older man cared for him in some way, even if it was a way he didn't like, didn't *want.*

He'd clung to the lie like a safety blanket. That Lawson *had* to care for him to make him do those things. Somehow, every bruise got tangled up in his mind with the ballet shoes Lawson had bought him for his sixth birthday, the trip to the zoo the man had pulled him from school to go to when his father had been away and the nights before his dad's heart attack, when Lawson had helped brush his hair, always too long for a boy's but he'd helped keep Shiloh's dad from cutting it.

It had meant the man loved him, just in a fucked-up way.

But clearly, it was a lie.

Shiloh saw it now with open eyes, the manipulation, the *grooming.* He saw it because of Gage. Gage would never touch his cheek so lovingly with one hand just to strike it with the other. He would never buy him a new leotard to apologize for the way Shiloh couldn't sit down for a week because of the tearing.

Gage would never hurt him, because Gage loved him.

Lawson didn't.

Shiloh had *thought* he knew that, but some naïve part of him had held the lie tightly with both hands, instinctively knowing that its loss would break him.

He barely noticed the icy water pelleting his skin like flecks of glass.

Chapter Fifty

Gage adjusted his vest as he stared at the unassuming cabin. It could be anyone's vacation cabin—small but not *too* small, plaid curtains visible through the front windows, a well-trodden path leading from the front porch into the wooded park around it. If Preston hadn't connected the deed to Lawson's firm, he wouldn't have looked at it twice.

Shiloh was in there. He had to be. Gage stayed back by the ambulance as he'd promised—the only way he could talk Preston into letting him tag along. It nearly killed him watching half a dozen officers circle around the sides and back of the cabin, covering all exits, while the rest stormed the front door while he did nothing.

He couldn't even pace back and forth because he needed to keep his ears peeled for any hint of what was going on inside. When he didn't immediately hear gunshots, but no police came out with Lawson either, he tensed. Either the cabin was a dead end or Lawson had Shiloh hostage. Each second that passed made his heart race faster. He was going to give them two more minutes before he went in, regardless of what he'd promised.

Before he had to break his word, Preston stepped onto the front porch and waved him up. Gage ran over, taking the stairs two at a time.

"We found him but he's unresponsive. I think he's in shock. I'm going to get the paramedics, but it might help if you try to talk to him," Preston briefed him in a low voice.

"And Lawson?" Gage forced himself to ask.

"Dead on arrival," Preston said over his shoulder as he headed toward the ambulance.

Gage raced into the cabin. A dozen cops were combing through the main room of the cabin, putting items in evidence bags, scanning a soggy mattress against the wall with a UV light. An officer pointed Gage to the connected room.

Gage hurried in, only to freeze in the doorway. Shiloh was crouched beside a full-size bed. His forehead was pressed hard to his knees, one arm curled tightly around his shins. The other was stretched awkwardly onto the mattress. A police officer was taking bolt cutters to the heavy chain that stretched from the metal headboard to the manacle around Shiloh's wrist.

Blood streaked from under the cuff, staining his boy's pale skin with shades of brown and scarlet. Gage's heart skipped a beat before it kick-started double-time and he was moving. He dropped to his knees in front of Shiloh, ignoring the body on the bed. A quick glance had told him all he needed to know. The red eyes, bluish skin and vivid bruising around Lawson's neck made it clear he'd been strangled, and the scratch marks down Shiloh's arms meant he'd put up a fight.

Gage's only wish was that he'd been the one to do it, not his boy.

"Shiloh," Gage murmured, hesitant to touch him. Heaven only knew what Lawson had already subjected him to. But when Shiloh didn't acknowledge him, against his better judgment he reached out, laying his hand against chilly skin.

Shiloh didn't react, so Gage slid a bit closer, running his other hand through the pink hair. It was damp against his fingers, which helped explain the boy's goosebumps, despite the Texas heat.

"Can someone find me a towel?" Gage asked without looking away. An officer went to look for one. They returned with a plain blue one just as the other officer, kneeling on the bed while he worked at the chain, finally managed to get the bolt cutter to break the link with an audible *crack*.

At the sound, Shiloh flinched hard, slamming back into the rough wood as his head snapped up. His eyes were wide and wild, unfocused as they darted around, but then they froze on Gage's face.

It was like time stopped for a second, just his eyes locked on Shiloh's, no one moving. Then Shiloh flung himself forward into Gage's chest, hard enough to send him back onto his ass, and Shiloh was sobbing. Then Gage was crying, running his hands over Shiloh's body for further signs of injury.

"You're going to be okay now," Gage promised, over and over, and Shiloh just kept crying, and Gage did too. Eventually, he pulled back just enough to let the paramedics look Shiloh over, but not too far. Shiloh kept at least one hand fisted the entire time in the bit of shirt that peeked over Gage's vest.

The paramedic twisted Shiloh's right wrist back and forth in his hands, examining the lacerations. It looked like he'd pulled on the cuff hard enough to cut into his skin, but it wasn't bleeding anymore.

"It's shallow enough I don't think it'll need stitches," the EMT mused with a frown. "It'll definitely need cleaned, though."

"I just want to go home," Shiloh said suddenly, the first words he'd spoken since Gage had come in. He looked up at Gage, his eyes pleading. "Please, can we just go home?"

Gage glanced at the paramedic. "Do you have stuff to clean it in the bus?"

The EMT's frown deepened. "It would be best to go to the hospital and get checked out." Shiloh whimpered and the man sighed. "But if you absolutely won't, I can take care of it here."

"Here," Shiloh demanded, his voice sounding stronger already.

"We'll need to get a statement too," Preston muttered from behind him.

"Does it have to be now?" Gage asked, glancing back.

Preston glanced at the body on the bed. Whatever Lawson had done to Shiloh, he wasn't a threat now. With all the evidence they had back at the precinct, even Gage knew Shiloh's testimony wouldn't be vital to closing the case. "Later is fine. We can schedule something in the next few days, after"—he cleared his throat—"after we've had time to process everything."

Shiloh shuddered, tugging on Gage's shirt until he looked at him. The boy's blue eyes were damp, fear easy to read in them. "I don't want to go to the hospital," Shiloh said quietly, just to him. "But…I need an STI test." Shiloh dropped his eyes, the shame flooding his face too easy to read.

"Hey, look at me," Gage said, voice stern. Immediately, Shiloh looked up. "We'll go together, whenever you want. We can go tomorrow if you're ready, but I'm not worried. Do you want to know why?"

Shiloh bit his lip before saying, "Why?"

"Because no matter what, I'll love you and I'll be here for you. Nothing, not even an STI test, is going to change that, no matter what the results," Gage promised, using his thumbs to swipe away the dampness on Shiloh's cheeks. "You are *mine,* and I'll take care of you."

Chapter Fifty-One

Six months later

Shiloh's feet struck the boards in time to the rapid drumbeats, faster and faster until he felt like he was flying. Then, just as the orchestra went silent, he leaped. For an eternity, he flew through the silent air, a hushed breath surrounding his body like a caress. As soon as his bare foot struck the wood, the violins came back in, filling the theater with a frenetic energy that pierced into his skin like electricity.

As the music neared the crescendo, Shiloh went *en pointe* into a *sus-sous* before collapsing slowly to the ground as the music dwindled into silence again.

The theater stayed quiet as he lay motionless, like a moment frozen, before applause broke it. The wood hummed beneath him with the intensity, and finally, he stood to take a bow. The stage lights were blindingly bright, but despite that, he could see the beaming faces in the front row. Teddy was there with Ian, both of them grinning wildly. His dad was there too, clapping just as hard. Even Mason and Ryder had flown from Seattle to see Shiloh's opening night.

Grateful as he was for all their support, it was toward Gage where Shiloh immediately looked. His boyfriend was clapping just as hard as the rest of Shiloh's makeshift family, pride written clearly on his face.

Getting there hadn't been easy. For weeks after what he'd taken to calling 'the incident', he'd flipped between extremes—one day barely dragging himself out of bed, the next filled with the fear that if he stopped moving, the world would end. Gage had been by his side through it all.

He'd gone with Shiloh to every therapy appointment, waiting in the lobby just in case he was needed. He'd dragged Shiloh out of bed and into the shower when he started getting that grungy, three-day funk. And when Shiloh was so hyped on caffeine he was literally shaking, Gage pinned him to the mattress and helped fuck away the excess energy. He'd held him when he'd finally broken down and sobbed, and pushed him to finish his degree, even when everything had seemed pointless.

Gage had been his rock through it all.

Shiloh's skin flushed when Gage lifted his fingers to his mouth to blow him a kiss, following it up with a wink.

Shiloh straightened fully and left the stage. Nerves birthed butterflies in his stomach at the thought of what was waiting for him in his dressing room—flowers from his family, of course, but also a small, velvet box with a simple silver band inside.

He'd been carrying it around for over a month, waiting for a time that felt right, and this was it. He wanted to remember today not just as the day he achieved his professional dreams, but as the day he made an even more important dream a reality.

Gage was already his everything, but he wanted to make it official.

Shiloh was going to marry him.

The muscle-bound meathead standing outside Shiloh's dressing room door planted a hand in the center of Gage's chest and shoved him back half a step. "Off limits to fans."

Gage grinned and socked the bodyguard in the shoulder. "I'm not a fan."

Phoenix lifted a ginger eyebrow. "Ooh, I'm going to tell your boy you said that. No nookie for you."

"Are you ninety now? Do we have to call it an early night so you can get your beauty sleep? Who even says 'nookie' anymore?" Gage pointedly glanced at his watch. "Now can I go in and see my boyfriend yet?"

Phoenix grabbed Gage's wrist and dragged it closer to peer at the watch face. "I don't know. Shiloh specifically said to give him fifteen minutes alone with Hot Daddy before I let anyone else in, so you'll have to wait."

Gage swatted at Phoenix, laughing when the big man cringed from his hands. "Let me by, asshole."

"Buy asshole? I don't think Shiloh would approve of— Ow!" Phoenix rubbed his stomach where Gage had pinched him. "Abusive much?"

Before Gage could reply, the dressing room door opened. Shiloh peered around it with a huff. "Hot Daddy says to keep it down out here. He can't— Hey!" Shiloh squealed as Gage pushed by Phoenix to throw the boy over his shoulder. He landed a loud but painless slap to the firm ass still covered by pale pink tights.

"I better be the *only* Hot Daddy in your dressing room, Boy." He used his heel to kick the door shut behind them. Shiloh's laugh was contagious as Gage carted him over to the vanity. He lay Shiloh atop it. A handful of makeup brushes clattered to the floor, but he ignored them.

Shiloh pressed back into the mirror as he clutched the edge of the table. His eyes were wide, his mouth parted on a gasp. Gage ran his thumb over the plump lower lips. "We've got fifteen minutes of alone time before the rest of your family shows up, baby. What should we do?"

Shiloh's moan was answer enough. Gage dropped his hands to Shiloh's knees, spreading his boy's legs until he could step between them. The sound of Shiloh's whimper as Gage slid his palms over his thighs was perfection. Gage dipped his fingers below the band of the tights at the same time he leaned down, licking a stripe from the jutting hipbone all the way up the bare chest to one perky pink nipple. He sucked it into his mouth, flicking his tongue over the bud before pulling away, blowing a breath on it until it tightened even further.

"Please, please, please, Gage…" Shiloh cried out as Gage gripped his cock in his fist. The shaft was hot and hard, throbbing against his palm.

"Fourteen minutes, Baby. Think you can come before then?" Gage kept his hand still until Shiloh's hips jerked upward, masturbating himself into Gage's hand.

"I can, Daddy. Just move your hand, please. I've been a good boy," Shiloh whined, moving his hips erratically, searching for any bit of friction he could get.

Gage shifted his mouth to the other nipple. When it was as aroused as the first, he lifted his mouth. "You have been a good boy, but what if I want you to come like this? Fucking into Daddy's hand like a good slut."

Shiloh whimpered, his shaft getting even hotter in Gage's hand. "Please, Daddy, I need you to move it."

Instead, Gage let go, pulling his hand out from under the tights. He ignored Shiloh's protest to grip the waistband and yank them off. He threw the nylons, along with the cream dance belt, over his shoulder and grabbed Shiloh's thighs, forcing them even farther apart.

Shiloh's dick bobbed on his stomach, hard and leaking. A drop of pre-cum beaded on his slit before slowly spilling down the bright red shaft. Gage caught it on his finger and lifted it to his mouth, swirling his tongue over it dramatically. "You taste so sweet, baby."

Shiloh just whimpered, shuddering against the mirror. "Daddy, don't tease me."

"I like teasing you, and your pretty little dick likes it too. Look at it," Gage said, gripping Shiloh's chin between his thumb and forefinger to angle his face down. Shiloh blushed beautifully. It made Gage's cock harden even further in his suit pants. He stepped closer, rubbing the obscene bulge against Shiloh's pink hole in a facsimile of fucking. They didn't have time for that, not with proper prep, but he loved to tease Shiloh.

"You're not looking, baby." Gage pulled away when Shiloh clamped his eyes closed against the sight. Shiloh whimpered and seemed to force them open. His face was red, flushed with arousal.

Gage wanted to tease the boy longer, have him begging to come, but they were running low on time, and honestly, all Gage wanted was to make his boy happy. So he dropped a bit awkwardly to his knees and swallowed the pretty cock bobbing just in front of his mouth, taking it to the back of his throat with ease.

Shiloh keened, arching his back as he clamped his thighs tight around Gage's shoulders, a series of nonsense words and sounds pouring from his lips—then he was spilling into Gage's mouth. Shiloh tipped his head back, striking the mirror with a dull throb as he cried out.

Gage swallowed the bittersweet fluid, keeping Shiloh in his mouth until the boy was squirming, too sensitive to continue.

Then, he dug into his pocket and pulled out a small velvet box. Still on his knees, he opened the lid, revealing the pink-diamond ring inside. "Baby, I have a question for you."

Want to see more like this?
Here's a taster for you to enjoy!

Out in Austin: Trusting Tennyson
KD Ellis

Excerpt

Then

The boy on the screen was pretty. Blond, with copper-lined blue eyes—cornflower, not steel—and pouty lips made shiny from gloss, he looked like a doll. Men would pay thousands to fuck him and even more to fuck him *up.* It wasn't hard to see why Master had picked him.

Misha hated him. Misha hated everything he stood for on the other end of a computer screen, thousands of miles away. He probably lived in some nice suburb with a white picket fence, with parents who paid for braces without complaint, drove him to swim classes and sat down for family dinners consisting of more than just oatmeal and water.

Misha hated his amateur videos that taught boys how to apply makeup, his comparisons of drugstore makeup brands and his mock fashion shows as he strutted around in skirts and heels and lacy blouses.

If the boy wasn't so pretty, if his videos hadn't gotten quite so popular, he could have stayed under the radar and Misha would still be Master's favorite.

The best whore.

The prettiest.

The most obedient.

The good boy.

Instead of sitting there, Master's breath damp on the back of his neck while Misha crept his fingers over the keyboard to lure in his replacement. The pretty boy must get thousands of messages a day. Maybe Misha's wouldn't register, buried beneath the rest. Maybe he'd get it but not reply, and Misha would be safe.

Master's attention on him, his hands on Misha's body, might terrify him, but not as much as the idea of losing it.

* * * *

Asher Downs rattled his bedroom doorknob for the third time, just in case it had somehow come unlocked. Then, and *only* then, with his heart pounding in his chest, did he drag out the old Nike shoebox from under his bed, the one that used to hold his soccer cleats. Now, it hid his makeup case.

It was plastic and cheap, much like the makeup inside, odds and ends he'd bought discounted at the drugstore on the corner with change he'd picked up from the sidewalk and pilfered from the ashtray in the Buick, one lonely quarter at a time.

With reverence, he carried the case over to his desk-turned-vanity. The mirror was a cheap thing, bought on sale because it was cracked, the glass spiderwebbed from the top of the frame down one side. When his parents were home, he kept it tucked in the back of the closet, under a ratty baseball jersey he'd outgrown as a preteen.

His phone was already secured in his makeshift tripod—leaning against a book, the bottom half-inch tucked behind a two-pound weight so it didn't slide forward. As soon as he laid out his makeup, he could start the video.

His lipstick was barely a nub of pink in the cracked tube, his eyeshadow more dust than pigment. Even his foundation wasn't *quite* right—a bit too dry and a little too light for his sun-kissed, boy-next-door skin, tanned from playing football each summer with the church youth group.

These broken beauties were his prized possessions, worth more to him than the collectible baseball cards in their little plastic sleeves on his bookshelf or the signed poster of Kobe that his dad had been so excited to hang up when Asher had started high school.

Before Asher got caught kissing the captain of the basketball team under the bleachers.

Before the mandatory after-school meetings with Pastor Luke twice a week to 'examine his soul'.

Now, his little brother Ryder wasn't even allowed in the same room alone with him, his dad could barely look at him without scowling and his mother locked the cabinet doors in the bathroom as if she needed to hide her feminine products from his perverted eyes. She *should* have locked her makeup away instead, back when he was a boy and had first discovered the magic it held.

The way a bit of shadow could make his eyes piercing, soften his jaw or sharpen his cheekbones… How a little color could make him look happy, even when inside he felt like dying.

He'd come a long way since the first time he'd decided to film himself doing this, a silent protest against his parents that had been devised under the influence of Dad's bitter liquor, pilfered from the expensive stash he kept on top of the fridge. He hadn't expected the video to go viral.

Now, he filmed sober, but nerves still birthed butterflies in his stomach. The fear of getting caught, which had him rattling his doorknob again, mingled with the excitement of watching his view counter tick steadily upward. He had almost a hundred thousand subscribers now, enough to put a little money into the secret bank account he'd opened as soon as he'd turned eighteen.

He could use it for better makeup or a ring light, but he was saving it to escape, maybe move out West, somewhere he wouldn't have to hide anymore. He'd dipped into it once already for a better laptop after his old one had crapped out. He was going to need to upgrade his phone soon, too—an expense he couldn't avoid but was delaying as long as he was able. His subscribers were already starting to comment on the graininess of the videos, and those wouldn't take long to become complaints.

Mom promised he could stay with them until he graduated, but that was it, leaving him with just over a month to get a plan in place. College was out of the question. Unlike his younger brother Ryder, he wasn't a computer genius who already had a dozen scholarships to choose from, and unlike they did for Ryder, Mom and Dad would never cover his expenses.

If he wanted out, he was going to have to do it on his own, a thought that finally motivated him to draw in a breath, plaster on a smile and push the red circle to start filming.

"Everything sucks and we're all dying, but I'm going to look pretty doing it. Who's ready to play with the pretty paint and give themselves a plus ten to their charisma check?" Asher jumped in with his quirky and somewhat nerdy greeting, smothering his real-world concerns beneath the joy that he got from doing makeup.

It wouldn't last long—only until the video ended—but for now, for these handful of minutes, he was going to enjoy it.

* * * *

Asher closed the live stream with his highest view count to date, and even when the camera stopped rolling, the little red number on his notification tab kept growing. He itched to tap it, to start scrolling through the comments and likes and shares. Even knowing many of them would be haters, homophobic assholes who couldn't live-and-let-live, didn't stop the curiosity.

He couldn't yet, though—not like this. While his parents, who were off at their evening bible study at Mrs. Worther's house, should be gone until evening, he couldn't risk it. If Mom got one of her migraines, if Dad got into another argument with Mel Geist or if Karen forgot the cookies again, they could be home early, and he would be fucked.

He wiped his face half-raw with the cheap makeup remover wipes, until it was greasy and red but makeup free before he risked, even in an empty house, crossing their hallway to the bathroom so he could wash it.

The house was still empty when he was finished, but he locked his bedroom door again, anyway. It was against the house rules, but he'd rather get grounded for that than the alternative. He dropped back into his chair and opened his laptop, pulling up the desktop version of his channel. Finally, he opened his notifications.

Half of them he could delete immediately. The slurs and insults, the propositions and dick picks, the crazy right-winged conservatives with their MAGA hats and conspiracy theories. He wasn't into politics to begin with, but if he *were,* he didn't think some guy from a reality show should be able to nuke anything that didn't come out of a microwave.

After his routine cleaning, he was still left with dozens of messages to sort through. It was probably his favorite part of making content, if he were honest with himself. Even when the message was more of a critique on his blending technique, like this one. Maybe he'd take the advice *@gayboy93$* gave him and try it out in a later video, just to see. If it worked, he'd learned something and if it didn't, he'd get a good laugh.

Just as he was about to log off, his computer pinged again.

@BoyInADress13 sent you a message.

Curious, Asher clicked the box.

@BoyInADress13: I know u probably get a bunch of messages, but I wanted to tell you that your videos literally saved my life.

Asher flushed at the thought that his videos would mean that much to anyone, especially a stranger. He clicked on the username to visit the user's profile, but it was pretty bare. All it said was that he was nineteen, and he was from Texas. The thumbnail image by the username was just a pair of shiny pink lips, clearly male but otherwise unidentifiable.

He went back to his messages, hovering his fingers over the keyboard for a long moment before he finally replied.

@ThemBoyFemBoy: I don't know what to say to that, except I'm glad they helped. R u okay?

@BoyInADress13: no but your videos help, so thank u. I wish I was as brave as u

@ThemBoyFemBoy: Not brave. Just dumb and drunk and got lucky. My parents don't know I'm doing this.

Part of Asher knew he shouldn't admit that, knew that talking to strangers on the Internet was dumb. Every single 'stranger danger' lecture talked about it, about how the person on the other end of the computer screen was never a teenage girl but some old, creepy pervert trying to lure someone into his trap, but it wasn't like Asher was going to tell him where he lived or anything.

@BoyInADress13: Still brave. My dad would KILL me. He says it's wrong. But I just want to be pretty.

Asher was going to reply, but before he could, another message pinged through.

@BoyInADress13: Sorry, TMI. U probably have better things to do than listen to me. Sorry… I'll go now.

@ThemBoyFemBoy: no, ur fine! I like talking to u. It's nice to talk to someone who gets it. My parents will be home soon, but we can talk until then, K?

@BoyInADress13: really?

@ThemBoyFemBoy: Yeah. what's ur name?

@BoyInADress13: Devon

They kept chatting, about everything and nothing. Somehow they went from discussing makeup to Asher trying to explain the new MMORPG video-game he'd started playing a few weeks before—an open-world fantasy game called EverQuiet that he was becoming obsessed with. They even made plans to play together after school the next day, if Devon could convince his dad to buy it for him.

He said he thought his dad would go for it, since video games were something teenage boys were *supposed* to be obsessed with. Devon said they'd probably be ecstatic that he was taking an interest in it in the first place.

Asher hoped he was right. Playing online was fun, but it was better when there was someone to play with. Besides, if Devon's dad *did* get it for him, they could talk on the headset and he'd know for sure that the other guy *wasn't* a creepy pervert.

The front door slammed loudly and Asher jumped, glancing at the clock in surprise. He felt like he'd only been talking to Devon for a few minutes, but it was already almost nine at night. He hastily typed out a goodnight to his new friend and shut off his laptop, unlocking his door only seconds before his dad stomped up the stairs.

He flung himself on the mattress with his chemistry book just in time for the door to swing open. Dad loomed in the open space, a dark silhouette backlit by the hall lights.

"It's almost bedtime. Shouldn't you be getting ready?" Dad barked, his arms crossed.

Heart thumping at the close call, Asher waved his chemistry book in excuse as he answered. "I have a test tomorrow and lost track of time studying, I guess. How was Bible Study?"

Dad harrumphed. "That idiot Mel wouldn't know how to interpret a verse if the Lord himself stood in front of him with a dictionary. Poor man."

"It's a good thing you and Mom are there to guide him, then," Asher tried to sound earnest instead of sarcastic, and he must have succeeded because Dad just nodded, thumping his fist lightly on the doorframe.

"That's true. Well, get to bed, son." He left, and Asher tried not to flinch. Dad rarely called him 'son' anymore. Rarely called him anything, to be honest. It was like, in moments like these, he could forget for a minute that Asher was a sinner. Tomorrow he would be back to ignoring him, unable to look Asher in the eye.

Asher tossed his chemistry book toward his backpack then rolled out of bed to shut his door again and flip off the light. He stripped down to his briefs and crawled under his comforter. It was only spring in Delaware, still chilly out, but Mom already had the air cranked up high enough to freeze his balls off. He used to argue that her hot flashes shouldn't leave him with frostbite, and she used to laugh. Since getting outed, though, he didn't dare.

Instead, he curled into a ball under the thick comforter and closed his eyes, his thoughts drifting back to his conversation with Devon.

About the Author

KD Ellis is a professional cat wrangler by day, and an author by night. She moved from a small town to an even smaller village to live with her husband and wife and their two children. She loves reading—anything with men loving men. She writes queer romance in between working her two jobs and cuddling her pets—all six of them, which confuses the turtle.

KD loves to hear from readers. You can find her contact information, website details and author profile page at https://www.pride-publishing.com

PRIDE
PUBLISHING

www.ingramcontent.com/pod-product-compliance
Lightning Source LLC
LaVergne TN
LVHW050922080826
845145LV00001B/172

* 9 7 8 1 8 3 9 4 3 7 5 4 0 *